Until Death Do You Part

An American Family Meets Their Sicilian Cousins

Wm. Hovey Smith

ISBN
978-1-956161-26-7 (Paperback)
978-1-956161-25-0 (eBook)

Table of Contents

Chapter

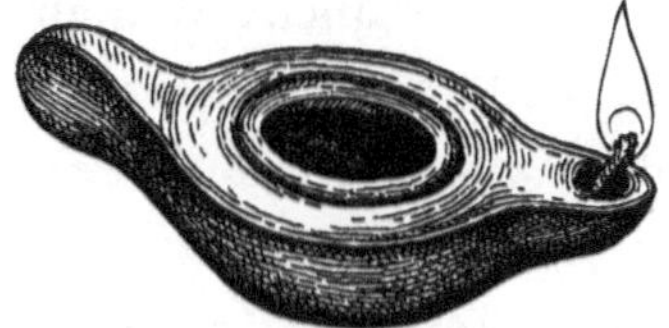

1

𝕾icilians in 𝕭aton 𝕽ouge

PRESIDENT AND FIRST LADY Ronald and Nancy Reagan would have felt at home had they visited the split-level ranch house owned by Ronald and Nancy Calsase in the Prospect Park subdivision of Baton Rouge. Although the ranch lands and open vistas surrounding the Reagan home in California were replaced by huge live oaks dripping with Spanish moss, the house was very similar to hundreds of thousands of such homes built in the United States during the 1950s. Ronald Calsase received his degree in Civil Engineering at Louisiana State and had been successful in helping to construct everything from oil refineries to subdivisions after World War II. He started his own residential company during the height of the building boom, sold that company, and now works from home as a consultant piloting companies through the increasing body of city, state, and federal regulations required to build their projects.

His wife Nancy also attended Louisiana State, but took an education degree. She specialized in sex education for middle and high-school students. Deep in the Bible Belt and among those for whom any talk about sex was socially forbidden, she had faced her challenges with the advent of AIDS. As there was no effective treatment or cure in sight, her advocating the distribution of condoms in high school was met with such an outcry that she was forced to leave the school system. She lectured on AIDS prevention at national and local events motivated by the climbing death toll, which had reached 3.1 million worldwide by 2004. Many teens

1

and parents still did not want to hear anything about the subject, even though most knew of someone who had died of the disease, including movie star Rock Hudson.

They are empty nesters. Mary, their daughter, lives in downtown Baton Rouge where she works with her uncle, William. They operate Calsase Hair Fashions on Florida Boulevard just east of the Historic District. One of their two sons, Frank, is a Marine Corps Captain who lost his flying status during the First Iraq War because of an injury, but was retrained as a forward observer who coordinated air strikes for ground units during the Second Iraq War. His brother Roger, the younger by a year, studied art at Louisiana State. He became fascinated with painting portraits in the style of Rembrandt. He had moved to San Francisco in hopes of finding wealthy patrons to support his art. He idolized his older brother as a kid, but, whereas Frank was quarterback of the Catholic School's Bruin football team, Roger was much more interested in art, music, and making props for one-act plays. Teachers at the school made him participate in sports, but his heart was not in the games. He liked hanging out with the guys, but whatever ball-playing skills were in the family's genes were passed to his brother.

Because he sometimes had leftover materials from his building projects, Ronald had continually upgraded his home. Gone were the original Linoleum floors which had been replaced with parquet wood, ceramic tiles, and carpet in the upstairs bedrooms. The original steel cabinets in the kitchen had been replaced with oak and weathered cypress cabinets with matching paneling, which also decorated the halls and den. One relic in the kitchen was an avocado green refrigerator, spared because, as Ronald said, "I can't see replacing a perfectly good appliance with a new one just because of its color."

Hanging from the walls were a mix of cowboy art and Louisiana scenes of marsh, boats, hunting, and photographs of some of Ronald's construction projects with the pipes and towers of a night-lit oil refinery presenting the most striking contrast between modern and historic Louisiana. Prominently featured on a wall facing the front door was a large painting showing Nancy sitting on a dock with marsh grasses and a live oak in the background. Although Roger had finished painting the figure, bench, and part of the dock, the rest of the painting remained a primed canvas with only penciled-in outlines of the composition's major elements. When Roger left for San Francisco, his mother had framed the painting to protect it until her son could finish it.

Well-drained land is at a premium in Baton Rouge, and the house's footprint and a huge live oak dominated the property. While the lot was twice the size of those in the downtown area, its 2.5 acres left little room for the shed where Ronald kept his lawn mower, tools, grill, and, most important to a Louisianan, his Low-Country boil pots and propane burners.

The newest addition to the house was a red tile patio laid on pea-gravel in front of the shed. This allowed the cooking stuff to be more easily rolled out and allowed water to drain and feed the roots of the oak, whose branches shaded the patio and back third of the house. None of the kids had seen this yet, and Ronald welcomed the chance to try it out.

Perhaps he would invite his brother and daughter over after they closed the shop on Friday and cook something for them?

"Nancy, do we have anything going for this Friday?" he asked as he stepped down into the kitchen from the den.

"Not that I can think of. What do you have in mind?" Nancy asked.

"I would like to invite William, Tim, and Mary for supper. I want to cook something on the patio."

"If they can come, it is going to be late. They are not likely to get here until around 8:00, and are going to be starved when they do arrive."

"That's fine. I would rather feed a hungry person than 'one with a coming appetite,' as my dad would say," Ronald mused.

"Was my brother in the shop when you went yesterday?"

"Yes, he fixed my hair, and we had quite a chat. He's worried sick about this AIDS business. He was telling me that many people he knows in the gay community are now dead, sick with the disease, or so scared that they don't get out anymore. He and Tim are tested regularly, so he knows they do not have it; but the weight of worrying about it really has William worn down. Tim has made caring for some of his friends a full-time job."

"William was always more compassionate than me. He put on a brave, funny face when our parents died a few months apart, but I know that it really tore him up. If he can come, I really want to see him. How is Mary doing?"

"Okay, I guess? I know that she dates, but I don't think that she has found anyone that she is serious about. I think she is looking for someone like Frank, but doesn't want a military guy – maybe a college prof, teacher, or something like that."

"Speaking of Frank, I think that we may have him at home for a visit since he and Jean are divorced," Ronald said. "He wrote that he had four months of accumulated leave. He said that he would like to visit and maybe go on a trip – like we did when we drove out West to see Yellowstone that summer.

"There is a trip that I would like to make. I would like to go to Sicily. I'm still in contact with Mario. He has invited us many times. I think that this fall is the time we should go. You, me, William, Mary, and the two boys. If we wait much later it could get too complicated if any of the kids start a family and/or have conflicting work obligations."

Ronald's long background in civil engineering had reinforced his innate organizational abilities, and he had been mentally planning such a trip. He wanted to meet his now distant cousins to reestablish contact with that side of the family. He never had the chance to go to Sicily, and the more he thought about it, the more certain he became that this was the time to make that trip. That would be one thing that he could discuss with the family when they came over.

When the doorbell buzzed on Friday, Ronald walked across the patio into the kitchen and down the short hall to the door. He was wearing a denim apron with "eat more crawdads" embroidered across the front in red letters.

"William, Tim, come on in," he said. "Is Mary behind you?"

As if to answer the question, he saw Mary's powder-blue Mustang drive up and stop behind William's old cream-colored Cadillac Seville. Compared to the Mustang, the Cadillac looked like a battleship parked in front of a sleek destroyer.

After William and Tim went in, Ronald closed the screen door behind them and stood on the sidewalk under the alcove porch that sheltered the doorway. Mary, carrying a bag that obviously contained a bottle of wine, walked between the two cars and paused.

"Dad, I brought a bottle of wine. It's Marsala from Sicily."

"Strange that you did," Ronald replied. "Because that is one thing that I want to talk to you and your uncle about – visiting Sicily this fall."

"That sounds exciting," she replied, blowing away the gnats and waving the mosquitoes away from her face. "Let's get inside before I get eaten alive. The bugs are really bad."

"The rain, welcome as it was, has really brought them out. I called the county to spray again, but they haven't made it yet."

"William, Tim, Mary, come in, come in, come in," Nancy said as she waved them in. "Have a seat at the table. Ronald has nearly got everything ready on the grill, and I know you are hungry."

"I picked up some wine for after dinner," Mary announced. "Let me uncork it so that it can breathe a little. According to the bottle it is supposed to be served at room temperature, although I suspect that they did not have ninety-six degrees in mind."

"I'm sure not." William chimed in. "Thank god for air conditioning. I don't know how we survived when we didn't have it. I remember summer nights when the pillows and sheets were soaked with sweat when we woke up – even though we had a fan in the room."

"Here we are," Ronald said as he walked into the kitchen from the patio with a covered cast-iron frying pan full of deer-burger steaks. "These have onions, bell peppers, garlic, and Portobello mushrooms just as you like them. I will put them on the stove until we are ready."

They started their meal with a cold tomato soup made from fresh tomatoes grown in their yard and dill-deer potato salad. This was one of Ronald's specialty dishes made with local potatoes, fried granulated deer burger, sweet relish, a touch of mustard, sparse mayonnaise, and a generous sprinkling of dill weed. It was something that his guests would take home if there was any left.

"Mary mentioned that you were thinking about going to Sicily?" William asked.

"What I was thinking about was that it is time for us to make that trip while I still have contacts with our relatives. What I have in mind is going with anyone who can come. I would like you, Mary, the two boys, and of course, Nancy and Tim to go – a family vacation like we used to do.

"I would love to," William said. "I need to get away from this AIDS business."[1]

---

[1]   With the advancements in treating AIDS since 2004, many do not remember the terror that the disease brought to society and to the Gay community.

"I can't go." Tim sighed. "I have become the funeral coordinator between the gay community and their families — many of whom didn't know, or will not admit, that their kids were gay. This has become a 24-7 job that funeral directors are paying me to do."

"I'm proud of the work you are doing," William said, patting his partner's knee. "You are stronger than I am. I need to think about something else for a time. Is it all right if I go on this trip without you?"

Tim clasped William's hand. "I am sure that I can manage without you for a week. I want you to go. Just don't run off with some Italian stallion," Tim chuckled.

The rest of the family burst into laughter at this unexpected bit of levity.

"Thank you for your consideration, Tim," smiled Ronald. How are you both doing with this AIDS stuff?"

"Is the question that you are really asking is, 'Do we have AIDS?[2] Is that it? The answer is NO, we do not!" William spat out.

Some insights into that time period can be obtained by viewing the 1993 Movie Philadelphia, in which Tom Hanks gives an Academy Award winning performance as a lawyer who fights an anti-discrimination lawsuit against his former employer, a powerful law firm.

[2] My connection with AIDS came because I was a young geologist-writer-journalist who lived in Middle Georgia, just 90 miles from where the First International Conference on AIDS was to be held in Atlanta. I attended and reported on that conference and published the first of three editions of *Plain Words About AIDS* on the subject. These were three of the first books available on AIDS, and they were published at a time when few journalists dared write about the subject. At the time of the first conference, I did not know anyone who was Gay or had AIDS. As I covered the first conference in Atlanta, the second in Paris and the third in Washington D.C., I came to know hundreds of people who had the disease, their parents, friends and the doctors, researchers, social workers, and activists who were involved. Although AIDS was a disease that the general public thought to be restricted to homosexuals, thousands were also infected through blood transfusions until a means was found to screen the nation's blood supply. By 2004, treatments with antiviral compounds were only partly successful in suppressing the virus. It would not be until 2012 that a combination of the drugs Tenofovir and Emtricitabine was approved that could indefinitely suppress the disease and act as a prophylactic against infection so long as a daily dose of the pill Truvada was taken by a non-infected adult. By 2015, 15,000,000 people worldwide were being treated for AIDS-related disease. This treatment helped

"We were lucky. We were together before this stuff started. We give blood, and it has always come back clean."

"William, I'm sorry. You are my brother, and I love you. I don't have the language to do anything other than ask. Have some Key Lime Pie, and let's talk about the trip."

"So when are we going?"

"It will be sometimes this fall when the weather is nicer. That is the time that Mario has always suggested. Frank has a long leave coming and said he wants to go somewhere. I don't know about Roger. I have no idea what his plans are, and I doubt that he knows either. At any rate, I suspect that he could put whatever projects he has on hold for a week."

"What do they do over there?" Mary asked.

"I don't know. It has been three generations since grandpa left, and there are a bunch of them. Mario has mentioned a vineyard, making olive oil, goat-milk cheese, farming, and growing lemons. I suppose they do mostly farming and something in the export market. It doesn't pay to question anyone in Sicily too closely about what they do."

"You mean they are in the Mafia — like in The Godfather?" Mary questioned.

"I do not have any reason to think that they are, but there are some questions best left unasked," Ronald replied as he looked at this brother, who nodded in reply.

"Let's have some of that wine before it evaporates," William said. "Tim is really the wine expert, and he can tell us about it."

"Starting, I think, in the 1800s, it became popular in the English export market as an after-dinner wine that competed with Port," Tim replied.

"I don't have but one brandy snifter, but I do have some Old Fashion glasses," Nancy said as she got up from the table, retrieved seven glasses from one of the cabinets, and set them on the table.

"Just pour a finger or so, because everyone may not like it," Tim suggested.

---

to extend and improve the quality of their lives. There is continuing work on a vaccine, but as of 2021 this elusive goal has not been achieved.

"If it is like Port, this is a sipping wine," Ronald said as he first swirled the amber liquid in the glass, sniffed it, and then took a sip as everyone watched.

"It has a little bit of a bite," Ronald replied after he tasted it. "I think it would go well with bar-b-que, and might do fine with spicy seafood."

"William what do you think?"

"I agree, it is not something I would want to drink a lot of, but it is a good way to top off a Low-Country Boil. It has got a kick, and just the right balance of sweetness and harshness. I think that they add some brandy to it."

"You are both correct. This is something to savor after a good meal and mellow-out with," Tim concluded. As everyone enjoyed their Masala, Nancy saw William glancing at his watch.

"I know that you have to go because you open early tomorrow."

"We do," William replied. "Even when I get there at 7:00, there will be people waiting in the parking lot. The Saturday morning crowd is something of a tradition. The same women come every week – it's almost like church. At least they talk about something other than the latest election squabbles between Bush and Kerry. With the primaries, I have already had more than enough electioneering. If we go to Sicily, at least we can get away from that for a week."

"Actually, voting won't be a problem. We can do that before we leave," Ronald volunteered. "I hate to see you go. It has been a good visit. I'll keep you both posted on the dates and who will be able to go."

"I'll put this wine in a screw-top bottle and keep it in the fridge, so we can have some the next time," Mary remarked as she started to clear the table. She found an empty wine bottle with a screw top, rinsed it out, and poured the Marsala into it before putting it into the refrigerator.

Ronald handled the goodbyes and saw his guests to their cars. After William and Tim had gotten into the car, he said, "Thank you for coming. Thank you, Tim, for agreeing that William should join us. We wish you could come. You are as much a member of the family as anyone else."

"Ronald, thank you for everything," Tim replied. "Just getting out and talking about something else has done me more good than you can know."

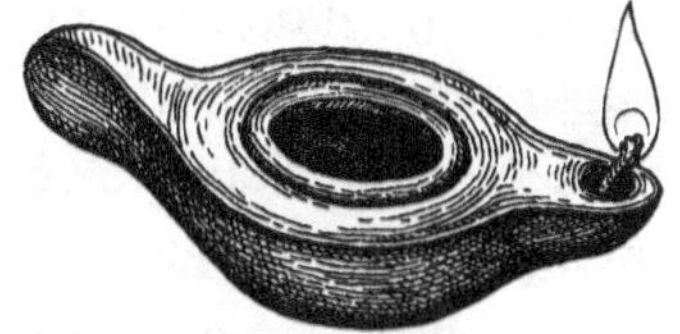

Moving Out of
Height-Asbury

ROGER THOUGHT HE WAS making reasonably good time because he had already crossed the Bay Bridge to Oakland and was proceeding towards Vallejo on his way to Willows, which was about half-way up the Sacramento Valley. The trip was only about a hundred miles, and if he could beat the city traffic, he should be able to make his midday appointment without any problem.

He had left Matilda asleep in their bed. His 1980 International Scout II was already packed with his easel, flip-chart, and a framed canvas along with some markers and pencils. All he had to do was get out the door, leave Clayton Street, avoid most of the construction, and get out of the city before the traffic started to build up.

"Damn," he thought. "Are they ever going to finish anything?" Although he knew the central San Francisco area fairly well, he was immediately confounded by more construction on I-80, which was to ultimately connect with Interstate I-5 to Canada.

Between concrete trucks, cranes, and flat-beds carrying huge concrete beams, the little Scout seemed like a blue beetle that was likely to get crushed between the huge trucks that were trying to get as much construction material in place as possible before the city woke up.

Finally, after passing field after field of planted vegetables north of Woodland, he stopped and went into a gas station to grab something to eat. This was a family-run station that was likely to be replaced by some of the newer fuel plazas. Most of the stores were located on a frontage road and could now only be accessed from off-ramps that were miles away.

"Times they are changing," he thought as he mentally quoted Bob Dylan's song. "A lot of these shops are going to be put out of business."

There were four gas pumps in front of the station. Inside was a counter, a few rows of groceries, and a cooler box with a drink machine against the front wall. They had a kitchen with a few tables in the back. Two cooks, who looked like a man and his wife in their forties, were making tamales, burritos, tacos, sausages, and hamburgers in preparation for lunch. Truck drivers and road workers would flood the place around noon to grab something to eat on the road or sit at the tables outside. The drivers mostly opted for a 'grab and go' so they could make as many miles as possible. Roger arrived just before the lunch rush.

"I'll have a tamale, burrito, and coffee," he told the girl running the register, who looked like she was about sixteen-years-old. He wondered why she wasn't in school, but decided that she must be older, and it was just her small size that made her appear to be a kid.

"Are you sure? They are huge," she replied.

"Yes, I'm sure. I have been driving since early this morning, and I'm starved," Roger replied.

"Some are just coming out now, and if you have a seat at one of the tables, I will bring them to you. Do you want some water?"

Roger replied that he would like some water and sat at a small wooden table covered with a finely checkered red and white plastic tablecloth. These were like the tables outside, but instead of having benches to sit on, there were cane-bottomed wood chairs.

In a few minutes, the cashier-waitress brought him his meal. It came on two large dinner plates with the banana leaf-wrapped steaming tamale lapping over the edges of one plate and a burrito that was four inches in diameter and a foot long on another. The coffee was served in a smaller cup than usual, and it looked like the boiling asphalt that they were pouring on the roads.

"I'll need a bag," Roger said with a hint of surprise in his voice. "I'll have that burrito for supper. I will also need some cream and sugar for the coffee."

Roger unwrapped the tamale. He found a thick layer of steaming corn meal and jalapeno peppers on top. Inside that layer was wood-smoked pork that was so tender that it pulled apart with a touch. He ate, eagerly enjoying every bite. He had eaten tamales before, but never like this.

The coffee was more of a challenge. He had been brought up on chicory-flavored Louisiana coffee, but this was something different. He diluted it with the milk, added a half-teaspoon of sugar, and got it down. He thought the coffee was more medicinal than pleasurable, but it would keep him alert.

For the first time since he started on this trip, he had time to rehearse his presentation for Valley Tomatoes. He was going to propose doing a painting of the company's founder, Ishido Yoshomoto. He had met Yoshomoto's son, Phil, at a job fair in San Francisco, and approached him about doing a portrait of his father, who was now in his nineties.

The old man had an expressive face that showed decades of working fields in the hot sun, the sorrows of internment during World War II, and his struggle to reclaim his business after the war. Fortunately, he had non-Japanese partners who were able to run the business during the war, and while he was in internment, his canned tomatoes were being consumed by U.S. fighting men all over the world.

Although he had never been there before, a sun-bleached billboard with the name Valley Tomatoes made it easy to spot the cannery. It was a large industrial complex covering fourteen acres with an asphalt-paved parking lot along the front and side. Phil had told him to use one of the visitors' parking spots near the entrance.

Still an hour early, Roger decided to get out of the heat and see if he could set up for the meeting. He went through the twin glass doors into the reception area and walked up to a lady sitting at a desk who was busily sorting the mail.

"I'm Roger Calsase. I have a presentation to give to Phil Yoshomoto at three. I need a few minutes to set up. Is there a room I can use?"

"Do you have a card?" The smartly dressed receptionist asked.

She was in her thirties with shoulder-length blond hair, blue eyes, and as his father would say, "All the right parts in all the right places."

"I could go for her," Roger thought. But a wedding ring on her finger proclaimed her status, and even more significantly, Matilda was waiting for him back in San Francisco.

Roger fumbled inside his worn billfold and sorted through some cards until he found one that proclaimed "Roger Calsase, Paintings in the Style of the Old Masters" and handed it to the receptionist.

"I see you are on his calendar. I will ring his secretary and tell her you are here. We have a large training room and a smaller conference room. Both are available. Which will you need?"

"I imagine the conference room will do fine." Roger replied.

"Will you need some help to set up?" she responded.

"I have a couple of large things to bring in, so if someone could help and show me where to go, that would be helpful." He did not want to show up for his meeting dripping with sweat.

"Roger, it's good to see you again," Phil said. "Do you have everything that you need?"

"Yes, I do. Do you want to get started now?" "Go ahead."

"I specialize in doing portrait paintings like the European Old Masters, but knowing something about your father, I would like to do something different. I want to show him with things that reflect his accomplishments."

Turning to the flip chart on his easel, he revealed a pencil sketch of a man in the center of the white sheet wearing a business suit.

"I don't think that this is your dad."

Flipping to the next page the figure had morphed into a man in a field holding up and examining a tomato with part of the composition showing rows of tomato plants with a canning plant in the background.

"This is truer to your father's life and experiences, and I think is a better rendition than the usual pose used in portraits."

Removing the flip chart from the easel, Roger replaced it with the framed canvas. When he removed the dust cloth the prepped white canvas showed a pencil sketch of Roger's concept. Unlike the flip chart where the major elements of the composition were vertical, the canvas was put on the easel horizontally.

"What I think might work best is this. Your dad's head takes up approximately twenty percent of the painting in the upper-right corner. On the other side is a painting of your classic Valley Tomato can, which is known all over the world. Between them is a tomato field with ripe tomatoes with your canning plant in the background. I think that this painting represents your dad's life and work. I'm also thinking about putting in a twist of barbed wire to symbolize his internment during the war."

"Roger, as a piece of advertising art, I think that this might work, but this is not what I was looking for to hang in my house."

"You're right. Where I had in mind for it would be to have it hanging in the reception room or here in the conference room."

"That has its own problems. We are going to sell out to Universal Brands, who will redo our line to focus on higher-value products like salsas and sauces, rather than on canned tomatoes.

"This factory is old and needs to be replaced. They still want Valley Tomatoes; but they also want tomato products that denote excitement, movement, progress, and fun. I'm afraid that they have no interest in expensive art related to Valley Tomatoes.

"How much would this cost?"

"Phil, I work with the old mineral-based pigments, and some like lapis and cinnabar which give deep sky blues and vibrant red and things like sperm oil, mummy, royal purple, and amber which are also scarce and expensive. The pigments alone are going to cost at least six-hundred dollars. The finished costs of a painting this size, with this much detail that will be suitably framed is going to be five-thousand dollars."

"I know that Universal Brands is not going to go for something like that for a company they plan to restructure. I will put you in touch with their art department, and maybe you can sell them on something for their new vision of the company.

"For me, my brothers, and sisters, we have plenty of photographs of Dad with us and grandkids. I doubt that they would pay three-hundred dollars for a portrait of grandpa. He is in the nursing home now and hardly knows anyone. I don't know if he would recognize anything in the painting if he were to see it."

"But you said," Roger interrupted.

"I know, but that was before I knew that we were selling out. My sisters and brother want their share of the money. This is going to run into the millions, and they just can't refuse. Although they want to keep dad's business, they don't want to do the hard work or take the risks of transforming it to be a leader in tomorrow's tomato market.

"Not me though. I will stay on through the transition and help get things restarted. Come back when the new company is running, and I think that we may be able to do something with you.

"I'll have accounting cut you a check for three-hundred dollars for your expenses. You can pick it up on the way out. She can cash it so you can leave with the money."

Although feeling betrayed and fuming inside, Roger assented with a nod, shook hands with Phil, and started taking down his canvas and easel.

With a parting, "Stay in touch," Phil left the room. Roger was already dreading what he had every expectation of being a real battle with traffic getting back to the apartment.

Matilda greeted him with a, "How did you do?" as soon as he walked through the door of the three-story walk-up. Because it was late he had to park nearly two-blocks away. The street-level bars, sandwich shops, and small retailers in the district were going full swing. He had been told that it was not at all like it was in the sixties, but in the gentrified, up-scale version of the district, one might hear jazz, rock and roll, country, and even an Irish tune on a tin whistle emanating from a doorway.

This section of Clayton Street was dominated by some of the "Victorian Painted Ladies" of San Francisco, which were typically three-story with a ground floor garage, steps leading to the front door, and a narrow hall that allowed access to steep stairs climbing to the upper floors.

Although it was thankfully cooler here than it was in the valley due to the ocean breeze, it was still hot. The only thing that he had carried in was the envelope containing the money and the stained paper bag containing the burrito.

"They didn't take the painting, but I got three-hundred dollars for working up the concept."

"That's all – three-hundred measly dollars. You spent more than a week on that stuff, and all you got was three-hundred? Where is the five-thousand dollars that you told me about?

"You owe me your portion of three-month's rent that I had to cover. That's $2,250 in case you forgot.

And all you all you brought back was three-hundred?"[3]

"Yes, but…," Roger stammered.

"Don't 'Yes, but' me nothing. I want my money now, or I want you out of here."

"But doesn't what we had together mean anything?"

"You want to know the truth, do you? I will tell you if you want to know it or not.

"You never finish anything. You said that you were going to do all sorts of things around the house. Outside of sweeping up and a little cooking, you have done nothing – absolutely nothing. You have been fiddling with your paints, with that junk Scout, saying that you are filing for grants with this art organization or that theater, but I don't see anything out of it. I need someone who can bring in income, not promises.

"It took me five years to get this apartment. I'm not going to lose it to a deadbeat, limp-dick like you or support you in the manner to which you would like to become accustomed."

"You know how to really hurt a guy," Roger replied. He handed the envelope with the remaining cash to Matilda.

"You keep it. You're going to need it. You can stay the night and sleep on the couch. But get your stuff out of here by noon, and don't forget that junk of yours in the attic. I want you and everything of yours out of here. Let me know where to forward your mail," with that remark, she turned, walked past the kitchen into the bedroom, and closed the door.

The metallic noise of a lock's bolt being thrown registered a note of finality in Roger's brain. This part of his life was over. Even before he moved in with Matilda, he had fairly well thrashed through every gallery in San Francisco seeking commissions to do portraits. Because he did not have anything to show, he was having a hard time competing against those

---

3 Apartment costs in San Francisco were very steep in 2004 and are even more expensive now. The problem of raising the ever-increasing rents often results in people sharing their rooms with other people or couples even though they are all making very good salaries compared to the rest of the country.

who could show a portfolio of their work instead of only a few sketches. The only thing that he had at least half-way finished was that portrait of his mother. Hard as it might be for him, one obvious thing to do was to go back home and finish it.

In the meantime, he needed to get something to eat and find a bathroom. He didn't think it was likely that Matilda would let him use hers, and he did not want another confrontation. Fortunately, Zippo's was open down the street. He could grab a drink there, eat his burrito, and think about what he was going to tell his dad.

It was nearly ten before he hustled his way back to the men's room carrying his stained paper bag. The place was crowded with men and women drinking, talking, and smoking. There had been periodic news stories about a ban on smoking in bars, but the bar owners had thus far managed to defeat it. They had installed a powerful exhaust fan. Even so, when he passed one table, he caught a whiff of something that did not smell like tobacco.

After leaving the men's room, he went to the bar, ordered a beer and a shot of Jim Beam. He slipped his burrito into the microwave at the end of the bar while he waited on his drinks. He also looked for an empty chair and spotted a couple who were apparently about to leave. He grabbed his sandwich and drinks and moved through the crowd in that direction.

As soon as the guy got up, Roger grabbed the back of the chair with an apologetic, "Sorry, it's crowded," as he balanced his two drinks in one hand while holding his sacked burrito against the chair.

The guy nodded in agreement, helped his date out of her chair, and brushed their empty glasses to the other side of the table. "We're leaving to catch a show," he remarked.

Surprisingly, considering the crowd, a busboy came, quickly removed the glasses from the table, and wiped it off. Sitting his drinks down and opening his burrito, for the first time that evening, he felt that he could relax. He had a plan; he knew what he was going to do – have his drinks, eat his burrito, go back to the apartment, and leave for Louisiana in the morning.

"May I sit?" Asked an older man who had a plate in one hand and a beer in the other. "There doesn't seem to be anywhere else."

"Sure," Roger said pulling, his glasses back a bit to make room on the small table.

They started a conversation as they worked through their meals. It developed that his dinner partner was a retired architect who had helped renovate many of the buildings in the district.

"This sometimes included tearing out some of the old walls while preserving as much original detail as possible, so steel reinforcing beams could be added, and modern electric, gas, and water lines run. That was tough because many of these buildings that were built in the early 1900s had hidden beams that were cracked or broken by the earthquake of 1904.

"I used to own some of these houses, but now I just keep an apartment," he concluded.

"I just got thrown out of mine – actually, my girlfriend's place," Roger said. "I'm an artist, a portrait painter, and I just could not make the rent."

"Corporate folks and lawyers sometimes have portraits done. Have you tried some of the studios?"

"Yes, but it is the chicken and the egg thing. I must have something to show them, and I don't at the moment. That is why I'm going to go back to Louisiana tomorrow."

"I'm sorry; I can't do anything for you. You are a good-looking guy, and I'm sure that you can get a horizontal proposition at any of the gay bars to get you a bed for the night, but not from me – just not the type. Here, here is one-hundred dollars to help get you back home."

"I can't take this. I don't even know your name."

"I don't know yours either and don't care to," his dining companion replied. "If I can help people out occasionally, I will."

With parting words of, "Good luck and good night," Roger's unidentified benefactor left the bar.

If he was going to leave by noon, he needed some sleep, so he piled out of Zippo's and walked back to Matilda's. He let himself in as silently as possible, walked up the stairs, and used his key to open the door. The deep leather couch looked a little more inviting as Matilda had provided a blanket, spread, and pillow. He lay down, hoping for a good sleep, and it quickly came. His very long day had finally come to an end.

"Get up, Roger, I'm about to go," Matilda said as she shook the sleeping form on the couch.

Sleepily, he pulled the covers off and sat up. He had just taken the hard stuff out of his pockets the night before and was still dressed in his shirt and pants. Matilda thrust a pair of socks, shorts, some cut-off jeans, and an old tie-died undershirt at him. "Take those clothes off, and I will throw them in the washer for you. You can shower and change after you finish packing."

He took off his clothes and stood up naked. "You still want me to go?"

"I like you, Roger. You are a good-looking guy, but I just can't afford any human toys. I'm going to the court house to file these eviction notices and then to the newspaper to put them in 'in the official organ.' I will be back after lunch, and I expect to find you gone."

With that, she walked up to him grabbed him by the shoulders, and gave him a kiss on the lips. She pushed away and walked back towards the washing machine, leaving Roger startled and uncertain about what to do.

Before he could even pull on his pants, he heard the door of the washing machine close, the machine start up, the sharp tap, tap, tap of a pair of high heels on the hardwood floor, and the lock on the apartment door click as it closed.

"Well, that's that," he thought. But things 'got'a end when things got'a end' – another useless mental platitude."

It wasn't that Roger had a lot of stuff to start with. Mostly, these were his pigments that he had been collecting since childhood. These included ocher from Indian paint pots, ground up cleaned turquoise, a few lumps of lapis that he had bought at the Tucson Gem and Mineral Show, and some poisonous arsenic, antimony, mercury, and uranium minerals that he had ground into ultra-fine powders using his prized possession – a fifty-pound granite mortar and pestle that his dad had bought for him from Fisher Scientific.

Most of his art books were still in boxes. Matilda had already taken his clothes and piled them on the bed. He had one suitcase to pack, some boxes, and a plastic bag. That was about it, except for some frames in the attic.

The first thing he had to do was to retrieve his Scout and get it somewhere closer. One thing about having a beat-up vehicle was that no one would think he had anything in it worth stealing.

Known as 'The Busted Beast,' the 1980 International Scout was too young to be considered an antique car, but so old as to have fewer parts available for it every year. Most of the parts that he had on it were junk-yard salvage and rebuilds. It ran most of the time, and he even got it past California's emission standards, but this cross-country trip was going to be a challenge.

"I think I better call home," he said aloud. "I better give my folks a heads up."

"Dad, this is Roger."

"Yes, Roger. What's up? Nancy. Pick up. Roger is on the phone."

"Hi Roger it's your mother. What's wrong?"

"I'm Okay. I'm still in San Francisco, but I want to come home for a time. There are some things that I need to paint in Louisiana before I can make a start here on the Coast."

"Roger, don't you remember me telling you something like that?"

"Yes, you did Dad, but I wouldn't listen."

"What about that girl you were living with," Nancy inquired. "Is she coming too?"

"No. Just me. We broke up. It was amiable. San Francisco apartments are expensive, and I wasn't able to pay my share of the rent. I thought I had something in the works, but it fell through. I need to come home and go back once I have a portfolio to show. Just like you told me, Dad, but I wanted to get out to the Coast and get started. I made some useful contacts, but they didn't work out."

"Is the Scout going to get you back?" his father asked.

"I have been working on it, and it is running fine at the moment."

"Plan to drive through Las Vegas. That's a twenty-four-hour town. If you break down they can patch you up and get you on your way. If something goes wrong when you are in the middle of West Texas, you're screwed."

"Do you have triple A?" "No, I don't."

"I'll fix you up with a package for your vehicle. Call me this evening, and I will give you the numbers to call and the number of your card."

"I don't know where I will be, but I will call," Roger affirmed.

"By the way, we are planning a trip to Sicily this fall," Ronald said. "I hope to have William, Mary, and Frank come with us to make it a family trip."

"That sounds exciting, but we need to talk about it later, I'm using Matilda's phone, and I don't want to run up the bill. I'll see you in about three days."

So he didn't forget about it, Roger took out a ten-dollar bill and put it under the phone. Matilda had treated him fairly, and he did not want to do anything to further damage their relationship.

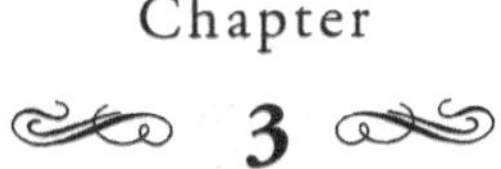

Death in Novo

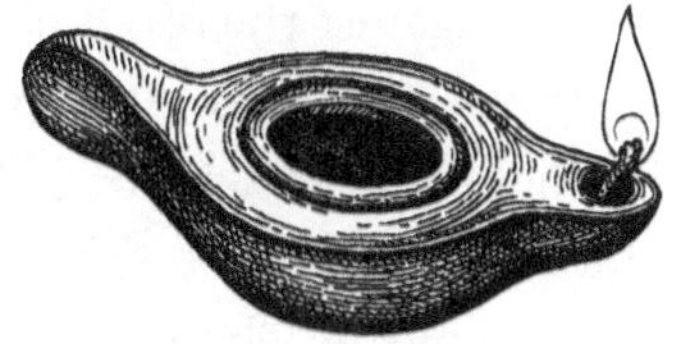

DAVIDE'S SHIFT AT THE Gelato shop was about over. His younger brother Paolo would soon get out of school. When Paolo arrived, he and his brother would pick up some groceries and walk two miles across the valley and up the hill to their family's home on a forested ridge leading towards the sea.

This was their weekday ritual. The only thing that made the day unusual was that this was Davide's 19th birthday. He could have asked for the day off, but his mother needed the money he earned to supplement what they got from her olive, almond, and citrus trees that were planted in terraces like giant staircases leading up the ridge.

"Happy birthday, Davide."

Davide turned from putting away some dishes to see Angelica standing in front of the counter. She was wearing a rose-printed flowing dress, with her chestnut-brown hair flowing over her shoulders. His attention was first drawn to her breasts bulging against the front of her frock, and then to her green eyes that sparkled with life and fun.

"You would think that you had never seen a girl before?" Angelica said as she spun around, letting her skirt lift above her ankles.

Davide, caught completely by surprise by his less-than-pure thoughts towards his childhood friend, blushed and stammered, "You've changed."

"You have too," Angelica replied as she looked over his six-foot frame, muscled arms, rippled torso, sculpted Norman nose, and blue eyes.

"I've just gotten back from Rome, and I will be attending the University in Catania. I'm staying with Uncle Luigi. Hope to see you around." With a wave of her hand and a jangle of the charm bracelet on her wrist, he watched her walk out of the doorway onto the narrow cobblestone street and heard her high heels click against the black paving blocks.

Davide's next customer was also a young lady, Cecilia, who Davide had also known since childhood. Although not so flamboyant with a teal skirt, apricot-colored blouse and low-heeled shoes, she could have passed as Angelica's sister. They were cousins who had been raised together after Angelica's father had died in the Mafia wars of the 1990s. Things got so bad that twenty to forty people were killed every day as the Mafia families fought over drug distribution territories in Italy. It was like the Middle Ages had been revisited, except this time with guns.

"Angelica's back home," Davide remarked to Cecilia when she came in.

"Now that she's back, I see that you only have eyes for her," Cecilia rebuked with mock indignation.

"No. It is not like that at all – as you well know. You are the one I love and have always loved. I will even buy you a bowl of peach gelato."

"It is your birthday. I'm supposed to buy you something, not the other way around."

"Gelato will have to do for now." He set out two bowls and dipped out some pistachio for himself and peach for her. He put a two-euro coin into the till, took the one she offered, kissed it, and put it into his shirt pocket.

"I'll keep here next to my heart."

Now it was time for Cecilia to blush, and they could have carried on quite happily for some time, except that Paolo came in. He plopped his book bag in the corner and loudly announced, "I'll have some chocolate."

Then, Paolo and Davide started what had become a daily ritual. Davide would ask Paolo how he was going to pay for the ice cream. Paolo would say that he did not have any money. Then, Davide would reply that he would have to earn it by helping him carry the groceries back home. With protest that this was in violation of labor laws and extortion, Paolo would agree.

Rugimento, the businesses' owner, came down from upstairs.

"Happy birthday, Davide. Which one is it?" "I'm nineteen today," Davide replied.

"Well, I've got you three times that and then some. I thought you were going to go to University somewhere this year."

"I might be accepted, but mother needs me right now. We have that land. It is too small to make any real money and too big to walk away from. Besides, it has been in my family for generations, and I don't want to give it up."

"Clean up your dishes, and get out of here." With that statement, he reached into the till and pulled out a ten-euro note. "Buy something for your birthday. See you tomorrow."

A few minutes later when everyone had left, Rugimento thought, "I'm going to hate to lose Davide, he is such a young, friendly boy – hell, a man now, and he draws the younger crowd into the shop."

Paolo had his book bag, and Davide had a backpack that he took to town to carry groceries home. The narrow streets were lined by two-to-three-story stone buildings, which often contained shops on the ground floor and living quarters above. They proceeded towards the market square, which was two blocks away. Although they didn't notice it, their progress was being monitored by men on the street corners who were talking into their flip-phones.

Davide's plan was to pick up the groceries and then take, as he usually did, the footpath down into the valley and then up the other side to his mother's house on the lower flanks of Mt. Etna. The footpath was much more direct than taking the road home but still left a mile's uphill walk to their house.

With the ten euros he got from his boss, he could afford to buy something special. He purchased some fresh swordfish, eggplant, tomatoes, and peppers. Onions, garlic, herbs, and wine, they had at the house.

Their grocery shopping completed, they left the streets and started down the steps on the paved pathway that would take them to their house. There was a bench by the creek that ran through the middle of the valley. They always stopped there for a bit before starting up the ridge.

Their farm's soils had been developed on top of the lava flows and ash from the mountain. Olive, pistachio, and fruit trees grew on terraces that had been installed over the centuries. Although ancient, they needed to be maintained so that the trees could get the maximum benefit from the water-diversion structures that had been built to funnel water to them. Some channels had been carved into the rock and those on the terraces were filled with small clean stones to allow water to flow underground to the roots of the trees. When these channels became clogged with dirt and roots, they had to be dug up, the stones cleaned and replaced. This was hard year-around work that the boys did most days after school.

Just last week, they had found a new branch of the channel leading to one of the lower terraces. It would take them a month to clean it out with the pick-mattocks and shovels they were using.

While they were talking about the best way to cook the fish, they heard several people approaching. Although it wasn't raining and too hot for such a garment, the leading figure was wearing a long raincoat.

As the group of five approached, Davide and Paolo got up to leave.

"Stop right there," the leading figure ordered as he pulled a sawed-off double-barreled shotgun from underneath the raincoat and cocked both hammers. The old Beretta still bore engravings on its side plates, showing pigeons, indicating that it had been used as competition gun for shooting live birds.[4] Now it had a shortened buttstock and twenty-four-inch barrels so that it could be concealed under a coat.

"What is this all about? We don't have anything worth stealing." Davide asked.

"This is about honor," the raincoat-clad figure replied.

"Rodrigo, we have known each other since we were children. What's going on here?"

"My father was nineteen years old when your father killed him. Family honor requires that blood be repaid with blood. Now that you are nineteen you must pay for this offense. I don't want to do it, but these other family members will kill me if I do not. It is a hard code, but it is what we live by."

"This is ridiculous. Your father is dead. My father is dead — whatever happened back then died with them. Neither of us had any part in it. I

---

[4]   Expensive, strongly built, side by side, double hammer guns were designed to be used for live pigeon shooting in Europe and the U.S. Typically these had no safeties as they were loaded only before the birds were hand thrown or released from traps. Large wagers were often made on the results of the competition. Clay targets, still often referred to as "birds," are now mostly used today instead of live birds, but the device used to throw them is still known as "a trap," and the modern version of the sport is known as trap shooting.

thought we were friends, or if not friends, at least got along with each other."

An older figure, Mario, stepped out from the group. "For my brother's life, blood must be paid," he said with an act of finality. "Family honor will not be satisfied until this debt is discharged, and Rodrigo must do it."

"Didn't enough people die during World War II and when the Mafia families were fighting it out? Now you want to kill me for something I never did?"

"It is a hard code that we live by," Mario said. "But when everything else is taken away, that is all we have."

"There is nothing I can do or say that will change your mind?"

"No." Mario said. "Our code demands blood for blood, and that is the way that it has to be. If Rodrigo doesn't do it, I will. There are no other options. We will spare Paolo and your mother if they keep silent. Otherwise, everyone dies."

Davide considered his options. If he ran and escaped they would find him and kill him along with Paolo and his mother. Even if he managed to get away, they would die.

"All right," he said with a sigh. "Then it is time to end it. There has been bad blood between our families for two-hundreds years, since some foolish dispute over a goat. Are you going to kill me over that?"

"It is about my father," Rodrigo said. "Either you die or I die."

"And then what? Is Paolo going to kill your son, and his son kill Paolo's son until there is no one left? Are you going to kill Paolo too, so my mother has no one to help her, or are you going to kill her too?"

"No. Paolo can go. No one cares about this sort of family business as long as we keep it among ourselves."

"I'm sorry, but there is no way out of it," Rodrigo said, although his voice cracked with emotion.

"Very well," Davide replied. "If this has got to happen, I will die like a man, not like a rabbit being run through the woods. I want you all to swear on my blood that this ends it with this generation – Paolo, you too."

"Each of you take my hand, look me in the eye, and swear. This was a hunting accident. Someone stumbled on a root, and the shotgun fired accidentally. That is what you all must say."

"Paolo, you first."

"I can't." Paolo said with tears streaming down his face.

"You have to, Paolo. Otherwise this killing goes on for generations. I want it to end with me. You've got to be strong and help mother. You are the man of the house now. There is no one else. Now, swear."

Paolo nodded, hugged his brother for the last time and stammered, "I swear."

"Take your bag and my pack and pull them out of the way."

"One by one the men came, stood in front of Davide, and took their oaths."

"Rodrigo you have to look after my mother. This burden is on you. Paolo is now as much your brother as he is mine."

Reaching into his shirt pocket, he took out the two-euro coin and put it into Rodrigo's hand. "Give this to Cecilia, and tell her that I love her forever."

Looking at the blue sky through the leaves of the forest trees, David turned his face down to look Rodrigo in the eyes, "I forgive you. I forgive you all. Now, if we must do this let's get it done."

"I can't," Rodrigo said.

"Come closer. Hold the gun up," Davide said. Rodrigo did as he was asked. When he stepped forward, Davide grabbed the barrels of the shotgun and yanked them to his chest. Rodrigo's fingers were pulled against the triggers, and both barrels of the side-by-side shotgun discharged into Davide's chest. Davide slumped to his knees and then fell forward on the ground, with a gaping jagged hole in his back.

Rodrigo recoiled back from the horror and shouted, "What have I done?" As he did he fell against some rocks and gashed his head which started to bleed.

Paolo threw himself across Davide's body as if to protect it, and tears rolled down his cheeks.

"You have upheld the family's honor and done your duty." Mario replied.

Mario began to organize the group. "Use some water from the creek to clean him up. We are going to take him and Paolo home. This was a regrettable but necessary business. We must never speak of it.

"Paolo, you have the heaviest burden. Davide took his life to preserve yours, your mother's, and unborn generations. That must be your and our secret. If what happened gets out, he cannot be buried in holy ground.

Because of this oath, we are all your brothers and are bound to protect you and your family for as long as we live."

To emphasize the gravity of the circumstances, Mario announced, "The vendetta is over."

As dusk fell like a wet blanket across the warehouse district of Naples, sounds like a screaming cat were heard from a corner building covered with rusted sheet metal. Up a steel suspended stairway in an office area, the sound became louder and then abruptly stopped. Inside, the office was as plainly appointed as the exterior except for a table covered with a lace-trimmed tablecloth on which an Italian cream cake topped with red cherries had been placed along with two small China plates and two sets of sterling knives and forks. Behind the table in a French Empire chair covered in red velvet sat Don Augustino, immaculately dressed in a blue pinstriped business suit.

Pasquale, naked, was strapped into a wooden cane chair with the bottom removed. There were wires running from his body to a small black box with a white dial set on top of the table.

"Please, not again. I will do anything you say," Pasquale whimpers.

"You say that that bitch, Angelica, has left Rome and gone back to Sicily?"

"Luigi ordered her to quit the University and return home."

"He was always a lucky bastard. How did he know we were planning to snatch her? Did you tell him?"

Don Augustino twisted the dial again slowly, and as Pasquale first squirmed, started to sweat, and then screamed louder than before he turned the dial back.

"Did you tell him?" "No. No. I swear."

"I want you to send me information about Don Carlos in Sicily, enough to get the authorities to arrest him. If you do not, you and your entire family will die. *Capire. Capire!*"

"Yes, Yes, anything you want."

Seemingly satisfied, Don Augustino plucked one of the cherries off the cake and chewed it up stem and all.

Just another little taste of the Hot Seat before you go. Don Augustino turns the dial more rapidly. Pasquale screamed and passed out. He pushed another button, and two men enter the room.

"Take that scum away. Clean him up, give him five-hundred euros, and let him go."

Turning to a dark corner of the room he asked, "Apachee, did you enjoy that?"

Apachee, a darkly tanned, lanky twenty-year-old with black hair tied around his head with a red band is dressed in cut-off jeans and a tie-dyed T-shirt. He approached his father drying his hands on a towel.

"I had a good one. I am puzzled, though. If you want to get rid of Don Carlos, what's this business about Luigi? He's old. What can he do?"

"Luigi will likely be called back to run the family's operations if Don Carlos and his *Segundo* are arrested. During the Mafia Wars, Luigi was Don Carlos' Enforcer. He killed some of our people with that knife of his," speaking as he cuts two slices of cream cake and handing one to his son.

"That wavy-bladed dagger that he carries?"

"The same. We took Luigi's wife and had fun with her. I was your age. We fucked that whore every way we could think of for three weeks. Then she hanged herself. She was a good fuck," Don Augustino concluded as he took another cherry and crunched it with enthusiasm.

"Would you give Angelica to me if we can take her? I could think of something special for her."

"Her and her cousin Cecilia too, if we can. She will be harder to get. She stays closer to home in Syracuse."

"I can't wait," Apachee replies as he rubed his cock.

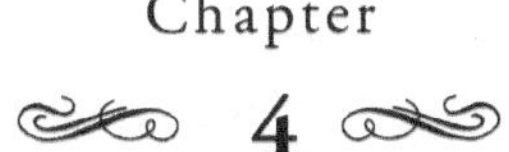

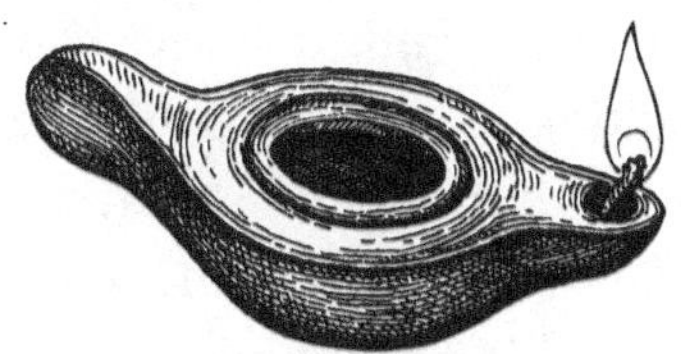

4

Confession

MARIO TOOK THE SHOTGUN from Rodrigo and gave it to Silvestre. "You are the best hunter among us. Here is the gun and some shells. Go kill a hare or something, and meet us at Davide's mother's house."

"Rodrigo, you go back to town and get a priest Ask for Father Flanagan.[5] He's just arrived from Ireland and doesn't know all this family history. He speaks Italian.

"Then go and get the Carabinieri. Tell them there has been a hunting accident. Say you stumbled on this root and the gun accidentally fired, killing Davide. Don't hide your feelings. Act as if you have just accidentally killed your best friend."

Paolo was so stunned that he was nearly numb. He let Mario hold him by the shoulder as they walked up the hill.

"Your brother did a very brave thing. We must honor his memory by going through with this plan. You must not tell anyone what happened here – not even the priest. Do this, and I will look after you like you were my son. Your and your mother's future depends on it."

Paolo listened, understood, but did not respond. Still wiping away tears so that he could see, he walked up the path. Behind Mario and Paolo, Davide's body, wrapped in Rodrigo's raincoat, was being carried as gently as could be managed by four of the men.

---

5   Father Flanagan was brought into the novel to point out that family distress because of cultural conflicts is not unique to Sicily.

Drops of tears and blood stained the dark rocks as they walked, marking the passage of Davide's last trip home.

The stone house was typical of many of the rural farms that dotted the Italian landscape before World War II. The ground floor contained the stalls for livestock, while the upper stories had an elevated porch and living quarters. The cooking and baking were done in an oven built into the house and at the end of the porch. Once fired, the stone oven was used to cook and warm food. Each of the upstairs rooms had fireplaces, which had been improved by installing wood-burning stoves.

Above the house and now obscured by oak trees, there was a bunker that had been built during World War II. It was designed to house a heavy naval gun to shell ships offshore. Although the emplacement had been built, the gun had never been installed. It was briefly used by Italian, German, and Allied troops during the battle for the island. The outside walls were pockmarked by small-arms fire, but the rooms inside the meter-thick concrete walls were intact. Naturally cool, they had been used to store hay, cheese, and feed for the cows, pigs, chickens, and geese owned by the family.

Not knowing if the Carabinieri would arrest him or not, Rodrigo first went to find Father Flanagan. As he crossed the square and started to climb the church's steps, he noticed splatters of blood dried on his shoes. Thinking it disrespectful for him to enter the church with blood on his shoes, he sat on the lowest of the seven steps to remove them.

This was not the first time that the church had seen members of its flock get blooded or even killed on its steps or within its walls. Sometimes this had been at the hands of invading Arabs from North Africa. On other occasions, earthquakes had rained the very stones of the church on those seeking spiritual and physical shelter against forces that they could not control.

Wracked simultaneously by guilt, fear, remorse, and shame at the enormity of what he had done, Rodrigo was in need of comfort.

Holding his cap and his shoes in his hands, he opened the central door and entered the village church's, cool, dark interior. This was not like the elaborately decorated churches that he had seen on his school trips to Palermo.

Instead, the church had a dark flagstone floor at the end of which was a cross holding Christ behind a painted altar. Other parts of the church walls were dedicated to the Stations of the Cross, although one of the stations by the door on the right side had been relocated. In its place was a shrine to a priest who had been murdered by the Mafia.

This shrine was of little comfort to Rodrigo, who came seeking a priest to help him assuage his guilt and shame.

A priest approached him, "Can I help you, my son?"

"I would like to see Father Flanagan," Rodrigo stammered. He was covered in sweat and visibly shaking.

"Sit, sit here," the priest replied, "I will get him. He just went out for a coffee."

Actually Father Donald Flanagan was having English breakfast tea at his favorite coffee shop, which was located on a small alleyway off the main square. He could drink the dark, bitter Italian coffee in its tiny cups if it was offered, but much preferred his tea.

As a young priest he had first studied in Ireland and then spent time in Vatican City in Rome, where he discovered that he had a natural ability with languages. In his three years in Rome, he had become conversant in Italian. When he returned to Northern Ireland, steps were being taken towards reconciliation, and he was able to assist young lovers and their families in healing the wounds of the Irish rebellion. With this experience he was stationed to Sicily to help restore peace between the Mafia families.

Flanagan's red hair and light skin made him stand out from the townspeople. He was also getting tanned, but was definitely more pallid than most who lived in Novo. Now forty-three, he was fighting a losing battle with his weight, and he was starting to develop a paunch due to his semi-sedentary lifestyle and the fact that everyone insisted on feeding a priest.

Father Flanagan was dressed in the traditional black suit with a white collar. He was reading the Catania morning paper whose headlines were about the latest arrest of Mafia figures and charges against local officials for taking kickbacks for awarding contracts to Mafia-controlled companies.

"No difference between what I experienced in Ireland and what I see in Italy," he thought. "It seems much the same. Whether it is Mafia killing or bribing this person or that or Protestants and Catholics fighting in Ireland, it seems much the same. Greed, hatred, and envy appear to rule the world. The better impulses of Your church have tried to correct this for over 2,000 years, but we do not seem to have made much progress."

Flanagan's chain of thought was broken were by the abrupt appearance of Father Bolsonaro.

"Father Flanagan, come quickly. There is a man at the church with blood on his shoes. He says he needs to see you right away. I don't know if he is a *mafiosi*, but he may be. He appears to be very distressed."

Grabbing his paper and laying some coins on the table, Flanagan got up to leave. He hated to leave his tea and the hot bread, but duty called. This was hardly the first time his meals had been interrupted, and this would not be the last.

Although the young priest pointed him out when they entered the church, Flanagan had no problems identifying the person in need. The young man, perhaps in his late teens, was sitting on one of the rear pews with his boots in his lap and holding his head in his hands.

In spits and starts, with much backtracking and repeating, Rodrigo went through his lines.

"It's Davide. He's dead. I accidentally killed him. He was my best friend. It was an accident. I shot him. I need to report this to the Carabinieri and take you to his mother's house. Can you come?"

"There are many Davides. Which one?" Flanagan asked.

"Davide. You know – Davide Francaviglia, who works at the gelato shop in the alley across the square. His brother is Paolo, and his mother has the farm across the valley on the ridge."

"I have probably seen them, but I can't say I know them. I haven't been in town very long. I'll go with you to report this to the officials. You may be detained while they fill out the paperwork. This is Italy. There is always paperwork."

The old convent, which now housed the Carabinieri was also located on the Plazza Centrale. This building, like the others on the square, had been damaged by the earthquake of 1693. It had been rebuilt in the style of the Spanish Baroque, but with a subdued façade more suitable for a convent than the much more highly ornamented former palace, now municipal building, which also fronted the square. There was an interior courtyard with a two-story row of thin arches providing access to the common rooms on the lower floor and the nuns' cells above.

The entrance hall was stark and covered with cream paint. There were pictures of some of the current officers and their awards hanging on the wall. To one side was a counter with one chair facing a thick glass wall behind which sat a bored Sergeant surrounded by plastic bins containing stacks of forms.

Benches filled the remainder of the room. When they arrived, a lady was loudly complaining about a neighbor's dog, despite being repeatedly told that this was a matter for the city police and not the Carabinieri.

Having helped people file complaints with the Carabinieri before, Flanagan took a plastic card with a number off the stack by the window and motioned for Rodrigo to take a seat on the first bench.

After the Sergeant had crumpled and thrown away the two forms he had started, he nodded to the priest and the young man to come forward. Rodrigo sat nervously in the chair.

"What is your business here?" the Sergeant asked.

"This young man has shot and killed his friend in a hunting accident."

"The man is dead?"

"Yes, he is dead," Rodrigo said with a sobbing sigh.

"Inside the city limits?"

"No. Outside," Rodrigo stammered.

"Then, the death is in our jurisdiction. You will need to fill out these forms," he said as he pulled four sheets of paper from different shelves. "After you have finished, you will need to talk to a detective."

"Priest, did you witness the event?"

"No. But he told me about it in the church."

"The detective assigned to this case will be Lieutenant," he paused as he consulted the duty roster for the day, "Lieutenant Sinatra who may wish to talk to you later, but for now, go back to your church. The boy must make his statement without any outside influences. I am sure you understand."

Father Flanagan understood only too well. He had picked up more than one person from British custody in Belfast who was interrogated to the point that he could hardly stand because of the beatings he had received.

Bending over to talk to Rodrigo, he said, "I will go to Davide's mother's house and see what aid I can do for the family."

"Priest, stay out of this. You are new here and may become involved with something you do not understand. These are dangerous people who will kill a priest as easily as anyone else."

Flanagan nodded that he had heard the warning. After a reassuring press on Rodrigo's hand, he walked out the door.

He would see if he could reclaim his tea and then walk over to the farmhouse. Whatever happened, it would be a stressful evening, and he needed to get ready for it.

Rodrigo stared at the papers on the clipboard that he had been given. As he looked, the lines began to merge, and the more he stared at them the more they began to swim. He felt a chill come over him and then a rush of heat. He was going to throw up.

Looking up, the Sergeant saw Rodrigo's ashen face and buzzed for assistance. Two officers entered the reception room through the locked pair of security doors. They grabbed Rodrigo under the arms.

His body was hardly responsive as the trio shuffled back through the security doors and down the hall towards a door marked *Bagno*. One of the officers opened a narrow stall. Rodrigo sank to his knees in front of the toilet and grasped the cold porcelain bowl in his hands. He puked violently into the bowl and felt the burning stomach fluids and bile in his throat.

That was the last thing he remembered. He collapsed backwards and fell through the door of the stall with his head banging hard against the terrazzo floor.

Not knowing what they were dealing with, the officers lifted him by the arms and dragged him down the hall to the infirmary.

The nurse looked at Rodrigo, noted the blood on his boots, and asked, "What's going on?"

"I don't know. He became sick in the reception room, threw up in the bathroom, passed out, and we brought him here." the senior officer said.

"Whose blood is that? Is he bleeding?"

"He said that he just killed someone named Davide in a hunting accident. He came in with a priest. That's all we know about him," said the Sergeant who had heard the commotion and had followed them to the infirmary.

"So, he is not shot?" The nurse asked.

"No. Not that we know of. He walked in. He was distressed, but apparently, not wounded."

"He's not drunk?"

"I don't think so. I think that it is just the heat and excitement that got to him," the Sergeant opined.

"Get him undressed, and get him in bed," the nurse ordered. "I am going to start an IV. It looks like he may just be dehydrated. Once we get him cooled down, he should be able to talk. Since we don't know anything about him, cuff his legs and arms to the bed."

Once again, Father Flanagan was sitting at his table with his paper preparing to enjoy his tea and bread when he heard the distinctive "wa wah, wa wah, wa wah" of the Carabinieri's van outside on the square. This was followed by the slap of hard-soled boots on the steps of the alleyway and two uniformed officers coming through the door directly towards his table.

"Reverend Father, would you please come with us? the young officer asked. "The man you brought to the police station collapsed before he could tell us anything. Do you know what happened?"

"I know only what he told me. He said that he had accidentally shot and killed Davide … Francaviglia, I think. He said that it was a hunting accident. He appeared to be in anguish about the event."

"Did he tell you where the body is?"

"He said that his companions were going to take it to Mrs. Francaviglia's house, that is on the ridge across the creek."

"Let me finish my tea, and I will come with you. They are my parishioners, although I don't think that I know them. It is going to be a long evening, and I need to eat."

Although eager to leave, the two officers sat down at the table and watched Flanagan drink his tea and eat his jam and toast.

5

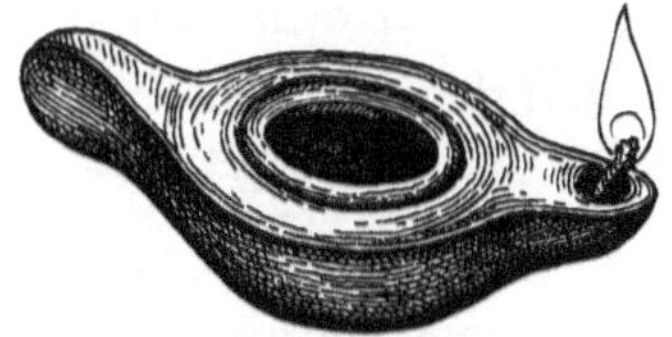

Mafia Crackdown

MICHAEL GOULEARIE WAS DRIVING towards the multi-story ultramodern edifice that was the *Direzione Investigatfiva Antimafia's* central headquarters on Via Alberto Biolitti in Rome. The new building was sprawled out like a snake with a stepped roof-profile similar to that of a Mayan pyramid on the ends with levels rising towards a summit.

This structure housed elements of the *Guardia di Finanza, Carabinieri,* and *Polizia di Stato* that had combined resources to combat Mafia organizations throughout Italy. The section to which he belonged, the AIA, *Association Interior Antimafia,* had branch offices throughout Italy, including Milan, Naples, and Palermo.

Combining the functions of investigating financial crimes, the breath of on-the-ground knowledge of the Carabinieri, and the advanced surveillance techniques and international contacts of the state police had been the conceived by Giovanni Falcone who became the organizations' first Director in 1991, just before he was murdered. The directorship was now rotated between the various branches, and the present director was Giuseppe Tavormina.

The AIA cooperated with international crime-fighting groups such as Interpol and the FBI in the United States because the Mafia families had extended their reach in the drug trade from the Far East into Europe and the Western Hemisphere. The various families had their origins as local organizations and sometimes fought each other over territories, but also formed mutually beneficial cooperative associations that now had international impact.[6]

Although the AIA investigated continuously and made busts of drugs and money amounting in the millions of euros, the seemingly insatiable demand for cocaine, heroin, and other drugs had made their efforts seemingly inconsequential. If they had a successful operation in Milan one month, and the next month made an even larger bust in Naples, they knew that the Mafia was still getting their drugs past them. There were fires to put out everywhere, including in Rome itself. Between having vast amounts of money for bribes and the added threats of intimidation, the Mafia had been able to recruit informants from nearly every law-enforcement organization. Safeguards had to be planned into any operation, least word of coming drug busts be leaked to their targets.

Michael presented his credentials to the guard at the entrance to the parking area. Driving to his parking spot, he noted with approval the fine finishing on the stone on the exterior of the building. Before entering, he again presented his I.D. and was passed into the building. In the lobby, in steel letters on the wall was the organization's motto, *Vis Unita Fortior*, Strength United is Stronger.

Michael knew that something was coming up and that he was to be involved, but he did not know any details. As he was a relatively new member of the organization and single, he was often sent on months-long assignments for some of the more elaborate sting operations.

As he worked his way deeper into the cavernous building, he saw more people wearing the distinctive blue AIA vest, including a squad of eight men armed with submachine guns and pistols who were obviously being deployed in an operation that morning. This was not unusual, as almost every day some arrests were being supervised out of the operation room in the center of the complex.

He glanced inside one of the rooms and saw banks of monitors on the walls showing pictures captured from cameras on the vehicles, worn by the officers, or from prepositioned cameras. But whatever his next assignment was to be, it was not at this stage. He was to meet in a conference room with other members of his team. He was nearly late when he went through the final security check and walked in.

---

[6]   Global Crime, 2004. Vol. 6, No. 1. p. 1931

There was a long table and the walls were decorated with photos showing Mafia members in cuffs or in the act of being arrested.

"Have a seat Michael. We are about to get started."

Looking around the room, he saw some people he knew and nodded at Vito, who he had worked with before.

An individual he did not know rose at the head of the table and spoke, "We are going to arrest two of the most significant figures in Sicily, who for now we are going to call Alpha and Beta. They have operations in Palermo and work the traditional businesses of extortion, prostitution, gambling, and more recently, cocaine and heroin. We want to locate and bust their labs and arrest the principals.

"Our operatives in Palermo have established a limousine rental business and have gained the confidence of the *mafiosi* by doing some not-so-legal services for them, such as pick-ups and drop-offs. This has taken years to establish, and whatever happens, we do not want to expose these people to reprisals.

"Michael and Vito, you are going to become drivers for this limousine company and report what goes on with the Mafia family directly to Rome. We have a branch office in Palermo, but you are not to make any contacts there or make any arrest yourself. Only go to them if your cover is blown.

"When we feel that we have the necessary information, the bust will be made by officers from Milan. To prevent word of this operation from leaking out, no one from the Palermo branch will know about it until the day the events are to happen. When it goes down, we will be assisted by an armored personnel carrier and heavy machine gun that are being lent to the operation.

"Your cover story is that you are brothers, which will give you an excuse to live together. You are distant cousins to the owners of the limousine company who had to come down from Milan because of some trouble with police having to do with the ownership of a car, which turns out to be stolen. You will go to Milan, be arrested, and processed. This will back up your cover story and provide suitable police documents. You will go to Sicily after your trial and start working for your make-believe cousin,"

"How long are we going to be in prison?" Michael asked.

"For a week or so. We need to have you seen there, to give you a good alibi that the Mafia in Sicily can check out."

"What last name are we going to use?" Vito questioned.

"It needs to be something common, so as not to attract attention," a voice from across the table volunteered.

"How about Rossi? That is the most common last name in Italy."

"You know we don't look much alike," Vito said.

"You can say that you are half-brothers. You are both from near Venice, so your accents are similar. I don't think that you will have any problems with your story, particularly with the suitably dog-eared ID papers we will make up for you. Throw away or store all possessions that don't go with a working car mechanic who is down on his luck – that should not be difficult."

Michael instantly thought, "With what we are earning, that will be no trouble at all."

"This is a high-risk assignment. Are there going to be some extra benefits?"

"No. You are civil servants. Your pay will be just like everyone else in your grade. However, if this is successful. there are transfer and promotion opportunities. In fact, we are going to be loaning some of our people to the FBI and Interpol, and there are benefits and extra pay involved with those assignments. "You are going to be held in the San Vittore prison in the old Gestapo wing where we confine suspected Mafia members. There are three individuals in there now with Sicilian connections, and I want you to get to know them. One will be released with you and can vouch for you when you get on the island. You will get to pick the one you are most compatible with.

"To increase your chances of making some meaningful contacts, you will be confined in different cells. This is standard procedure when we arrest relatives or members of the same gang.

"Don't stay in your cell. Circulate. Don't accept even as much as a cigarette or candy bar from anyone because the only way you can pay anyone back is with sexual favors, and we already have a problem with AIDS in the prison population."

"If we do this, we are going to have to leave the country," Michael said.

"AIA is aware of this, and that is the reason that those assignments with the FBI and Interpol will be waiting for you."

Despite its medieval appearance, the prison was built in 1897 at a location that was then on the edge of town but now was well inside Milan. It had been somewhat modernized to meet changing conditions with the walls and towers of the prison being covered with special materials to make them more difficult to climb. It even had an underground railroad siding where Jews were transshipped to German death camps from 1943-45, unseen by the city's population.

The six, three-story wings inside the prison were painted an institutional white, which had become grimy in the city's industrial atmosphere. The red tile roofs provided a small touch of color and also projectiles that were thrown during prison riots, such as those that took place in 1946 which nearly brought down the government.

"Car thieves?" The gruff processing officer questioned.

"No," Vito said. "It's all a mistake. We bought a Mercedes at a good price to work on and resell, got the paperwork, but when we tried to register it, it turned out to be stolen."

"That is what they all say," the officer said. "I see you are to be confined with your own kind in some of our best accommodations. Enjoy your stay in what we like to call the Grand Hotel San Vittore.

"You," pointing to Michael, "will be No. 447892, and you" flicking his hand towards Vito, "are No. 447893. Here are some tags with your numbers to put on your clothes, which will be washed, bagged and stored for you when, and if, you leave. Both of you are on the road detail until you earn the right to work in one of the prison workshops because of good behavior." Still wearing their civilian clothes but in shackles, the pair were marched through a pair of security gates to the reception area where they were to be examined by a doctor and issued their prison clothing.

Like everywhere else, the room had bare walls. The only furniture was a long bench on one wall where they were unshackled, told to remove their clothing and put them in bags with one set of their new prison tags.

Whereas before they had only seen guards and members of the police, now prisoners in grey pajama-like garments performed many of the necessary functions to keep the institution going.

The examining Doctor had on a white coat and green hospital scrubs and was pulling on a pair of rubber gloves as they came in. After that, he grabbed two clipboards.

"You," pointing at Vito," "sit on the bench and fill out this paperwork. Answer the questions as fully as you can. If you become sick or injured, I need to know something about you."

"But we are only supposed to be here while our case is being investigated," Vito said, "Maybe just a few days."

"It's time you face reality," the Doctor replied. "Even if what you say is true, this is not the City Jail. Those who are confined here stay for months, years, or even for life. It is best if you get accustomed to the idea. Italian justice moves, but very slowly indeed."

Turning to Michael he motioned towards an examination stall with a curtain over its door, two chars, and a table. Not bothering to close the curtain, he proceeds to examine his eyes, ears, and hair. Reaching down he grasps Michael's scrotum.

"Turn your head to the left and cough," he ordered.

Michael complied.

Picking up a stainless-steel bedpan, he put it in Michael's hand and asked, "I am going to examine your rectum. Do you need to take a shit? Do you have anything in there?"

For the first time, Michael was somewhat embarrassed about the procedure because he knew what was coming next. Prisoners often tried to conceal money, drugs, or weapons that they had pushed up their anus.

"No, I hope not. It is going to be rather painful if you do. Turn around and bend over."

Michael did as requested and bent over. He was startled when he felt the doctor's finger probe inside his rectum and winced when he fingered his prostate.

"Okay, that's over. It looks like you are healthy and will do well here, however long you stay," the Doctor said as he stripped off his gloves. "When you leave you will be given some soap, two packs of cigarettes, and four condoms. We are having real problems with AIDS in this institution. Avoid sex, but if you cannot, use condoms. Finish up the forms, and I will look them over before you leave."

Michael almost expected a "Have a nice day," from the Doctor, but the physician was too busy to engage in such meaningless ribbing. He felt that he had found someone that he thought he might trust.

Next, they were escorted to an open window where they were to be issued their prison clothes.

"Let me see your tags," the inmate behind the counter said.

After the two presented their tags, "You two get our fashionable gray striped outfits." As the prison clerk grabbed a pair of trousers and a pull-over top from the bins behind him, Michael asked, "What are the other colors for?"

"So you know, the red ones are for those who will likely kill you, the orange stripes are for those who may kill you, the gray stripes are for those who will beat you up and rob you, and the yellow stripes are for trustees who will likely only cheat and steal from you.

"Get dressed, and go get your haircuts."

The barber shop consisted of six barber chairs with torn seats and foam showing in the headrest. The inmate barbers kept their equipment and work area clean and swept after each inmate's head was shaved.

By the time he was through, Michael's scalp felt like it had been worked with a rasp, like a piece of wood. He was surprised that he was not bleeding.

The next room in the processing center was a shower with three stalls, of which only one worked. The two shared the room. When the cold water hit their freshly shaved heads they uttered a surprised yelp, to the amusement of the guards.

Now through processing, they were to enter the cell-block where they were to be confined. The hallways connecting the six wings provided a long walk with the entrance into each wing having a separate desk manned by a guard. A double-doored entry-way led first into the guard room and then the cell block itself. Between the cell blocks was an exercise area with soccer fields and a running track that inmates with exercise privileges could use.

"You, 447892, are in cell 347 on the third floor. Number 44793, you are in 126 on the ground floor. Inmates on each floor are fed at different times. One buzzer is for meals and exercise for the first floor, two buzzes is for the second floor and three for the third floor. Each door is individually locked and unlocked by the guard."

Michael was walked up the stairway to the third floor, where he and his paperwork were presented to the floor warden.

"Got cigarettes? Give me five."

Michael did not protest and opened the pack and presented him with five.

"I'm to be in cell 347. Who is my roommate."

The guard pulled out a ledger, turned to the listings for the cells, and flipped the pages. "You got Alexie who is being investigated regarding a Mafia killing of an informant in Sicily. That guy had his arms and legs cut off while he was alive and was then burned to death. To make a point, the Mafia Don made everyone in the gang eat some of his roasted legs, or so they say.

"Don't worry; he has not eaten anyone for the last three months."

Not much comforted by this information, Michael was walked down the block to his cell which was nearly at the end of the building. This wing was painted white on the top half of the floor and a sea-green on the bottom. They still had the old cell doors, which had bars on the upper half and a steel plate on the bottom.

As the pair walked down the hall he was greeted with catcalls, whistles, and comments like, "Hello handsome" and "Fresh meat coming down."

Fumbling with his keys, the guard announced, "Here is your new roommate. Neither of you wants to go to solitary confinement for six weeks, so play nice."

"What they got you in for?" Alexie asked as he looked up from the book he was reading.

"Car theft," Michael said. "My brother and I got this Mercedes with a banged-up front end and repaired it for resale. But it turned out to be stolen and implicated in a crime, so we were arrested. We did not know it was a hot car, or we never would have bought it. They took the car, we lost the money we put into it, and now they have locked us up. Maybe they will let us out soon?"

"Don't count on it. Soon, quick, and fast are words that don't exist around here. I've been here for three months, although my lawyer, the greasy S.O.B., has been saying all along that I should be released any day.

I don't know if he is doing anything for me or not, although he wants his money every month. It's people like him that really need to be behind bars. We get a few hundred euros and those stuffed shirts and politicians steal millions."

Michael and Vito spent three weeks at San Vittore. They only got to see each other when on the road gangs and even then could not speak. Michael was making reasonable progress in getting to know Alexie. One day, he and Vito were called to go before the court. He found himself represented by a lawyer that he did not know.

"Your Honor," the lawyer argued before the magistrate. "While it is true that these two brothers worked on and attempted to sell a car that turned out to be stolen, they were tricked into buying it and are innocent of any serious crime – outside of being in possession of a stolen vehicle.

"For that crime, they have already paid by having the vehicle confiscated and lost not only the money they paid for it but also the money they could have made had they been working on someone else's car. They have been vouched for by a cousin, Renato Ciatti, who owns a Limousine Service in Palermo. Here is a letter where he offers to hire them as mechanics-drivers and pay court costs.

"I would like to suggest that they be immediately released to their cousin and under the supervision of authorities in Palermo for a period of six months."

"Do the prosecuting authorities agree to this arrangement?" he asked the representatives of the state sitting at the other table in the courtroom.

"We do, your Honor. They have been model prisoners while they were confined here, and nothing in our investigation has indicated that these two brothers have been involved, except as unknowing participants, in any crime other than being in the possession of stolen property."

"Very well, for that they will be sentenced to time served and ordered to pay court costs of three-hundred euros each. They have seven days to settle their affairs in Milan dend then will report to the Carabinieri in Palermo who will arrange for their release to their cousin."

Now addressing Michael and Vito, "The conditions for your release are that you remain employed, are not arrested for any crimes, do not associate with any criminal elements, and report weekly to your supervising officer in Palermo. You will be processed out tomorrow.

"Do you understand the conditions of your release?"

Both Michael and Vito replied in the affirmative. They enthusiastically thanked their legal counselor and were hustled out of the courtroom as the Judge was preparing to hear the Alexie's case.

"How did things go?" Michael asked when Alexie was escorted back to his cell.

"For once, that scumbag of a lawyer was right. The case was dismissed for lack of evidence, and I am to be released under supervision in Sicily."

"Vito and I will be going to Palermo in a week to work for our cousin. We have an old Fiat 500 that we are making into a rally car that we are going to repaint like the old Sicilian donkey carts. We want to rent that out for weddings.[7]

"Our cousin wants us to work as mechanics and drivers for his Limousine service. He says he knows of a cheap apartment that we can rent.

"I'd offer you a ride, but there is just room in that little car for us and our tools."

"That's fine. I will be picked up here and driven down. Perhaps we can meet in Palermo and have a nice seafood meal, something I have very badly missed."

The check-out from San Vittore was just as functionary as the check-in. They were given five euros for their work on the road crew and had to sign a release that they had been paid. They were taken to another sterile room where a trustee in a yellow striped uniform recovered their bag of clothes. Then, they were allowed to change and escorted out into the street. The steel door closed noisily behind them. They had much to talk about but dared not speak. There would be time enough on the long drive to Sicily.

---

[7]   These are known in Italy as "auto cerimoni."

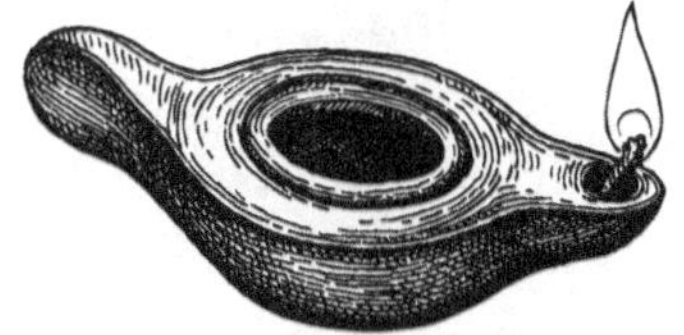

Across the Mojave

BY THE TIME THAT Roger got underway, it was nearly 10:00 A.M. He had the Busted Beast's back seat and bed packed with his clothes, frames, and pigments. Among the last things that he put in was an old GI Jerry Can filled with water. He was going to cross the Mojave Desert, and temperatures of over one-hundred-and-ten degrees were forecast.

His route would not take him through Death Valley, but he would go from San Francisco to Bakersfield, east to Barstow, and then up to Las Vegas — between five hundred and six hundred miles. With luck, he could drive the worst of the desert at night and make it to Vegas by midmorning.

The Busted Beast got its name during his college years because whenever his friends wanted him to take them somewhere, he would often reply, "I'm sorry, but it's busted. I need to replace the (fill in the blanks)." On any given day, it might, or might not, run.

This was the only vehicle he had ever owned. He, his dad, and his brother had been working on it since he was in high school. It was advantageous that 1980 was the last year that International Harvester made the Scout. That year's redesign of the Scout II continued the shift towards appealing more to city dwellers, rather than staying true to the original Scout's purpose as an off-road work vehicle for farmers, ranchers, and outdoorsmen.

While in High School, they took the Scout down to Venice for fishing trips, and one year they went to Texas with their dad on a deer-hunting trip at the King Ranch. He and his brother Frank shared the vehicle until Frank left for college.

Since he had not wrecked it, Roger's dad had thoroughly serviced the vehicle as a graduation present before he left for California. The transmission, air conditioning unit, gas tank, belts, and hoses had been replaced as preventative measures. One lagging problem was the radiator. Although it had been rodded out to remove some of the accumulated crud and corrosion, the Scout still tended to overheat.

His version of the Scout had a 345 liter V-8 gasoline engine, but not the Diesel or turbodiesel that his dad would have preferred. Although the once-dark blue paint had now faded, the plaid seats were somewhat worn, and the exterior dented from off-road use, his father had made sure that the vehicle was running well before he left Louisiana. Always an engineer, his father was more interested in functionality than appearance. His dad's only concession to cosmetic factors was to have the underside steam cleaned and undercoated to prevent salt-water corrosion should he ever drive it on the beach, which he was forbidden to do. At times, Roger thought that his dad might be more attached to the old Scout than to him. Whatever happened, he had better bring that Scout home in one piece.

By driving to Las Vegas he would avoid the more serious mountains he would have encountered had he headed east towards Reno. The Scouts, as a class of vehicles, were not built for speed, and he had learned that the red fifty-five on the speedometer was apparently meant to be a reminder that this was the designed sustained operating speed for the vehicle. Even the turbodiesel version, which used a Nissan engine designed for forklifts, was made for durability and reliability, rather than roaring down the highway at seventy mph. Although some Scouts like the Rally-e and the Midas Models had been fancied up with sharp-looking paint jobs and extra options – none were noted for great speed.

As he approached Bakersfield, Roger thought, "That's strange. Every radio station seems to play the same song."

Sounds of the long musical introduction to The Eagles' Hotel California seemed to sync with the vibrations of the vehicle.

"On a dark desert highway, cool wind in my hair Warm smell of colitas, rising up through the air…"

"Well I am not going to stop at any hotels in the desert until I get to Vegas, regardless of what they do in the master's chambers," he thought. "There are some really strange people out here. Maybe it's the heat and tortured landscape that drives them mad."

Still, he had to stop in Barstow for gas, a cold drink, and something to eat. This time a burger, fries, and a milkshake would have to do. He took his time to allow the Scout to cool down. It would not restart unless he allowed it about thirty-minutes to recover.

While he sat at a table in McDonald's, a giant man with dark shoulder-length hair dressed in filthy coveralls approached his table. This was definitely not one of the "pretty, pretty boys" from the song, but he looked more like a member of a cult who would be only too happy to use their "steely, steely knives," on a traveling stranger and leave his body in the desert.

Grabbing his half-eaten burger, fries, and shake he went out to the Scout and turned the key. The engine ground "ennnnnn, ennnnnnn, ennnnnnnnnnnn," and then finally sputtered, backfired, and started to run. His exit was none too soon because he saw the same man waving at him as he scratched out of the parking lot leaving a cloud of white limestone dust in the Scout's wake.

When he was back on the road, he turned on the radio and the lines "heard the bellman say. You can check out any time you like, but you can never leave. Welcome to the Hotel California...." filled the cab, followed by the song's long guitar riff.

This song had become an ear-worm, and he kept hearing it repeated in his head. About half-way across the desert, he was in a dead zone and could not pick up anything. He turned the radio off and could still hear, "Welcome to the Hotel California," in his head as clearly as if he was listening to a cassette tape.

"Maybe this means that I am destined to come back someday."

Now in the central part of the desert, the landscape had progressed from trees to twisted shrubs to dry grasslands to patches of dry white lakebeds that were too hostile for anything to grow to rocky and sandy patches where a few tufts of dried vegetation stood as twisted tombstones that marked the last rainfall and bloom. He had heard that these blooms were spectacular but had never seen one.[8]

Late in the night he reached the eastern edge of the desert, and he noticed that the Scout's engine was laboring as it started to slowly climb hill after hill. Each progressive ridge and valley providing him with a net elevation gain as he approached Las Vegas. Occasionally there would be a ranch exit road, and once in the moonlight, he could see a perfectly round area of green, where a pivot irrigation system watered a patch of ground to raise feed for the rancher's cattle and horses.

When climbing up a grade, he heard a loud clank and felt the vehicle lose power.

"That's not good," he thought as he steered the Scout to the side of the road. He tried to give the engine more gas, but although it revved up, all that happened was an increase in the sound of clattering from the rear half of the vehicle.

He was not reassured when his mental playback of Hotel California came to the lines, "You can check out any time you like, but you can never leave."

Rummaging in his center console, he found a tiny flashlight and used it to look underneath the Scout. He discovered that the rear driveshaft had sheared off at the universal joint and was dragging on the pavement.

Looking at his watch he could see that it was now 3:00 AM.

"I don't know if dad is a prophet, but at least he gave me this AAA card."

From his vantage point on the hill he could see down into the valley and saw a pair of headlights slowly approaching him. Whatever it was, it was big, slow, and miles away.

He took out his flip phone and attempted to call the AAA number. Considering his location, he was not surprised that it reported, "No service." Moving from one side of the road to another or up and downhill did not help. No tower had been installed within reach of his phone.

"Maybe I can get a lift with this trucker," he thought as he watched the vehicle slowly grind its way towards him. He turned off his flashlight to preserve what battery life it had and waited in the Scout with the windows

---

[8] As a geologist, I worked for several years in the wild country between West Texas and Southern California and commonly drove the route I describe. For someone who grew up in the lush Southeastern states, it was strange and wonderful country indeed. For one thing, you could actually see some rocks

down. The desert was cooling off, which would be good for the vehicle if he could get it going.

When the noise and lights got closer he saw approaching was a huge Peterbilt wrecker that was pulling a loaded 18-wheeler behind it. On the side of the cab was painted, "Long Haul Truck Recovery, Las Vegas." From its speakers, he could hear the music from some British grunge rock band screaming out over the landscape with a force that almost overpowered the throaty blasts emanating from the wrecker's twin chrome stacks.

Roger waved his flashlight up and down. When the trucker pulled alongside, he turned off his music, rolled down the window, and asked, "What's wrong?"

"Broken rear driveshaft," Roger replied.

"You got four-wheel-drive?"

"Yes, I do," Roger affirmed.

"I can't stop on this grade. If the rear axil can rotate freely, wire up the driveshaft to the frame and get to Vegas using your front-wheel drive. Can you do that?"

"Yes, I can," Roger replied.

"When you get to Vegas, go to Don's Four Wheeler. He specializes in Scouts, Jeeps, and Broncos. He will be able to get you going. Good luck."[9]

As the wrecker pulled away with sounds of gears grinding and wheels bucking, the Scout's headlights illuminated the large side mirrors on the wrecker. The long-haired driver was none other than the scary-looking guy dressed in coveralls that he had seen at McDonald's.

Bending a coat hanger, he brushed the ground back and forth to make sure he was not crawling under the truck with any snakes or scorpions. He prepared his expedient repair. What he was going to use two coat hangers that he had twisted together with pliers and wire the broken driveshaft to the frame and limp into Vegas as the wrecker driver suggested. Even though he did not have much room to work under the vehicle, he got the job done.

His clothes were now grimy with sweat, sand, and the ever-present desert dust which he could feel inside his nostrils. He tried to blow his nose, but everything was caked dry, and nothing came out. With an

---

[9]   After the flood of surplus World War II Jeeps went to the scrap heap, Jeep, along with the International Scout, and Ford Bronco dominated the market for agile, small, four-wheel-drive vehicles that could take on the rough mountain trails of the American West.

involuntary shake, he thought, "It is going to feel good to get out of these grimy clothes and take a shower, or even a hot bath."

More worrisome than the grime was an increasingly aggravating pricking feeling in his back caused by minute cactus spines that had worked their way into his clothes as he lay on the road. When he sat back in his seat, they were pushed further into his skin, so he had to sit uncomfortably erect for the rest of his trip to Vegas.

Once back in the cab, he used the second shifting lever to engage 4-wheel drive and then shifted to low gear to pull away. Whatever had happened, the rear wheels still turned, and the Scout pulled onto the highway and continued to climb the hill. He would get to Vegas plodding along at forty mph. As long as his supply of coat hangers held out, he was in good shape. That hot bath would have to wait.

He was relieved to see the "Welcome to Nevada" sign beside the road. "Maybe I have left the California jinx behind me," he thought as he continued his slow creep towards "the gambling capital of the world." He was not particularly reassured when he saw signs describing places like Dead Man Gulch and Bad Water Bill's. He had just left California and still had to travel across Nevada, Arizona, New Mexico, and Texas before he was home.

It was daylight before he crested the hills west of town and looked down on the sprawling city of Las Vegas. Even from his distant vantage point, he could see "The Strip," with its neon-lit casino signs.

"Maybe I could win some money," he thought. Instantly, he thought better of the idea. He had better find Don's Four Wheeler and get the Scout fixed. That might take all the money he had, and who knows how long that repair might take?

He stopped at a gas station, fueled up, and asked about Don's. He was told that the shop was located just four blocks off "The Strip" north of Fremont Street. Inquiring about where he might stay, he was told there were many hotels, casinos, and motels within walking distance.

Don's shop was made of concrete blocks with two large garage doors that opened up to a grease-stained concrete floor containing hoists, lifts, and pits. It was big enough that four vehicles could be worked on at the same time. Over each workstation was a swamp-box cooler that kept the immediate work area somewhat cool, despite the usual hot weather. It was forecast to be over one-hundred degrees today.

Roger saw a person talking on the phone in the office part of the shop wearing a grease-stained baseball cap with "Don's Four Wheeler" embroidered on the front. He motioned Roger over.

"I have a Scout II with a broken rear driveshaft.

"Can you fix it?" Roger asked.

"Where is it?" the man asked, cupping the phone's mouthpiece in his palm.

After replying that it was outside, Don told Roger to bring it in and park it over an empty pit, and he would take a look at it. Don resumed his conversation. He was apparently ordering some front-end parts for a Bronco.

"At least I have come to the right place," Roger thought.

Like a surgeon giving a diagnosis, Don discussed the problem. "Apparently the universal joint failed and caused the drive shaft to shear off. You are lucky. I have a junk Scout II in my yard and can salvage the parts. It will take a day to fix it, and cost eight-to-nine hundred if nothing else is damaged. That is getting close to what the vehicle is worth. Do you want to fix it?"

"I'll have to call my Dad and arrange for payment."

"You can use the shop phone. Once I have an approved credit card number, we will start work on it. Otherwise you can drive it like it is, or I will buy it for five-hundred dollars."

Roger called home, and his dad agreed that Roger could put the charges on his new card. The details of the repairs were discussed with Don and the financial arrangements finalized. At the end of the conversation Don asked Roger, "How did you hear about my shop?"

"A wrecker driver told me about it."

"Was it Long Haul Truck Recovery?"

"Yes it was."

"That's my brother, Frank. He got sent to Nam, and I went to Alaska – something about not having brothers in the same combat unit. He got really messed up over there – he won't talk about it, but he was never the same again. He tried to work with me for a time but could not be around customers. He started this truck-recovery business so he could mostly work by himself and is doing well with it. He has always had a fondness for Scouts and has owned several of them. In fact, I am pulling your parts from one of his old Scouts."

Roger checked into the Plaza Hotel. This was one of the oldest hotels in Vegas, a hangout for some of the Mafia families, but it offered good room rates, good food, and was located "where the action is" downtown. Like everywhere else in town, there were slot machines ready to take your coins everywhere, even in the men's room. Any reasonably-agile guy could take a whiz and drop a quarter into a conveniently available slot machine at the same time.

His room at the Plaza Hotel was rather ordinary. There was a huge bed, a desk, TV set, closet, and bathroom with a tub and shower. Its style was perhaps best described as 'hotel functional' with a few nice pieces of furniture in the halls and public rooms, but simple wooden pieces in the rooms. The only unusual thing was that there was a five-foot-tall mirror on one wall and another over the bed. Anyone on the bed could have a full view of their bedroom activities.

He threw his suitcase on the bed and opened it. What he needed more than anything was that bath, some food, and a beer or three. There was a steak house in the hotel, but he thought he could find something more interesting on Fremont Street, where he had spotted a number of formal and informal eateries.

After he showered, he tried to scrub across his back with a bath towel, but the cactus spines between his shoulder blades were sticking him to the extent that he quickly relented. Looking at his T-shirt, he found more spines. Although some were stuck on the shirt, a sufficient number were in his skin to the extent that any pressure on them was painful.

He threw the T-Shirt into the trash can and the towel on the floor of the bathroom. He did not want to use either of them again.

Dressed in cargo shorts, a loose-fitting short sleeve cotton shirt, and tennis shoes, he ventured down Fremont Street during mid-afternoon. It was too late for lunch and too early for supper, but he was hungry and thirsty anyway. "Beer and whisky ought not to be too difficult to find in Vegas," he thought. "Food might be a little more of a problem."

The midday inhabitants of Fremont Street consisted of tourists and performers working the street who were there to see and be seen. One group was setting their instruments and amplifiers up on stage for their event that evening. Lining the street on both sides were shops selling everything from fine arts to the gaudiest of Las Vegas trinkets – many of which were very similar to Mardi Gras beads.

One Glen Campbell impersonator was belting out Rhinestone Cowboy, while an African drumming group beat out a driving rhythm from somewhere further down the street. The diversity of the noisescape was equaled by the variety of costumes. Having lived in San Francisco, he was not surprised to see guys dressed in black leather and chains as well as drag queens sporting formal dresses from all periods of history. For now, the most revealing of the costumed characters were still mostly clothed, although some had breasts and butt cheeks exposed. The performer showing most skin was wearing only his jockey shorts, an Indian headdress, and snakeskin cowboy boots. He was belting out country songs and accompanying himself on the guitar doing a version of "It Never Rains in Southern California."

He spotted a pair of apparent nuns from the rear and wondered what the holy sisters were doing in such a place. When they turned around, he was startled to see that their habits had been cut away and their breasts were exposed which sported blue tattoos. They smiled when they saw the surprised expression on Roger's face. He smiled back and proceeded down the street following the scent of curry emanating from somewhere past the cotton-candy vendor.

Selecting a bar stool to keep from irritating his back, he looked at the photos of the dishes posted above the bar. He wanted something that he had never had before.

"How is your goat curry?" he asked the barman.

"It's good. We can make it as hot or mild as you like. I should warn you that it has bones in it because we cook them with the meat to extract all the nutrition from the animal. It is one of our most popular dishes. We can cook it for you now, but it will take about half an hour. We usually don't start cooking until later in the day."

"Make mine mild, please. In the meantime, I'll have a Coors."

While nursing his ice-cold beer from a frosted mug, he looked at the bottles behind the bar. These contained a variety of liquors that he recognized and some, presumably from India or the Far East, that he did not. One bottle stood out. It was bright red with golden tassels[10] hanging from its neck.

The first frosted beer was so satisfying that he quickly ordered another. As he was lifting the second frosted mug to his lips, a hand brushed his back, and he recoiled from the surprise touch and the cactus spines prickling his skin.

"Hello, Handsome."

Setting the mug down on a napkin to catch the spilled beer, Roger turned to see a heavily made-up face wearing bright red lipstick, purple eyeliner, and inch-long eyelashes framed by a flamboyant wig of blond hair.

"I'm Dixie Crystal."

Taking a closer look, he saw a large-breasted figure wearing jeans and a blouse supported by silver six-inch heels. On her arms there were rows of jangling bracelets, and around her neck a necklace with rows of square white beads resembling sugar crystals.

"I'm Roger," he replied.

"Buy a girl a drink?" She asked.

"If it is not too expensive, I'm about broke." Roger had been hustled in more than one bar. "I'm just driving through, and my Scout broke down."

"Poor thing. I'll just take a little white wine," she replied as she once more ran her hand down his back, and he winced.

"What's wrong?" Dixie asked.

"I have got cactus spines in my back, and I can't reach them to get them out."

"Oh, Honey, I know all about that. Once in West Texas, me and a guy thought it would be fun to do it under the stars, and we found out better. We were picking spines out of each other for days.

"I have just the thing to help."

Reaching into a cavernous handbag, she pulled out a pair of eyebrow tweezers and a bottle of nail polish remover.

---

10   This reference is to Chinese White Spirits, which I think is the most wrenched, terrible, foul-tasting distilled liquor known to man. It is now illegal to import it into the U.S., although it is the most popular distilled sprit in the world. I have a video about it on YouTube. It is frequently employed during business negotiations in China for the Chinese to gain advantage over their Western business partners.

"We will need to move out into the sun so that I can see the little buggers; besides, they don't like half-naked men running around inside until after dark."

"Ahmed, we are moving to a table outside," Dixie shouted to the barman.

"That's fine. I will serve you out there."

"The poor thing has some cactus spines in his back, and I am going to help him get them out."

"You are a good-looking guy. What are you doing running around Vegas without a woman?"

"My last one threw me out," Roger said.

"I can't imagine why," Dixie said as she ran her hands over his shoulder. "Take off that shirt and sit here with your back towards me."

Roger did as he was told. The relatively odd sight of a jean-clad drag queen picking something out of a guy's back and painting it with nail-polish remover did not warrant more than a passing glance. There were many stranger sights than that to be seen on Fremont Street.

Each time Dixie's finger brushed a spine, Roger could feel it. Dixie pinched up the skin and pulled each of the tiny thorns from his body. All told there were ten, and when Dixie was finished Roger felt a hand run along his back without the pricking feeling.

"Here's my meal. I'd better eat. Do you want some?" Roger offered.

"No," Dixie said. "I have already eaten, and a girl has to watch her figure."

"Do you want to have some fun?" Dixie asked.

"No. I have been up all night and need some sleep."

"I can help with that."

"I'm sure you can. I want to thank you for helping me out."

"Believe me, Honey, the pleasure was all mine." With that statement, Dixie put a hand on his crotch, bent over, and kissed him on the lips.

"Look me up the next time you are here and have some cash. It's a shame to let a beautiful guy like you get away."

With that, Dixie turned and walked away, leaving Roger with his bowls of steaming curry and rice. He put his shirt back on and turned to enjoy his meal. After pouring the curry over the rice, he started to eat, picking out the bones as he went. The dish was mild, and he enjoyed the mix of exotic flavors. In its own way, it was as flavorful as a Louisiana Gumbo, but with a different color, smell, and feel in the mouth.

"Glad to see you made it," Roger heard a voice behind him. "Don told me that you were likely headed down this way."

Roger turned to see Frank, the burley wrecker driver, who had the look of an NFL linebacker, but was now also dressed in cargo shorts and a T-shirt.

"Yes, I did, thanks to your suggestion. Can I buy you a beer?"

"Sure, I'll take a frosty Miller Lite in a mug," he said as he sat down.

"What I wanted to tell you in Barstow was that you have a small leak in your radiator. I looked at it at the shop, and there is a rotten spot down near the bottom. How far are you trying to get."

"Louisiana."

"That is really pushing it. You still have a thousand miles to go and that thing could go at any time. Are you going to go through Van Horn, Texas?"

"Yes, that's on the way."

"I've run Scouts too, and haven't been able to get new radiators for years. There is a guy in Van Horn that will replace your old core. He makes custom radiators for hot rods, racing cars, dune buggies, and such. If you are lucky, Don can call him, and he will have one built by the time you get there."

"How much is this going to cost?" Roger asked. "The last one I got was two-hundred-fifty."

"That's reasonable enough. I've been nursing this old one along with Stop Leak for months. Thanks."

"Think nothing of it. I am glad to see those old Scouts on the road.

"What was Dixie doing to you? I've seen her make some strange pick-ups over the years, but that was a new approach, even for her."

"Oh, nothing sexual. I got some cactus spines in my back when I crawled under the vehicle, and she was picking them out."

"Have you known her long?"

"She is a regular on this street. His usual daytime job is designing and building custom kitchens. He will remove the old cabinets, replace them with wooden units, and put in a central cooking island, which is the newest trend in kitchen design. You would not recognize him when he is swinging a hammer.

"When he feels like it, he will put on his drag outfits and work the street. He must be between jobs to be here this time of day."

"I've seen enough gays in San Francisco to suspect that he was a guy in drag, but that would come as something of a shock to the tourists." Roger shared.

"I'd like to hang out with you sometime, but I have got to get some sleep. I have been going hard for the past couple of days, and I am about to nod off in this chair." Frank said.

"Got a card? I would like to call you when I come back through in a few months. It looks like my family and I are going to make a trip to Sicily, and I should have some interesting things talk about."

They exchanged cards, and Frank left. When Roger got up he looked up the street and saw his hotel. With warm food and three beers in his belly, he knew that a bed was going to feel awfully good even if he was its only occupant.

Chapter

7

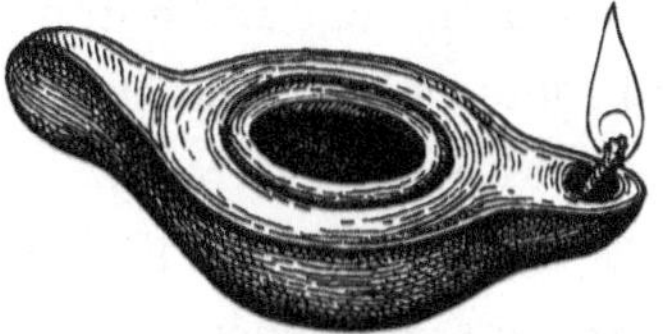

Luigi and Archimedes

FROM HIS HILLTOP VILLA, built against the ancient city wall of Syracuse, Luigi could see the heart of the old city on the island of Ortygia. This historic city had been one of the most powerful in the world until it was overwhelmed by the Roman Army and made a part of the Empire.

This event in 212 B.C. was remembered by the Romans and city residents because of the employment of several defenses devised by Archimedes. These included devices to lift Roman galleys out of the water to dash them on the rocks and polished mirror shields that acted like a magnifying glass to focus the sun's rays on the ships to set them afire.

Because this hill had such a commanding view of the harbor, Luigi thought, "Perhaps some of those polished shields were employed from this very spot."

Luigi slightly shifted the palette that was strapped to the stub of his left arm and dabbed his brush in the deep blue pigment before applying it to the cloak of a Roman soldier on a three-by-two-meter canvas supported by two easels. He had carefully positioned the painting so that the light coming from the window struck it at a forty-five-degree angle providing maximum contrast to the details of each stroke of his brush.

Glancing out the window, he saw a red Ferrari kicking up dust as it drove up the narrow road to his house.

"That could be no one but Angelica, driving that way," Luigi thought.

"Estavo, open the gate. Angelica is coming home. I can't stop. I have just prepared the paints. Show her in when she arrives."

Estavo did as he was told and opened the gate to the walled compound to allow the car to enter. The wall was three meters tall with a stone platform built on either side of the gate and four others at the corners. Each of these contained small rooms which were used for storage and to house guards that rotated on eight hour duty cycles.

Keeping an estate of this size required a staff of about twenty-five, including cooks, housekeepers, gardeners, drivers, and mechanics who kept everything in and about the house working.

"Angelica, Angelica, I would hug you, but as you see, I have my hand full. It is good to have you back home. How was the drive from Rome?" Luigi asked.

"Why did you send for me and cut off my University money? I was doing fine," Angelica huffed.

"I am sure you were child, but I did not like what I was hearing about you, including your partying all the time, getting stopped for drunken driving, and hanging out with an African. All that told me that you needed a little closer supervision.

"As my brother's daughter, I have given you the life of a princess and held back nothing since you were a child. Now I think that I need to apply some constraints for your own safety, and for the honor of the family. As always, it is for your best interests that I am concerned.

"When I was your age, there was nothing but grime, dirt, and poverty. I gave you better than that."

"I know, Uncle, but those were my friends. Don't I deserve a life too? I don't want to die an old maid. There was nothing going on between me and the 'African' you mentioned. He is a Chadian who worked in the South African Gold mines, was involved in a labor movement against the Apartheid government, and had to flee the country. He managed to go to the University where he was studying government and international affairs. He will return to Africa someday and be an important person."

"He sounds like a fine young man, but that is not our fight. Our family is descended from the earliest Sicilians who fought invaders whose only purpose was to exploit our poor island, steal our women and children, and enslave the men.

"In my generation I fought the Germans and lost a hand. The government in Rome has done much the same in that they have taken much and given little back. In Sicily we get cast-offs and second-bests, like an unwanted stepchild.

"Protecting what we have is challenge enough. No one has any need to go to Africa to find something worth fighting for. This is what I have done all my life. I have lost my father, brother, wife, and son in this struggle.

"You and Cecilia are all I have left. I want to keep you safe so that you can pass on these traditions when you start a family of your own. I am old now, and I would like to see that happen before I die."

"You are not old, and you are not going to die."

"Unfortunately, Child, death is a debt that all men must pay." Luigi concluded.

For the first time Angelica looked at the huge canvas. She saw a scene in a room with a large window overlooking a burning city. There were three figures in the room. Two were dressed in the garb of Roman troopers, and the third was a bearded man wearing white robes.

One of the soldiers was now sketched out in charcoal. He was standing in the doorway with his hand out as if to grasp an arm that was too far to reach, while the other was standing over the white-robed figure that was on his knees holding his intestines in his hands. The attacking soldier held his bloody *gladius* upright, preparing to deliver a death blow to the kneeling man.

"This is the biggest painting you have ever done.

"What is it all about?"

"This portrays the death of Archimedes, the most famous Sicilian of all who was killed by the Romans when they took Syracuse. The Roman commander ordered that his life be spared, but the soldier, filled with hatred for a despised enemy who had caused the death of many of his countrymen, killed him anyway."

"The soldier just killed him?"

"As the story goes, Archimedes was ordered to come with them, but he replied that he was busy. He was working on some problem, discovering how to determine the volume of a section of a cone, and was using a sand table on the floor and large protractors to help solve it.

"He published at least five books on higher mathematics and was considered, even by the Romans, as being the Einstein of his age. The Roman commander gave him a burial in a tomb outside the city walls and supported his family after his death."

"What are you going to do with it?"

"I am going to give it to the city of Syracuse and have it put in the same museum that houses some of the relics that I helped American archeologists dig up after the war."

"You have told us you were hired by the Americans and that work kept you alive during those years."

"I worked in Syracuse, Palermo, and elsewhere helping them document the finds they were making while clearing away the bombed-out buildings. This was hurried, necessary work. You never knew what you might find. The next thing you might dig up could be Roman, Greek, Norman, Spanish, Arab, or even something from the even earlier inhabitants of the island. Some of these were the Sicels, who fought everyone to protect what they had on this island. It is from these people that you are descended."

"I guess I have something of that in my genes, too," Angelica mused. "I want to be a restoration architect. I want to learn how we can keep up these old buildings."

"For now, you can study at the University in Catania. When you are ready, I will put you in touch with professors in Florence and plan out things from there.

"Did you stop on your trip here?"

"I went into Novo and saw Davide at the gelato shop. Is Cecilia still sweet on him?"

"They are waiting for him to get through University before they get married. I understood that he was supposed to go this year, but did not to help his mother, who owns some olive and lemon groves."

"How was Davide? I don't see him very often, but I like him."

Angelica tried to suppress a slight blush at her carnal thoughts towards Davide but was unsuccessful. "He has grown up to be a really good-looking guy. I am sure he and Cecilia will be very happy."

"I am going to have to do something that you will not like. That red Ferrari is going to have to stay locked up for a year. That was part of the arrangement I had to make to get you off that DWI charge. My driver will take you where you need to go."

"You what?"

"Otherwise, you were going to jail. There is nowhere to park a car like that in Catania where it would not be stolen or wrecked. That car was made for long trips on good roads, not the donkey paths we have around here. My driver will pick you up after school each day."

Angelica knew better than to argue with her foster father, who had such a streak of Sicilian stubbornness that his reputation as an implacable foe had made him one of the most feared men on the island.

Adding to his reputation was Luigi's wavy-bladed dagger that was described by the Greeks as being used by the Sicels. Since his retirement, it had spent most of its time in a shadow box on the wall.

Although a terrible instrument, there was no doubt that it was beautiful. Damascus steel formed contrasting bands on its wavy blade, and its hilt was made of richly figured olive wood from Sicilian trees.[11] Even the steel used to make the Damascus had been salvaged from old blades used throughout the island's long history. Even when new Luigi's knife carried a tangible record of the island's turbulent past just like the scars on its owner's body that it had collected from gunshot, knife, and bomb fragments.

When she was about sixteen, Luigi had shown her the knife and explained what it meant to him. He expressed the desire that he, like the warriors of old, wanted his blade to be buried with him.

She heard the telephone ring and snatches of conversation as Luigi spoke in hushed tones. After he hung up, she turned to see Luigi, approaching her.

"Angelica, that was Cecilia. She is in Novo. She said Davide has been killed in a hunting accident. We need to go right away."

"That's impossible. I just spoke to him four hours ago."

"Nonetheless, it is true. Cecilia is devastated. Get ready to go. I will have my driver bring the Mercedes around."

---

[11]   Although I looked while in Sicily, I could find no such dagger in museums and built the knife shown on the book cover and may make the knives used in the movie.

8

The C-130 Chariot

THE LOADMASTER ASKED, "SIR, do you have your orders?" as he was checking his manifest for the names of those who were loading up on the Lockheed Hercules for their flight to the U.S.[12] Some, the injured who were already aboard, would go for hospital treatment in Germany, while others would be booked on commercial aircraft to take them to their stateside destinations.

"Yes, I have you. Captain Frank Calsase. Since you are a flying officer, you might want to sit up front nearer the cabin where you will have a chance to talk to the pilots and flight engineer. It will be about a fourteen-hour flight to Germany, and there are no in-flight movies," he quipped.

Against the cavernous aircraft's walls was a row of nylon-web jump seats that folded down from the bare aluminum walls of the aircraft that were broken only by a few windows on each side. The windows were there, Frank supposed, so that the inside would not look quite so much like being in the belly of a flying whale. Not only were there no movies, there would be no meals except what you brought with you. This aircraft was like a huge flying cigar tube with wings and four Rolls Royce turboprop engines. Although they could be outfitted to carry troops or even as a gunship with a 105mm howitzer, this was a cargo plane that had delivered supplies to the Qaggarah Airport West, the former Saddam Airport, and was now

---

12   During my service time in Alaska, I spent many hours in C-130s.

deadheading back to Manheim. It could carry wounded, but fortunately, there were only four on this flight, and a nurse was assigned to them.

"I know all about that," Frank thought. "When my hand and eye were injured, I was evacuated in one of these C-130s." Even then, the aircraft was the oldest military aircraft in continuous production anywhere in the world. The first models had been made in 1954 and produced ever since. This workhorse had been designed to fit the largest battle tank in the U.S. arsenal, which it could tote anywhere and land on unimproved runways.

There were no problems landing at Qaggarah because Saddam had built it for the French Mirage fighters that he had acquired. He kept them in concrete hangers. Many of the hangers survived the bombing campaign at the start of the war, but most of the aircraft were destroyed. Now in allied hands, the base handled both American and British flight units without having to compete with civilian air traffic.

Frank braced himself for what he knew was to come. He heard the engines roar to full power, the aircraft start down the runway, and began a steep vertical spiral climb to gain altitude as soon as possible. Although powerful, the lumbering aircraft could not climb near-vertically like jet fighters; but clawed through the air, as if scratching its way up an enormous screw towards the heavens. This maneuver was being done to lessen the possibility of being exposed to enemy fire.

During the first Iraq war, Frank had flown Harriers from Dubai, and took a near-fatal hit from an anti-aircraft gun near the Iraq border. He had managed to put his stricken plane down in the desert next to a road that was occupied by American troops. Two marines attached to an artillery unit pulled him out of the aircraft. His left hand and left eye had been injured, and he was bleeding from both. In the treatment center in Kuwait, he was informed that he would likely never gain full vision back in the damaged eye and that although his hand was still usable, he would probably loose significant feeling and flexibility. "Consequently," he remembered the words very vividly, "You will never fly again."

During rehab, he found that these predictions were all too accurate. He faced the choice of either being mustered out with a thirty-percent disability, or taking a desk job or maybe a ground combat position.

Although this job was mostly done by junior officers, he wrangled and cajoled for retraining as a forward air controller that would be attached to combat units. As a former pilot, he had a leg up in that he knew from a flyer's actual experience what aircraft and weapons systems would be most effective against a given target and which to call in for close support. Theory was fine, but he found the reality was to call upon whatever aircraft happened to be available at the time if the unit he was with was under intense fire, as they were several times during the push to the Baghdad airport.

This time, instead of dealing death in an antiseptic way from the air, he witnessed the gruesome impact of high explosive, white phosphorus, and napalm on live targets, including unintended hits on the civilian population who only wanted to get away from the firefight. His orders were to avoid civilian casualties, but when his marines were being fired upon from hospitals, mosques, and apartment buildings, he had little choice but to order strikes on them. He found that, sometimes, his requests were denied — not from superiors on the battlefield, but by officials in Washington who were attempting to micromanage the battle, according to Rumsfeld's latest whims.

Being a Captain instead of the usual Lieutenant in such a position, he was also tasked with being on the lookout for the "Weapons of Mass Destruction" that the Bush administration used to justify the war. He even had a map that purported to show storage depots, launch sites, R&D facilities, etc. where these weapons were supposed to be located, but he found none. As Baghdad was approached and the noose tightened around Saddam, the consensus was that he would start to use gas shells or bombs, as he had done against Iran, but none were deployed — although all the troops carried gas masks and protective anti-chemical gear just in case — adding to the seventy-to-ninety pounds of gear that each marine carried in the desert heat and dust.

The droning throb of the engines and the vibration of the aircraft inclined his mind to wander to his wife, Jane. He remembered when he was in Kuwait reviewing the location of Saddam's hidden weapons when a missile hit the sprawling allied base.

He opened his laptop to tell Jane that he was fine if she should see something on the news, and he found:

Dear Frank,

I'm sorry, Frank. I am filing for a divorce. I won't be here when you get back. After five deployments, I just can't take it anymore worrying about you all the time and not knowing if you are living or dead. I want a husband who is here when I need him — not God knows where doing God knows what.

I have met another man. He is a Sanitary Engineer for the city of Baton Rouge. He has college degrees, loves me, and comes home every night. We had good times, and I am sorry it had to end this way. This has nothing to do with you personally, but I just cannot live this life anymore.

Regretfully,

Jane.

"Damn. Damn. Damn." During his military career, he and Jane had some really good times together. Maybe the best was when he was stationed at Miramar Naval Air Base in California, where they managed to get on-base housing while he trained on the new F-14s. On weekends, they went to San Francisco, enjoyed the beaches at San Diego, or even slipped down to Baja California.

Jane was a child psychologist, but the frequent moves had not enabled her to set up the private practice that she always wanted. The only opportunities she had was doing volunteer work at whatever base they happened to be assigned. He thought that she always enjoyed their time in bed together, and sexual satisfaction was never an issue. Maybe, he thought now, she just felt unfulfilled living the life of a naval officer's wife with receptions, command appearances at parties given by his superiors, and being involved in what she saw as meaningless activities on post. She had started drinking more than she ever did, and he could see her turning more to vodka as a means of getting through the day. She may have been on her way to becoming an alcoholic, a condition that plagued more than a few of his fellow officers' wives. There was treatment, of course, but she was not ready to admit that she had a problem.

Maybe the best time of all was when they had gone to Paris for a week after he had participated in an Air Show. During that week, they could play civilian, sleep in, join the night crowd when things started happening at 2:00 AM, visit the museums, the royal palace at Versailles, and eat some really good food. He found out that she was not quite up to eating a whole suckling pig that was on a rotating spit in one of the shop windows or to a fish served with the head attached. The pastry shops, the little neighborhood groceries, and the small specialty shops of all sorts fascinated her. Sometimes they just browsed around the square, picked up interesting items, returned to their room with what they had gathered and a bottle of wine to enjoy an intimate supper overlooking the rooftops of Paris.[13]

Jane, who also had a traditional religious Catholic upbringing, was captivated by Rome. They went to Saint Peter's and walked through the doors that were only opened every thousand years. They toured the cathedral, went down into the crypts where the popes were buried, and like everyone else were overwhelmed by the Sistine Chapel. They walked the ruins of the Forum and visited the Coliseum where the Christians were martyred.

She was not a museum person, but he was. Jane tolerated being dragged around through the museums. Frank guessed that he was influenced by his brother, who insisted that the family visit every museum that had paintings in it. He guessed that even without Roger, that tradition stuck as a thing that he ought to do. He was always more athletic than Roger, but Roger had been the better artist. He wished that Roger could have been there too, and he bought the museum's guides and videos to share with him.

He had to admit that of the things he and Jane had seen, he missed what all the fuss was about concerning the Mona Lisa in the Louvre. He saw it as only a small portrait of a lady, but he could really appreciate Michelangelo's marble sculpture of David, and the fact that the same artist had done the Sistine Chapel. Only a very few people in history had been that multitalented.

---

[13]   My late wife Thresa and I enjoyed our 5th wedding anniversary by spending a week in Paris and this segment reflects our holiday

Even sitting in a noisy, rattling, aircraft he could imagine he and Jane making love again, naked body against naked body, and he savored the thought.

"Well maybe there is someone else for me?" he found himself asking. "Maybe somewhere there is?" This was his final thought before he drifted off into sleep.

He was booked on a commercial flight from Frankfurt to Atlanta, and, from there, to New Orleans. He had changed into some clean fatigues, and was relieved not to fly in his dress uniform. He was reconciled that Jane was leaving him and did not know what to say during the divorce proceedings. He had agreed to an uncontested divorce and alimony payments until she remarried, which he understood would be in a few days. She had said that he could come to the wedding, but he thought he would pass on that one. No way was he going to put himself through the bother of explaining who he was and why he was there – just so Jane could show that she could attract a "trophy husband," and her present choice had better fly straight.

He had completed the divorce proceedings electronically in Iraq, and that was the end of that. Jane was on her own.

He looked forward to seeing his mother and father and spending some time with them. He had heard that his dad was thinking about a family trip to Sicily but did not know if it was psychologically safe for him to go. He knew that he had suggested some sort of trip earlier, but that was before a nightmarish couple of weeks when he was tormented by combat, had a near miss by a shell in camp, and the divorce was finalized. He was haunted by what he had seen in Baghdad. Terrible, sometimes frightening images were prompted by random events. He could not predict when they would come or know how to stop them when they did.

Although he had once been briefly on liberty in Palermo and had seen the island from the sea, he really did not know much about Sicily. He did not get much beyond the bars on Lincoln Avenue that catered to seamen. There were other establishments on Lincoln Avenue, but he did not patronize those because the last thing he wanted to do was to explain to Jane how he had "accidentally" got a venereal disease. The old-time stuff like syphilis and gonorrhea were bad enough, but now there was herpes and AIDS to contend with. As horny as he might be, he wanted none of it. The Navy issued condoms by the barrel-full to those going on liberty, with the expectation that they would be used. Treating STDs aboard ship was possible, but no one he had ever known said that they enjoyed the experience.

Once for a group of junior officers who were always boasting of their sexual conquests, a sweet tropical punch was spiked with a green dye. When they returned from their shore leave, they started pissing shamrock green and reported to sick bay. There, they were examined in detail by two nurses who were in on the joke and placed in embarrassing positions while the details of the progression of venereal diseases were explained in excruciating detail. After this ordeal and painful treatments, little more was heard from this group about their sex lives.

Although he could have hopped a connector to Baton Rouge, his parents agreed to meet him at the airport in New Orleans. They would spend the night in the city, allow him to get over his jet lag and have an enjoyable two-hundred-mile drive back home. He didn't have much baggage – just a duffle and a carry-on.

There was one item that he shipped some weeks before he left. This was an Arabic flintlock rifle that seemed to western eyes to have an impossibly long barrel. The style was called a Jezail. This gun had a large number of bone inlays, five brass barrel bands, a distinctive curved stock and weighed twelve pounds. This rifle was used to snipe at British troops from three-hundred yards, far outside the range of their Brown Bess muskets. Jezails were largely responsible for the defeat of the British during the Second Afghan War because the Pashtun could sit behind rocks and fire at the columns of redcoats with impunity.[14]

This gun had a flintlock that had been salvaged from a British East India Co. gun and had the date 1792 and the company's rampant lion stamped on the lockplate. Although somewhat rough and battered, the lock still worked, and he hoped that he could restore it to shooting condition to hunt deer and wild hogs once he got home.

He had carefully boxed it up in a wooden crate and hoped that it had safely arrived at home. Since it was a muzzleloader, rather than a cartridge

---

[14]   This event was real and happened at the battle of the 1842 retreat from Kabul where an entire column of 4,000 British troops were wiped out by tribesmen with their awkward-looking, but accurate, rifles.

gun, he didn't feel that he should have any trouble with customs. After all, what reasonably sane person would attempt to rob a bank with a gun that was nearly 6-feet tall and was capable of firing only a single shot that had to be laboriously reloaded with loose black powder and ball.

Frank liked muzzleloading guns and belonged to the NMLRA, the National Muzzleloading Rifle Association. He had shot matches with that organization both on base and at regional competitions.

Changing his line of thoughts, it would feel good just to get the smell of grease and the desert grime off his skin and out of his hair. Although he usually took showers, a good long soak in a hot tub would do the trick, he thought

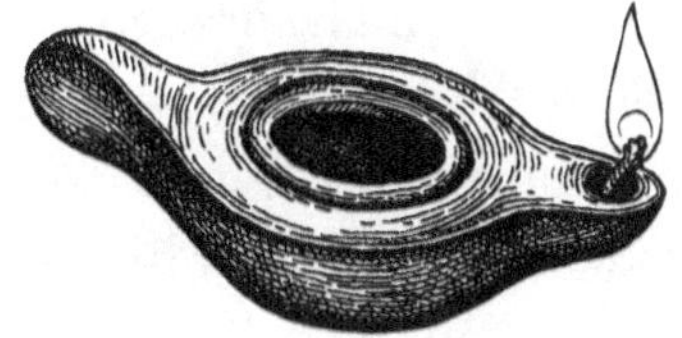

Homecoming

FLORA FRANCAVIGLIA HAD JUST taken the cannoli shells out of the hot oil, and was preparing to stuff them with sweetened ricotta cheese when she heard the sound of several men outside the house. She was expecting her sons Davide and Paolo to come in from town, and was getting ready to have a small celebration for Davide's 19th birthday. She heard the front door of the house open, and a strange man's voice call her name.

"Signora Francaviglia," Mario called. "There has been a terrible accident."

"What? What?" The startled woman asked as she burst into the room. She was wearing a white apron that was dusted with flower and powdered sugar over her floral house dress.

Mario was standing just inside the door with his cap in his hand. "It's Davide. He has been killed in a hunting accident. We have brought him home."

"My Davide. Oh, my Davide," the stricken woman sobbed as she sank to her knees on an oriental rug. It seemed like the weight of having her husband killed a decade ago and her brother two years later, combined with this new tragedy was too much for her body to withstand. She felt as if she wanted to sink into the carpet and dissolve among the woven threads.

"He is outside on the porch."

Mario stepped forward to comfort the woman, but she suddenly rose and pounded him on the chest with both fists.

"You Mafia thugs, you killed him, didn't you? This was his 19th birthday. Why today? Couldn't you give him just that? He never did anything to hurt anybody. Why did he have to die? Now, I am all alone."

"No you are not. You still have Paolo, and we are going to help you. Rodrigo will be your new son and act as an older brother to Paolo."

"I don't care what you do you will never be able to replace my Davide."

"I know we can't, but we can make life easier for you and plan to do that. There were five of us who were there, and each of us is going to look after you and Paolo for as long as we live. I swear. We loved Davide like he was a brother, and that extends to you and Paolo too."

"I want my Paolo, and I want my Davide. Send Paolo to me."

"Mother, Mother," Paolo said as he rushed into the room and threw his arms around his Mother. "It was a terrible accident. I saw it. Rodrigo stumbled on a root, and the shotgun went off into Davide's chest. It was an accident. It was an accident."

"I have sent for the police and a priest. They should be here shortly."

Almost as soon as Mario spoke, the sounds of the police and ambulance sirens could be heard from further down the valley. Their bleating notes echoed against the mountain, making the very air seem to compress and decompress as they approached.

Emotionally spent, and sensing the chaos to come, Fora gathered Paolo in her arms and sank down in a sofa, lowered her head, and sobbed. The tears flowed freely and seemingly came in exhausting waves accompanied by wails of grief. She did not know if she had the strength to even look at the body of her dead son. She had seen more than enough death already, and that was not the image that she wanted as her last glimpse of her beloved Davide in the house that had protected and nurtured him for nineteen years.

The first car that drove up to the ancient stone farmhouse contained Chief Homicide Detective Stefano Maccari and Father Flannigan. Between the time that Mario had arrived with Davide's body and the Carabinieri drove into the yard, Silvestre had rejoined the group with two dead hares.

These lay on a flat stone in front of the house that often served as a table, with the unloaded shotgun broken open and lying on top of them.

"Who saw what happened?" the detective asked even before the other officers got out of their cars.

"We did," Mario replied, gesturing towards the two others beside him. "Rodrigo accidentally shot Davide, and we brought him home."

"Where did this happen?"

"Down by the creek at the foot of the path. We were hunting, and Rodrigo was showing Davide how he shot those hares, and when he swung around he stumbled, and the gun went off. We all saw it, including Paolo, Davide's brother. They were bringing groceries home from town."

"So there were five of you plus Davide and his brother? You realize that it was a criminal offense to move the body before we had a chance to investigate a potential crime."

"Yes, but the only thing we could think of at the time was to bring him home to his mother."

"Where is she now?"

"In the house. She is very upset. Perhaps the priest can comfort her."

"Father Flannigan, I will need to talk to Paolo as he was a witness, but go and see what you can do for them. This is a terrible business."

Knowing that he wanted to secure the scene as soon as possible and prevent a potentially bloody retaliation, Maccari called for a roadblock to be set up at the foot of the road that climbed up the mountain from the valley. He knew that, soon, the area would be flooded with people who had nothing to do with what might turn out to be a crime, and he wanted to get statements from those who were directly involved.

"I want three cars blocking the road down at the first stitchback by the gas station, including an armored car with a machine gun. This may be a Mafia killing, and there might be an attempt at retaliation which would put our officers in danger. Unless they can prove that they live on this road or are in official vehicles, let no one pass until I tell you differently."

"I want to get this body out of here. Take it to the morgue. It has been moved, and there is nothing useful that we can learn from it here."

Once the body had been removed, he pulled out a voice recorder from his pocket and put in a new tape to take statements from the witnesses. The sooner he could get these down, the better. As some of his officers found a hose and washed the blood from the stone floor of the old farmhouse, he questioned the witness one by one. By the time he had finished, it was long past dark.

"I have called for a van to take you back to town. Come to the station tomorrow and give your formal statements. There will be an inquiry into the matter before the magistrate. This is a terrible business, and I want to resolve it as soon as possible. Davide was a well-liked individual. There will be many who have questions about his death."

There were many questions when the dark Mercedes pulled up to the gas station where blue lights and an obvious roadblock prevented travel to the Francaviglia house up the ridge.

Luigi spoke quietly to the driver and Angelica. "It will be best if no one knows I am here. I don't know what's going on with this killing."

"Angelica, try to find Cecilia. I suspect that she is here and we need to take her home. The police are not going to let anyone go to the house until they are done." When Angelica had left, he spoke to the driver.

"Go up to the roadblock, ask what happened, and see what you can find out. Say you are a cousin, saw the commotion, and are curious. Look for any Mafia members and question them. Whatever happened, I need to keep Cecilia and Angelica out of it."

A few minutes later, the roadblock was opened and an ambulance passed through. It did not have its flashing lights on, and appeared to be in no hurry as it proceeded back towards Novo. "There is no need to rush," Luigi thought. "Davide's only appointment is with the grave."

"I've found her," Angelica said. "She won't leave. Maybe you can persuade her. I have told her there was nothing she could do here, but she will not listen."

"I'll go," Luigi said. "Where is she?"

"Down by the station in front of the door. She is asking everyone if they know what happened."

Walking into the crowd, Luigi quickly found his daughter.

"Cecilia, you've got to come with me. I will have my driver take your car to the house. You are in no condition to drive."

"I won't go until I know what happened to Davide."

"I have my driver questioning the police at the roadblock. I saw the ambulance take the body away. There is no reason for you to stay." Gently, Luigi put his arm around her shoulder, and led her back to the car where Angelica and the driver waited.

After an exchange of keys, the driver found Cecilia's car and left the parking lot. Luigi was taking the two girls back to the villa, and he left with more questions than answers.

"All my driver was able to find out was that there had been a shooting, Davide was killed, and it was claimed to have been an accident; but that some of the people involved had known ties to the Mafia, as do many men in the village."

"I just saw him today, and he was fine," Angelica said.

"Me too," Cecilia sobbed. "We were going to be married, and now he is dead. We had such plans – such plans. I don't know what our life would have been like, but it would have been wonderful."

"I liked him too, "Angelica responded. "Everybody did. He did not have an enemy in the world, and now he is dead. I am so, so sorry," Angelica put her arm around Cecilia, allowed her head to rest on her shoulder, and held her cousin all the way back to the villa. Except for the rumbling of the tires on the road and the whispers of the wind blowing against the car, there was a somber silence in the vehicle. Everything that could be said had been said. Now, only nothingness seemed to remain as the foreboding landscape of Mt. Etna loomed to their left, and the sea crashed against cliffs on their right as they made their way back to Syracuse.

As if moving in a macabre play, Davide's mother busied herself preparing the birthday dinner that she had planned. There would be an empty chair for Davide, but whether he was present in the flesh or only in spirit, the swordfish and vegetables would be cooked, the wine served, and the cannoli finished as the cycle of life and death in Sicily once more came full circle.

After all, she had guests. There were two policemen who would stay the night, and she had Paolo and a priest to feed. Davide's birthday present, his letter of acceptance at the university, would remain in the box that she had wrapped it in, and it would be buried, like his dreams, with him.

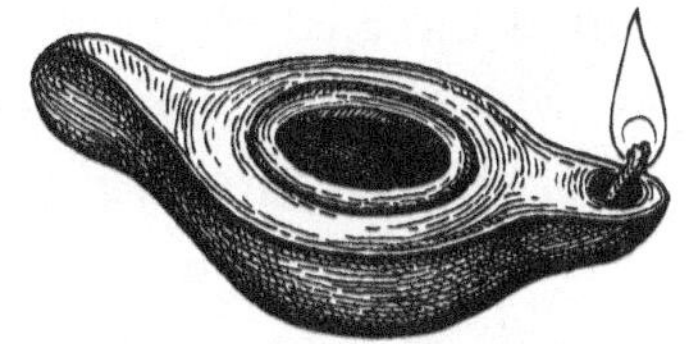

Getting Home

DON'S PARTING COMMENT AS he ran the credit card was, "I won't claim that she is as good as new, but that drive shaft will get you wherever you need to go. You might luck out with that radiator. It is going to be cloudy and rainy today, and Robert Duval will have your new radiator ready for you in Van Horn when you get there."

"I certainly want to thank you and Frank for helping me get on my way. I would hate to be stranded in the middle of nowhere."

"I will admit there are some desolate places out here, but there are more desert rats around than you might suppose. There are a certain number of people who do well in the dry, desolate parts of the world."

"Yeah, there sure are," Roger thought, but he kept that remark to himself.

"Why are the Western States so damn big?" Roger questioned as he and the Scout slowly ate up the miles across Nevada and New Mexico as he headed towards El Paso. Tacked onto the end of the state almost as an afterthought, El Paso sits on the hills around the Rio Grande. The west end of the town is dominated by the smelter, which accepts ores from all over the southwest, to extract the valuable lead, zinc, silver, and gold.

Smelting ores has always been a dirty business. In El Paso, this resulted in huge artificial plateaus of once-molten slag piled onto the land while one of the tallest smokestacks in the western hemisphere belched gases into the atmosphere. Nowadays, these gases are scrubbed to remove sulfuric and other acids, but for most of the 1800s and mid-1900s, the stack's discharges were nothing short of deadly – maybe not instantly, but eventually. Prevailing winds took the discharges mostly northeast across a barren landscape of limestone outcrops, which helped neutralize the acid vapors.

Miners always distrusted the analyses they received for their ores. American Smelting and Refining, one of the largest smelting companies in North America, was often referred to as American Stealers and Robbers, as the miners' ores were frequently discounted in value for containing unwanted materials like arsenic, or too much of this or that element, etc., so the net value of their ore was often quite different from the figures that they received from independent assays of the same material.[15]

Roger was cognizant that these same toxic materials, arsenic, antimony, mercury, lead, and their oxides and compounds were the same pigments that he employed in his art. Being mineral-derived, they were more stable than organically produced colors, did not fade nearly so fast in sunlight, and if you used the appropriate oils, attached better to canvas and paper. He often ground his own pigments from minerals that he purchased at the Tucson Gem and Mineral Show.

He really wanted to spend some time in Tucson to pick up some azurite, malachite, turquoise, and cinnabar; but only stopped at two roadside rock shops. They did not have much that he could use. Besides, he was already loaded up with nearly as much as he could carry in the Scout and didn't have any money to spare. Instead of rocks, he had a radiator to buy, and who knew what else he might need for the Busted Beast before he got home?

Outside of El Paso, but before the string of roadside motels ran out, he stopped at the Roadrunner Motel, which had an attached diner and private club. Although the string of rooms around the parking lot had obviously

---

[15]   I first heard this comment when I was working in the Chicken District in Alaska which is on the Mosquito Fork of the 40-Mile River where a miner was complaining about the returns he received from his gold ores. Ores sent to custom smelters come from many mines and each one often has a different composition. The smelter mix, like a bread recipe must be changed to obtain optimum results. In practice this is not often done and the ores are run using less than optimum mixes results in the metals being only partly recovered and/ or needing additional refinement before they could be sold.

seen better days, the parking area was freshly paved, they had a new neon sign, and all of the lights on the Roadrunner's tail were working.

"How many nights?" the night-clerk asked. "Just one."

"Here is your key and club membership card so you can use the bar which is in the next room over there. The restaurant closes at 10:00 and the bar at midnight."

After finding room seventeen and putting his bag inside, Roger thought that he had better get something to eat.

"What would you like?" the bartender asked. "A Coors, Bourbon and water, and some food."

"The cook is off today. I can grill you a flank steak with peppers and onions, slaw, and some rolls if you like, and I have some homemade coconut cake. Will that do?"

"That will do fine. I just need to get something in my stomach. In the meantime, do you have some chips?"

The bartender pulled a medium-sized bag of chips from under the counter, set them on a white plate, and placed them on the bar. "Help yourself. That's about all we've got here. It will be better if I let your steak thaw a little before I grill it. Is that okay?"

"Sure, I'll work on my beer and the chips for a while."

Now that his eyes had adjusted to the dim light inside the bar he could see that the walls were hung with paintings of cowboys and western scenes with price tags attached. These were obviously the products of a local artist.

"Who is the artist?" Roger asked between bites of chips.

"I am," the bartender replied. "I stay here and paint, bartend, and cook a little. I also show in a couple of places in town. I can't say I rake in the money doing this, but it puts a roof over my head, food in my belly, and gets me buy for now."

"I paint too, portraits mostly. I tried my luck in San Francisco but did not do very well. I use oils and natural pigments, in the manner of the Old Masters, although apparently I haven't mastered anything yet."

"I understand Partner. This artist business is shaking a very lean bush. I sell some nice pieces every year, but most people who pass through want to buy things for thirty or forty dollars, and I can't paint them for that. Hell, I can't even frame them for that. All they have to do is to go across the border to Mexico and buy all the velvet art that they want. I can't compete with that and don't try."

"It's photography and the ability to print things directly onto canvas that is doing me in. Anyone with a camera and the ability to pose a picture can 'paint' portraits these days."

Roger pushed back from the bar, grabbed his beer, and moved away to take a closer look at a painting of a cowboy standing in the snow with his horse by a corral.

"Sorry, you can't do that in Texas."

"Do what," Roger asked?

"Walk around with a beer in a bar. If you want to move to a table, a waiter has to bring your drink to you. It's just one of those crazy Texas laws, like me having to serve you with sealed mini-bottles to prove that I am not diluting your whisky."

"I remember now that you remind me. Each state has some strange laws regarding how, when, and to whom liquor can be served, and Texas has some of the strangest of the lot. Outside of airplanes, I think that the first time I ever saw mini-bottles was when we used to sneak across the border from Louisiana to Texas to go to some of the clubs that didn't check your IDs too closely.

"How did you do this one? It looks different."

"That was done with a palette knife using thick pigments. An Arizona artist named Florence Sackett[16] uses that method. I tried it on that painting, but it uses so much pigment that I can't afford to do it. The paint is applied very thick and takes a long time to dry. I can do two paintings using conventional oils before I can complete one smaller one with the palette knife."

Looking closely at the surface of the canvas, Roger saw how the dabs, scrapes, and smears of the pallet knife had been used to outline and texture the figures on the canvas reminding him somewhat of the French impressionists, but with a fresher, brighter, look that approached a three-dimensional depiction of the subject material – an ideal technique if you wanted to highlight a portion of the painting.

---

[16] Frances Sackett (1927-2012) exhibited in galleries in Arizona, California, Washington, and Oregon. When I was working in Tucson, I purchased one of her paintings. Some still appear in art auctions.

Hearing the sizzle of the steak on the grill, Roger returned to his stool and drinks. Soon, he had his beef, potatoes, and slaw served up, and although the flank steak was a bit on the chewy side, it did well enough smothered in onions and green peppers. Not wanting to tempt fate, he sampled a small sliver of the jalapeno pepper on the side of the plate, knowing that some were much hotter than others. This one had a manageable level of heat, and he added bits of it to his meal.

Remarking that he liked the bartender's art and wished he had the money to buy some, he paid his tab and left for what he hoped would be an uneventful night's sleep. In motels like this, it was not unknown to have a 2:00 AM fight and maybe shootout in the parking lot. Whatever happened, he wanted no part of it.

Cold cereal, stale store-bought donuts, and coffee awaited him for breakfast the next morning. He sat at a table this time, and in better light, took a closer look at the paintings. There were six oils on display, and he could see some scuff marks on the walls where others had been hung, hopefully sold, and removed.

"Why can't I do that?" He questioned. "Is it that I am so fearful of failure that I can't stand the thought of finishing something, having it judged, and found lacking? I have seen people buy terrible pieces of art for enormous amounts of money. Is it that I can't stand the thought of being rejected? He is making a living. Millions of other artists are too. Why can't I?"

Grey skies, light rain, and wind with a little bit of a bite in it greeted him when he left his motel room. It was shortly after 7:00 A.M., and he should make Van Horn in time for the radiator installation to be done that day, provided that he had no further trouble. The Scout, seemingly recovered after a night's rest, started promptly with just a touch of the key as if it was eager for more "adventures in travel." Roger was not so sure that he was ready for more such "adventures." The brick road that he saw patches of was red, and not yellow like in the "Wizard of Oz," but he was thankfully on his way.

"Don't see many like this anymore," Robert Duval remarked as he reached in over the Scout's grill to pull the fan and shroud away from the engine block. He needed to do that so that he could get at the four bolts and hoses that connected the radiator to the engine. "Once I get this off, I will have a little room to get at those bolts. Sometimes, those can be seized to the point where I have to pull the entire engine to get them out."

"While I have the radiator out, take a look at that fan motor, and see if you want to replace that too. As old as this vehicle is, that may be a good idea."

From the decades of accumulated bug, bird, asphalt, and small animal parts that were stuck to the back of the fan motor, Robert could hardly distinguish where the electric leads went into the motor.

"I've got a twelve-volt power supply we can hook it up to for testing to see how it is. If it is starting to drag, spark, or anything like that, it is time to replace it."

"I am going to drain the antifreeze out of the block and flush it to get all of that Stop Leak out of the system, or as much as I can. Just doing that should help the engine run better and put less strain on the water pump."

Looking around the shop, Robert could almost imagine that he was in a sculpture gallery. Around the walls were assembled radiators and cores, formed from hollow aluminum slats that were folded from one piece of once-square aluminum stock, so that they now had diamond-shaped cross-sections.[17]

"Making the cores this way eliminates a large number of welded joints," Duval responded to Robert's questioning look. "I am the only one who does radiators this way. The racers like them because they can pump a larger volume of fluid through the system and usually use them with a more powerful cooling fan and water pump.

"I use to cut and weld every joint by hand, but now I set up a jig on this table so that I can bend the tubing at the bottom and top and only weld when I start with another piece of ten-foot tubing. Once I get the ventilator tubes accordioned into shape I can box it in with steel, weld on the hose connections and filler cap, and I am done. I usually have to do

---

[17]   I don't know if anyone ever made radiators this way, but it seems to be an interesting possibility.

some grinding and fitting to install it. With these old vehicles, it is not unusual for the front of the engine compartment to be out of line.

"My insurance won't let me have you in the shop, so go sit in the waiting room. If I need you to help me bolt it in, I'll come and get you."

The waiting room had a TV set that no one had bothered to turn on and a radio tuned to a local station that was giving the morning market report which included everything from soy beans to mohair.

Although he had seen some occasional irrigation pivots and fields planted wherever there was flowing water, this was undoubtedly ranching country. In the morning, he had passed ranchers fighting their continuous battle against small cedar trees that were forever encroaching on the sparse grasslands that their stock needed to survive. He had also passed some grazing antelopes as well as cattle and horses, which gave this country its distinctive appearance. He had started to appreciate how the bartender could find ample subject material to paint in a landscape that some would describe as desolate.

"I have some good and bad news for you. I got the radiator in, and tested it, and everything is good and tight. That fan motor is about on its last legs, so I replaced it along with new hoses, clamps, thermostat, and wiring. Your total is going to be $266.30."

"That is a bit more than I expected. Take two-hundred from the card, and here is the difference in cash."

"I see that I am not the only one who has turned a nut on that vehicle."

"No. My brother, father, and I helped keep it running over the years. I don't know that we have replaced quite everything on it, but we are certainly getting there."

"How far are you going?"

"To Baton Rouge."

"So far as I can see, you should make it with no problems. I put in new antifreeze too. You are good down to zero degrees, which should be low enough so long as the Scout stays in the Southeast. It is a good little vehicle and should last you for years.

"I have a thirty-thirty guarantee on my work." "Thirty days or 30,000 miles?" Roger asked.

"No. Thirty minutes or thirty miles. If it leaks during the initial thirty-minute run I will repair it, or if it fails within thirty miles of here

I will tow you back and fix it. I suggest that you let it run here for a time before you start off."

After alternatively letting the engine idle and then revving it up through several cycles, Roger pulled away, splashing a little mud and water from the puddle outside of the shop. Roger was once more on his way. "Maybe I can still make it to Dallas tonight. That will give me an easy one-day drive home."

Rain that had originated in the Gulf of Mexico and swept up along the Sierra Madre Mountains into Texas had noticeably greened the countryside as he headed east on I-20. This was a string-straight road that seemed to extend from horizon to horizon through some of the most sparsely populated counties in Texas.

These enormous tracks of land in Hudspeth and Culberson counties are home to those who operate ranches on marginal ranchlands, who through decades of family experiences, have managed in dry years and wet to hang onto their property. They capture surface water when it is available in tanks with earthen dams, and built windmills to continuously pump into steel tanks that allow them to pipe water to more distant parts of their operations.

Managing and working such lands have resulted in the accumulation of internally-held knowledge about these properties such as when to move what livestock to better graze and where to take them, the best-producing water sources, where the best trees are to be found for firewood and timber, best rock for building, sand for cement, etc. This intergenerational knowledge often makes the difference between running a profitable operation and a failing one.

Desert species like mule deer, javelina, the small Coues deer, and, somewhat surprisingly, the European wild boar are found in the small rugged valleys extending up to the highlands. These are capped by stunted oaks and, ultimately, by Ponderosa pines if sufficient elevation is obtained.

Pushing towards Midland and Odessa, Roger encountered a new type of beast on the landscape, as he entered the oil-rich area of the Permian Basin, which was, and remains, one of the most productive oil-producing areas in the nation. The seahorse-shaped heads of pumping wells dotted the landscape. Some were producing wells, and others were not. Periodically a new drilling rig appeared that was either servicing an existing well or drilling a new one., Fortunes had been made, lost, given away, or stolen from speculation in lands and oil rights in the Basin. The most obvious presence of the oil companies outside of the wells themselves were the refineries and petrochemical plants with their cracking towers and smokestacks covering acres of industrial parks along the Interstate, and the penetrating smell of oil was everywhere.

The idea of "miles and miles of nothing but miles and miles" kept running through Roger's brain, but as he progressed first in fading light and then through the night towards Fort Worth, small towns like Colorado City, Sweetwater, and Merkel appeared with more regularity. He finally decided that Abilene was going to do for the night. There was no way he wanted to tackle the traffic going through Fort Worth and Dallas in the dark. He still had five-hundred miles of tough Texas driving to the Louisiana border and then another two-hundred-fifty miles to Baton Rouge.

He selected a Best Western motel with a bunch of big rigs parked in the lot. He generally found that truckers were a no-nonsense bunch of people, who were more interested in making miles and hitting their schedules than getting into any sort of trouble. This motel also had a club-bar-restaurant that featured steak and potatoes. "What else?" he thought. Although he did enjoy an occasional steak, he had already grown tired of steak, baked potatoes, and store-bought rolls.

After selecting a table and sitting down, a waitress wearing a pearl-button western shirt with a cactus pattern on it came to offer him a placemat with drawings of the available meals and side dishes.

"What do you have other than beef and potatoes?"

"We do baked and fried fish on Fridays and baked or fried chicken on Sundays, but steaks the rest of the week.

"Honey, if you want something a little different we have mesquite-smoked beef ribs with a homemade green chili and tomatillo sauce that is real good. Those ribs have been slow cooking all day, and they go real fast when we have them. We can put either a hot or mild sauce on them."

"I'll take a tall Lone Star, some of your homemade bread, butter, and fries with the ribs in the mild sauce."

Nursing his beer and working on a small loaf of bread and butter, he started looking around the room. The dining room was done up in old wagon wheels, saddles, and tack with faded black-and-white photos of cowboys with their guns and horses along with stern-looking photographs of ancestors. The last had a central European look to them, reflecting large-scale immigration between the Civil War and World War I. The men wore black coats with white shirts that were buttoned tightly at the neck, and their wives were similarly dressed in somber clothing. Their appearances were not unlike the weather-beaten fence posts that had withstood decades of West Texas weather. They had held their children when they died of diseases, seen their sons killed by Indians and outlaws, and even by the very horses and cattle that they were raising. No wonder these folks looked as stern and unforgiving as the land in which they lived. If your court case ever got to trial, you could expect no mercy from them.

Over the mantle in the main part of the dining room, were a pair of double-barreled muzzle-loading shotguns that were patched together with baling wire, tin, and leather. Obviously these had seen hard use on the homestead, keeping hawks and predators away from the chickens and shooting quail and small game for the table.

"Frank would be more interested in these than I am, and I really look forward to seeing him," he thought.

A platter of steaming ribs emerged from the kitchen along with an empty plate for bones, a bowl of pinto beans, his fries, and an entire roll of paper towels.

As he prepared to dive in, he felt something like a caveman preparing to feast by the campfire.

Hitting Dallas in mid-morning was about as good as could be managed between the city traffic and attempting to navigate the incomplete sections of the interstate. Always keeping a look out for signs directing him to I-20, he chose to drive straight through the heart of Dallas, where things were further complicated by construction cranes working on high-rise buildings.

Roger saw an occasional gallery, art shop, and antique store, and toyed with the notion of stopping; but thought better of it. As long as the traffic was moving he wanted to move with it. Like salmon migrating upstream, he had to go with the flow or likely spend hours on a series of side streets trying to find his way out of the city.

Three hours later, he and the Busted Beast were finally out of the worst of the traffic, and he felt that he could start to breathe again. He thought that the Busted Beast felt so too. He had watched the temperature gauge rise while he was in the stop-and-go traffic in the city, but although moving into the lower part of the high range, the engine did not overheat.

Stopping at a new-looking filling station, he went in for a bathroom break and to grab a Coke. When he returned, he opened the hood to check the radiator and its connections. There was no sign of leaks anywhere inside or on the pavement where he had parked. With his new tires, new drive-shaft, and repaired cooling system, he and the Busted Beast could push on towards Shreveport.

Somewhere around Tyler, Texas, he noticed for the first time that grits were listed among the breakfast foods. He had crossed the Grits Frontier and was a little over a hundred miles from the Crawdad Frontier at the Louisiana border. These unseen cultural barriers were markers that Roger was indeed, getting closer to home.

After he had gone through customs and made it to Baggage Claim at the International Terminal at the New Orleans Airport, Frank heard a woman's voice call "Frank, over here!" He turned to see his mother and father standing outside the rail beyond the airport turnstiles where the bags were coming off the conveyer belt.

Frank waved in acknowledgment and waited for his duffle to come down the shoot. He had to be careful because he was not the only serviceman traveling this season, as others standing around the turnstile in their uniforms could attest.

Seeing his nametag on the bag, he grabbed it and made his way to the exit, where an attendant checked his bag before letting him through the exit.

"Mom, Dad, it is good to be home and see you." Unsaid, but meant, was, "it is good to get myself home and find that we all are still alive and healthy." He had seen enough death, disease, and destruction for several lifetimes on this tour, and he had a renewed appreciation of the visual affirmation that his loved ones were safe.

"What do you want to do?" his mother asked.

"I just need to get somewhere, shower, and collapse in bed for a few hours. I am just double-dog tired."

"I brought some of your old clothes from the house," Nancy replied. "I selected the largest sizes, but I have no idea if they will still fit."

"Mom, I am sure they'll do. I weigh less now than I did in High School. I'll pick up my clothes from a storage unit where Jane put them tomorrow. Right now, a stiff drink, and a cool soft bed, is what I need."

"I got us rooms in the Airport Hilton, so we are taken care of on both accounts. Do you still drink George Dickel?"

"I do when I can get it."

"I picked you up a bottle, and you can take that up to your room with you. Let's see if we can get out of here and to the hotel. It is not far, but I will need to get out of airport parking and into the hotel's lot."

"That box you shipped arrived last week. What in the world is it? It looked like a huge curtain rod, but much heavier."

"That is a Jezail, a flintlock rifle that was used in the Afghan War against the British. I'll tell you about it when we get home.

"Right now, I could really use a drink and a bed." Shortly thereafter, Frank, at long last, had both.

The plastic-wrapped glasses beside the sink were made of real glass, and his dad had filled his ice bucket when they had checked into the adjoining room.

With an "I'll see you sometime tomorrow," Ronald had left him alone in his room with his whisky and his thoughts.

Frank poured himself a half glass of Dickel, plopped some ice in it, and collapsed in an upholstered chair. He took a sip of the whisky and thought, "I had better get to bed, or I will go to sleep right here." Stripping off his clothes and leaving them in a pile on the floor, he pulled back the covers, relocated his drink on the side table, and climbed between the sheets. The cool sheets felt good against his bare skin.

He nursed his drink for a time. His eyelids got heavier and heavier. Although his drink was unfinished, Frank could no longer fight sleep. He turned off the light, snuggled down into the bedding and soft pillows and fell into a deep sleep.

Frank awoke to a persistent knocking on the room door, with a Hispanic accent, repeating, "Housekeeping."

It took a few seconds to register that he was not in tent quarters in western Iraq, but back in his home state, and he needed to do something that did not involve grabbing a pistol. He had enjoyed the feel of clean, cool sheets against his naked body, but decided to wrap a towel around himself before unlatching the door.

"It's check-out time, Senior," the voice called through the crack in the door allowed by the security chain.

"I'm just back from Iraq. Give me a few minutes to shower and dress, and I will be out of here."

"Take your time, I will come back later." The voice replied.

After rummaging through his duffle bag for his shaving kit, he stumbled into the bathroom to see if he could wash the smell of sand, dirt, oil, smoke, and God only knew what else off his body. As many times as he showered in Iraq, it seemed that he could only get rid of the smell of burning jet fuel for only a few minutes at the time. He imagined that this was like living in London with the choking coal dust during the turn of the early 1900s, except this residue was oilier and sticky. Before he started his shower, he loaded up the in-room coffee maker and looked forward to having a cup as he dressed.

For the first time since his deployment four months earlier, he enjoyed sitting down on a clean commode and having a good crap in a sparkling clean bathroom surrounded by towels that were so thick that you could sink your toes into them. There was even a bathrobe hanging on the door and a pair of disposable slippers. It would have been a shame to rush through his shower, and he did not.

The clothes that his mother brought more or less fit. More in that he now weighed less and had an inch-smaller waist, and the pants were nearly an inch too short. "Well, I've changed. At least I am not wounded this time out."

He noticed that several pieces of paper had been slipped under his door. One was a bill for the room, the other some breakfast coupons, and the last was a note from his mother.

We are going to do some shopping while we are in town. Your room has been paid for. We will meet you in the lobby around noon and then go out for lunch. If you need to buy some things, we can visit some stores here in town before we go back to Baton Rouge.

Frank looked at his watch. "Things were sort of working out. It was 11:00, so he had time to dress and meet his parents without rushing. He flipped on the TV, but, on the news shows, everything seemed to be about whether Kerry's service in Vietnam was altogether what he claimed it to be, or if Bush had really served in the Texas National Guard.

He noticed the half-finished drink on the side table and thinking, "I am not going to waste good whisky" slugged down the now-warm and diluted mixture.

"That is still as good as it ever was," he remarked as the burning liquid made its way down into his stomach. Somehow, it made him feel clean internally.

"There he is," Nancy told Ronald after they had passed through the revolving door and entered the Hotel lobby. As she approached her son, who was sitting on a posh red-upholstered day bed with an ornately carved back, Frank got up and they embraced.

"Where do you want to eat, I can imagine that you are hungry?" asked his dad.

"I want some Cajun seafood. I have really been missing it. Even the worst fish shack in the state has to be better than what I have had lately."

"I know a neighborhood place on the lake that caters to longshoremen and railroad workers. They specialize in fresh seafood, and now everything is in season. It is called Jubilee, and they have a seafood platter to die for. Your mother and I usually split one. They serve their meals along with a bowl of gumbo and a length of boudin made with smoked alligator meat, sausage, and spices. Everything is so good that it is hard to get out of there without stuffing yourself. They also serve the best hushpuppies in the state made with old-fashioned coarse yellow cornmeal and lots of onions – not sweet like some of the boxed mixes."

Jubilee[18] was as advertised. Set in a parking lot shaded by huge old live oaks, the place was made of white-painted plywood sheets with tables set both under the oaks with a view of the levy, and in the elevated dining room you could see the lake. All of the tables with a lakeside view were filled, but Frank was more interested in the smells emanating from the kitchen than the lake.

Knowing that his stomach could likely not handle a huge platter of fried food, he ordered his meal grilled, except for the oysters, which he

---

[18] Sorry, Jubilee does not presently exist, but is a composite of a number of neighborhood restaurants in New Orleans.

wanted raw. Those were brought out first with the Bud Light he ordered. These were enjoyed and the shells were thrown through a hole in the center of the table, where they would ultimately be returned to the Gulf to help serve as a foundation on which the next crop of oysters could grow.

The taste of salt, sea-grass, and clean air washed over his palate, and he teared up as he said, "Thank you. Now I feel like I am really home."

Knowing that he had boxes of clothes that Jane had put into a storage locker along with his tools and sporting equipment, Frank said that he just wanted to get home. Until he sorted through his stuff and threw out things that no longer fit or were hopelessly outdated, he was neither in the mood nor had the need to buy anything new. If they needed to go anywhere fancy, he could always put on his uniform. Unlike the returning vets from Vietnam, he received a good reception wherever he went. Seeing what he had seen and knowing what he had done, he wondered how long that would last. The nation seemed removed, or not to care, about what was going on in those confusingly named countries in the Middle East, even though Americans were being killed almost every day. The war might have been declared a victory, but the fighting was not over.

Chapter

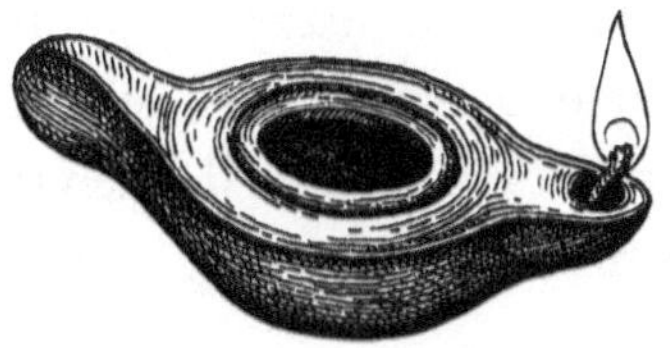

11

𝕽eunion

ROGER HAD THE COMFORTING thought of "Home today," as he crossed the Louisiana border headed towards Shreveport. It was near enough to lunch time that he was looking for signs advertising sea-food. He knew what he wanted. He was looking for a small-town seafood place that served "real food" and not the pre-packaged stuff that was opened from its foil packets for the tourists. About fifteen miles in, there was a sign indicating that the place he was looking for was three-miles away on a state road. "That's good enough," he thought.

Hank's Seafood met Roger's expectations. They had a gumbo, which was served boiling hot. He ordered a bowl, a side of rice, and a pound of boiled crayfish along with fried paddies of cornbread. This was a meal he had been looking forward to ever since he left California.

"I'll have a Bud Light and a glass of unsweetened iced tea. I would love a second beer, but I've got two-hundred-fifty miles to travel yet today."

"Where are you headed Hon?" the waitress asked. "Baton Rouge."

"Nice place, or so I am told," she said as she put her pad down on the table, placed her hand on his shoulder, and licked her lips.

These actions instantly registered: *Small town girl wants to get out anywhere with anybody at any cost* with Roger.

"I'm sorry, I have other commitments," Roger replied.

97

"Why is it that the good ones are already taken," she complained as she picked up her pad and went back to the kitchen to place her order without waiting for an answer.

Her response was a welcome relief for Roger because he didn't have an answer to her question. He felt an instant empathy because he knew what it was like to not to be able to put one's life together.

Such considerations quickly dissipated when the serving tray appeared that was heaping with fresh food smelling of butter, garlic, onions, and fried cornbread.

"Some seafood sauce, please. It has been a long time since I have had a meal like this, and I am really going to enjoy it."

"I am sure you will," the waitress replied in a matter-of-fact voice. "You're a little early, and it was all cooked minutes ago. We have customers who drive out from Shreveport to eat with us every week."

The meal did not disappoint, and Roger left a twenty-dollar bill on the table. He felt gratified not only with the meal, but even that a young woman would think him appealing enough to consider him as a ticket out of whatever private hell that she was in. He did not know what her problems were, but whatever they were, they were likely worse than his.

"Thank you for that hotel room," Frank told his father after they had started their trip back to Baton Rouge. "I needed that time to decompress. Dad, I am not sure that I am ready for polite society, and I would really like to keep things on a low key until I get my head on straight."

"That is exactly what we have planned this week – just family stuff," his mother replied. "Mary and William will come by tomorrow, and Roger is driving in.

"He might be here tonight or tomorrow, depending on the Scout."

"He's still got it? Frank asked. "We had some good times with that vehicle on our hunting and fishing trips."

"I got updates as he left California. He put in a new drive-shaft and rear-end in Las Vegas and a brand-new radiator in Van Horn, Texas, of all places."

"Do tell. I didn't know that Roger had gotten all that mechanical all of a sudden."

"I guess that necessity is the mother of invention. Faced with either being on foot, or fixing the Scout, he has kept it up," Ronald replied.

"I thought he was living with his girlfriend, Matilda, in San Francisco?"

"As I understand it, she threw him out because he could not pay his share of the rent. He thought he had a piece of commission work, but that fell through."

"So he is coming home to regroup and think about what he is going to try next."

"And finish my portrait," his mother added from the back seat.

"Tell me about this trip to Sicily?" Frank asked. "It seems like if we, as a family, are ever going to go; now is the time." Ronald began. "When you boys were in high school and college, I was working full time, and it could not happen then. Now you have a long leave, Roger is free, and Mary and William can get away for a week. Your mother and I are not getting any younger, and we want to go while we can still get around well enough to enjoy the trip."

"I don't know if I am ready to go anywhere after this last week. I was really in some bad stuff in Baghdad and can't seem to get it out of my head. I feel like I want to curl up in a closet. Dad, did you have something like this after Nam?"

"Yes, I did, and I found that a change of scenery helped. I guess that is why they gave you four months' leave. You don't have to go if you feel like you really can't, but I would really like you to come with us.

"I have been corresponding with Mario, who is a cousin of some sort, and he has invited us many times. The plan is that, next week, we fly to Palermo, meet the family, and tour the island for a week.

"The family is going to arrange all the tours, guides, hotels, meals, everything. Apparently, there are a number of great-great uncles, aunts, cousins, etc. scattered all over the island.

"Who knows? You two guys might even meet some nice Sicilian girls and have better luck with them than with the women over here," Ronald joked.

"What do they do?" Frank questioned.

"They have always been a little vague about that. Mario writes me about import-export businesses, fishing, vineyards, olive oil, cheese making, lemons, blood oranges, and such things, so I suppose that some members of the family are involved in all of this."

"I have seen a little of Palermo and a bit of the island from the sea and air. It would be good to have the time to enjoy the visit rather than rushing through on tours," Frank added.

"That is why I want to stay all week, rather than take side trips to Rome, etc. Mario has assured me that there is more than enough food, drink, art, sports, and culture, to keep you and Roger occupied for a week. Hearing of your interest in hunting, he even wants to take you on a boar hunt while Roger is busy with runs, museums, and painting. In fact, one of the family in Syracuse is also a painter."

"It sounds like it is going to be a great trip – a family vacation that we never imagined when we were kids, but I still don't know if I am ready for it. After all, people were trying to kill me just four days ago – almost did too."

Then, he had another thought that he did not express, "Maybe Baton Rouge has too many memories of me and Jane right now until I get over her. It is going to be tough enough when I get the key to the storage shed. Dammit, I don't want to disappoint the family, but I don't want to embarrass them either. Buck up Marine, you've got to do what you need to do. You are a Captain of Marines!"

The sign to Prospect Park Lane was partly obscured by a beard of Spanish moss from the huge water oaks that were scattered throughout the subdivision. When the car pulled up to the Calsase family home, there were some things that Frank instantly recognized, but there was also a new patio and shed.

"When did you build that?" Frank asked, pointing at a bit of patio that he could see beyond the corner of the garage.

"I just finished that last month. I thought it would be good for outdoor entertaining so that when the weather was nice we did not have to have everyone in the house.

"Do you want me to take you to Jane's house now?"

"Not really, but I suppose we should. She said she would leave the key and the contract for the storage shed under the flowerpot by the door, so I could clean out my stuff and pay any fees. I really don't know if I want to talk to her right now or what in the world I would say.

"Yeah, let's get that over with."

The divorce and the move had been complicated. During their marriage, they had moved four times and had sometimes managed to stay in on-base housing. But with the divorce, Jane moved back to her parent's home in Baton Rouge, and all their belongings went with her. Jane had packed "his" and "hers" boxes as she called them and designated them with different colors of tape. All of the clear-taped boxes were hers, and the black-taped boxes were his.

Jane's new husband, Bill Woozenburger, had helped Jane sort through the things and made up some new boxes for Frank that contained items like a stereo and speakers because Bill already had a sound system in his house. Frank did not want to meet him, however good a guy he might be. A hidden key would do fine.

The trip to the Woozenburger residence took them across town, which was good because that distance reduced the chance of accidental encounters. It would have been bad had they lived just a few doors down the street and would jog on the same streets, visit the same stores, etc. Since they were divorced, he wanted to make the separation as clean as possible outside of murder and mayhem. Frank still had a soft spot in his heart for her, despite the divorce.

As they drove up to the house, it looked like they were both still at work. Not wanting to trip any alarm systems, as gently as possible he lifted the pot and retrieved the envelope. After removing the key and billing invoice, he wrote "GOT IT. THANKS" on its back and placed the empty envelope on top of the pot. Relieved that this task was done, Frank was pleased to go back to his parent's house and maybe catch some more sleep.

Roger pulled up at a Howard Johnson's for a last gas-up before he got home. "I guess I had better call my folks," he thought.

"Mom, this is Roger. I'm in Alexandria. I'm going to make it home around suppertime, provided I don't get held up by construction."

"We picked up Frank at the airport last night. He and his Dad have gone to pick up his things. Tomorrow night, we are going to have William, Mary, and Tim over. Are you all right?"

"I'm fine, and you can tell Dad that the Scout is too. It is running better than ever. Tell my no-account brother that I owe him a whipping for scaring us all to death when he came home wounded last time."

"You know you never could when you were kids."

"'I know, but damn, I miss Frank and the time we had growing up together. You sure he is all right? I hear that it was terrible over there, and this time he was in ground combat."

"So far as I can tell, he is fine – just worn out. He flew to Germany and then to Atlanta and finally back here. He said that he brought plenty of pictures of art stuff for you to look at. I've cleaned out your old rooms, but I don't know what we are going to do with all your and his things."

"I don't have much – just my clothes and art materials. Maybe we'll rent a storage shed or something. We'll solve that when I get there. Tell Frank and Dad that I am really look forward to seeing them.

"Do you want me to pick up some crawdads if I find some along the way?"

"If you can buy about six pounds that would be good? We can have them tomorrow night."

"I've been passing some roadside vendors. I'll see what I can do."

Not long after he filled up, he saw "Crawfish Billy's" on the other side of the road. Although he would have to go down, cut across at the next intersection, and backtrack to the old gas station, he decided that this was the place he needed to be.

"Crawfish Billy was a large black man in his sixties. He stood behind a counter on which were displayed jars of pickled eggs, pig feet, pig lips, and peppers along with fried pork skins and cracklings."[19]

"Do you have some fresh crawdads?" Roger asked.

"Sure do. Do you want them for fishing or for cooking?"

"I would like some large ones for cooking – about six pounds worth."

"You got a cooler?"

"Yes. Let me get it and wash it out."

"There is a hose by the pumps that you can use. The water is a little smelly, but it is fine. I'll give you a shot of filtered water and ice, and that will keep them fine. How far are you going?"

"Baton Rouge?"

---

[19]   Every part of the hog is utilized for something. The pickled tails, feet, and lips were commonly sold in grocery stores and may be eaten as snacks or used in soups, stews, or even to give a little acid spice to salads

"No problem. Just put them in a fish tank or the fridge, and they will do fine."

"My dad has an old bathtub with an aerator that he uses for his crabs."

"Do you want some fish meal?" Billy asked.

"We are going to cook them tomorrow night, so just an ounce will do."

Once the cooler was about half-filled with water and a scoop of ice, Roger helped Crawfish Billy take it to a tank in the back of the shop and put it on a scale. Moving the weight bar over six additional pounds, Billy started dipping the struggling crawfish out of the tank and putting them in the cooler. These were four and a half-inch crawfish, which Billy claimed were really the best size for eating.[20] Once the cooler was brought up to full weight, it was put on a dolly and pulled out on the building's concrete floor to where the gas pumps once stood. It was quickly loaded into the Scout where Roger had cleared out a hole for it.

With the assurance that "You can buy them cheaper, but you can't buy them better," Roger dug into his wallet and his change to make up the $12.68 that Billy wanted for his crawdads, ice, water, fish meal, and conversation. He considered this transaction to be as much entertainment as it was a financial exchange.

Having completed the diagonal slash across the state on I-49, he now joined I-10 at Lafayette and Roger felt that he was now truly on home ground. He was only an hour away from the city where he had spent most of the first twenty-years of his life. When he was growing up, Port Allen, on the west side of the Mississippi was like a foreign country. Unless you were in the shipping business, no one had any reason to go there. In the opposite direction, the arrow-straight run of the Airline Highway was the edge of the world so far as development was concerned. The city, unable to expand to the west, built towards the east first along the roads that later evolved into Interstates 10 and 12 and then added the connecting streets to the north. His dad had done a lot of engineering for the factories and businesses that were developed, and, as boys, he and Frank had gone with their dad from job site to job site and got excited by the visible and

---

[20]   There are many species of crawfish some of which can grow to a foot long. These mini-lobsters can survive in a variety of fresh and brackish water habitats and even in salt water as we will later see in Sicily.

continuing expansion of their home town. Ronald had bought a 180-acre farm that was considered too far from the river to be developable, but as the value of the land increased had sold portions of it. Selling this land had largely paid for his and his brother's college.

As Roger drove through the town towards the Prospect Park subdivision, happy memories of his childhood and youth swept over him. His trip down memory lane was interrupted; however, when angry honks from people behind him served as a reminder that the light had changed.

When he turned down Prospect Lane, the Busted Beast seemed to know that it was on its way home, and Roger's eyes started to tear up as he pulled up in front of the house. The driveway in front of the garage already had two cars in it, but there was still enough room for the Scout to pull in behind and clear the street. In this case, being a smaller-than-usual vehicle had its advantages.

Almost as soon as he stopped, he was greeted by a black mixed-breed Lab, whose head came all the way up to mid-window. Roger did not know this dog, and he was not so sure that he wanted to. The dog looked like it weighed over one-hundred-twenty pounds, was draped in fur that hung halfway down to the ground, and from what Roger could see, had teeth long enough to rival those of a cave bear.

Frank ran out of the side door of the house, wrapped both his arms around the huge dog's neck, and with a bit of a struggle pulled him away from the car.

"This is Bear, Momma's new dog. He is just a little over a year old and wants to play with any new humans that happen to come by. He might slobber all over you, but he is not going to bite."

"You're sure? Positive? That dog is big enough to do some real damage."

"Yeah, he's fine. We were wrestling on the lawn before you came up. I am sure you and he will have a good time sleeping together."

"I don't know about that," Roger said as he tentatively opened the door and held his hand out for Bear to sniff.

Now that Roger was safely out of the vehicle and Bear was at least temporarily obeying Frank's stern command to sit, Roger grabbed his brother and gave him a hug. "It's good to see you Brother, I missed you. What has it been, three years or more?"

Before Frank could answer a stranger carrying a dog leash with a massive clasp walked up, hooked it on the dog's collar, and said, "Bear, have you been good to our neighbors? I'm Bob, I live two doors down. I'm sorry if Bear gave you any concerns. He is as big dog, but he would not hurt anything, except maybe a squirrel if he could catch one."

"So he doesn't belong to Mom and sleep in my bed?" Roger said as he cuffed his brother on the shoulder with the flat of his hand.

"No. I was just pulling your leg. You know Dad would never let us have a dog, even though we always wanted one."

"Thanks for letting us see him. He is a fine dog, and someday, I would like to be in a position where I could have one," Frank said as he gave Bear a parting scratch before his owner took him home.

"Let's go inside. The folks will be glad to see you."

"I hope so. Matilda threw me out of her apartment in San Francisco."

"Mine too, sort of. It seems that besides being brothers, we have a lot more in common. Strange how things work out that way."

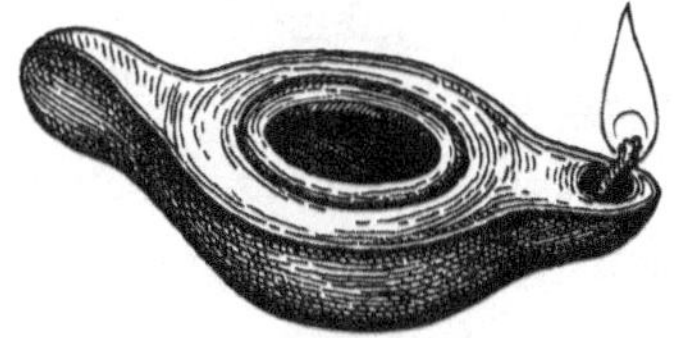

The Sting Gets Planned

MICHAEL AND VITO USED their two-day trip down the length of Italy from Milan to Palermo to work on their new life story as the Rossi brothers. They decided that Michael's biological father was dead, and the other had taken off after Vito was born. They had been raised by their mother, Maria, who did inventory accounting for Fiat. They invented a story that she had used her connections to get them into some auto-mechanic training programs with Fiat, and later with Mercedes.

This was close enough to their life experiences to be true. Their first contact with the AIA had been as mechanics in the Motor Pool, and they had received training at both Fiat and Mercedes before they became officers in the AIA. They had to get their certificates updated with their new names and stuck back into their old frames so that these documents looked as if they were owned by mechanics that moved around a lot.

Although they were interested in how the Fiat was performing on the road, they spent many hours fabricating their backstory, so that they could be consistent if questioned about their past lives. They decided that Maria had married a Rossi, who fathered Vito and adopted Michael. Then Maria's new husband had gone to work in the Libyan oil fields and abandoned the family leaving Maria to raise her two sons.

As the mother did not have time to cook, the two brothers were taught to cook pasta, use local vegetables like eggplant, make spaghetti sauce, seafood dishes, and generally get by in the kitchen. Learning to cook in real life was a skill that they had mastered on their own as single guys who had to fend for themselves.[21] They also came up with expressions that their supposed mother might have said, such as, "If you are going to eat, you are going to have to feed yourself;" and "If you are going to eat well, find the dishes you like, and learn how to make them."

This was good advice that they would pass on to their children, if they ever had any. Raising kids on a policeman's pay was not going to be easy, judging from the problems they were having supporting themselves; but, at least, they had jobs.

On their journey, they mostly traveled down A-1 to Bologna. Then, they continued to Rome and from there down A-3 to catch the Caronte ferry from Villa San Giovanni to Messina, which put them some hundred miles from Palermo.

Had anyone been watching from the air, the little Fiat would not have been difficult to spot. It still wore a coat of rust-red primer and was towing a black trailer stacked with the pair's tool boxes, a welding outfit, and a few household appliances that had been lashed together and covered with a blue tarp. They were stopped twice on the trip and had to remove the tarp once so that the officers could inspect their car and its contents.

The car was different from a stock Fiat. Starting from the ground up, the tires were wider, an inch taller, and mounted on aluminum rims. A water-cooled, 180 hp. turbocharged 1.4-liter engine was crammed into the front of the car, and sat on reinforced mounting brackets. The front drive wheels and caliper brakes were attached to new threaded drive shafts, that were firmly secured by cross-pins and supported by a beefed-up front end, suspension, and springs.

These changes necessitated that an air scoop be welded onto the hood, complemented by two new light mounts on top of the fenders and steel front and rear bumpers. With another one-thousand pounds of weight added to the front end, steel plates were welded behind the rear seat to provide rigidity and cover an area where an additional fuel tank might someday be installed. For now, this compartment contained Michael and Vito's official IDs, two

---

21   Although I did not hear this from my mother, as a man who ran bush camps and lived alone for much of his life being able to cook a variety of interesting meals was definitely an asset. I quickly learned that I could cook better than I could buy. I consider cooking a survival skill for guys that needs to possess, beyond putting something on a grill.

Beretta .380 semiautomatic pistols, and encrypted flip phones, that provided a secure line to their headquarters. These were secured by padding, bolts, and screws, to prevent vibration, and discourage detection.

The inspecting officers were more interested in the modifications made to what they considered a third-line vehicle so that the extra compartment between the rear seat and trunk went unnoticed, as did another bolted onto the fame behind the skid plate on the underside of the vehicle.

There was no spare room in the engine compartment. The transversely-mounted engine with its turbocharger and radiator necessitated that the entire front bumper-light assembly be removed to access the engine. All of the modifications that the agents had made were permissible in the small-car class of rally racing cars, with the added storage compartments thought of by the brothers.

Normally, a Fiat's four-cylinder engine would have struggled to pull itself, and this heavy trailer over the hills. Unlike the smaller branch roads, highways were carefully graded, and many millions of tons of rock had been removed to keep the hills at as low a grade as possible.

The Fiat, with its unfinished look and trailer, surprised several truckers when it passed them as they strained to get their loads up some of the steeper grades.

"Running well, isn't she?" Vito remarked to Michael, who was driving. "Yes she is. As long as we don't get her too hot, she should do fine. I don't know if I am ready to take her racing over the Alps, but on these roads, she is doing fine."

They had started driving at slower speeds to let the engine go through its break-in period. Once past Rome, on straight sections of road, they kept it at average highway speeds so as not to be ticketed. Although not the fastest car on the road, it handled crisply, the brakes were holding up well, and the cooling system was managing the added horsepower without boiling over.

"It has been dry, which is good. After all the work we spend on getting it primed, I would hate to have to do it again before we have it painted. I want to put the car cover over it, if we can't get it inside the ferry."

"This is supposed to be a covered ferry, so that will be no problem. We should manage without getting it wet, particularly with salt water. I am glad our roads are taking us away from the coast, except for this last stretch to Villa San Giovanni."

Through southern Italy, they passed a number of derelict factories and clusters of now-abandoned stone buildings that had once been small farms. It seemed that most of their occupants had left as if attempting to eek a living from the stony ground was no longer worth the effort, compared to better opportunities in the regional cities like Naples. Still, there were a few active farms, and the two would-be brothers wondered how many supplemented their agricultural income with wages to keep them going.

Before they left the mainland, they were instructed to call in from a pay phone to see if there were any last-minute changes to their assignments. One of the older truck plazas a few blocks from the ferry was still popular, not only because it had food that was cooked in front of you, but also because it still had pay-phone booths that could comfortably hold two people. This feature was popular to visitors to the island in order to call their families with better approximations of their arrival times. They were also much used by the Mafia, who commonly arranged deliveries of smuggled goods on these phones, and for an increasing numbers of refuges, who were typically attempting to contact family now that they were in Europe.

After Michael connected through the secure AIA line, Vito could hear half of the conversation. It was short, but he got some tantalizing hints that their sting operation was being re-written on the fly.

He heard phrases like, "black formal outfits," "funeral," "take them on the road," and "let them load whatever they want."

Answering Vito's questioning expression, Michael replied, "I will tell you about it in the car. Something has happened, and perhaps we can take advantage of it."

Once in the car, and with their conversation shielded by the noise from running truck engines, Michael felt he could be more responsive, "I don't know the particulars, but day before yesterday a young man was killed in Novo. There was Mafia involvement, but it was said to be 'a hunting accident,' although everyone has their suspicions about that. For whatever reason, members of different Mafia families are attending the funeral. We are going to be driving representatives of our target family from Palermo to Syracuse, where the plan is to intercept them on the road after the funeral."

When they approached the dock, Michael could see the ferry positioning itself against the dock so that the vehicles that had loaded aboard in Sicily could drive straight off. These ferries' names were not so much imaginative as descriptive, such as those run by the OK Ferry Line, which operates all over Italy.

The site where the ferry landed was likely the same location where Roman galley-ferries had operated for centuries to transport Sicilian grain and livestock to feed the population in nearby Naples and even Rome itself. Over the centuries, the ferries had evolved from being propelled by oars, to sail, to steam, with some of the more picturesque being the paddlewheel ferries of the mid-1800s. The exposed paddlewheels were efficient in that they were located in the center of the boat so reversing their motion was all that was needed to change the ferry's direction of travel. However, the paddlewheels were somewhat delicate and subjected to damage when storms swept through the straits. Although more complex gearing was needed for the later screw-propeller ferries, these were more reliable in rough seas.

As a line of demarcation between the European and African continental plates, these straits were always treacherous, such as in 1908, when an earthquake and tidal wave killed some 80,000 Messina residents as it devastated the town. Ships from the American Great White Fleet that were making their world tour rendered assistance. Nonetheless, because of the town's location, it was quickly rebuilt over the bones of the dead.

"Who knows what is going to happen at this funeral," Michael said. "These Mafia events can easily go south, and we are not going to know anything about it until the shooting starts. Whoever they are, they are not going to like being arrested.

"The concept is that, with the army and their heavy machine gun, they will not resist."

"No one is going to take on a tank with a pistol," Vito responded hopefully.

Approaching the port of Messina, the first thing seen was the white pillar with the statue of Madonna della Lettera, which was set atop a round fort on the end of the spit that protected the inner harbor. With the city's history of earthquakes, tidal waves, conquest, and retreats, there was little doubt that any gesture evoking divine protection was welcome.

A rather more practical approach was taken by German and Italian forces when they withdrew from Sicily after the allied invasion of the island. Unlike the British losses at Dunkirk, the Axis forces were extracted under the cover of dense anti-aircraft fire without the loss of a single ship sunk by enemy fire. As a military operation, this event was an unqualified success for the German and Italian units.

Once off the ferry, the pair began driving the completed parts of A-20 towards Palermo. Sometimes, they were in sight of the rugged coastline where cliffs reached down to the sea, occasionally broken by coves that had sandy beaches.

The Fiat and trailer were holding up well. "It looks like we are going to make it without any trouble with the car," Vito remarked as they approached Palermo. "I have had it up to ninety mph and there was no problem, although I would not like to push those wheels at that speed for very long. There will not be much left of us if we lose a wheel in this thing."

"Rally drivers do it all the time, but I will admit that they try to keep their high-speed runs to a minimum. We have put in the best parts we could get, so it should hold up fine. We will have to see if we can find someone in Palermo who specializes in the kind of paint job that we want. We need something that is not only traditional and colorful, but that will be durable."

"One thing for sure," Vito added, "We are certainly not going to be able to sneak around. Then again, I suppose the police would think that no one would attempt to smuggle anything in a vehicle that would be so easy to identify. It will give us some reasonable cover for circulating in various parts of the community."

Hemmed in by craggy white limestone mountains to the west and north, Palermo had expanded in modern times to the less-rugged terrane on the western edges of the city, away from the historic buildings near the harbor. This section of the city was noted for making the transition from orchards, vineyards, and fields to residential and industrial areas. It was home to numerous small shops and independent businesses needed to support a thriving port city, including the former factory, which was now their faux cousin's repair shop and rental business.

The narrow streets of the residential part of the neighborhood led to a flattened ridge nose, where a factory has been erected prior to World

War II. The building was nearly leveled by Allied bombing, and rebuilt in sections. It had gone through several owners and was now looking "like the house Jack built." Sections were made of different construction materials, mostly steel and concrete block, with some walls made of stone salvaged from the war's debris. Since it was never much to start with, repurposing it into an auto shop was an organic evolution – a pit dug there, a wall taken down here; doors and windows stuck in where needed; electric and air lines run; a forge set up, and a tire repair area designated. The result was not fancy, or necessarily safe, but workable.

The office was in one of the most solidly-constructed buildings on the property. It had windowless two-foot thick concrete walls spanned by wooden beams and a tin roof that had once been used to store volatile solvents and potentially explosive materials.

When they pulled up to the front of the office, they were greeted by the business's owner, Renato Ciatti. "You must be Michael and Vito," Ciatti said. "The authorities in Milan said that you would be arriving. I did not know that you would be driving that," pointing to the Fiat. "I am surprised that it got you here."

"The little Fiat is doing fine. We completely rebuilt it before we left. We are going to have it painted in the Sicilian fashion and rent it out for weddings."

"If you rebuilt that thing, then you are real mechanics and can do me some good. Come inside, we have some things we need to talk about. I have a driving job coming up for you tomorrow, and we need to rent you some clothes."

When Michael and Vito walked into the office, they saw that the stark exterior of the structure was matched by an equally barren interior, which was not unlike the prison that the brothers had recently left.

"Close and lock the door. This is the only secure building where we can talk. If you want to talk business, do it in your car on the road. I am going to take you to your apartment tomorrow and get you settled in. For tonight your car and trailer are going to stay locked up in the shop. The Mafia is everywhere. Assume that your apartment is bugged and that the phone in your apartment is tapped. It might be by the Mafia, it might be the police, and it might be by a policeman who is an informant for the Mafia. Got that?"

The two nodded their heads in agreement.

"There is going to be a funeral in a small church in Novo on the other side of the island near Syracuse. You are going to pick up a Mafia Don and his bodyguards at a filling station. You will take two of the Mercedes, which have two sets of rear seats. When you arrive, park the cars one behind the other, and put this magnetic flag on top of the car. Leave your trunk open, and go inside for coffee. When you come out, you will have passengers, and the trunk will be closed. Do not ask about their cargo or touch any bags. They have the car for as long as they need it. Take them wherever they need to go, and you stay with the vehicle.

"After they leave the church, there will be a roadblock that will be reinforced with an armored personnel carrier, and a heavy machine gun. You will open the trunk when you are ordered to do so. Make a protest, claim you are just a driver and don't know where the key is. Ultimately, open the trunk. The Mafia members will be arrested, and you will be allowed to bring the cars back here."

"What if there is nothing in the trunk?" Michael asked.

"No difference. Arrest orders have already been drawn up for several of people that you are likely to carry. These include Don Carlo and his second in command Leo Catochi. They both may have bodyguards with them. This is an opportunity to take them when we can get them out in the open.

"We don't have much time. Let's get you to the wedding shop. The tailor is a friend of mine, and he doesn't like it when I bring his garments back with bullet holes in them." On seeing the shocked look on Michael and Vito's faces, Ciatti continued.

"I'm joking. Everything about this operation should go fine. Just keep to your story. You are just drivers. You are not to take any part in the operation, except to drive the cars. If you have an opportunity to do something for one of the Dons, do it. The more they trust you, the better."

At the wedding shop Ciatti outfitted them with matching formal outfits with tails and top hats so that they could be easily be told apart from their Mafia passengers. The only thing distinguishing them from a visiting musical troupe was their lack of instruments.

"I am glad I don't have to wear this all the time; I feel like a penguin," Vito remarked. "I sort of look like one anyway, and this adds to the effect."

Somewhat to his embarrassment, no one disagreed.

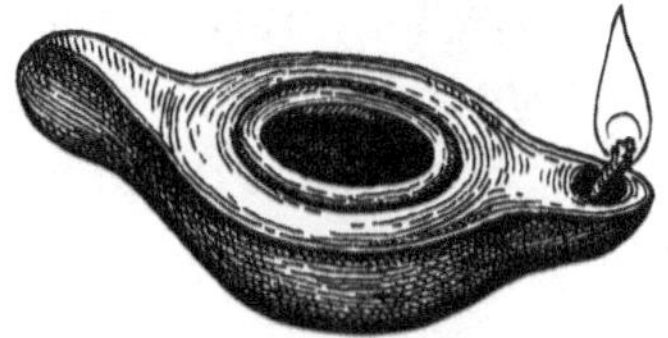

Capture of the Dons

ANGELICA HAD POSTPONED THIS question as long as possible, but she knew Cecilia would never ask, "What's going to happen at the funeral?"

"I really don't know," Luigi replied. "Cecilia is devastated. She was looking forward to a life married to Davide, and if anything, their feelings for each other had grown even stronger while you were away.

"I am unsure as to how and why Davide died. Everyone says it was an accident, even his brother, but I think there is more to it than that. I hear that members of the family are coming in from Palermo, and I fear that this could start another round of fighting between the Mafia families."

"But Davide had nothing to do with the Mafia! I know that. Everyone loved him, and I did too. If I could not have him, I looked forward to being an aunt to his children. I hate to think about the life he and Cecilia will never have."

"Will she talk to you about Davide?"

"She is at the stage that she can accept that he is gone forever, but she cannot look forward to doing anything with the rest of her life, or even looking at another man. Every man she looks at, she says, 'I see as a faint reflection of Davide. Not one is as loving, as caring, as handsome.' Then the tears come. She says that she maybe wants to become a nun, and perhaps that way can find some peace."

"Having someone be a priest or nun is an honor to the family, but that is not the life that I would have wanted for either of you."

"Where will the funeral be?"

"It will be at the Church of Saint Lucia in Novo not far from where he worked. Many people knew him because they grew up with him, or they met him at the gelato shop. He will be buried on his family's land, near his house. We will go to both places if you like, so you will have your chance to say your goodbyes."

Michael and Vito pulled their black Mercedes touring cars into the parking area at the refueling plaza, placed their flags on top of the cars, and opened their trunks. They parked among the buses and trucks, which were often towing flatbeds with containerized freight. In about fifteen-minutes, they returned to their vehicles to find their trunks closed and passengers inside.

"Are you ready to go to Novo?" Michael asked one of the dark-clad passengers.

He received a gruff, "Yes," and the two darkly colored Mercedes with their tinted windows made their way down the highway looking like a giant ant on wheels. They had approximately eighty miles to go to Novo. Michael could hear a low conversation taking place behind the glass privacy window, but could not make out what was said. He put on his earphones and plugged them into his radio. Whatever was being said behind him, he did not want or need to know. All he had to do was get them safely to Novo, find a place to park, and wait for them. That, he could do.

Another Mercedes disembarked Luigi, Angelica, and Cecilia at the foot of the north road leading to the town plaza and the church up a side road. Only official traffic was permitted on the Plaza, which hosted another church, the town hall opposite it, and the Carabinieri and police station on the other sides.

Coffins going to San Nicolo/San Lucia were manhandled up the steep road to the smaller church and then down the aisle between the pews. This transport sometimes required that pall-bearers be hired among the young men of the town. Davide had sometimes picked up a few extra euros this way, but now, his part in this play of life was reversed, and it was he who was being carried in the coffin.

This point was not lost on Cecilia, who saw Rodrigo, the man who shot Davide standing among the men at the altar, ready to take up the coffin and carry it out of the church. He had his back to the congregation so she could not see the expression on his face. She knew what she had been told, but she was not so sure that she believed it, even when Paolo had told her.

Standing on steps of the building that housed the Carabinieri, Lieutenant Sinatra was approached by Rugimento, the Gelato shop's owner, who was on his way to the funeral.

"Lieutenant Sinatra, is anything more known about Davide's death, other than it was supposed to be an accident?" Rugimento asked.

"Not unless you know something, or remember something, from that day that can help."

"It was a special day, Davide's 19th birthday. I gave him an extra ten euros. As usual his brother Paolo came by after school. Cecilia, Luigi The Claw's daughter, was leaving as I came down, but there was nothing unusual about the day that I can remember.

"Rodrigo told me that he stumbled on a root, and accidentally shot Davide by the creek on the path to his mother's house. He seems to be really torn up about it."

"I questioned Rodrigo and the others. This is a strange business; but everyone agrees that it was an accident. Perhaps so and perhaps not, but without some other evidence, we had to release him. He is one of the pall-bearers at the funeral and has agreed to work for Davide's mother as restitution.[22] Everyone involved maybe had Mafia connections, and I do not know if we will ever learn the whole story. This is a sad day for the town."

Rugimento nodded in agreement and crossed himself in an almost involuntary motion. Then, he proceeded across the Plazza to walk up the steep inclined road to the church.

---

[22] The tradition that a man who unlawfully kills a family's breadwinner is then responsible for the family's continued support goes back to medieval times.

Once inside and standing in a pew, Luigi felt a nudge from behind him, and turned to see Arbenaro, one of the Mafia Dons from Palermo, in the pew behind him. He watched as Arbenaro mouthed, "we need to talk," and Luigi nodded in assent. He did not know what that was about, but supposed it had something to do with Davide's death.

Paolo and his mother were the only members of the Francaviglia family to walk down to the front pews of the church. The boy's father had been killed years before, and their other relatives had either disassociated themselves from the family or were working out of the country.

The funeral was brief. Father Flanagan said the necessary words, and the coffin was quickly borne out of the church. No one spoke on Davide's behalf because of the suspicious nature of his death. When they walked past, the pallbearers had stoic expressions on their faces, except for Rodrigo, who was fighting back tears.

"He looks really remorseful," Cecilia thought.

"Go back to the car," Luigi told Angelica and Cecilia. "I have something to discuss with Don. Arbenaro."

Stepping into a nave, Luigi and Don Arbenaro had a quiet conversation in a darker corner of the church that was illuminated by votive candles and a representation of the station of the cross where Jesus stumbled and had his cross taken up by another man.

"Luigi, you and I have known each other for many years. I want you to know that neither I nor anyone else in Palermo had anything to do with this boy's death."

"I live closer to this family that you do, Cecilia was going to marry him, and I don't know anything either. I am told that it was an accident, but I find that hard to believe. Whatever happened, it apparently is a close family matter and did not involve any of the Mafia families in Sicily. I am content to let things stay as they are."

"I do not want to be in any way involved, but here is an envelope with ten-thousand euros for the benefit of the family. This money is paid not out of guilt, but to ensure our continued good relations." Don Arbenaro concluded.

"I understand completely. No one wants to stir up the Mafia Wars again. That was a terrible time, and many good men were killed for no good reason. I don't know, but maybe Davide's killing was somehow related. I will see that the family gets the money, and your name will be kept out of it."

"I don't know if I can live here anymore," Cecilia said when she and Angelica were back in the car. We were to be married in that church, and now Davide is dead. We had our whole life planned. This is more than anyone ought to bear. Right now, I want to leave this place and never come back."

"I know exactly what you mean. I thought all the killing was behind us, something that happened decades ago, but it is still with us and seems like it always will be," Angelica agreed.

"Do you feel like going to the gravesite?" Luigi asked.

Both replied in the affirmative but had nothing more to say as the driver navigated the car out of the town and up the road leading to the Francaviglia farm. There were a number of cars there already, and the driver had to park in an awkward downhill slant, making it a bit treacherous to get out of the vehicle.

The driver helped the two girls out and gave Luigi a hand so that he could obtain a firmer footing on the gravel road where the dark lava gravel road was beaten nearly flat by the traffic. As they were walking up, the coffin was being lowered into the rocky soil by the pallbearers who were supervised by Mario.

Maria Francaviglia who had said nearly nothing all day, spoke. "Priests may tell you that this is not holy ground, but as God made it, I declare that this ground is as holy as any other and fit for my son to rest in for as long as body and bones endure. He was a good boy. Before he had his chance to grow into a young man, he was taken away from me, by what everyone says was an accident.

"Rodrigo held the gun, and Paolo tells me it was an accident. Four others swear that it was an accident. Maybe it was. If it was not, it is their burden. Rodrigo says that as he is responsible, he will act in Davide's stead, and be my son and brother to Paolo.

"I accept that this will be so. Rodrigo will sleep in Davide's bed, wear his clothes, and do his work, and I will come to love him as if he were my own. Davide leaves a sweetheart Cecilia, who I was looking forward to welcoming into the family. She is also welcome here whenever she wishes to come.

"For now, let us put Davide to rest and remember what he was to all of us."

After that speech, there was no need for anyone to say anything else. Father Flannigan gave the final benediction and threw a handful of the black pebbly soil on top of the coffin. As they walked past, others at the event did the same. Luigi, Angelica, and Cecilia complied with the custom as a sign of respect and expressed their condolences to Davide's mother.

"I am so sorry that you did not have a chance to get married," Mrs. Francaviglia said to Cecilia. "You would have made a wonderful couple and a fine daughter-in-law."

Luigi pulled Rodrigo and Mario aside. "I have ten-thousand euros for the family that I will give to Mrs. Francaviglia tomorrow. I also want to rent that bunker above the house for 25,000 euros a year. You can tell her that I will use it for storage and set up a small laboratory in it. This will help her and Paolo over the years."

Mario replied, "I have collected another eight thousand from members of the hunting party, so that will amount to a healthy sum when it is put together. It won't replace Davide, but it will get some bills paid."

"I will help out too as I can," Rodrigo added. "I am going to be living here so I can look out for everybody."

"Rodrigo. That is exactly your job. Keep everyone out of trouble, particularly Paolo, and help Mrs. Francaviglia make this farm viable, or at least livable – just like a son would do. That is the pledge we made, and you must live up to it for the sake of your unborn children. Davide did a noble thing, and we must honor his memory." With that solemn remark, Mario left, leaving Rodrigo standing by the grave.

Cresting a hill, the two black Mercedes were confronted by a roadblock manned by twenty Carabinieri. By the time those in the car saw the roadblock, the roadway was hemmed in on both sides by a deep cut through a hill.

Rolling down his window, Michael pulled out his identification, which included his driver's license and a card with the name of the rental company on it.

"I am a paid driver and am taking these passengers back to Palermo from a funeral in Novo."

"Everyone out of the car," ordered the officer as three others approached with their submachine guns pointed at the vehicle. "Spread your legs and place your hands on the top of the vehicle."

"This is an outrage," Michael said. "We are coming from a funeral for God's sake."

From behind him, he heard a voice that he knew. It came from the same officer that briefed him and Vito in Milan the month before. He never did know his name and dared not look at him now, lest some flash of recognition come across their faces.

Two large black duffle bags were taken from the trunk. When they were opened, they contained a variety of pistols, two submachine guns, and enough 9mm ammo to sustain a considerable firefight.

"Don Carlos, do you know anything about these?" "No they must have been in the car when we got in. I don't know how they got there."

Looking at Michael and Vito he asked the same question.

"No," Vito said. "We picked up these passengers at a fueling plaza, and I did not see anyone put anything in the trunk. It was open when we went into the plaza and closed when we got back. It does not pay to be too curious about such things."

"You," pointing to Michael. "Do you know anything about the contents of the trunk?"

"Only that it is supposed to have a spare tire and tools in it. Otherwise, it is just as Vito said."

"Search them."

Two of Don Carlos' bodyguards were carrying pistols, and the Don himself had a small .32 Walther PPK stuck in an inside pocket. When asked about these, Don Carlos replied. "All of these are legally licensed. We live in dangerous times." Of the entire group, only Michael and Vito were unarmed.

"You are all going to be arrested under suspicion of possession of unregistered weapons."

"We haven't been paid," Michael said.

"Ok. Pay the drivers. How much is it?"

"It was 1,200 euros for the cars, and 400 euros for us, for a total of 1,600 euros."

"I will pay them" said Don Carlos. As he counted out the money to give to Michael he whispered in his ear, "There is a note in an envelope under my seat. See that it is delivered. Here is an extra two-hundred for that service."

"You can take the cars and go now. Your business here is concluded."

Michael and Vito returned to the cars, buttoned them up, and thankfully drove away from the roadblock. They had all the jail time that they wanted and were gratified that the arrests had gone so smoothly. In one operation, the AIA had taken two of the most powerful Mafia figures in Sicily.

Midafternoon the next day, a strange vehicle was approaching Luigi The Claw's compound in Syracuse. It was an old Fiat that looked like it had been dipped in tomato sauce. It was stopped at the gate.

"I have a message for Luigi from Don Carlos," Michael said. While Vito was getting their apartment ready and their tools stored away, he was delivering Don Carlos' message.

The car was inspected, let inside the compound, and he was searched.

"He's clean," the guard said. "Wait here."

The arrival of this strange vehicle and its driver provoked Cecilia's curiosity. She had seen many vehicles come and go in the compound, but none that looked like a ripe strawberry with an air scoop in the front.

As she approached to get a closer look at it, she felt an involuntary shudder because the driver looked so much like Davide. He had the same color eyes and hair and a similar slim build.

"Nice car, or at least I think that it is going to be," Cecilia remarked.

Surprised, first because she had spoken to him and secondly because she seemed to care about cars, Michael gasped because she was so breathtakingly beautiful even though plainly dressed in a pair of slacks and a blouse.

"We are not through with it yet. It is going to be painted in the Sicilian fashion like a wedding cart. My brother and I are going to rent it out."

"I thought that I was going to be married, but my fiancé was killed."

"I know. I was at the funeral."

"I didn't see you there."

"You would not have. I did not go to the grave. I am a driver for the limousine rental company and stayed with the car during the funeral."

"I'm glad you didn't because you look so much like Davide that it's scary."

"I don't know. I never met him. My name is Michael Rossi, and I came down with my brother Vito. We just arrived in Palermo yesterday and started work with our cousin."

"I have a message for Luigi. Your father?"

"He has been father to my cousin Angelica and me since we were little girls. He is a stern man, but a good father."

As Luigi approached, Cecilia said, "This is Michael Rossi, and he has a message for you."

"Yes sir. This is from Don Carlo, and he asked that I give it to you."

"How did you come by the message?" Luigi asked.

"That is perhaps a matter that we need to speak of in private."

"Just so. I like a young man who shows a little thoughtfulness in such matters. Come inside."

Once inside, they sat down in the reception room of the house.

"Tell me what happened?" Luigi asked.

Michael explained that they had left the funeral in two cars with Don Carlos, been stopped on the road by a force of police, and Don Carlos and everyone with him was arrested. He said that Carlos had the opportunity to slip a note under his seat before his arrest and asked him to deliver it.

Luigi retrieved a curious-looking claw-shaped knife from a side table drawer and used it to open the envelope. He frowned as he read the contents.

Look after the family while I am away. Carlos.

Those few words were quite enough. He had just been designated as the acting head of this branch of the Sicilian Mafia family. He would have to go to Palermo and reconnect with the family operations. Like in any business, there were opportunity costs and obligations to be fulfilled even if its Chief Executive Officer and his designated successor were temporally out of the picture. Other crime families might attempt to grab parts of the weakened organization, and it was his job to prevent such undertakings. By establishing firm control over the operation, Luigi could illustrate that nothing significant had changed.

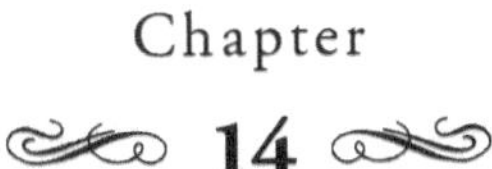

Family Matters

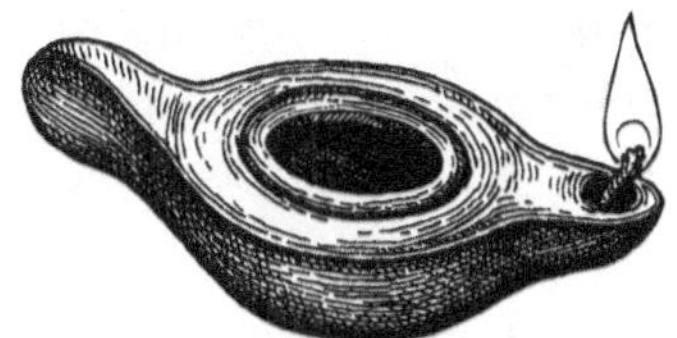

RONALD AND NANCY ONCE more had their two boys under their roof. They were excited to receive a letter from Mario that Ronald was to read to the family that evening. He had told his wife, "Basically what the letter says is that there has been some legal trouble concerning taxes, and some of our several-time removed cousins and uncles have been arrested. However, they still want us to come in November. They plan to show us the island and introduce the boys to some nice Sicilian girls.

"We can hire a van to take us to New Orleans, connect to Delta, and fly to Italy. We land near Rome and then take another flight to Palermo. We just need everyone to take their passports, and we should be fine. We have ours, Frank has his, but I do not know about Roger, William, and Mary."

Now that the much-anticipated meal of homemade gumbo with fresh boiled crawdads and hushpuppies was concluded, Ronald stood at the head of the table. He pulled an envelope from a side table drawer and opened it with a flourish of his hand.

"For three generations we have kept up a correspondence with our relatives in Sicily. In my time this task has fallen to me and one of our cousins named Mario. He writes in English, and I reply in Italian.

My Dear Cousin,

There has been some trouble with the family businesses due to a change in the Italian government and supposed violation of tax laws to the extent that some members of the family have been arrested on false charges. With these Italian bureaucrats, these sorts of things happen with each new batch of officials – all of which is tied to keeping Sicily a sort of Roman colony to be exploited for the benefits of the stuffed-shirts in Rome.

Even so, there is no need for you to postpone your trip. I have talked to other members of the family, and they are all looking forward to meeting you and showing you around.

We also have some special things planned for your sons. Luigi will be your host in Palermo and Syracuse. Luigi also paints, and for Roger, who I understand is also an artist, he will take him to some local museums while Frank goes on a boar hunt with me.

Some nice young ladies in the family are going to escort your sons on the tour and maybe participate in a bit of the nightlife, if there is time.

You will also have a chance to sample some of the varied foods that we have in different parts of the island. There will almost always be seafood, but there are also many vegetable dishes that you will get to try. We also have some of the best wines in the world, drunk in the very vineyards that made them, olives like you have never had, and some unique goat cheeses that are so valued that they are seldom exported from the island.

Our shared culture is rich and variable, and we are all looking forward to showing it to you. This will take seven days from the time of your arrival in Palermo to your departure. Even so, this is just a sampling, and the start of what I hope will be the first of many trips to come. Our family has been too long separated, and we all look forward to catching up with our American relations.

In eager anticipation,

Mario

"Wow. That is quite a letter," Roger said.

"I agree," William replied. "I am certainly excited about going. I am disappointed that Tim can't go too, but I will keep him posted on what happened when we get back."

"What did you tell him about our marital difficulties?" Frank asked.

"I told him that you were both unattached at the moment."

"He didn't mention me. I am a member of the family too, you know," Mary said.

"I am afraid that Italian men don't think of women as we do here in America. I am very sure that the women in the family will ensure that you are very well looked after," her father replied.

"I am not going to Sicily to be locked in a convent or wash dishes in someone else's kitchen," Mary said. "I want to have some fun too."

"I am sure that something can be arranged for you that will suit your interest in fashion and design, even if it might not be making lace and milking goats."

That remark brought a general chuckle to everyone around the table, and the conversation progressed to the nuts and bolts of getting passports, which dates would work for everyone, how many stops the van would have to make, and what kind of clothes they needed.

"Dad, Roger and I had a chance to talk about things last night. I am still decompressing over this Iraq business and am not so hot about going anywhere. Roger wants to go so badly, and he wants me to go with him and so do all of you. I am still a bit unsettled with the war and breaking up with Jane, but I'll go. I have decided that some new experiences will maybe help me forget some things I don't want to remember."

"I am glad to hear that Frank, it would certainly not be the same without you – now back to Mario's letter.

"According to Mario, the island's weather can be very changeable in November," Ronald warned. "There can be rain, and it can snow in the higher parts of the island. You need to take at least one set of clothes that you can be warm in when the temperature is about freezing. Your Louisiana winter clothes should be about right. I would take at least one dress-up outfit and another that you can walk around comfortably in for when we visit the vineyards and ruins."

Although not as accommodating as his villa, Luigi had moved into a suite of rooms in a Mafia-owned hotel in northeastern Palermo while Cecilia and Angelica remained in Syracuse.

Mario came into a part of the suite that served as an office and presented an envelope to Luigi who was seated behind an ornate Spanish Baroque desk. "I got this in the mail yesterday. It is from Ronald Calsase. He wants to arrange a time to bring his family, six of them, over from America. With everything else that is happening, do you still want them to come in November? They haven't bought their tickets, so there is still time for them to postpone their trip."

Luigi handed him the letter back, "Read me the letter. I want to hear what he had to say."

Dear Cousin Mario,

I have talked it over with everyone. If the invitation is still open, there will be six of us. Me, wife Nancy, daughter Mary, brother William, and sons Frank and Roger.

Nancy and I will much enjoy meeting the family, touring the ruins, visiting the sites, including Mt. Etna, and sampling the food.

Frank, who is a black powder enthusiast says he is really looking forward to the boar hunt and wonders if he can do it with a black-powder gun. He would really like to take a boar with either an original or replica flintlock musket. He is an expert with such guns and has been using them since he was a child.

Roger, the artist among us, would like to see paintings and artwork as well as having an opportunity to meet Luigi, who, I understand, also paints.

Getting away would be a great help for the boys, who have been having relationship issues and are looking forward to meeting the women you mentioned.

William, who is gay, is interested in food and art as well as AIDS prevention education. Generally, I think, he will hang around doing whatever Nancy and I do.

Mary, my daughter, is feeling a little left out of the planning, so we will need to find some things that interest her. Like most women she enjoys clothes, shopping, unusual foods, jewelry, etc., but she was also an active participant in sports.

We are all excited about coming for our week's visit. What dates would be most suitable?

Sincerely,

Ronald Calsase

"Mario, there may be an opportunity here. Set up a conference call with Cecilia and Angelica for this evening. I want to see if they are willing to marry these Americans. If bad stuff starts going down between the families, it would be good to have them out of the country.

"Angelica, Cecilia, I want you to listen closely. I am going to be stuck in Palermo most weeks for as long as Don Carlos and Leo are in jail. There is a possibility that other Mafia organizations may try to move in on our territories. There has been a sort of peace between the family operations in southern Italy and Sicily for twenty years, but trouble could blow up anytime.

"These things usually start with a bombing, or ambush of some leaders of opposing families, and I do not want you to be involved. Stay in the villa. Only go out with my bodyguards. Angelica, do not drive your car. That Ferrari is too conspicuous.

"There may be a way to save face and get you two out of the country. We are going to be visited by a Sicilian family from America who have two young men who are single. I propose that we arrange marriages between these men and you two. That would get you out of the country.[23]

"One of these men is a U.S. Marine Captain, and the other is an artist. If you don't like them, you can divorce them after a period of years and retain your U.S. citizenship."

"Why can't you just send us to college in Europe or the U.S.?" Angelica asked.

---

[23] I had several conversations with college-aged students at the University of Catania on the subject of arranged marriages. Their feelings about them were almost universally negative. Part of this was based on the fact that these were often between men who were decades older than their brides. This was something that happened in their grandparent's day, but not to modern Italian women.

"That would be seen as a sign of weakness. If you are married to two Sicilian Americans, that would be thought of as a sign of strength, and a collaboration between two potentially powerful Mafia families across the ocean. Believe me, for your own safety, this is the best way out of this problem. I wish it were otherwise, but you both need to take advantage of this. If you marry them, you can go to the states and be safe."

"This is preposterous," Angelica interrupted. "I know I told you I did not want to be an old maid, but we don't even know if we like them? What if they are old and ugly? What if we can't stand each other?"

"From all reports, these are handsome men with good reputations. After a period of years, if the marriage does not work, you can easily get divorced in America."

"It's too soon. Much too soon." Cecilia interjected. "I will love Davide forever. I can't even think about anyone else right now."

"I know. But it is time for you to move on. I will arrange that you both will continue your educations and that you and your husbands will be supported. I can't protect you here."

Unseen by Luigi, Angelica and Cecilia clasped hands and exchange looks. Angelica was the first to reply. "I don't like this one bit. I want to at least see them. This isn't the 1600s, you know?"

"You will meet them tonight."

"If it seems like our lives really depend on it and that we could love them, maybe. Cecilia, don't you agree that we should at least have a look at these men first?

"Father you don't seem to be giving us much choice. I agree with Angelica. If we can get divorced and after we take a look at them, maybe. But I still can't think of being married to anyone but Davide."

"Yes. You can be divorced in America after you have been married for five years. That is not such a long time, and you may come to love them. Your very lives depend on this decision.

"I will start making preparations for a wedding in Novo. I want to make it look as if this was in the planning for years and that it is going forward even though members of the family have been arrested."

"What if the men don't like us or we just can't get along?" Angelica questioned.

"There are two of them, and there are two of you. You will work it out. The thing is to get you married and out of the country."

"Ok, if we must," Angelica answered. "Cecelia, what about it," Luigi demanded.

"It's too soon after Davide's death to think about such things. No one can ever replace him." Cecilia said.

"For me it does not matter. I am an old man. I have had my failures and successes, loves and heartbreaks. I think of you both as my daughters, and I want to keep you safe. The best that I can do to show that the family is still strong is to marry you to those Americans. I want that more than anything. Davide would want it too. Do it for both of us." Luigi pleaded.

"Where do they live?" Cecilia asked.

"Their father is a Civil Engineer in Louisiana.

"They live in a city near New Orleans."

"That might be fun," Angelica commented.

"If our lives depend on it, I guess I will, provided that I can get out of the marriage if things go badly." Cecilia reluctantly agreed.

"It is settled then. They will arrive on a Monday, and the weddings will be in Novo on Friday after they have had a chance to meet you and tour the island."

Listening to the tape of the recorded conversation at the AIA headquarters in Milan, Chief Detective Roscotti remarked, "It looks like The Claw is going to marry off his daughter and niece to members of the American Mafia. Check with the FBI, and see what we can find out about them. They may be bringing in new blood from the States to take the place of Don Carlos and Leo. Do we still have those agents, Michael and Vito, in Palermo?"

"Yes, we do. They did a good job with the arrest and their cover is still solid. Michael even delivered a letter from Don Carlos to The Claw in Syracuse."

"I want them to keep us posted on anything they can find out about this wedding. Luigi is a level head and only wants to keep the situation between the families stable. We don't want another round of Mafia Wars in Sicily. It is not so much that I care if one member of the Mafia kills another, it's the innocent people who get swept up in all of this that matters. Nothing happened in connection with the funeral, so perhaps things will stay on an even keel. In any event, I want to monitor this situation very closely."

"FBI, Agent Williams speaking."

"I am calling on behalf of Chief Detective Roscotti of the AIA in Milan. We have a situation that is developing in Sicily that may involve members of the American Mafia who might be starting an alliance with one of the Mafia families in Sicily.

"The short version of the story is that two weeks ago, we arrested two major members of the Sicilian Mafia. From a wiretap, we have learned that the family is trying to arrange a marriage between two Sicilian women and two men from what may be the American side of the family.

"We request that you investigate them and let us know if there are any Mafia activities associated with this American family, and what their possible interests might be in Sicily. I am going to send you the paperwork in a diplomatic pouch. We have agents on the ground, and I do not want to compromise them."

"I can run a background check on them at this end but can do nothing else unless we can establish some legal justification. Just suspecting someone of an undefined crime or associating with members of a crime family, will not pass muster with our judges."

"A background check will do fine for now. I will keep you posted when we learn more."

Chapter

15

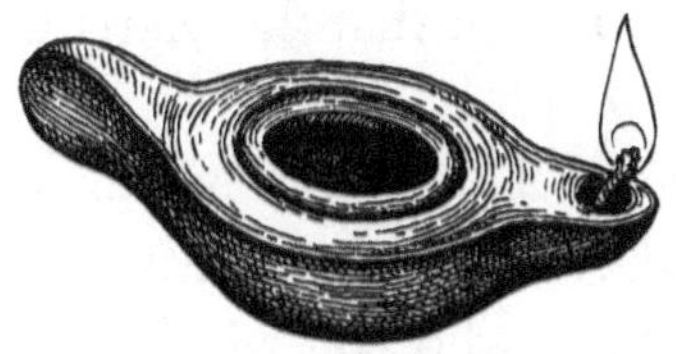

Departures

AGENT ROB WILLIAMS HAD a somewhat puzzled look on his face, when he asked Agent Howard Smith, "Do you remember Ronald Calsase, that the Italian Anti-Mafia Association wanted us to do a background check on awhile back?"

"Yes," Williams replied. "I don't think we got anything too serious on him. He was a witness in some cases about zoning regulations, but nothing but a traffic ticket on the criminal side. So far as I can tell he's clean. He has a son who is a Marine Captain with a top-secret clearance, another that is an artist, and a daughter who works with his brother as a hairdresser. So far as we can tell they do not have any criminal records."

"The AIA has intercepted a telephone call between a Mafia enforcer in Palermo and his daughter and niece. He had apparently been brought out of retirement to oversee one of the Sicilian mob's families after the AIA arrested the head of the family. It seems that he wants to arrange weddings between his daughter and niece and the Calsase's two sons.

"Now, we have learned that six members of the Calsase family have booked flights to Palermo in November. The AIA has also told us that this enforcer, Luigi, The Claw, has been frantically booking places and making arrangements for them to be married in Novo, which is a small hill village near Mt. Etna. These places are often booked years in advance, and he is leaning on some people to free them up for his weddings."

"What are we supposed to do about it? Isn't this something for the CIA?"

133

"Because of our ties with the AIA, they want us to come, bring some of our surveillance equipment, and cooperate with them regarding our nationals. The Italians will make the arrest, provide the manpower, and direct the operations. What they don't want to happen is fighting between rival Mafia families or that the Mafia family in Sicily be taken over by Americans."

"It's going to be tricky. The AIA in Milan is running this operation because of widespread infiltration by Mafia informants. There are two undercover AIA agents who you will be working with in Palermo. Otherwise, no one is to know why you are there. You are to pose as American contractors associated with the U.S. Air Force doing training on new weapons systems at the joint services base at Sigonella, which is west of Catania. When you leave the base you will do so on military transport or by giving a call to this limo rental service for a car. Request either Michael or Vito for drivers. They are the only people that you will be able to trust, and those cars are the only safe places where you can talk. These two agents are also driving the Mafia people around so they can keep you posted on what's happening.

"Button things up in a hurry. You fly out of Andrews the day after tomorrow. It is going to be a thirty-hour flight."

Don Augustino, dressed in one of his usual expensive suites was sitting at a table in a fine dining restaurant overlooking Naples' harbor as his son approached. Apachee was wearing a tight-fitting suite and black shoes with three turquoise stones set in silver on the outside heels and a red tie – the epitome of a young, aggressive Italian businessman.

"I am ordering octopus. What do you want?

"I'll have squid. That is always good here.

With a nod, the waiter accepted the orders and rushes back to the kitchen.

"I have received several pieces of interesting news from Pasquale. A man that Luigi's daughter was going to marry has been killed. Don Carlos and his Segundo have been arrested, and the most interesting of all…"

The waiter returned with wine, bread, and oil and sat them on the table along with small side plates. As Don Augustino broke and dipped his bread into the oil, he thanks the waiter and continued.

"Luigi and Donna Carlos are frantically making wedding plans for his daughter and niece to be married to two Americans."

"I suppose that we don't want that to happen?

Right?"

"Quite right. I want you to take the plumbing van and six men and do everything you can to see that this wedding does not take place."

"I get to be a wedding planner! That sounds like fun. Are these Americans Mafia?"

"I don't know these people. They are not in their territory, and they don't need to be in Italy. I want you to teach them that."

"Can do. Can do. I have been wanting to look at some American wild horses from a breeder in Sicily for my next movie. I'll buy a paint if he has one."

"Be careful that those bit movie parts don't get you hurt."

"Don't worry. I let those fool stuntmen do the falls. I don't need another broken arm."

"Here comes our meal. I want you to leave tomorrow."

The waiter proceeded to put a large platter down on a folding table and serves his two guests.

"Enjoy your meal, gentlemen. We are honored to have you. There will be no charge."

With a bend of his head Don Augustino put a ten euro note in the waiter's hand and replied, *"Millegratzi."*

The logistics of getting six people who lived in three different locations in the same vehicle and pointed in the same direction at the same time was not lost on Ronald Calsase. The Louie Armstrong Airport Transport Van had been ordered for 5:00 AM and was just pulling up in front of their house in Prospect Park. Ronald, his wife and sons, had been up since 3:00 and had their bags sitting by the curb shortly before the van arrived.

Checking for what seemed to be the fourth time, "Has everyone got everything – bags, passports, tickets, money, medicines, topcoat, everything?" Ronald asked.

"Yeah, we got it Dad," Roger replied. He thought that the last time he had said those words under similar conditions was when he was taken off to college for the first time. He remembered that he had felt full of anticipation, and fear, of being the last to leave home. He had seen his brother and sister off, and now it was his turn. This was a pivotal point in his life that had not gone too well. He was supposed to be living an independent life, and now he found himself starting over again. He could not fight the memory, and he had a lump in his throat as he got in.

"Roger, you all right?" his mother asked.

"Yeah, I'm ugh, fine. I just had a bit of a flashback of when I went off to college. I'm all right now."

"Away then." Ronald ordered. "William and Mary will meet us at the shop downtown. I don't want them being there any longer than necessary this hour of the day. It is fifteen minutes there, an hour and a half to the airport, another hour at least to get checked in at Air Italia, and then get off the ground at 9:35. We have ample time, but none to spare."

"Don't they want us there early to go through security?" Nancy asked.

"Yes they do, but at this hour of the morning there should be no problem with the TSA people. They have just put in some new baggage inspection restrictions. Remember guys, no pocketknives in your carry-on luggage. You can put one in your checked bags if you like."

The lights were on at Calsase Hair Fashions when they arrived.

"Hi William, is Mary here?" Ronald asked.

"Yes. She is just putting my pistol in the safe. I always carry one when I come to town this time of day. We can load up the bags."

Soon, the driver had the bags in the back of the van, and Mary was locking the door.

As she got in, she made an act of counting heads and, with a flourish, announced, "We are all here. Let's go."

"Go. Go. Go." Ronald added, and they proceeded to launch their drive to the airport. The traffic was moderate, became somewhat more congested as they approached New Orleans, but thinned out a little when they pulled off on the new approach to Louie Armstrong.

"We need to go to the International Terminal. Our flights are on Air Italia to Rome."

"That's no problem. It may be a Delta flight that takes you over and an Air Italia flight that brings you back. Look at the departure signs. They may have more than one flight number listed for these shared carrier routes," the driver mentioned as he accepted his tip.

At least now it was daylight. Frank who had not spoken during the drive over, said, "I'll grab a cart, we will have to check our bags in at the counter for these international flights. Some of the people returning to Europe buy a lot of stuff, and their bags are often oversize and overweight. Once we get checked through, we should be fine. I will put them all on together if I can, but everyone will need to have their own bags put on their tickets.

"I didn't think we could get all these bags on one cart. Put some of the larger ones flat on the bottom, and then, we can pile them up and get more on."

"Roger it is going to take two carts. Why don't you grab that one?" Frank directed.

"I am glad that you boys did learn something from me," Ronald said laughingly. "At least you can stack luggage."

Roger thought that remark cut a little, but he held back his reply. After all, this was supposed to be a fun family trip, and he did not want to cast a dark shadow on anything before their vacation even got off the ground.

Arriving at the check-in line, they found a dozen people in front of them trying to board the early flights. There were individuals, families with small children, students, businessmen in their suits, and service personnel traveling in their uniforms. As this was a family event, Frank had decided not to wear his uniform, although he did have one packed in his luggage as well as some fatigues for his boar hunt.

"You may have two checked bags, a carry-on bag and a personal item such as a handbag or briefcase," the Delta clerk stated. She was a handsome brunette who was trying to process the lines of people in front of her as quickly as possible.

"This is my family behind me. There are six of us, and we are all headed to Palermo," Ronald said.

Glancing up and seeing that they were all adults, the clerk said, "Since there are no minor children, all of you will have to check in individually. You can take your bags to any of the other clerks when they are open. I assure you. All of your bags are going to wind up at the same place."

Remembering horror stories about bags intended for Anchorage, Alaska, winding up in Ankara, Turkey, Ronald was not particularly comforted but nodded in assent and dug out his and his and Nancy's bags for processing.

"Thank God for roll-a-way bags," William thought as he pulled his bag down the long hall towards yet another set of lines for TSA security scanning.

Seemingly, even more people were queued up in front of the four security scanners than were at the ticket counter. With tickets and passports in hand they put their carry-ons on the conveyor belts. William, Mary, and Roger had laptops, and everyone had phones. Ronald had arranged that everyone's phone programs be expanded so that they could connect with each other in Italy.

Outside of the hassle of having to prove who they were three different times, they were finally at the gate with a few minutes to spare to catch their collective breaths before starting their long flight to Rome.

"I hope that they have a good movie this trip," William said. "The last time I flew, there was only one choice, and I brought a book along just in case."

"Things have changed a bit now. There are usually several movies and some other entertainment channels to choose from. They also serve you a few drinks so you can relax a bit," Frank replied.

"I hope that they give us something reasonable to eat," Mary said. "It looks like we are going to have lunch, dinner, and breakfast on our way to Rome, and nothing between Rome and Palermo."

"Did anyone get a bulkhead seat?" Ronald asked. "I think that Roger and I did," Frank replied.

"That's good because you have the longest legs. However, William, your mother and I may need to swap out with you during the flight if we start to have leg cramps. Those are no fun on these long flights."

Finally, after all of the check-ins, preparations, and preliminaries, they were escorted on board the European Air Bus. The six had a block of adjacent seats on the right-hand side of the aircraft. Frank and Roger took the two seats behind the bulkhead, their parents were behind them, and Mary and William were in the third row.

William elected to take the window seat and remarked to Mary, "During the flight, I want to go up and talk to Roger. We have not had a chance to seriously talk in years, and I want to see what's going on with him."

"I know. He seemed a little upset when we left the house – like he was really trying to get his head around some problem. I think that he was really disappointed that he had to leave San Francisco. Frank doesn't seem quite right either. Maybe you need to talk to both of them."

As the jet engines started up, conversation became more difficult.

"At least we don't have to push it off the runway, like they did in *Flight of the Phoenix*." Ronald quipped. This was one of Ronald's favorite movies, which starred Jimmy Stewart. In the movie, a designer of toy aircraft rebuilds the crashed plane, and Steward flies it out with the passengers strapped to the wings.

Three movies were featured on the flight. The most recent in the Harry Potter series was *Harry Potter and the Prisoner of Azkaban*, *Sideways*, and *Aviator*.

Not unexpectedly, the different movies appealed to different family members. Frank, a pilot, had a strong preference for *Aviator* as did his dad, William thought that the characters in *Sideways* were not unlike some of his customers in his beauty shop, Mary was taken by the strong female characters in the Harry Potter production, while Nancy was fascinated with the food and wine scenes appearing in all three movies, Roger was blown away by the enormously expensive production methods that must have been used to make the Potter movies and *Aviator*. He thought: "Paying the actors and extras was only a small part of this production. It took thousands of people to produce these Harry Potter movies and budgets of tens of millions of dollars. By comparison *Sideways* was made for pocket change but was nonetheless an interesting adult film. Maybe I could work on something like that someday."

"Estavo I want you to call the limousine rental company and order two of their large Mercedes for the week. I want one of the drivers to be that young man with the Fiat who brought me the note from Don Carlos. I want him to take a limo and pick up Cecilia and Angelica. He is to bring them here with enough clothes for a few days while we tour the island with the Americans.

"Tell the driver that he may make several trips back and forth with the girls and that each time he is to take a different route. I don't want to make it easy for someone to ambush that car."

"Who would do that?"

"I don't know. It might be someone out for a revenge killing, another Mafia family, or maybe an independent operator for money. I have invited many of our business associates to the wedding, and they have accepted. As long as I can see them, there is less likely to be trouble."

"This assignment is not going to be so bad after all," Michael thought as he pulled up at the front gate of the Sigonella AFB and signed in. He explained that he was to pick up two civilian contractors, Rob Williams and Howard Smith, and take them to Syracuse. He could brief them on the way, drop them off in town, and they could take a bus back to base. At noon, he was to go back to Luigi's villa with the limo, pick up the two women, and take them to Palermo. He hoped that one of those would be Cecilia. He would enjoy seeing her again.

"This has all happened very abruptly after we arrested Don Carlos." Michael began once he had the two agents in the car. "Luigi announced that his daughter Cecilia and niece Angelica are going to marry two Americans from Louisiana. They are to arrive on Sunday – tomorrow. This may mean an alliance between the American and Sicilian branches of the family that they are going to cement by establishing blood ties. This sounds like a Royal wedding, and I suppose that it might be that sort of thing. The Sicilians apparently like to cling to traditions, or at least what they construe them to be.

"Vito and I are going to be driving them around and can keep you informed on where they are going. There was a killing in Novo that involved the Mafia. This was claimed to have been an accident, but no one really believes it. Nothing has happened yet, although this is a sort of powder keg that could explode any time. Almost everyone on this island knows someone who is in the mob, and is aware that they pay well for useful information. That is why these cars are about the only place where we can talk."

"Our role is strictly to assist," Agent Williams replied. "We brought some surveillance gear and some secure satellite phones. I have two, one for you and another for your partner. Can you hide one in these cars?"

"Yes, I have a hidden compartment under the dash where I can put a phone and a small pistol. I can't carry one unless someone in the mob gives one to me. I will phone in when I can. It might be very late. Sometimes, these events can go on well into the night.

"Here is the bus station. I need to go to the villa, and pick up the two women."

When Michael pulled up to the villa he was met with a small mountain of boxes and suitcases piled in front of the door including two huge trunks used by passengers on ocean steamers.

"You do look like Davide," Angelica blurted out. "I don't know. I never met him," Michael replied.

He spoke quietly so as to lessen the impact on Cecilia's feelings. She was coming out the door struggling with another large box, and he hoped that she had not heard the exchange.

"Let me help you," Michael said. "Is there anything else?" Judging from the pile outside, it seemed like they had emptied the entire house.

Thinking of how much stuff there was, even for the limo, Michael said. "I can take you, or I can take all this stuff. There is not enough room unless we put some of the smaller bags on the passenger's seats and you both ride on the front seat with me. It will be a little tight, but we can do it."

The two girls looked at each other, Angelica winked, and the loading began.

"Be careful with those trunks, they have our wedding dresses in them."

"You are both going to be married?" Michael questioned with a hint of feigned surprise in his voice.

"Yes. It is a bit of a rush-up affair," Angelica said. "My Uncle apparently worked a two-for-one deal and he is going to marry us off to two Americans on Friday. We are going to have to find a dressmaker in Palermo to do the final fitting on our wedding outfits."

"You have never met them?" Michael asked disbelievingly.

"No, we haven't," Cecilia said. "But that's fine, arranged marriages happen all the time."

"I'm from Venice, and they don't do things like that anymore – at least not since the 1800s. I guess things are a little different down here."

"I will chaperone this young lady," Angelica announced as she occupied the middle of the front seat next to Michael. "It's not good to have a handsome guy so close to a prospective bride."

"This is not the way we usually go to Palermo," Cecilia said.

"I have been told to take you a different route. We will still be there by mid-afternoon. You are going to the Crystal Hotel. There is a tailor around the corner that will fit your dresses."

While making small talk on the drive to Palermo, Michael felt a hand on his thigh slowly creeping up to his crotch. He shut his legs, but when the creeping hand persisted, he relaxed to enjoy the experience.

"Whichever guy this gal marries, he is in for one hell of a wedding night," he thought.

Chapter

16

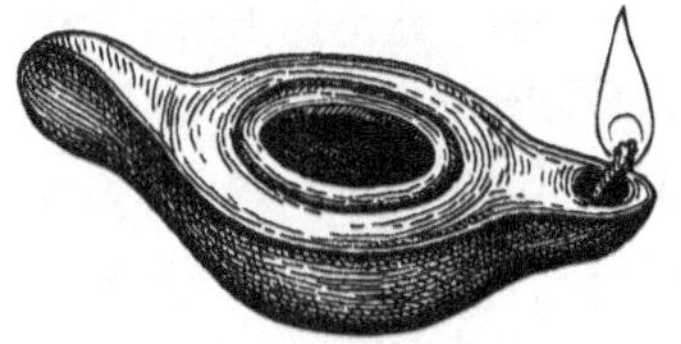

Arrivals

WILLIAM HAD SWITCHED SEATS on the plane with Frank and was now sitting next to Roger.

"Roger, we have not had a chance to talk for a long time, and I wanted to see how things were going with you. I heard that you broke up with your girlfriend in San Francisco and haven't been able to get much of anywhere with your art."

"That's true. Matilda threw me out after a deal I was working on fell through. Fact is, I never could make my share of the rent or get in any galleries because I didn't have anything to show."

"I can teach you to do hair, and you can come and work in the shop with me and your sister. You can start just making appointments until I can get you trained and pass the state exams. You can just work on men's hair if you like, but the real money is in women's hair."

"Believe me, I have thought about that ever since High School, but the idea of fiddling around with people's hair just gives me the willies. I'm interested in the crafts and arts of what I do. My problem is that I come up with lots of ideas, but never can seem to finish them."

"I know that, and maybe there is a guy here who can help. He is Luigi, who goes by the moniker 'The Claw' because he lost a hand as a child during World War II. He was taught to draw and taught English by American archeologists who did salvage work on the island after the war.

143

He retired, but I understand from a letter your dad got that he has been brought back to run the family businesses.

"When he retired, I got notices that he had been exhibited in some major galleries in Italy. He may be able to introduce you to people who might be able to help. At least, as you heard, he is going to take you to some interesting places which have been drawn and painted for centuries."

"That is part of my problem. Because I paint in the classical fashion, almost everything that I consider doing has been done more famously, and often better, that I can do. That's why I like doing portraits – each one of them is a different face, with a personality to go along with it.

"The project that I tried to sell in California was of a Japanese-American who was put in an internment camp during World War II who started a tomato canning company that supplied tomatoes to U.S. servicemen all over the world. I would not be surprised to find some of his tomatoes in mess halls on the island today. The guy wasn't over here, but his tomatoes were.

"Frank brought me back some photos from the Middle East, and I am thinking about putting some Persian and Assyrian-inspired themes in my art. I am sure I will get some ideas from this trip too."

"I want you to know that I am always here if you need help with something. If you get something painted, I will hang it in my shop. Some of these ladies have serious money and might be interested in having portraits of their children or grandchildren. You just have to be able to get along with them and finish the work."

"Thanks. I appreciate that." Roger said with all sincerity, but deep within himself, he wondered if he ever could.

"Prepare to arrive," came the announcement in both Italian and English, and the Air Bus began its descent towards the sprawling National Domestic Terminal outside of Rome. One problem with the tickets that Ronald had noticed was that their departure gates were not indicated for the connecting flight to Palermo.

Once off the gangway, they were immediately directed towards lines where they would go through immigration. There was a separate line for travelers from the U.S. and Canada. With an apparently perfunctory stamp of their passports, they were literally off and running to they knew not where.

This uncertainty ended when Frank spotted a flight board, and started looking for their connecting Air Italia flight to Palermo. He found one with the corresponding departure time and announced, "Gate D-12, this way."

The way led through a series of duty-free shops where they did not stop but pressed on to make sure they made their tight connection. This was the High Season in Sicily, and they knew if they missed their flight, the chances of being able to put another batch of six seats together was almost nil.

On they pressed. Roger could imagine a cartoon showing a bunch of drawn characters with their roll-a-way bags striking sparks on the marble floors as they hustled down the seemingly endless hallways towards their gate.

Ultimately, they did arrive, but the flight number did not correspond with the numbers on their tickets. Eventually, their flight did show up as a Delta flight, following other listings of the flight under the names of a variety of European airlines, who apparently also had cooperative agreements with Air Italia for flights to Sicily.

"This is our plane after all," Ronald said with a sigh of relief. "They start boarding in ten minutes. We made it."

In his mind's eye Roger saw a three-engine corrugated-metal propeller Ford Trimotor aircraft on the other side of the loading gate. His brother Frank envisioned a fighter aircraft. Dad saw the reality of a twin-engine jet, with the engines mounted near the tail instead of on the wings. Whatever they were flying in, real or imagined, they were all very glad to be a significant step closer to their destination.

Mario was prepared with a sign, "Calsase family." at the baggage claim area in Palermo. Unlike the huge airports that the family passed through in New Orleans and Rome, the airport in Palermo was more like an enlarged family living room. Even before all of their bags had been plucked off the discharging conveyor system, Ronald spotted a man with a sign approaching, and he held up his hand in recognition.

"Hello, I'm Mario."

"It is good to finally meet you after all these years. I would like to introduce you to the rest of the family.

"This is my wife Nancy, my daughter Mary, brother William, and those are Frank and Roger grabbing bags off the conveyer."

"Once you are sure that you have everything, we have a van outside to take you to the hotel. It will be about a thirty-minute trip, and we will get you checked in. This is our driver Vito, and he will help us get you loaded. I have a little something special for you once we get in the van."

When they were in the van, Mario brought out a bottle of clear liquid. "This is Grappa.[24] Like our Greek ancestors would say, 'all things in moderation.' This will settle your stomach after the flight, generally relax you, and provide you with a good night's sleep to help with jet lag. You have a busy day tomorrow, but for you stay at the Crystal Hotel tonight and sleep in. I will call for you at 9:00 AM. We will work out of this hotel tomorrow, and stay local, so you don't have to pack up to leave in the morning."

Mario poured about an inch of Grappa into seven plastic cups and passed them around. "I suggest that you sip it, as it will give your system time to adjust to it as it goes down. It is harsh at first, but it gets better as you go along. I will leave you the bottle, but I suggest that this one shot will do until you become accustomed to it. A Grappa hangover is a terrible thing. I know because I speak from too many sad experiences as a young man."

"This is the High Season at the Crystal,[25] and we are tight for rooms. We have a room with a king-sized bed for Mr. and Mrs. Calsase, a room with three single beds for the gentlemen, and a separate room for the young lady. Will these be satisfactory?" the young lady who was manning the hotel desk asked.

"At this stage, any bed anywhere will do," Ronald replied. "Can you give us a wake-up call at 7:00 AM?"

"Yes I can. There will be a complimentary breakfast at the restaurant on the basement floor starting at 6:00: AM. We have a small bar here, and you may have drinks or coffee anytime. There are also drinks and a

---

[24]   Grappa is the Italian equivalent of moonshine except it is made from the residue of the grapes after they have been crushed. It has a little bit of a harsh bite in either the red or white varieties. Among the first thing that Italians like to do with American exchange students is to give them the "grappa experience" which is usually their worst experience in Italy. After that, anything else that happens is often not so bad.

[25]   The Crystal Hotel was one of several that I stayed in Sicily and is also where the roof-top bar is located.

coffee maker in your rooms. You may take a bottle of water to your rooms if you like. There is also a music bar on the top floor with open seating on the roof, and you can get a pizza and sandwiches there after 7:00 PM."

"Enjoy your stay."

No more than two people and their bags could fit into the elevator at the time.

"I will grab a drink here at the bar before I go up," William announced. "I am a little hungry too, and a sandwich sounds good. After I put my bags in the room, I'm going to check out the bar upstairs."

"Turning to the clerk, he said, "I'll have a Heineken when you have a moment. That dry airplane air has parched my throat."

When William got to the room, he found that Frank and Roger had already left. This room had a living room with a couch that had been folded out into a bed and a bedroom with two double beds which the boys, as William still thought of them, had put their suitcases on. After making a stop by the bathroom, he went to the elevator and pressed the button for the top floor.

He could hear loud music through the door of the elevator. Even though it was 8:00 P.M., there were very few people in the bar, and the staff appeared to be still in the process of opening. He got the impression that things did not really start happening until after midnight.

Walking through the bar area and going outside on the roof, he saw that a table on the corner of the building was occupied by Frank and Roger.

"How are you two fairing?" William asked.

"Hungry, thirsty, and tired," Frank replied. "I am certainly not in a party mood. That Grappa helped, but now I want a beer, some food in my stomach, and that bed looks good."

"I think that is true all around," Roger added. "Dad and Mom looked worn out, and no wonder. They have been working night and day for more than a week, putting all of this together. What's up for tomorrow?"

"I really don't know. Some museums and local sights, I guess." William said. "We are going to meet the rest of the family at dinner. Most of the people work, and night is the time that they usually get together on weekdays."

"They have four-hour dinners here," Frank said. "So be prepared for that. Don't stuff yourself with bread, *antipasti*, and wine because the real meal is coming up."

"Thanks for the warning. If I can attract a waiter, maybe we can get some food."

"What will you gentlemen be having?" the waiter asked.

"A large sausage pizza with some onions and black olives, and another round of beers will do for starters," William said.

"Our kitchen is just opening, so it will be a few minutes. I will bring you some bread and olive oil if you like."

"That will be fine," William said.

"Looking over the skyline, there were modern concrete and glass buildings, that were mostly storefronts lining the streets. Smaller buildings with red-tiled roofs in various states of repair and the spires and domes of what were obviously churches dotted the skyline. The main street was well lit, with several lamp posts on each block, marked areas for pedestrian traffic, and covered bus stops.

"Except for the palm trees lining the streets, this could be almost anywhere in Europe," Frank said. "It reminds me of Portugal."

"The baroque architecture certainly fits in," Roger said. "If the streets were wider and they spoke Spanish, I could easily think that I was back in Southern California."

"You have had more exposure to Spanish than the rest of us. Can you understand what they say?" William questioned.

"Not really. I have better luck trying to read it, but many of the nouns are different even though both languages are derived from Latin. Thank goodness, most of the people we have seen speak excellent English."

The pizza arrived. It looked like something that had come out of a box from a third-rate supermarket in the U.S. It had a thin crust, a smear of tomato sauce, sprinkling of pepperoni, cut black olives, a minimal amount of cheese, and generally looked like a pizza that had gone on a diet.

Seeing the look of disappointment on his brother's face, Frank quickly spoke up. "Compared to the way the pizzas that we have in America have evolved, the original things here in Italy are generally poor sisters. Don't argue with the Italians about them.

"They made them, this is their dish, and they don't appreciate Americans telling them how bad they are. If you want a good pizza go to Chicago or Detroit or New York; don't come to Italy for one. The best that you will have here is, by American standards, second rate."

"I have heard the same thing from some of my friends who were trained as chefs in Italy," William added. "They also say that the way to enjoy an Italian pizza is with red wine, but we have already started with Grappa and beer, and I don't think it would be wise to put wine on top of that – maybe next time."

Sleeping alone was, at this juncture, the most desirable state for the three as they returned to their room for the night. After their long flight and eventful days that preceded their trip, a soft bed in a room that did not move was very inviting indeed.

The arrival of the Calsases was not unobserved. Two hours before the family arrived, Michael had brought Cecilia and Angelica to the hotel, checked them in, and helped them get their bags and trunks up to their rooms.

"I understand that I am to pick you and some others up here at the hotel tomorrow morning at 9:00 AM."

"Not us, I don't think. We have our wedding dresses to be fitted and some shopping to do before we meet our future husbands at dinner. They are also to arrive sometime today with their family."

Passing through the lobby on their way down to the restaurant, they noticed an older man with a beer sitting in an overstuffed chair with his bags beside him while two younger men got on board the elevator.

"I wonder if those are our husbands?" Cecilia whispered in Italian.

"No. I am sure that yours is the older man that is sitting down." Angelica kidded. Although Frank and Roger did not realize it, they were being examined as if by a butcher, looking at a carcass before deciding how to chop it into pieces.

"I like the taller, tanned, more athletic-looking one," Angelica said as they were having their dinner.

"Don't be foolish," Cecilia said. "We don't even know if those men are the right ones or not. We will have a few days to sort things out."

A Small Favor

AFTER LISTING A SERIES of events on a note pad, Luigi remarked to Estavo, "Our visitors will have a busy day today. I want the ladies picked up at the hotel after breakfast and taken shopping, and the men brought here. I need to tell them about the wedding, and what I expect of them.

"Angelica and Cecilia are there too. They are to have their wedding dresses fitted this morning, and their dressmaker is just around the corner from the hotel.

"I don't want them and the Calsases to meet until tonight, after everyone has been clued in. Mario will take them to some of the shops near the train station. There is so much for them to see that they will just have to pick a couple of places to visit. I will want to take them to some of the cathedrals, and maybe a museum today. Tomorrow, we will start our driving tour around the island and show them Monreale."

Sitting at one of the tables on the side of the dining room, Ronald and Nancy sipped some *café American* while they waited for the rest of their crew to trickle down for breakfast. Mary soon joined them, and she was soon followed by William, Frank, and Roger.

"Did you all have a good night?" Nancy asked.

"I slept like I was dead," William replied. "We had some pizza and a couple of beers upstairs at the bar, and that was about it for me."

"Us too," Frank added. "That trip really took it all out of us. I'm hungry now, and it looks like they have quite a breakfast buffet."

"They cater to international tourists, so there is bacon and eggs for the Americans, a variety of breads and spreads for the Europeans, and a selection of sliced meats and sausages along with pancakes. No grits, though. Those have apparently not crept into Italy yet," Nancy observed.

"You have your choice of three coffees or tea," Ronald added. "There is *Caffe' American,* which is something like we drink, ordinary coffee which is in those small cups and very strong, or expresso."

Once they had served themselves, a waitress came around with a plate of cannoli which looked like small open-ended fried eggrolls filled with sweet cream and cheese.

"These are a Sicilian specialty," Frank said. "I have had them before. They are not too sweet and complement their strong coffee. They are a little messy to eat, but everyone should try one."

"They are good," Mary said. "I see the tour groups are getting together. They look like they are going out in some of those buses we saw. I am sure that we will see more of them as we go around the island."

"To be sure," Frank said, "I spent a little time at the joint naval air base at Sigonella, and they were everywhere around Catania and at the tourist sites. Those huge buses are really a problem on these narrow roads which were made for donkey carts. I feel safer flying, than I do on some of these roads."

"They sound like they would be interesting drives," Roger said. "Do they have rally races here?"

"I have not seen one, but I am sure that they do. The Italians like their cars, and they love to race them."

"It's about time." Ronald declared. "We all need to do our bathroom things and meet upstairs so we can load up and get out of here. The weather is fine, so we don't need to take much with us. Just a light jacket will do."

"We have two cars. One for the ladies and one for the gentlemen," Mario said. "You ladies will have a chance to do some shopping. Luigi would like a few words with the gentlemen before they get started. We will all get together for lunch and visit some of the sights here in Palermo, then return to the hotel, give you a chance to rest, and then meet the family at dinner this evening.

"Ladies, this is Michael, he will be your driver. He is going to take you to some of the better shops in town, and arrange to have anything you buy delivered to the hotel. One of the events you will be going to is a wedding so you will want to pick up a modest dress suitable for wearing in church. The clerks will be show you what is fashionable. Don't be concerned about the costs. Michael has a credit card to take care of that."

"Who is getting married?" Nancy asked.

"It is going to be a small affair in a country church. We just thought that you would like a look at this slice of Sicilian life. Let's say they are your relatives. It is going to seem like everyone on the island is related to you somehow. That is not quite true, but it is close enough to work with."

"That sounds like fun," Mary said. "I enjoy getting involved with aspects of local culture. This is something that the average tourist would never see."

The black Mercedes pulled up to a pink-painted multistory building in the northeastern part of Palermo. The Calsase men were escorted into the plainly-furnished lobby. A dour-looking man behind the hotel desk said, in Italian, "You are expected," and pointed to one of two elevators at the end of the lobby.

As the party walked towards the elevator, the clerk left the desk, took a key, slid open a steel lattice-work door, and pushed the button to open the main elevator door. He then stepped inside and inserted another key into a slot labeled *attico*.

"That is the penthouse, where we have our company offices," Mario said.

It was a somewhat jerky, noisy ride up to the top floor. When they arrived, the walls were freshly painted and the hall was hung with paintings and photographs of Sicilian views. A vineyard, olive groves, citrus trees, factories, salt making, and shipbuilding were included in this collection. Halfway down the hall was an ornate wooden door. To the side of the door was another man dressed in a dark suit, seated at a table. He rose, entered a combination on the lock pad, and the door opened.

Frank noticed as he went inside that the inside of the door was solid steel with a wooden covering. "They don't want anyone getting into this place," he thought.

The furniture, computer, printer, and monitor screens in the reception area were definitely up-to-date. Three people were in the room. A receptionist was sitting behind a mahogany desk. Her blue eyes matched the color of her cut-away dress and were further complemented by an aquamarine necklace. Another lady was entering data in a computer, and a rather large sour-faced individual rose as they entered and unbuttoned his coat was stationed against a rear wall.

"It is all right, Andrew, they are expected," the receptionists said. She pressed a button on the intercom and said, "Your guests are here."

"I'll come out," came the reply.

With a loud click, another door swung open and out stepped a man who looked like he was in his forties, but was actually in his 70s. He wore a dark blue suit, with a blue-checked white handkerchief in his pocket. His appearance was notable, in that his left hand was missing.

Extending his right hand first to Ronald and then to William, Frank, and Roger, he said, "I am Luigi. I am so glad to see you here. Come inside. We have a lot to talk about.

"Mario, see that we are not disturbed."

Once in the office, he shut the door behind the group. Again, this door closed with the finality of a bank vault. This impressed even Ronald who was close enough to the construction trades to appreciate good doors. "That door is heavy enough to be on a bomb shelter," he thought.

"Please sit down," Luigi said as he motioned to a semi-circular set of folding chairs that had been arranged around his office table. Unlike the office-furniture look of the receptionist table outside, this table was made of an extremely well-figured wood, with a variable grain that Ronald had not seen before.

"That is a magnificent table. What kind of wood is that?"

"This table is custom-made from olive wood that is hundreds of years old. We get occasional huge olive trees that will no longer yield fruit. They are cut, and their wood is usually carved into decorative material and cooking tools. Sometimes, a craftsman will make a fine piece of furniture out of it, like this desk."

"I hope that you had a good trip, and a good night last night."

After receiving a general assent from the group, a more serious look came over his face.

"Gentlemen, these are serious times, and I am going to tell you some things that you must never tell anyone else. Your very lives may depend on it.

"You likely don't know it, but you are closely related to one of the most powerful Mafia families in Sicily. Don Carlos and his Secondo, Leo, have been arrested. Because of this, other families and gangs may try to move into our operations if they perceive that this has weakened the family.

"I have been asked to put up a strong demonstration that our organization has not been broken and is more powerful than ever.

"I have a daughter, Cecilia, and a niece, Angelica, who are very dear to me. They are in danger of being kidnapped to make me give concessions to the other families. This I cannot allow.

"Your visit comes at a fortunate time. It lets me show that the family is so secure in its position that it will arrange an elaborate tour around the island which will end with your sons marrying my daughter and niece on Friday."

"Say what! You expect us to marry two women we have never met on Friday?" Frank exclaimed.

"These are two of the fairest flowers of the island. They are both working on university degrees, and they will come with a dowry of 100,000 euros a year. If you find yourselves incompatible, you can get divorced after they achieve their American citizenship."

"Frank and I have kidded about this sort of thing with Dad, but I did not think that it could happen."

"Arranged marriages have worked for centuries. There is no reason to believe that yours would not be a good match. My niece and daughter's lives depend on it. If you don't get along, divorce is much simpler in the States than it is in Italy. What have you got to lose?"

"It is not as if Frank and I have not tried and failed before. I'm willing. Frank?"

"No way. I am still getting over my last combat tour. I haven't got myself under control yet. I don't know if I am fit to be around anyone right now – much less a new wife."

"Cecilia has undergone trauma too. Her Davide, the man she was going to marry, was killed days ago. You can comfort each other."

"And the women agreed to this?" Roger asked.

"Yes, they have agreed," Luigi confirmed.

"Out of courtesy, I will meet them, but no promises," Frank replied haltingly.

"Me too." Roger assented.

"Then, gentlemen, everything is set for your visit. Shake my hand on it."

Both Frank and Roger rise from their seats, and reaching across the wide table, shook Luigi's hand while the remainder of the family sat in silence trying to digest the events of the last few minutes that would alter their lives forever.

"With them married to two Americans and moved out of the country, they will be safer, and perhaps another Mafia War can be averted," Luigi concluded.

"I am sorry to ask this small favor of you. Ronald, you likely don't know it, but it was Mafia money that sent your Grandfather to Louisiana in the first place, to provide a sort of insurance so that the family could survive.

"It worked too. After the war, your dad sent us money to keep us from starving, and it was us who provided the money for your college degree. We also arranged for you to get some building contracts in Louisiana.

"Now, we need to get my daughter and niece out of harms' way. Even as we speak they are having their wedding dresses fitted. They agreed to the marriages, largely because of Davide's killing.

"None of the other families have started to move in yet, but it is only by putting up a strong front that we can prevent possible violent outcomes. Once the killing starts, there is no stopping it.

"I have invited our competition to the wedding and some of the events. This wedding needs to happen or everyone is in grave danger."

"I can hardly support myself. I can't afford a wife." Roger said.

"As I said, both women will have independent incomes of 100,000 euros a year that is already arranged. This marriage will not cause you any financial hardship."

"That is certainly generous. Can Frank and I have a chance to talk about it after we have met the girls?"

"You will meet them tonight at dinner when the wedding will be announced."

"Mario is going to take you to the tailor to have you measured for your outfits. Each of you, including William, is going to get some sharp-looking Italian clothes.

"William, I know you are gay, which is fine. The family has operated a gay club for many years. However, Italy is perhaps not as hospitable towards gays, as is the U.S. When you go out, I will send some bodyguards out with you. Should anyone bother you they will be taken care of. I want to get the word out that no one in this family is to be messed with."

The tailor shop had a glass front with a series of shirts, suits, and formal outfits displayed in the window. It was not a large place and looked like it might have been built in what was once an alleyway in that the entire structure was long and narrow.

"Welcome, welcome," said Palazzo, the shop's proprietor. "Signore Luigi called and told me that you were coming and needed some clothes for a wedding on Friday. I would have loved to have made you some custom outfits, but there is no time for that. I have some rentals that we can fit for you and have ready by Thursday.

"These will, unfortunately, all be black, but as this is mid-Winter, that will be appropriate. Who are the grooms?"

"These two, they are my sons Frank and Roger," Ronald said.

"Don't you think that this is rushing it a bit? We haven't said that we would do it yet, and now we are to be fitted for wedding clothes," Frank said. "I have heard of shotgun marriages, but isn't this a little ridiculous."

"Boys, come over here for a second," Ronald said. "I have heard enough of these characters from my father and grandfather. If we do not go through with it, or at least play along, this would be considered a grave insult, and none of us may leave this island alive."

"You mean they would kill us," Roger said.

"Maybe not directly, but the entire family might meet with an unfortunate accident on one of these narrow roads in the hills. Go along for now, and maybe we can find a way out of this if you decide you don't want to marry these women. It is not as if either of you had not had relationships. Some work and some do not. For all you know, this one will. With the dowry and annual payments, he has certainly made an attractive offer."

"I am a Marine officer. I can't marry a Mafia member and stay in the service," Frank protested.

"They were about to kick you out with a disability after your accident. It was only because there was a war that you were taken back in and put in a ground combat unit. You will never fly again. It is time that you considered starting over, and certainly, 100,000 euros can go a long way towards that. We can talk it over later. For now, let's play along. All of this might work out. This is no place to talk about it."

"Gentlemen are you ready?" Palazzo asked.

Measuring Frank and Roger with his mind's eye he said, you gentlemen are a little taller than my average customers – about a thirty-six waist and thirty-four inseam, to use English measurements. Is that about what you wear?"

"Something fairly close to that," Frank said.

"I am a little smaller than my brother and usually take a thirty-four waist and about a thirty-three inseam."

Going back to a rack Palazzo picked out two sets of trousers and set them aside.

"What about coat sizes?" he asked.

"About a forty-two in American sizes," Roger said. "I think that we can still wear about the same size coat, although Frank is a little broader across the chest than I am."

Gathering a complete outfit including a shirt, vest, coat, and trousers, Palazzo said, "Go inside the dressing rooms and try them on. I will then pin them up so they can be altered."

Turning to Ronald and William, he said, "You two gentlemen will be sitting in the audience, and I have a variety of business suits that you might like. You can pick something out on the rack over there, and I will see if I have one that we can alter to fit."

"I also have some shirts, slacks, and sweaters for you to look at. Signore Luigi wants his American visitors to be smartly dressed."

"What are these white shirt collars all about? I have seen them in old pictures, but did not know that they still made them."

"They are indeed old style, but have now come back into fashion. I am to outfit you all with three of them."

Returning from their dressing room, Frank and Roger were measured and fitted.

"What is the lining of this vest and coat?" Frank asked. "I haven't seen this fabric before."

"That is, how you say, Kevlar ballistic cloth. It is designed to resist bullets.[26]

There are two layers in the garments-one in the coat and one in the vest. These will prevent the penetration of the 9 mm and even the .45 ACP. Unfortunately, we live in dangerous times."

"What is this inside pocket for?" Ronald asked. "That is for a small pistol, like a Walther PPK or a .380 Beretta. Sometimes it pays to be armed, even at weddings."

For the first time the realization that they might be in real danger sunk in.

"Everyone here knowns how to use firearms," Ronald said. "Where do we get them should be need them."

"I am sure that Signore Luigi can supply whatever might be needed."

"I'm sure he can," Ronald thought.

"How did you boys do with your shopping?" Nancy asked when the group had returned to the hotel. If anything united her husband and his sons, it was that they absolutely hated to go shopping with her and Mary. Maybe, she thought, they did better by themselves.

"We did all right," Ronald replied. "The boys got measured for rental outfits for the wedding, and William and I picked out some suits for us to wear. We got some shirts, slacks, and sweaters as well."

"Why did Frank and Roger get something different?" Mary asked.

"As it turns out this wedding is going to involve someone that you know very well," her dad replied.

"Who?"

---

26   I don't know if this fabric is used in ballistic armor, but Kevlar sheets are used to wrap ammo in transit to the battlefield in hopes of protecting it from being exploded by small arms fire from outside an aircraft.

"Us," Roger replied, motioning his hands to point to himself and his brother.

"You two? You don't even know anyone over here. We just arrived last night. I know you guys might hook up fast, but this is a new record, even for you."

"There are two ladies who need to get out of Sicily. We will explain when we get back to the hotel."

"And they agreed to this?"

"Apparently, they did. We will have a chance to meet them tonight at supper."

"Well, I have heard of blind dates, but this takes it to another level," Nancy exclaimed. "It looks like you are going to have the chance to find out for yourselves. It is a little early for Champagne, but I think I'll have a Manhattan."

Mario, obviously wanting to change the subject, asked, "What are you going to have to eat? There is going to be a heavy meal tonight, so I would suggest a sandwich for now. They have some fresh tuna, chicken salad, or some good ham with some of our local cheeses and soups."

They placed their orders along with a variety of drinks, including a Bourbon and water for Ronald. "After this morning, I feel like I need a good drink," he said.

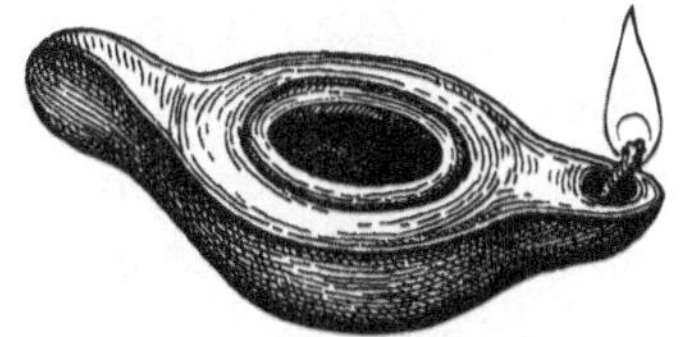

Meet the Family

PICK-UP AT THE HOTEL was to be at 6:30 P.M. By this time, packages that had been ordered at the stores and the shirts from the tailor had been delivered to the rooms and tried on.

"These shirts seem to be made of fairly thin cloth. I'm glad that we have some sweaters to go with them, it was fine today with just a light jacket, but I am going to wear both tonight," William remarked.

"I like the look of the shirt, but these stiff white collars are going to get dirty in a hurry," Roger said.

"Did you notice these snaps? They are detachable so that these collars can be taken off and washed separately," William added. "Otherwise, they would have been sewn back on each time they were washed. I suppose the fashion reason for wearing such shirts was to demonstrate that the wearer was a gentleman who would never sweat enough to soil his collar.

"How do the pants and suspenders feel?" William asked Frank.

"I have never worn suspenders except on combat gear. They do feel a little strange, and I find that I want to wear a belt along with them."

"Me too," Roger added, "I am not accustomed to something swinging around my waist. I guess the gals get use to dresses and such, but I want something around the middle."

"Speaking of women, what do you think that our brides are going to be like?" Frank questioned.

"They were described as, what was it? 'Two of the fairest flowers of the island,' so I suppose that they are not old ugly hags and are something close to our ages, or younger. Who knows? We will find out soon enough," Roger volunteered.

Once assembled in the lobby, Mario moved them into a quiet anteroom off the main floor and spoke quietly. "Let me give you an idea of what is going to happen. You are going to meet some twenty-five members of your extended family, and there will also be some invited guests, some of which are not necessarily our friends. Whether you speak Italian or not, always reply in English and assume that everyone understands every word you say. Only if they do not, do you try what Italian that you may know.

"One person that you will meet is Donna Carlos, who is the wife of Don Carlos. She has largely planned this wedding and your visit. She is a powerful and dangerous member of the family. Take what she says seriously. It is said that she and Luigi were once lovers, but that was many years ago, and that relationship is well known by everyone. Beware of our Sicilian women. They can be more dangerous than the men."

"What about our brides-to-be?" Frank asked. "Are they like that?"

"No. They are nice, attractive young women that most of the guys here have been lusting after for years. You are very lucky to have them offered to you. You would be wise not to disappoint them or the family."

The restaurant was a fifty-minute drive, from the crowded streets to the more rural area outside of town, where there were olive trees, citrus orchards, and scattered vineyards. The two limousines drove through an iron gate, beyond which was a walled-in parking lot. They disembarked in front of the door and were greeted by the doorman. Inside, all of the tables had been set end-to-end, to make a single long table. About thirty people were already seated. Conspicuously situated among the few empty chairs was a row of six vacant seats near the head of the table. Sitting beside Luigi was a stately women dressed in a striking velvet dress that could be none other than Donna Carlos.

Heads turned, and conversations stopped as the Calsase family made their way up to the head of the table. When they arrived, Luigi stood and made the introductions.

"Donna Carlos, this is Ronald Calsase, his wife Nancy, his brother William, their sons Frank and Roger, and their daughter, Mary. This is my daughter, Cecilia, and my niece Angelica. We would all like to welcome you to Sicily and to the family."

"Gentlemen and ladies," Donna Carlos said. "This is a joyous occasion, where we announce the engagement of two members of the American side of the family to two of our own, who are the beloved daughter and niece of Luigi. He has been part of our Mafia family for more than thirty years. He started as a boy, who grew into manhood, and now has reached maturity, as have I. Over the next few days, they will visit with you around the island, and I direct that you extend every courtesy to them. If it is not so, I will hear of it. Please be seated and enjoy your meal."

"Where do we sit?" Roger asked.

"There are place cards," Mary said. "You sit here and Frank, there, next to you."

Once seated and looking across the table, past the place setting, through the wine bottles, and over the green centerpiece, Frank and Roger saw that they were seated opposite two women who were both wearing white linen dresses and pearls.

"I'm Frank."

"I'm Roger."

"We know," Angelica said. "Luigi just told us."

"We are to be married, I guess," Roger responded.

"We know that too. What we don't know is anything about you," Angelica said.

"Us neither," Roger replied.

"Across a table is not the best way to become acquainted," Frank added.

"I agree," Angelica said. "But this is what we have for now."

A smartly dressed older man stood up from the other side of the table, and placed two small boxes on Frank and Roger's empty plates. Opening them, they saw that these were engagement rings set with one-carat colorless diamonds that fairly well matched the colorless expression that came over Roger's face. Not knowing what to do, he pushed it aside, so the box now lay beside his salad fork.

He noticed that Frank had discretely shipped his into a coat pocket, and quickly did the same. These rings were obviously to be presented sometime tonight, but this moment did not seem to be the time.

"I hear that one of you is a Marine officer who was wounded in combat and served in Iraq?" Angelica asked.

"That's me," Frank replied.

"And the other is an artist?" Cecilia questioned.

"I'm that one," Roger said. "Your uncle told me that he paints too. I look forward to looking at some of his work. By coincidence, it seems like we both paint in the style of the 1600s."

"Indeed we do," Luigi replied. "I don't have anything here in Palermo, but I have my studio in my home in Syracuse. I am working on a painting now, and maybe we can do some work on it together. I understand that you specialize in portraits."

"I do, but I have not found much demand for them in the U.S."

"That is a shrinking market. Portrait painting is still done here in Italy, but these are usually by a few painters who have political or family connections with those they pain or won a national competition."

"Would you like to paint me and Angelica?" Cecilia asked.

"Of course I would. But that is not something I can do in a day. Even if I had all of my supplies, it takes time to work up the pigments, apply the base layer, stabilize the canvas, and get everything ready. To say nothing of your posing for it."

"Can't you work from photographs?" Angelica asked.

"I can if I must, but the best portraits are done the old-fashioned way, from sittings."

"Well, I think that we may have the rest of our lives to get them done," Angelica remarked.

"Each minute, day, and hour is different. I would want to capture your images on canvas as you are now and as you progress through life."

"Frank," Cecilia hesitated as if getting accustomed to saying what might be her future husband's name for the first time. "Frank, what is it like being the wife of a Marine Officer?"

"I was deployed on aircraft carriers, but now I am more likely to move from base to base around the world because I no longer fly. There is a problem that if I marry into the family, I must resign my commission."

"No one has to know."

"Believe me, they will find out. The FBI will do background checks on you. If I cannot maintain my security clearance, I can't remain a Marine officer. I can accept a partial disability and maybe get a small pension. I am going to have to find something else to do. Maybe I will go to work with my dad."

"We have talked about that since Frank was wounded. There is room in my company for Frank, and maybe even Roger, but not as an artist," Ronald said.

"You know you two are supposed to decide who is going to marry who tonight, and give us the rings," Angelica teased, clearly enjoying their intendeds' discomforts.

Roger whispered to his father beside him, "Which one?"

A booming voice erupted from the end of the table as Luigi spoke, "No difference. Choose!"

Silence suddenly swept over the room, and Roger squirmed as seemingly every eye focused on him. To postpone the decision, he picked up his fork and started to sample his food. One item among the sliced meats was a red pickled onion that was obviously added as a color accent to the thin-sliced salami and prosciutto of the *antipasto*. When he put his fork on the onion in an attempt to cut off a portion, it rebounded off the lip of the plate, gained altitude, passed between the necks of the wine bottles, cleared the centerpiece, bounced in Angelica's plate, and landed in her lap.[27]

Angelica shrieked and stood to remove the napkin which held this unexpected projectile before it stained her dress. Roger, mortally embarrassed, stood and in the process knocked a glass over on the table, which dumped water on his leg.

"They have chosen!" Luigi announced.

This statement was followed by a round of applause as everyone in the room stood and clapped their congratulations to the new couple.

"Give the rings," Luigi ordered.

---

[27] I have witnessed pickled peaches, onions, and hard frozen wedding bells made from ice cream go sliding off porcelain plates to wind up in the laps of unsuspecting guests. This seemed to be an ideal way to solve the brother's bride selection problems, although I would put it in the category of not being a recommended method of choosing a future spouse.

Roger dug into his pocket, pulled out the ring box and, straining a little to reach Angelica's out-stretched palm, placed the box in her hand. Frank also gave Cecilia her ring, but she set the ring beside her plate, put the napkin to her face and sobbed.

"What did I do?" Frank asked.

"She is overcome with happiness," Luigi replied. Luigi rose and went to his daughter while the waiters came to replace the table cloth and reset the table. While the waiters were exchanging the place settings, Frank remarked to Roger, "Brother you really did it to us that time. Do you want to change places?"

"Yes. That would seem to be better."

In the meantime, Luigi and Cecilia exchanged a few quiet words on the other side of the table. "Davide was supposed to give me these. It is too soon."

Luigi took the ring and slipped it onto Cecilia's finger. "Do this for me and do it for Davide. He would want you safe as much as I do."

With a sigh, Cecilia reoccupied her seat. Again seated, Frank and Roger were more interested in the women across the table than the food. Angelica now stood and handed the engagement ring to Roger who also stood and slipped in onto her finger. It was a little tight and did not quite fit over the knuckle.

The jeweler was prepared and erected a small table behind the two girls, where he sized the rings using a small hammer and a mandrel. Soon, Angelica and Cecilia were sporting new white diamonds on their ring fingers.

"That wasn't so hard," Ronald remarked.

"No, but I think that we had rather chosen our future wives, rather than have them selected for us by a red onion," Frank replied. "Brother, you really got us into it this time."

The *primo*, which was fittingly an Italian wedding soup, was served next.

"This is Italian wedding soup. We have this in America too," Roger observed.

"What would you expect, Brother, minestrone?" Mary questioned.

"I had a chance to read up a little bit about their cooking before I came," William said. "Some heavier meat dish will be coming next. Since this is Sicily, it might be swordfish, sea bass, lamb, goat, pork, or beef. They could also serve some chicken here, but there will also be guinea fowl, squab, duck, or even turkey on occasion. What is not native was brought here by the Arabs from the Middle East or with the Spanish from the Americas or even Asia."

Frank and Roger were not interested in hearing about what they might have next on their plates but were staring at their future brides across the table.

Frank saw that Cecilia had brown eyes, brunette hair with tints of gold, a thin finely-sculptured face and petite nose, under which were bright red-painted lips that slightly parted to expose a row of evenly matched white teeth. He found himself with the thought, "Her mother must have really been a beauty to have produced such a girl."

Cecilia, knowing that she was being intensely stared at, lowered her eyes and did not look at Frank. She nervously played with the food on her plate and ate deliberately so as not to embarrass herself.

"What are you looking at?" Angelica questioned Roger sharply.

"Well, you. You are without question one of the most beautiful women that I have ever seen."

"You are not so bad yourself," Angelica replied. She unbuttoned the top of her dress, declaring, "It is starting to warm up in here."

Before Roger could think of a reasonable reply the waiters were bringing the next course which was sea bass with a side dish of brazed winter vegetables that included carrots, radishes, onions, and turnips.

Plunging a fork into a carrot that was in the *contorno*, Angelica thrust it into her mouth and looked straight at Roger as she lustily bit off the tip.

Roger winced at the obvious implication and mentally agreed, "Angelica is right. It is getting warm in here. No wonder that they had orgies in Ancient Rome."

"Angelica, when will we have a chance to be alone?"

"Not until our wedding night," she said. "My family is very traditional. We will be escorted everywhere we go."

"Well, until then," Roger said, raising a glass. Angelica did likewise. They touched the rims of their glasses over the center of the table and drank, much to the amusement of Luigi and Donna Carlos, who thought that their plans seemed to be going along very well.

"I think a little delayed gratification may be in order here," Luigi remarked to Donna Carlos.

"I quite agree. The two couples seem to be doing well for a first meeting."

Frank, now knowing that only two weeks ago Cecilia had buried the man who she had every reason to believe was the love of her life, found himself wanting to reach under the table, grasp both her hands, and tell Cecilia that things would be all right. She needed comforting, and he wanted to take her into his arms and provide it. Maybe things would work out with this business after all.

Although eating was not what the two couples had on their minds, they managed to maintain a degree of decorum through the meal, as it progressed through the salad, fruit and cheese course, which included blood orange slices from trees near Catania, and the dessert.

Roger selected a raspberry gelato and was surprised at the gritty texture. Looking at Angelica with a questioning expression on his face, she responded.

"We Sicilians like a little resistance in our foods. Our gelatos, chocolates, and even vegetables will often have some coarse salt, sugar, or ice crystal to provide a bit of a crunch when we eat. Some say that this is to remind us that life has its difficult parts – as if we had not been learning that lesson for thousands of years."

"In the South, we like our crunch in our foods too– like crispy fried chicken, grits, and fish fried with coarse cornmeal. We eat grits, something like you eat pasta, although most often in the morning with eggs and bacon."

The drivers, waiters, and kitchen staff were served in a separate building that was connected to the kitchen by a covered breezeway. Here there were also tables and chairs, but these had been retired from service in the main dining room. Against one wall was a long oak table, on which fresh food was placed periodically. There were also a couple of bottles of wine, but these were not replaced as they were emptied. It was understood by all but the rankest of drivers that they might have a glass with their meals, but their main responsibility was to be ready to safely drive their rides back home at any moment.

As members of the kitchen staff came in and out, there was a running commentary on the proceedings inside the dining room. This was much like calling a ball game, except here, instead of innings, the courses were announced as they were served.

A couple of times the Chef came in, to make sure that there was sufficient food for everyone. He did this because he knew that tourists depended on their drivers for recommendations, and a well-satisfied driver would return again and again. This was his most direct means of advertising, which had the considerable advantage that it was paid for by those dining inside.

"Better than we had in prison," Michael remarked.

"Yes, it sure is," Vito replied.

"When and where were you two in prison," an anonymous voice asked from the rear of the room.

"It was all a big mistake over a stolen car that we were working on. We were in for a short time at Saint Vittore in Milan before we came here to work for our cousin. It was not a big deal, but we are glad to get out of that dump."

"As are nearly all of us, most have served time for something, somewhere. A guy's got to do what a guy's got to do to get by in today's world, where people like those stuffing themselves inside have everything, and we pick among the crumbs."

"Shut up, Alberto. You have a cushy job, are eating good food, and drinking free wine. What have you got to complain about?"

"Michael, Vito, is that you?" Alexi asked from across the room. "We spent some time together in that Fascists hotel in Milan."

Before they could answer, there was a burst of submachine gun fire and two pistol shots at the front gate.

"Stay inside. That is none of our business," Alberto ordered. "If those mobsters want to kill themselves off, that's fine. They will come for us when they want us."

After a burst of shots peppered the roof, the lights were turned off inside the restaurant and there were shouts of "Get down." When there were no more shots and no explosion following the initial burst of gunfire, Luigi went outside and then returned.

"He turned on the lights and said, "Please be seated. Some of our competition just wanted to give us a warning. That burst of gunfire was not meant to hurt anyone and did not.

"Sit down please, enjoy your coffee, and help us welcome our American cousins."

Among those retaking their seats and trying to suppress a smile, Don Augustino enjoyed this aspect of his son's handiwork.

Roger, who had never experienced being shot at, excitedly asked Frank, "Do you think they will come back?"

"Not a chance," Frank answered. "They know that they are expected, and did you see all of those guns come out when the shooting started? It's like Luigi said. This was a warning – about what, I do not know. Maybe this is about us getting married, or some supposed connection with the American Mafia. It could be anything."

"This sort of thing is exactly why Cecilia and I want to get out of this mess," Angelica said. "Somebody we know is being threatened or killed all of the time. We just want to live a normal life."

"Cecilia, are you all right?" Frank asked as he attempted to move around the table to take her in his arms. He was stopped by Luigi, who sternly warned him, "You may not embrace until your wedding night."

"No. No. I am not all right. I hate this place and I love it. I don't know what to do. Every time I turn around, something bad is happening."

Again, Frank felt an urge to go to take Cecilia in his arms, but it did not happen. It could not happen – at least not tonight.

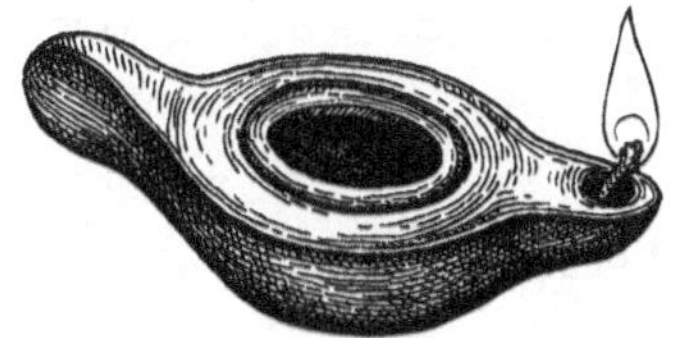

Palermo and Monreale

AT THE OFFICE THE next morning Michael asked Renato Ciatti, "Who do your think shot up the restaurant last night?"

"I have no idea. Mafia members are not often loved by many people because they have squeezed nearly everyone on the island at one time or another," Renato answered.

"You say that another driver told you that Luigi thought this was just a warning from another mob?"

"Yes, he told me that Luigi said that the shots were fired high over the cars and buildings and that they had apparently not intended to kill anyone. Although, some shots were fired back at the vehicle, so I suppose that there may be some bullet holes in it. No one saw enough of it to even tell what kind of vehicle it was, except that it was large enough that the lights blinded the guards at the gate."

"The one responsible might have been one of the guests on the inside," Vito said. "If you were responsible for a shooting, what better place to be than among those who were fired on? I am sure that Luigi is just as puzzled as we are."

"Did anyone report the shooting?" Michael asked.

"Apparently not. The restaurant is in a secluded location, and the *mafiosi* are not going to say anything about it. A few gunshots fired in the middle of the night are so common as not to draw attention. Not on this island, anyway," Renato concluded.

"Today, you both are going to take cars, pick up Luigi from the hotel where you were yesterday, and then get the Americans at the Crystal. You are going to take them sightseeing around Palermo. Luigi is going to be the guide. Try to pay attention to what they say and what is going on – particularly if any mention is made as to who arranged the shooting. Luigi is well connected with those who have operations all over southern Italy. Be friendly, and talk to them as much as possible.

"These are our big Diesels, and they will hold six in the back and two in the front seat.

"Michael, as you have already made contacts with Luigi's daughter and niece, see if you can drive them, and find out what they think. If they are like any women I know, they are not going to want to be pushed into this marriage, and they may give us some insight into what is going on."

Returning to the pink hotel, the agents parked their limos on the street and went inside.

"Signore Luigi is expecting us," Michael said.

Without a word, the desk clerk got his keys to operate the elevator, walked them over, and then started them on their journey to the penthouse.

Once in the office, they met a sharply dressed secretary and noticed on her desk two small suitcases such as might be used to carry fine cigars.

"Open the cases, fill out, and sign the documents you find inside, and put your driver's license numbers on them," the secretary instructed.

When they opened the cases they found two stainless steel 1911 .45 Colt semi-autos[28] with two extra seven-round magazines and another longer one that held at least twenty rounds.

"What are we to do with these?" Vito asked.

"Defend yourselves if necessary," answered a voice from the rear of the room. This voice was connected to Alberto, the same driver that they had met last night.

---

[28]   I was in the Colt 1911 army when I served my active duty time during the late 1960s in Alaska. I owned and carried my own pistol while I was there which harkened back to older times in the U.S. Armed Forces when officers were expected to furnish their own uniforms, which is still true today, and their own swords and pistols. I also had a .22 L.R. ACE conversion unit for the gun which was very helpful in allowing me to dispatch some rodents that would get into our tents in the field.

"Do you know how to use them?"

Michael replied that he knew a little about them, and Vito said that he had hardly ever seen one.

"Come back tonight. We have a range in the basement, and I will check you out with them. We don't want you shooting yourselves or any of us, and we are not going to let you carry them until we are sure that you know how to use them," Alberto concluded.

"We aren't getting paid for this," Michael said. "You will be," Alberto said. "We are going to pay for your licenses, and you will get something extra when you carry a gun."

"We can't do anything for you," Vito remarked. "If we do we go back to prison."

"Not to worry, we have the judges in our pocket around here."

Luigi walked into the room in time to participate in the conversation. "You two men are going to be part of our security staff. The cars have bullet-resistant glass. You need that level of protection when you tour VIPs around the island.

"I want to warn you how these vehicles are attacked. Often, it will be by a driver on a scooter or motorbike. He will drive alongside the car and attempt to shoot a tire or the driver. If anyone approaches your side of the car on a scooter, run him off the road before he can get alongside. By the time you see a gun it will be too late. Now let's go pick up our visitors."

I will be down in a moment. I need to have Estavo help me put on my jacket. Please send him in when you leave.

"Estavo, bring me the knife off the wall, and get my prosthesis – the one with the hand on it." In the vest he wore, there was a special sheath that held the long-bladed knife inclined against his left side, so that its handle was in a comfortable grasping position for his right hand and the point of the scabbard was positioned slightly behind the armpit. When wearing a coat and gloves, only a keen-eyed individual would notice that the grip on his left hand never changed. Perhaps, someday he might even be restored with a hand that had movement, but the doctors had told him that he had lost his limb too many years before for the nerve endings to be functional. Having lived for most of his life with only one hand, Luigi declined the operation. "If I have gotten along without a hand for this long, I do not see why I cannot for the next twenty years or however long I have left."

Arriving at the Crystal Hotel, Luigi told his visitors, "I must apologize for our dinner being interrupted last night. It may have been some men just having a bit of fun, so think nothing more about it. We will have two bodyguards with us who will be on the look-out for anything suspicious. You are going to see some marvelous sights and one of our Italian markets today."

"Let's enjoy the tour," Nancy said. "After all, that is why we came."

"And for the weddings as we find out," Frank added.

"Yes, the weddings too, but everything will work out." Luigi asserted.

Luigi sat beside Michael in the front seat of the first limousine, which also carried the other men in the Calsase family. Nancy, Angelica, and Cecilia were in the second limo, along with an older lady dressed in black and two burly bodyguards, who had suspicious bulges under their coats.

"When we get to the attractions we will try to park together, but here in the city that will not often be possible, so let us out in front, find a place to park and wait for us in front of the building," Luigi told Michael and Vito. "When we leave, you can go get the limos and pick us up again. I want the two bodyguards and us to be moving as a group all the time."

"Angelica, since you have studied our architecture, tell us about this," Luigi said when they arrived at the *Plazzo dei Normanni.*

"I am not prepared for this," Angelica started, but it was soon apparent that she knew what she was talking about.

"All of the buildings have been damaged by war or natural disasters such as earthquakes or tidal waves. In the field of historical reconstruction that I am studying, we repair, and, in some cases, rebuild, buildings that have been damaged by these events."

"Wow," Roger thought. "This lady has a head on her shoulders."

"Sometimes, they were originally built in the Romanesque style, and over the centuries, their exteriors were modernized to fit the fashions of the period, particularly the Spanish Baroque. The outside of this particular building is very businesslike, as is fitting for a seat of government. In fact, it was the Royal Palace. However, its rather plain exterior is deceiving as some of the most spectacular interior decorations in Europe are inside."

When they went inside, they found a two-story colonnaded courtyard with thin marble columns supporting delicate arches. Unusually, the top row of arches is two-stories tall, whereas the bottom floor has columns of the same diameter supporting only a single story.

"During each time period, there was a desire to outdo one's predecessor. Hence the departure from the usual Roman construction, where the taller, stronger, and thicker columns are on the bottom and the lighter-weight, thinner columns and arches are on top. Here the expected pattern is reversed for visual impact, but this was not a wise choice for a building located on an island with frequent earthquakes."

Once inside the Royal Chapel, Luigi directed Roger to talk about the jaw-dropping mosaics and ceiling decorations.

"There are two styles of decoration used in the chapel," Roger began. "The lower part of the chapel is done in the Arabic style, with geometric decorative patterns since pictorial depictions of The Prophet are forbidden in the Islamic traditions. They also favored natural stones for their work.

"These enormously bright-colored, figured mosaics are done with gold and colored glasses. It is nothing short of amazing how the craftsmen were able to both produce and use very life-like colorations for the skin textures and do shadings to match folds in the garment. This work was done by Byzantine craftsmen and is more detailed than the famous mosaics in Hagia Sophia in Istanbul, which predate them. Even today, we would be very hard-pressed to duplicate the work."

"I have never seen anything like this," Nancy said. "This tradition still exists in the Greek Orthodox churches in Eastern Europe and Russia, from what I have seen," Frank added.

In contrast to the elaborate decorations at the Royal Palace, the Church of San Francis d'Assisi is unadorned on the inside, with plain stuccoed walls. The most famous feature of the church is the rose window and frescoes done in the 1600s.

"This is fitting for a church dedicated to a saint who led a simple life," Angelica said. "After an earthquake in 1823, the façade of the church was restored to its simpler Romanesque style from the 1300s. Descriptions, old artworks showing the building, and construction elements recovered during rebuilding were all used in the restoration. Doing this sort of detective work is an interesting part of rebuilding an historic structure."

With more churches, monasteries, and cloisters to come, Luigi gave the tour a change in pace by visiting the Antonino Salinas Regional Archeological museum.

"This is another of our repurposed religious buildings. This was originally a monastery that was converted into a museum starting in 1866. It contains many relics from centuries past. These include things from the Phoenicians who founded the city, through Roman times, and objects recovered from Pompeii. After the war, I helped excavate some of the sites that were uncovered during the rebuilding of Syracuse, and a few of the things that we recovered are in this museum. I did not do any digging because I had already lost my hand, but I drew many of the objects, designs, and exteriors of the buildings we were working on.

"Inside, you will find many Greek vases with elaborate drawings of the times, which I was often asked to copy. There are also many pieces of sculpture, a few remains of helmets, swords, and spears throughout the ages, as well as an extensive collection of coins. You can imagine, if cities are destroyed time after time over the centuries, almost any dug site will reveal hundreds of years of historical records in the manner of the artifacts that were left behind."

"This building, as you will see from the photographs, was heavily damaged by an earthquake and rebuilt. We live on a very turbulent island. No one ever knows what might happen next."

"Appealing to the Gods for protection was one reason why there were so many temples and churches on the island," Cecilia added. "Many were converted to secular use after Italy became a state, and church properties were confiscated."

Frank saw what Luigi was doing on the tour. By encouraging them to showcase their knowledge about the locations they were visiting, Luigi permitted them to learn more about each other and bond while keeping them in a closely supervised situation. The way Angelica was looking at Roger made it apparent that she was more than curious about him. Cecilia was more reserved, but Frank felt the desire to comfort and protect her. She would give him a sly glance from time to time, but they were not allowed to even touch.

One of the rooms in the museum showed a painting of the destruction of Pompeii along with plaster casts of the bodies recovered from the ruins. Frank staggered, collapsed on a nearby bench, and held in hands in front of his face as if watching a movie play on the backs of his eyelids.

"I'm sorry, Frank is having trouble. We need to get him out of here, and he will be fine." With these words, Ronald put his arm around his son's shoulder and walked him out of the museum where the others joined him after their tour.

"Frank, are you all right?" Nancy asked.

"I'm sorry everyone. A few weeks ago, I was in combat in Baghdad, and it came back on me all of a sudden. I'm all right now. I was afraid that this might happen."

Cecilia had a look of obvious concern, and in response Ronald said, "This is PTSD. I had a touch of it after I got home. This sort of thing will pass in time. It is scary when it happens, but Frank will keep it under control. It just takes time."

Shortly before lunch they visited the central market, where among the usual fruits and vegetables was one meat stall where a man with a two-foot-long butcher knife was cutting steaks from a swordfish. "We use different knives in Sicily for different things, and this has always been so. One of the most famous was a knife with a flame-shaped blade, used by ancient Sicilian tribes who were here even before the Phoenicians.[29]

"Now, let's go to one of the cafés and have lunch."

The café that Luigi selected had small tables where two diners usually sat, but in this case, Frank and Cecilia and Roger and Angelica were joined by their grim-looking lady escort and Luigi respectively.

"Cecilia, I wanted to tell you that I know about Davide and what he meant to you. I wanted to comfort you after the shooting but did not have the chance," Frank said, as he extended his hands across the table in an invitation for Cecilia to grasp them.

An explosion of Italian erupted from their chaperone, who took a fork and rapped Frank's hand hard across the knuckles. Not since Catholic school, when his hands were smacked with a ruler, had such an event occurred.

---

[29]   While true that the knife used by the ancient Sicels was not later made by the Greeks, I do not know if it was actually banned by convention or law. The design I came up with was based on descriptions and artifacts from old tombs and knife styles of the time, although I could not find one of the actual blades.

"Ow" Frank said as he snatched back his hands.

His chaperone looked him in the eyes and wagged her index finger back and forth in a manner that instantly communicated, "No. No."

"This is going to be tough," Frank thought.

His brother was having no better luck with Angelica. He looked at his sandwich and saw that it contained three types of meats, fresh-ground mustard, a splash of mayonnaise, and greens in a small loaf of homemade bread that had been split lengthwise and then cut in half at a diagonal. This allowed the first bites, at least, to fit more easily in the mouth.

"What do you call this in America?" Luigi asked. "This is a Hoagie." Roger replied.

"That is a strange name. What does it mean?"

"I heard that it was named after a sandwich made by Italian immigrants in Philadelphia. They worked at the Hog Island Shipyard during World War I and called their sandwich the 'hoggie.' The pronunciation changed over time."

"Angelica, do you cook?" Roger questioned.

"Not very much. I did a little while I was away at school, but at home, we always had cooks who would run me and Cecilia out of the kitchen. Consequently, we were never really taught how to cook."

"I am afraid that is true," Luigi said. "When I was young, I had to learn to do simple cooking to survive, but, as time progressed, I did less and less. Except for maybe raiding the refrigerator after the cook has gone, I can't say that I cook much anymore. Looking back now, I see that I should have been more attentive to that aspect of the girls' lives."

"With only one hand it must be difficult to do things like chopping, pouring, beating something, and so on," Roger said.

"It is, but you learn how to work around it – like when I paint, I use a special palette that I attach to my arm."

"Frank and I are both fairly good cooks. We were taught by our dad and mom. My dad is really the master when it comes to cooking Louisiana seafood and wild game. We hunt, so we almost always have some fresh game and fish in the freezer."

"You don't shop every day, like we do?" Angelica said.

"Not like you do here. Usually, we go to a supermarket that has everything right there, rather than going to the fishmonger, butcher, baker, and so on. It is much more efficient, and we usually shop only once a week and get everything we need. In the bigger cities, there are still specialty shops, but not so much in the countryside anymore. The big chains have run them out of business."

"If Frank is fortunate enough to get a wild boar, maybe he can cook some of our Southern bar-b-que for you. This is pork that is roasted over oak coals and basted with a sweet-sour tomato or mustard sauce."

"I look forward to us cooking together," Angelica said, fully aware of the double-meaning implied in the statement.

"Me too," Roger agreed.

At Michael and Vito's table, Vito motioned with a finger to point at a well-tanned young man dressed in faded jeans, plaid shirt, cowboy boots, and a buckskin jacket carrying a boom box who was sitting at a nearby table. Michael watched his reflection in his wineglass as the man sat and arranged his boom box, put in earplugs and turned it on.

Michael nodded his head in agreement and mouthed to Vito. "That guy is a phony. He is trying to listen to us."

Vito rises, goes to Luigi's table and points to his watch. "We have an appointment. It's time to leave."

Not at all liking the interruption, Luigi responded, "I make the appointments around here."

With his body between Luigi's table and the young man, Vito indicates with his hand, and Luigi spotted the boom box. The man appears to be listening to the races while filling out his betting card. Luigi motioned to Vito to go to the other tables to ask the others to finish their meals.

Once away from the café, Luigi announced their next destination, "We are going to Monreale which is in the hills above Palermo. This was used as a summer residence for the royal families and to hunt the stags and wild boars in the rough country and in the mountains. There we also have a notable cathedral, as well as a cloister."

Once they arrived, Cecilia was selected to act as a guide. "You can see clearly the different styles used for the entrance of the Cathedral. The mosaics are every bit as beautiful as those in the Royal Chapel and much more expansive with illustrations showing biblical events in the apses and the largest figure being Christ below which is Mary and child flanked by angels and the apostles. We also have two stone coffins containing the remains of two Norman kings, William and Roger.[30]

"The elaborate visual displays were done for the benefit of a largely illiterate population who listened to services said in a language they did not know. They were threatened with eternal damnation should they dare to cross their religious or political leaders, as Kings were anointed by God, and could do no wrong.

"Difficult women could be sent away to a cloister where they would remain for the rest of their lives. Some of them even had children sired by priests. In the higher ranks of the church of the day, it was not uncommon for bishops to openly acknowledge their sons, as these were among the few people that they could trust in the constant intrigues of church and political life. I don't think that Angelica and I would have fitted in very well."

"Indeed not. A woman like me, who would dare to think of becoming anything other than a wife, would have been burned as a witch or a heretic," Angelica interjected.

"That does it for the day." Luigi said. "We will go back to the hotel, where we will eat in the dining room. You will need to pack tonight because we will be staying at other hotels as we tour the island."

"Where are the women?" Frank asked, once they were back at the hotel.

"I don't know. Luigi may have moved them elsewhere," Roger replied. "He doesn't seem to trust us together."

"With good reason brother. With good reason. Those gals are hot, and I would happily make love to either of them or both." Frank asserted.

"Me too, Brother. Me too."

Now unpacking in their new hotel rooms, Angelica and Cecilia had the first opportunity to talk about the new husbands-to-be. Angelica opened the conversation.

"What do you think about Frank, your new husband? Mine is an artist, and that sorts of fits with what I want to do in architecture. He doesn't

---

[30]   Being a William as many from England are, I may be a descendent of this William as royalty of the day would bed any woman they found attractive.

seem to be as strong as Frank – maybe the younger-brother syndrome. Still, he is a good-looking man. Perhaps not my first choice in a husband, but so far, he seems like a person I could get along with and maybe come to love."

"Mine is handsome, a Marine, an officer, and seems to be sympathetic. He has lost someone, and I have lost Davide. Maybe we need each other?"

"You got all of that from tonight? What about Michael, the driver?" Angela asked.

"It almost tears my heart out to see him. I look at him and there is Davide until he says something. Only their voices are different. It is as if he had come back to me, but that can never be. I am sorry, I am about to cry just thinking about it. I feel like I am betraying his memory – cheating on him. Sorry, I just can't talk about this now."

"I am going down to the bar and get a drink. Do you want to come?"

"No. I had rather be alone."

Angelica gave her cousin a comforting hug, picked up her purse, and took the elevator up to the disco bar which had a spiral stairway to the roof. As the elevator rose she heard the low disco beat reverberating down the shaft. When the doors opened she was hit by a kaleidoscope of colors cast by the disco ball, and the throbbing beat of the music penetrated her body. The room was crowded with young people dancing to the music as she worked her way towards the bar. Suddenly, she felt strong hands on both shoulders as someone attempted to drag her back into the elevator.

"Come with me and there will be no problem," she heard through the noise. Through one of the mirrors on a column she saw a dark-skinned slim man wearing cowboy boots and a leather jacket. She planted her feet and opened her purse to retrieve her knife.

"Who are you?"

"Someone who you are going to get to know very well," Apachee replies.

"I think not." With this statement she dropped to her knees and broke the man's grip which allowed her to rise and with the now-opened blade which she uses to slash him diagonally across the chest. The razor-sharp blade cut through the coat and ran along the top of his ribs. The man turned to get away from the stinging steel and she lunged and gave him another cut across his butt, leaving him hobbling towards the elevator with one hand clutching his chest and the other holding his backside.

With the commotion the DJ stopped the music and turned up the house lights. As Angelica put the knife away she was approached by the club's Manager.

"Nothing happened here. Please give the staff a few minutes to clean things up. Have a drink on the house." Turning to Angelica he said in quieter tones. "I saw what happened. There will be no police. I don't know who that was. There may be more. Please leave and give my regards to Luigi."

The manager escorted her to the elevator and when the door opened fresh blood on the floor and walls indicated the effectiveness of her defense.

"Bring a basin and water and clean this up," he ordered.

Once that was done, Angelica, now with a bottle of wine grabbed from a nearby table, returned to her room, where she closed and bolted the door. Cecilia was already asleep. Angelica sat by the window and, by the light of a streetlamp coming through the window, drank from the bottle. She had come close to killing a man, and maybe she should have.

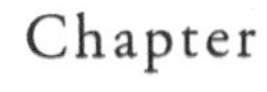

20

Colt's 1911

MICHAEL AND VITO RETURNED to the pink Mafia headquarters with Luigi after they had dropped off their passengers at the Crystal Hotel and relocated Angelica and Cecilia to another hotel five blocks away.

"Before you go out on the road with my family, I want Alberto to give you some training with the .45 Colts that you will be carrying in the car," Luigi said. "We have a range in an old air-raid shelter in the basement where you can shoot."

Michael wondered how many people might have been tortured or killed in such a conveniently secluded location.

"Go ahead and take your pistols out of the boxes. I want to show you how to disassemble and clean them, and then we will check them out," Alberto said. "These are brand new guns. Our people prefer the 9 mm because they are generally easier to conceal and often carry more rounds."

"Michael, you said that you knew something about them?"

"Only by reputation. I have read about the 1911 Colt autos in magazines, know something about their history, and that they were the handguns used by the Americans during both world wars. I have never had the opportunity to shoot one. Those that I have seen were behind glass in sporting goods stores or exhibits about the war. They are generally considered to be heavy, reliable, powerful pistols, but more difficult to shoot than the 9 mms."

"All that is true," Alberto said. "That is why I am going to start you off at fifteen yards. When you can, you can come down here and shoot some more – out to twenty-five yards.[31]

"This range is courtesy of the U.S. Navy. It was in a shipment intended for their air station but, somehow got lost along the way. They searched for it, but never found a trace. They supposed that it had been broken up and used to help rebuild some factory in Sicily. They thoughtfully even included the ventilation fans needed to exhaust the lead dust and smoke along with the lights and targets – thoughtful people, those Americans.

"Now go ahead and take a look at the pistols."

"I am surprised that these are stainless steel."[32] Vito said.

"There are a couple of reasons. One is that the brightly finished guns are intimidating and might, prevent a gunfight by just being shown. The other is that we sometimes must stash these guns in exposed places and want them to come up shooting when needed. As you know, using a stainless gun is helpful in that situation.

"Since your guns are going to be kept in a vehicle, the gun's size is less of a problem, and I expect you to keep them operational at all times. Your lives may depend on it. When you are on the road, you are exposed even though you are in a hardened vehicle."

"What if we are stopped?" Michael asked.

"Here are your carry permits. There is a place to hold your guns in the door panel of those cars."

Alberto took one of the guns placed it on a towel and got a brass brush and cleaning rod. "When Browning designed the 1911, he saw the need to have easily removable barrels. I can swap out this barrel and put a longer barrel with a silencer on this gun that muffles the gun but does not completely deaden the sound. At any rate, you don't need one. They would just get in the way."

---

[31] The shooting instructions are for those who have never been exposed to either military or police training. New shooters are always started out at short range, slow fire exercises. I like to start shooters, as was illustrated here, from sitting, rather than off-hand shooting from a standing position.

[32] Stainless steel 1911s were available from a variety of commercial sources during 2004, and are somewhat more common today. The gun I used to aid me in writing this section was a stainless 1911 R, made by Remington in their new factory in Huntsville, Alabama, which is now closed.

Obviously, Alberto was enjoying his job. While the thought, "Too much information, let's get down to the shooting," flashed through Vito's head. He could not appear too knowledgeable about the subject or shoot too well to keep from blowing his cover.

"The first thing is to remove the magazine and clear the gun. Then allow the slide the run forward. Do you see this checkered button beneath the barrel? Press that down while rotating the barrel shroud which will allow the spring to be removed. Then take out the slide-retaining pin and the slide will slip off in your hand, exposing the barrel and operating parts for cleaning. This is all you really need to do to clean and maintain your gun. Once you have it disassembled put some alcohol on a patch and clean the shipping grease out of the barrel and off the parts, and then put a light coat of oil on them. Don't try to ease the slide forward when you load the gun. Let it fly forward under spring pressure to make sure that the gun loads and locks up properly.

"Practice putting it together and taking it apart a couple of times, while I get some ammo."

"My gun feels a little stiff," Vito said. "I suppose it will loosen up when we put a few hundred rounds through it. Like a car, it takes a little while to break it in."

Returning with a G.I. ammo case, filled with boxes of .45 ammo and three sets of earplugs, Alberto remarked, "We have an unlimited supply left over from the war. Shoot all you want. The objective is for you to become sufficiently confident with your skills to take on a man at close range – from vehicle to vehicle on the highway or across the room. Don't believe what you have heard about the knock-down power of the .45. You still must get good hits in the body cavity for the round to be effective."

Although working the other side of the law-enforcement spectrum, Alberto was gaining Michael's respect because of his exhaustive knowledge of firearms and his skill as an instructor. "We could really use him in AIA," he thought but quickly dismissed it. He dared not become too attached to his new Mafia friends because they could at almost any time face each other in a gun battle.

The first magazine-full was shot downrange without any attempt to hit the target. This was just to check the functionality of the guns. After successfully completing that stage, a man-sized silhouette was installed, and the pair tried to group their rounds as close to the center of the target as possible.

"Pay attention to your sights. Let the target blur in your vision and keep the sights aligned and level. Then practice breathing, and your trigger pull. Don't yank the trigger. Use the ball of the thumb to get the best trigger pull possible. When everything is right, squeeze the trigger and be surprised when the gun fires. Do all of this, and your shot will go where it needs to go. Rush things and just go bang, bang and the shots will wind go over the place. With practice, your skills will improve, and your ability to place accurate rapid shots will increase. For now, do what I tell you to do. Try to place your shots as closely as possible to the center of the target."

"This doesn't have as much recoil as I expected," Vito said. "It wants to move in the hand when I shoot, but it is not too bad."

Overhearing the comment, Alberto said, "Grasp the pistol firmly, and attempt to keep the hand and fingers in exactly the same place for each shot. This will greatly increase your accuracy. Eventually, your hand will come to know the gun, and take that position automatically each time you pick it up."

Alberto brought up two folding chairs and sat them down. "What I want you to do now is to sit in the chairs, place your right hand across your body as if you were shooting out a window and, by feel, try to place your rounds on the target – just as if you were trying to shoot the driver in another car beside you. You will have your left hand high-center on the steering wheel, and your right hand will be below it."

After they tried that exercise with only four and five shots respectively for Michael and Vito hitting anywhere near the center of the target, Vito remarked. "That is considerably more difficult, and we were sitting still. It is going to be even tougher when we are driving a vehicle, and trying to control it at the same time."

Michael gave Vito a look that carried the message, "I hope that we never have to shoot like that."

Chapter

21

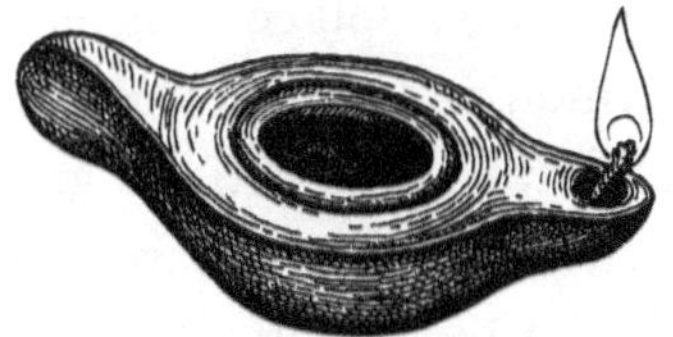

𝕾alt and 𝖂ine

STANDING NEXT TO BOTH limos as they prepared to leave the hotel, Luigi outlined the day's activities. "This morning, we are going to visit a bay where they have made natural sea salt since the days of the Greeks, and also view some of the best-preserved Greek and Roman temples on the island. These are the ruins that you have most often seen in pictures and ads about Sicily. We will load your luggage in the trunk, and go pick up the girls at their hotel. They brought enough stuff to stay for a month. I will send one of the drivers back for it and have him take what they don't need back to Syracuse."

After collecting Angelica and Cecilia, the two limos started their trip out of the city. At a stoplight, Angelica looked out her window and saw a trimmed tree whose branches had been cut in such a fashion to resemble a man, with two outstretched arms and a raging erection.33 She giggled and touched Cecilia who was sitting facing her, and pointed towards the distressed figure. "I wonder if the fellows that we are supposed to marry are like that?" she questioned.

Cecilia blushed as she got a full view of the tree. "I suppose," she replied.

"Well I am going to find out," Angelica said conspiratorially.

"Nice girls don't think about such things," their chaperone rebuked.

---

³³ I saw this suggestive trimming from our bus as we were leaving Palermo, and could not resist including it.

187

"Sure we do, all the time," Angelica thought, but did not bother to reply.

"Sicily has a mild climate and fertile soils, but is often hilly, rocky, and difficult to farm," Luigi explained to the Calsases as they traveled east of Palermo towards Trapani. "The very steepest ground is left to forests, the next steepest, if there is sufficient soil cover is planted in vineyards. Then come the olive groves, lemon and orange trees, and finally row crops on the least rocky ground. Cattle are sometimes grazed on the flatter parts of the island in the interior, and we also have sheep and goats that roam the less hospitable portions. Over thousands of years, people have tried to extract the most from the island, and it was literally the breadbasket of the Roman Empire."

The windmill on the skyline on the salt pans of the *Saline di Trapani* evoked the Netherlands to William and Mary, Spain to Roger and his mother, and the Moulin Rouge in Paris to Frank and his dad.

"I really didn't expect to see one of those here," Ronald said.

"That mill was probably built by the Spanish during the Baroque period," Angelica said. "I don't know if they invented that style, but they certainly spread that design through Spanish possessions all over Europe and the world. I would not be astonished to discover that they also built them in Mexico and California."

"One thing that was completely unexpected to me is how much some of this country looks like parts of southern California – even the same cactus," Roger observed, remembering his intimate contact with the plants.

"The cactuses were brought over by Spanish sailors from the New World to provide the vitamin C needed to prevent scurvy. A ship's crew's diet mostly consisted of grain products and perhaps salt-cured meats and fish a couple of times a week," Luigi explained. "Many things were first brought here, tried, and then spread from Sicily to other parts of Europe – like potatoes and tomatoes for example. They even have Sicilian-sounding names.

"It was, and is, no coincidence that salt recovered here was used all over southern Europe and even today is exported worldwide.

"There were many artifacts recovered from the salt pans, including some from very ancient times, but anything metal was corroded almost beyond recognition. Organic material like leather, human remains, and wooden tools are better preserved."

"Are these salts used for salt-curing fish and meats as well as for general cooking?" William asked.

"This salt is used for all of those things as well as for industrial uses. However, the best quality and highest priced salt is packaged as a cooking ingredient. There is one technique where a whole fish is cooked completely surrounded by a thick bed of coarse salt. This technique can be thought of as cooking before aluminum foil, but there was the significant difference in that it is the fish's skin that helps keep the fish moist rather than a metal foil. The result is a well-cooked slightly salt-tasting fish. It is not briny as might be expected or as salty as salt cod. I will see if I can order such a fish for supper."

"Who is the wine expert among us who wants to talk about Marsala's famous wines?" Luigi asked.

"I suppose that I could," volunteered Mario who was serving as a bodyguard that day.

"Very well. Tell us about the Marsala made here at the winery," Luigi said.

"Like many businesses on the island, this one is built in a repurposed monastery. An Englishman, John Woodhouse, started a vineyard here with the idea of exporting his wines to England. He started mixing them with brandy to give them a greater alcohol content and make them last longer when they were shipped. He also aged this mixture in charred oak Bourbon barrels from American distillers to make his products more like the Port from Portugal.

"Ultimately, he was successful, and now the Marsala wines are aged up to twelve years and exported in various grades all over the world. The brand became so popular that it is protected, like Champagne, so that a wine can only be called Marsala if it is made from grapes grown in this region and made here.

"This winery is among the world's largest producer of Marsala wines, but not the only one."

"We have branches of the family businesses that own vineyards and makes wines scattered all over Sicily," Luigi added. "And we will visit one of the more rustic operations. Here, everything is done with new industrial equipment."

A young lady dressed in a formal dress conducted them through the tour. Because this was a repurposed building and the desire was to conserve the original architectural elements, the group found themselves climbing up a steep, narrow defile of stone stairs.

As Frank was about to take a step, he received a sharp pinch on his backside. He almost stumbled at this unexpected physical encounter and whispered back without looking, "I thought only Italian men did that."

"Not so, brother-in-law-to-be. Not so," Angelica whispered in his ear.

This interchange was followed by an effusive eruption of Italian from the chaperone, who gave Frank's butt a hard slap as if that might erase the infraction.

"Luigi, surmising what had just occurred from further back in the line, chuckled and said. "All in good time, Angelica. All in good time."

"What do you think of it?" William asked Nancy when they had arrived in the tasting room. "It does taste something like Port, but my palate is not sensitive enough to tell the difference between a cheap bottle of Gallo Port from California and this. I can drink it and enjoy it in small amounts, but it is not something that I would want to drink by the bottle."

"Just so," Luigi said. "This is not a wine that you drink every day. This is a holiday wine that is consumed to relax you after a good meal while you discuss ancient history, philosophy, religion, or some similarly deep subject. The ancients thought a little wine lubricated serious discussion. I will buy a few bottles for later."

Mario and Vito had strict instructions to stay with the limos anytime they were parked on the street.

"That is a nice-looking black Fiat Coup that they have parked inside," Vito said.

"Yes it is, but we needed a back seat so that we can carry the bride and groom in the car," Michael replied.

"How much do you think that we will be able to get for it when we rent it out?" Michael asked.

"I'm thinking one hundred or one hundred-fifty euros depending on how far we have to drive. We have to make our money for gas as well as something for ourselves for what may be most of a day's work by the time we take people to a wedding during the day, and a reception that evening," Vito said.

"That sounds about right," Michael agreed.

After three bottles of ten-year-old Marsala had been loaded into Vito's car, the tour was again on its way.

Luigi leaned back over the seat and said, "We are going to Agrigento, where we will visit the *Selinunte e Cave di Cusa* archeological park and the Valley of the Temples. Unlike Syracuse and Palermo that have been built and rebuilt several times, these cities were abandoned during classical times and never reoccupied. That is the reason these sites are so well preserved."

Stopping in the parking lot among the usual tour buses, the two cars were unloaded. Michael and Vito took the cars to another parking area about two miles away, where the walking tour through the ruins would end. They parked the limos at an edge of the lot where the cars could only be approached from directions that they could observe. Thus far, at least, the tour had gone without any attempted interference. "But one never knows," Michael thought. "At least, with their passengers inside of the archeological park they were less likely to be attacked."

Once the fees had been paid, the group was funneled into a museum-like building which had exhibits showing some of the objects that had been recovered from the city and a presentation of the ancient town of Selinunte. Notable were the large temples built within the walled city on the hill which was separated by a valley from another group of temples in The Valley of the Temples.

When the group left the building, the November weather was partly cloudy. The occasional gust of wind was sufficient to blow a little sand around the standing columns and cobblestone streets. With a little imagination one could see streets and cross-streets among the low stone walls that marked the foundations that once supported its markets, bakeries, wine shops, and two-story buildings where small merchants had their shops on the bottom floor and lived above them.

"These people did the same things as we do today." Angelica said. "As a schoolgirl I came out here and volunteered to work at cleaning, sorting, and filing objects that were uncovered during the digs. Most were common items. Occasionally someone would uncover a fragment of a fine sculpture, group of coins, jewelry, or something like that.

"Although the museum is more modern and shows scenes of the city and models of structures in the Valley of the Temples when they were occupied, the park is continuously appealing for money to preserve the site."

"When I was working for the American archeologists in Syracuse, we did not have time for all the niceties. It was dig, document, conserve, report, and most generally pack up what we had found for shipments to museums all across Sicily and Italy. These objects helped the museum reestablish their collections after World War II and replace items that were damaged or looted," Luigi said.

"The oldest temples are here in the city, and as you saw inside, are designated as A, B, etc., because no one knows to which gods they were dedicated. The best preserved is the Temple of the Concord across the valley, and the largest is the Temple of Zeus, which would have been the most impressive temple built during the Greek period, had it been finished."

"What trees are these?" Nancy asked. "I recognize the lemon and orange trees because of the fruit, but what are these others?"

"Those are almond and olive trees," Roger said. "I saw a lot of them in California."

"You are correct," Luigi said. "Just as the Spanish brought American cactus and other plants from the New World here, they also started the olive and almond orchards in California and Mexico. This was a true cross-pollination.

"Some of these olive trees are hundreds of years old, as you can see by the size of some of their trunks. Several generations of a family may have gathered olives from the same tree. This is the season that the olives are ripe, and are pressed for their oil."

One thing that seemed startlingly out of place in front of the Temple of the Concord was a larger than life broken bronze nude male statue, that had been done by Igor Mitoraj. Scattered around the site were sculptures by other Italian artists which contrasted with the weathered stone blocks from the ruins which had been there so long they looked like an organic part of the landscape, except for their rectangular shapes.

The statue's nudity shocked the chaperone who attempted to direct Angelica and Cecilia towards a nearby goat pen, but Angelica resisted. She walked up next to the statue of the fallen Icarus and asked, "Take my picture?"

"I'll do it," Roger said, but Angelica said that he should be in the picture too, so there was a camera hand-off between Roger and Frank. Roger then joined Angelica, who positioned him so that the statue's male attributes would be fully exposed.

After the photo, Angelica faced Roger, reached her hands below his waist, groped his genitals, squeezed, and rapidly stepped away.

A noise somewhat between a loud swallow, belch, and yelp erupted from Roger's mouth, which he alleged to be a burp and apologized.

"Cecilia, do you want Roger to take our pictures with the statue?" Frank asked.

Cecilia's face turned red, and she said, "With the temple would be fine," implying that she was uncomfortable standing so close to the nude statue.

Roger, now somewhat recovered, said, "Let me get down and take a photo, with you in the foreground and the columns of the temple behind you. That way the fence will not be so obvious."

That photo was quickly snapped, and now the family's full attention could be paid to a family of goats that were kept in a pen on the site.

"These are goats that are only found in Sicily, and they give us milk and cheese," Luigi said. "If we are fortunate, we may have a chance to see that done or even try your hand at goat milking."

"I can't wait," Angelica said mockingly.

"I'd like to try that," Mary responded. "I have always been curious about how cheese was made."

"Dad, look at the size of these capitals," Frank said as he approached the Temple of Zeus. "How did they ever move and erect an object this size and precisely place it on top of a column?"

"It looks like someone anticipated your question," Mary said. "There is an exhibit here that tells how they quarried and moved the column sections, and put them up using manpower and animals by employing ramps, levers, wooden scaffolds, and large cranes."

"Have you noticed the packs of dogs running around? Some of them look like Labs or Lab-Shepherd crosses," Nancy observed.

"No one knows where these dogs came from. They may have originated from dogs whose gentlemen owners did these excavations in the 1700s, and they have been here ever since," Luigi responded. "I would not try to approach them unless one comes to you and indicates that it wants to be petted or given some food. Some assert that these dogs are inhabited by the souls of those who once lived here, but most people discount that legend, although anywhere in Sicily, we are literally walking on the bones of the dead. Many thousands lived and died on every patch of ground where we might stand."

"That's creepy," Roger said.

"That's true," Frank replied.

Michael and Vito had been on continuous alert at their cars. It was cool enough that they could comfortably sit inside the cabs of the vehicle. Suddenly, two motorbikes driven by two men dressed in black leather and helmets drove up, turned as if to look at the vehicles. When it was obvious that the vehicles were occupied, they sped away.

"I think that they made us," Vito told Michael.

"I agree," Michael said. "I think that we need to get out of here as soon as possible. In fact, here come our people now."

"Luigi, two men on motorbikes came by, and I think that they spotted us. We need to get out of here."

"Let's load up and go. We will go to one of our vineyards, which is down a long private road. We can call in help from Syracuse. You did good, Michael; I will phone from the car as we go."

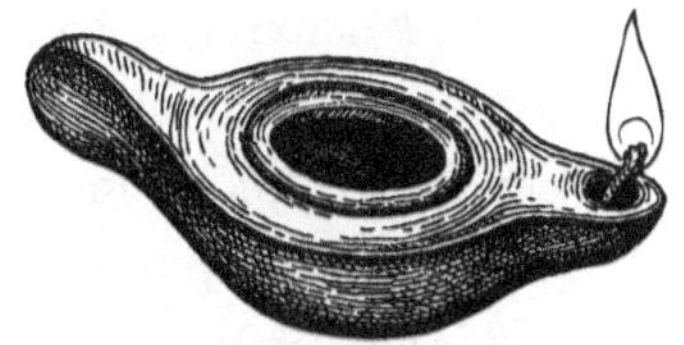

22

Agrituristmo

SET AMONG THE WHITE hills, the main feature of the vineyard was a walled compound containing a group of buildings which consisted of an ancient stone farmhouse, a newer building to house the winery, car garage, and various sheds. Surrounding the compound were rows of staked-up grape vines interrupted by plantings of olive, pistachio, orange, lemon, and pomegranate trees. Interspersed among the rocks were large prickly pear cactus and agave plants. Everywhere it seemed where life could find a foothold, something edible or useful was being grown – from a clump of fennel to an enormously old olive tree in the center of the patio.

Soon four other cars and a flatbed carrying what appeared to be a refrigerated shipping container arrived. The flatbed trailer, with its container on top, was parked crossways to the gate. When a panel was removed from the side facing the road, Michael saw the barrel of a 20 mm cannon inside, and a crew of three men to service it.

"That is to prevent uninvited visitors," Luigi told Michael. "I want you to take the chaperone back to Palermo, pick up the girls' things, and take them to my villa in Syracuse. Stay there overnight, and come back here in the morning.

"Vito, go to Novo and find Father Flanagan, the Irish priest, who should not be too difficult to spot. Inform him that he will be joining us for an island tour for the next few days. Tell him that the wedding we talked about for Friday is still on. Stay the night in my villa, and come back in the morning with the priest. Pick up a bottle of Grappa for him. I understand that he uses it to soothe his stomach.

"Here are 200 Euros for you. Take care because you will have a long night ahead." With that admonishment, Michael and Vito were sent their separate ways. Whoever was trying to follow them, would be looking for two large limos traveling together and not single vehicles going in different directions.

Angelica picked up her duties as an architectural tour guide without being asked. "Farmhouses like this were common all over Sicily by the 1400s. Although different in detail, they had a barn on the ground floor where livestock was kept, a second floor where the family lived, and sometimes a third floor which was used as bedrooms.[34] Most had porches where work, like food preparation could be done with a brick oven situated outside for baking. The large rooms on the ground floor were used as a kitchen, which included a large open fireplace and access to underground storage in a basement. Much later, things like this cast-iron wood-burning stove with its water heater were installed, and running water and electricity run into the house. Heat generated by fireplaces and small porcelain heating stoves in rooms aided in keeping the house warm during the winter."

The farm's operator, Gorgio Antonio, welcomed the group. "I run an *agrituristmo*, a tourist's farm, where guests can come and stay with us and work as if they lived on one of these isolated farms. Practically everything that is used is made on the farm. We do wood felling, timber making, cheese, wine, olives, and even a little hunting of wild game, such as pheasants and pigeons.

"But first, we have a meal for you. The featured dish which Signore Luigi requested is a carp raised in a nearby pond that we have cooked in salt from Trapani, which you just visited – one of our national treasures. This is supplemented with wild mushrooms, fresh grapes, hazelnuts, pesto, and wild boar sausage. For the most part everything that we serve is made, and as much as possible, raised here. This includes the wine, milk, cheese, breads, honey, meat dishes, seasonal nuts, fruits, and vegetables. Salt, flour, rice, and sugar are about the only things we buy.

---

[34]   This experience was provided for me during a boar hunt with muzzleloaders sponsored by Pierangelo Pedersoli and described in my book X–*Treme Muzzleloading.*

"What we do is very labor-intensive, and if we had to pay wages no one could afford to come here. So we teach our tourist guests the skills of their ancestors, provide them with some useful outdoor exercise, and they get to eat what that they helped gather and cook."

"Is this where I am going to do the boar hunt?" Frank asked.

"We get an occasional boar here, but you are going to hunt in a better place that is surrounded by a huge nature preserve, the *Parco Regionale dei Nebrodi,* that is on the northeast side of the island near Mt. Etna."

The large carp had been placed in a metal pan with 6-inch sides and surrounded by the coarse salt crystals. The top layer of salt was carefully scraped away, revealing a layer of green herbs, coarse pepper, and a sprinkle of coriander on top of the unscaled fish.

Once the excess salt and spices had been removed, the fish was completely exposed, and the two-foot-long fish lifted from the salt and placed on a plank where Gorgio deftly removed the skin revealing the flesh beneath. Once the fish was transferred to a platter, he took a knife, cut down to the backbone, removed the fish steaks, and served them in about three-inch portions to his guests.

"This is delicious," Nancy said.

"We have plenty of these at home, but no one eats them. They are considered 'trash fish,'" Frank said.

"These fish were brought from Asia by the Romans," Gorgio explained. "As exotic and sometimes colorful fish, they were highly prized by the Roman Emperors. The plainer varieties of carp came to be raised all over Europe as food fish and were exported from Europe to the Americas where they are now considered pests and even endanger some of your native species, as I understand. The best tasting are the grass carp, which feed on vegetation, but all are edible although they admittedly have different tastes, depending on what they eat. Carp are the most commonly consumed source of protein on the planet.

"After we bake a fish like this, we either use the carcass and do a fish stew from the remains or take off the flesh and do a carp salad, like a tuna-fish salad, but far better because it does not have the oily or tinny flavors that you get when you use canned tuna."[35]

---

[35]   I have the recipes for baked carp and carp salad in my book *Practical Bowfishing.*

After their meal, they were assigned their rooms. The bedrooms had mostly been arranged for families to stay together in the same room. Ronald and Nancy were assigned one room. For the first time, Angelica, Cecilia, and Mary were billeted together, and William, Frank and Roger were put into another bedroom on the ground floor of the house. This was a part of the house where livestock had been originally kept but was now converted into lodging quarters and a sitting room as the stock had been moved to a separate barn. As a concession to modern life, each room had its own bathroom with a tub and shower.

"That gal can pinch," Frank said as he examined a purple spot on his left cheek.

"She got you too?" Roger asked. "She grabbed me by the balls when we were standing by the statue."

"So that was what was going on. I know you sounded a bit strange when you spoke," William remarked.

"Brother, what are we going to do with these women?" Roger questioned. "Sure, I would like to sleep with them, but what about later? What happens when we get them home? Are we going to have to run and hide from some Mafia goons for the rest of our lives? These folks will slit your throat without even thinking about it. The money, the dowry, sounds wonderful, but at what costs to us?"

"Don't you like Angelica? If you don't, I will certainly take her. She looks like a handful, but I think that I can stand it for five years or so."

"And give up being a Marine?"

"I don't like the prospect of leaving the corps, but since I no longer fly and cuts are likely to be made after this war is over, I am almost certain to be requested to retire with a service-connected disability. Either that or I go back to the Middle East somewhere. Now that we are in that mess, we are going to have a hell of a time getting out. I am afraid that none of that is going to end very well. Being a partner with dad does not sound like too bad a deal, particularly with that extra money coming in for Cecilia every year."

"The problem with taking that money is what are you going to be asked to do for it?" William interjected. "And do you realize where that money comes from? It comes from illegal drug sales, prostitution, extortion, rackets, wholesale thefts, contract murders, and who knows what else? If there was ever such a thing as blood money, this is certainly it. It's like, 'If you take the King's shilling, you are the King's man.'"

"That may be," Frank replied, "but I really don't see any alternative."

Do you want to talk about what's tearing you up so? I won't tell anybody and I think it would do well to get it out of your system.

"Perhaps. Did that bottle of Grappa wind up in here?"

William pulled the bottle from a bag and handed it to Frank. Frank took a long pull and returned it to his Uncle.

"Fighters in Iraq were using civilians as human shields. When we were taking fire in Baghdad, I would call in an air-strike as soon as a potential target was I-Ded. One time, a building was collapsing in flames. Burning women and children came out of it. We were still under intense machine-gun fire and could do nothing to help. Simultaneously, we had a burning vehicle, and a wounded marine was in it. I got him out, and my body armor was pinged twice from an AK. When I was pinned down, I watched those people burn alive as a result of what I had done. I could hear their screams, feel the heat, and smell their burning bodies. These are the images that I can't get out of my mind."

Roger did not immediately reply but took the bottle from his uncle, pulled the stopper out of the bottle, and took a deep swig.

"That's tough Dude. That's really tough. I would have a hard time living with that too."

"That's a grim story," William added. "Your Dad had to work through something similar. He would have nightmares about it and would sometimes call me in the middle of the night and talk about it. Just talking through this stuff worked better than alcohol and hard drugs. He got no help from the VA, but that has changed. There are support groups and directed counseling now that didn't exist then. If you need that or need a therapist, they are trained and out there. If this stuff doesn't go away, seek them out. You helping Cecilia get through her trauma may do you as much good as her."

Father Flanagan was sitting at an outside table, taking advantage of an unusually warm November afternoon. He had just ordered a clam stew and looked forward to enjoying a rich mixture of clams, potatoes, corn, and aromatic spices such as garlic, rosemary, and oregano with a splash of sour provided by fresh lemons and a hint of sweet from the onions and pomegranate molasses. In a culture where many dishes contain large amounts of tomato products, this stew was a welcome relief, in that it had the garlic that was almost mandatory in every meat or fish-containing dish, but lacked the strong acid smack of tomatoes on the palate.

When he first arrived in Sicily, he had eaten so many tomato products that he had blistered the inside of his mouth from the radical change from his potato-rich diet in Ireland.

"Father Flanagan," Vito asked. "I have been requested by Signore Luigi to ask you to join us on a tour of the Island and meet the family whose sons you are going to be marrying on Friday?"

"This wedding has been arranged by Donna Carlos. I suppose that I could go, although I would need to have some reason."

Thinking rapidly, Vito briefly considered telling him of his connection with the AIA, but rejected that idea. "Cecilia, Luigi's daughter, who you have met, is still getting over Davide's death, and it would ease her mind to have a chance to talk to you about it."

"Can't this wedding be put off for a time until she is more comfortable with it?"

"No. The man is a U.S. Marine Captain, and his family are here now and are to return to the states this weekend. All is arranged. It would be considered a great favor to the family if you would come."

"Very well, meet me here after I have breakfast tomorrow morning, and I will go with you."

"Father, bring some warm clothes. They haven't told me, but I suspect that we will be visiting Mt. Etna, and there is snow around the summit. I am to spend the night in Syracuse and will meet you here tomorrow morning."

Flanagan contemplated his cooling bowl of stew after Vito left, "Why do people always interrupt me when I am eating?" It was still, fortunately, hot. He closed his eyes and enjoyed the fragrant aromas rising from the dish and the rich flavors of clams, herbs, and crushed peppers in his mouth. "Life cannot be much better than this. Truly, a merciful God has given us dishes like this to ease our passage through life."

A long pull from a glass of white wine from a vineyard less than two miles from where he was sitting served to complement the stew and lessen his concerns.

Michael got back to the garage in time to see Renato and get to the concrete office, where he made a phone call back to the AIA in Milan.

"What we suspected about their American relatives is true," Michael told the situation officer on the phone after he had been transferred to the control group that had been assigned to the operation. "An American family of six has been brought over. Two brothers are to be married on Friday, but I don't know where. Maybe Vito does, but I don't. Another mob family is apparently shadowing the family. A family gathering was shot at yesterday, but no one was hurt. Now they are at a farmhouse north of Agrigento. They have brought in more men and a 20 mm cannon on a flatbed to block the gate. They don't know who is responsible for the shooting, but they are taking no chances. Apparently, someone is trying to move in on their territory. They sent Vito to get a priest, but I do not know what that is all about. He is said to be an Irishman, can you believe?"

After briefly assessing the information, the voice on the other end of the line replied, "These people might do anything. Two American FBI agents can meet you in Syracuse. Maybe they can set up somewhere and monitor what is going on at that farm."

"I would not advise it. Luigi and his group are now reinforced, on full alert, and have lookouts to monitor any movement on that road or nearby. They would surely be spotted, tracked, and killed. Putting anyone there would be a bad idea."

"We can have them in a work party at the Villa del Casale, which is a world-class attraction near where they are and a place they are almost surely going to visit."

"I think that they will spend tomorrow night at the vineyard, but when they might visit the villa is anyone's guess – tomorrow afternoon or the next morning, I don't know. I have to end this now, as I have to drive back to Syracuse tonight."

"I hope those Americans agents don't get in the way," he thought. "This entire situation could turn very messy in a hurry. If they got into trouble, I do not know if I could help."

With two armed guards placed in the upstairs hall, the three women were locked in their room.

Always the more direct one, Angelica immediately started questioning Mary about her two brothers.

"Can you tell us something about what they are like, and what was it like growing up with them?"

"My parents had us three, bang, bang, bang. I am the oldest, then there was Frank and lastly Roger. My mother tells me our birth order was not particularly planned that way, but that was how it happened.

"Frank was always bigger and more athletic than Roger. They always enjoyed some of the same things like hunting and fishing with their dad and working on cars, but Roger was always the more artistic type who liked his music, drawing, and even in High School, painting.

"Frank, like his dad, went into engineering whereas Roger, taking more after mom, I suppose, gravitated towards fine arts. I don't know why, but Roger was such a perfectionist that it took him forever to finish anything. His instructors were so exasperated at him that they threw him out of the program but then invited him back. The work he did was excellent, but his assignments were late or never turned in. It was only when he was forced to complete something on the spot that he would actually finish it.

"Frank took ROTC and became a Marine Officer, a pilot, and was wounded during the First Gulf War. He could have gotten out of the service with a disability but went back in as a forward observer for ground combat units during the second war. He witnessed some very heavy combat in Baghdad, and is now on leave from his unit in Iraq. He will be going back in January if his unit is still there.

"Frank was married, has been recently divorced from his wife Jane, who left him for another man with a more stable future. She could no longer tolerate worrying about him after he was repeatedly deployed to war zones.

"Roger's most recent was a woman named Matilda, who had an apartment in San Francisco, where he lived until she kicked him out because he could not pay his share of the rent.

"Neither of them have had any children, and Dad thinks it is about time that he had some grandchildren while he could still enjoy them, although this marriage business has caught us all as a bit of a surprise."

"They did not know?" Cecilia said. "Luigi told us that they had asked for the marriage."

"Perhaps they did in a kidding, joking way; but Luigi definitely seized the opportunity to make this a firm commitment. My brothers, because they have had such poor luck getting and keeping wives on their own, agreed. The rest you know better than me."

"What do you want to do?" Mary asked the pair.

"I want to continue my schooling and become a restoration architect," Angelica said.

"I want to become a teacher so that I can perhaps show young people that there can be a life outside of this Mafia business," Cecilia said.

"While you are a Marine officer's wife, finishing a university degree and working in that field would be difficult," Mary commented. "Although I suppose that you might be able to do some of the coursework online where Frank might be stationed. Since his tours are usually for two years, you would often move from place to place around the world. There are schools for children on the larger U.S. military bases. If Frank were stationed at one of those, you might be able to work in the school.

"Once you are certified in the U.S., Cecilia, you could teach practically anywhere after having your credentials approved in the state and by the school district that hired you."

"What have you heard that they are like in bed?" Angelica asked.

"I don't know. Like most men, I suppose that they think that they are fabulous bed partners, but like all men, I think they have enhanced opinions of their own capabilities. A fair appraisal would be to assume that they are reasonably athletic and agile – particularly Frank, he weighs less and seems more fit than he was in High School. Somewhat above average in the love-making department, I would suppose. Beyond that, I don't know."

"Haven't you been able to find anyone?" Cecilia questioned.

"As a beautician, the men that I mostly meet are gay, so that limits my opportunities. I have nothing against marriage. I am still looking, but I haven't found anyone. The ladies who come to the beauty shop are trying to fix me up with their sons, grandsons, and nephews. However, I never date them. That is just poor business."

"Luigi asked us to recommend an escort for you, and we both agreed on Michael. He's here, he's handy, he's good looking, and Luigi says that he feels like he can trust him. He and his half-brother Vito, the other driver, have just arrived in town, so they don't know anyone."

"I look forward to it"

"Do you want William and me to help with your hair?" Mary asked.

"No. Donna Carlos, has all of that arranged," Cecilia said. "And as you might suppose, no one disappoints her. Since her husband's arrest, she has gone all out to make this wedding happen.

"She and Luigi are said to have been lovers at one time, after Luigi's first wife was killed.

"Whenever and however, this was resolved years ago. She remained married to Don Carlos, and Luigi and Donna Carlos never saw each other again, at least not in a sexual way. Don Carlos, who had known other women, apparently extended the same sexual liberty to his wife. He found Luigi too valuable to the organization to take reprisals against him. The result has been that they have remained lifelong friends, and Luigi is one of the few people that Don Carlos really trusts.

"I am sorry that you and your family have been drawn into the mess, but knowingly or not, and like it or not, you have; and this is a dangerous game that we all play and have played for centuries. Welcome to our family."

Now, with his body parts stitched back together and covered in heavy bandages, Apachee had been relocated to a hotel room in Palermo. There, he lay on a large bed dressed in an open-backed hospital gown and propped on his side by an array of pillows.

"That bitch cut up my best leather coat. Now I have scars and can't even sit – much less ride. I have to have an anesthetic before I can even shit. Oh. Am I ever going to get her for this."

"What do you want us to do?" Alexie asks.

Apachee rose up slightly, winced in pain, and waved for the men to come closer.

"Take the plumbing van, and see if you can plant a sticky bomb on the car and blow them all to hell. Act like you are doing something with the toilets in a rest room, fixing a sewer, or something like that. Call me when they are ashes by the side of the road."

"You don't want us to try to take the women?"

"It would be delightful if you could. I think boiling in oil, salt water, or sulfur in a big pot heated with olive wood would be in keeping with the theme of their wedding, don't you think? I can imagine them twisting, while suspended over the pot as they are lowered millimeter by millimeter."

"While I am sure the thought is satisfying, and boiling in oil was often threatened as a punishment, but it usually ended badly after the body exploded. It ruined all that good olive oil and meat and often set the building on fire."

"What do you suggest?"

"Sausage. They should yield about forty-pounds each. That way you could snack on them anytime you wanted. I think that small heart-shaped sausages flavored with a touch of licorice and smoked with cherry wood would be appropriate."

"I like it. I like it!" Apachee starts to wave his arms in enthusiasm, but cries out in pain as he flops onto his back.

"Straighten me up. Now!"

Proceeding as carefully as they could and as rapidly as they dared, Alexie and the men return Apachee to his side resting position while trying not to touch any of his wounds.

"If I ever get my hands on that whoring bitch, she will wish she was never born. Now go make something happen."

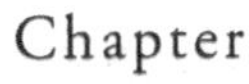

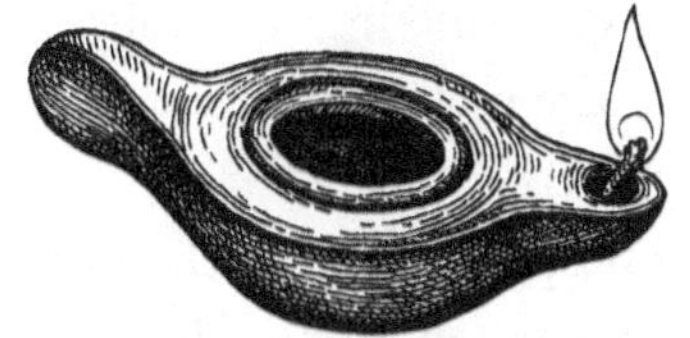

23

Goat Milking

QUEEN WAS THE FIRST goat to come from the pen to the milking stand that had been set up inside the barn. The stand allowed a sitting person to be at eye level to the goat's two teats. Gorgio had already put feed in the trough in front of the stand, and dropped the block whose two limbs went over the goat's neck to restrain it. He then took a cloth from a bucket of soapy water and washed the udder. Donning rubber gloves, he put his thumb and forefinger around the teats, and in a rhythmic motion, forced the milk to stream into the stainless steel bucket which made a sound like a boy peeing on a piece of roofing tin.

"These goats think that they are royalty," Gorgio said. "They demand to be milked at the same time in the same order, twice each day. Queen is the boss goat. She is one of the best producers and gives half a gallon of milk each day if we keep her kids from nursing. We bottle feed them twice a day. By using a bottle, we make sure that all of them get an equal share.

"We store the milk in a cooler, and what we do not immediately sell, we save until we have enough to make a batch of cheese, which is a six-day process. We will start making cheese with the milk we gather today, but will actually eat some that we made last week."

Gorgio's explanation had been punctuated with the steady and somehow comforting squirt, squirt noises of the milk falling into the bucket. He concluded by squeezing some yellow liquid on his palms and smearing it on the teats.

"This is from the Mexican agave plant's leaves. It is non-toxic, all-natural and serves to lubricate the udder and teats. I use this instead of commercial udder balm. The goats seem to enjoy it."

Although he made no comment, the corollary of a prostitute washing her John's genitalia after sex came immediately to Frank's mind.

"Who wants to milk the next goat?" Gorgio inquired.

"I do," Mary volunteered.

Queen was let out and put back into the pen, and the next goat that was let in, Princess, immediately climbed up on the milking platform and began hungrily feeding from the box into which had been poured a mixture of chopped greens and grain.

Gorgio washed the goat's udders and positioned the bucked and stool for Mary to sit.

"Don't be afraid. Grab the upper part of the teat with the thumb and first finger and pull down and squeeze. Let the first squirt go on into this cup to clean the teat's opening and then aim for the bucket. Go for a rhythm, left hand, right hand, left hand, right hand. That is soothing for the goat. When the flow of milk slows, bump your fist into the udder to stimulate more milk to drop. Don't worry. You are not hurting the goat. Their kids really ram it hard with their heads."

Somewhat hesitant at first, Mary began and soon had a satisfying rhythm going. After she was done and had a half-bucket of frothy white milk, Princess was led away, and the next goat in the herd, Lady, was escorted in.

"It takes about two hours to feed and milk the goats. I'll let my sons take over now. Let's go inside, and I will show you how the cheese is made. The goat milk is very fragile, and we have to either make cheese out of it or refrigerate it in a hurry, or it will take on an undesirable ammonia flavor. If you handle it correctly, it is just as mild as cow's milk."

Inside the kitchen, Gorgio's wife, Flavia, had already started making cheese. Heating on the wood-fired cook-stove were two large pots filled with hot milk.

"I was a textile designer for a factory that made rugs before Gorgio and I married. I handle the cheese, jelly, baking, honey, spinning, weaving, and about half the cooking, while Gorgio takes care of the carpentry, animals, repairs, wine, brandy making, and generally running the business. We are blessed with three sons and two daughters, and they all help keep this place running."

"Everything is kept as clean as possible to keep wild strands of yeast and molds away from the cheese. We use ancient techniques described by the Roman writer Pliny The Elder, which use cardoon, a native weed, and fig sap to coagulate the warmed milk and promote the formation of curds which are pressed to make the cheese. Since everything is living, the milk is not allowed to boil.

"Once the curds are separated, they are pressed and allowed to drain for two days, then coated with salt and ground charcoal and allowed to cure to the point where they are coated with mold and dry enough to cut and serve.

"The key is to keep the humidity down and the temperature from getting too hot. Either condition can spoil a batch of cheese. Gorgio is going to take you through our wine and brandy making, and you will be able to have some of both for lunch. This need to keep the cheese at a constant temperature is why caves and cellars are valuable to anyone who ages cheese.

A separate building was used for wine making. Like the others, it was built of stone and had a red-tiled roof. Inside was a floor that was covered with split stone flags that were sufficiently level for barrels to be rolled over them. One end of the building had a large roll-up door that could accommodate trucks.

The tour started under an open pole barn that contained a twelve-foot diameter barrel that had been cut in half.

"When the grapes were harvested two weeks ago," Gorgio said. "They were put in here and crushed in the traditional fashion by women's feet. The juice is then piped into fermentation barrels for about six days, depending on the weather, and then transferred into barrels to age. Like you saw in Marsala, we use American oak barrels for aging. Unlike the commercial vineyards, we might add apricots, peaches, or pears to our grapes during the fermentation process to give our wines a distinctive flavor. No two batches will come out the same, which is fine. We either consume or sell all we make. I also have a still, and will do brandies or make our version of Grappa from the spent husks and grapes. "You can taste some of the fermented juice now.

"This is not quite ready to bottle. We will add more or less sugar to the juice to raise the alcohol content. You will find it very dry. We will add additional sugar after fermentation is over and before we bottle it because sweet wines outsell dry varieties, although I personally prefer the drier wines over the sweet ones.

"Commercial wines will be carefully filtered to remove any solids and treated to keep sediment from forming in the bottles. We don't filter our products quite as closely and leave in the cream of tartar sediment to make it more of an artisan-produced wine. It does not have quite as good a storage characteristic unless we add some brandy to it as well, but it does make each batch uniquely its own. This is a wine that needs to be drunk the same year it is made. It is interesting for us to make it this way and our customers love it. No disrespect to the California and Australian wine makers, but if someone wants their wine to taste more nearly the same each time they buy a bottle, they make millions of bottles of it that are inexpensively priced. But you did not come to Sicily to drink California wine. Now let's have some lunch."

Vito had been shown a bed in a small bunk room in a wing of Luigi's villa, and even if less than ideal, slept well. Michael arrived somewhat later and was escorted to another bunk. Roused with the household at daylight, Vito fed on some bread, jam, and coffee before heading back to Novo to pick up Father Flanagan while Michael was to remain to take Frank on his boar hunt. On the way out of Syracuse, Vito picked up two bottles of Grappa, one white and one red, for the good father as he had been directed.

Vito found Father Flanagan at the same café and sat down at the table.

"Have you eaten?" Flanagan asked.

"Yes, I ate before I left Syracuse. Whenever you are done, we can leave. Do you have your clothes?"

"Oh, would you give a man far from his sainted country a bit of time to have a taste of home?"

With this comment Flanagan reaches into his bag and takes out a jar of Chivers Black Current Jam, opens it, and carefully spreads a half-teaspoon of it onto each side of his split roll.

"Whenever you are ready, Father."

"I have everything that I need in this bag," he said, motioning to an old leather bag with a wide belt strap reinforcing its metal latches.

"That's fine. There is plenty of room in the car now that I have unloaded the women's boxes out of it. You know women, they want to take everything they own everywhere they go."

"So I have heard," Flanagan replied.

Once Flanagan had finished his roll, jam, and an orange, Vito took the suitcase and carried it back to the limo around the corner where he had been lucky enough to find a parking place. Before starting the car, he opened the hood, looked at the engine, and checked the oil. Then he took a mirror on an extendable arm, and looked at the tires and under the wheel wells, and the underside of the car.

Only after this inspection was completed did he open the trunk and place Flanagan's suitcase inside.

"Would you like to ride in back or up front with me?" Vito asked.

"With you, if you don't mind. I would like some conversation, and the front seat will offer a better view."

"What do you know about what's going on?" Flanagan asked.

"Very little. My brother and I just arrived in Palermo last week and went to work for our cousin as drivers and mechanics. We were assigned this job taking some Americans and their Sicilian family members around the island. He is driving the car with the Americans, and I am driving the Sicilians. They most often speak Sicilian in the car, so I really don't know much about what they say."

"I met both the ladies at a recent funeral," Flanagan said. "One of them, Cecilia, I think, was to be married to the young man that I buried.

"I am surprised that Cecilia is to be married so soon after the funeral. I don't doubt that she needs some support to help her get through such major life transitions in so brief a time. Frankly, this sort of stuff sounds like something that might have taken place in the 1800s."

"I don't know, Father. I just get paid to haul them around. About the only thing that I can say is that they are beautiful, smart young women. I don't think that I would mind marrying either of them myself, but that is certainly not going to happen, no matter whatever else does."

Another vehicle that was on its way to the *Agrituristmo* that morning was driven by Alberto. He was carrying a long rifle box across the back seat of his Fiat hatchback that was covered by some smaller boxes and bags. He had spent much of the past three days working on the gun, and it was time to see if this American could actually shoot it. He also had the two .380 PPKs that they would carry in their coats.

Rather than consider this an imposition, Alberto enjoyed working with guns and teaching people how to use them. Unlike most of the people he taught, it seems that this American, Frank, was the expert, and he looked forward to this as being as much of a learning experience as a teaching one.[36]

He had phoned ahead, and when he approached the gate to the Agrituristmo, the flatbed with the shipping container on it had been pulled away from the gate. As soon as he was inside, he could hear the back-up bells ring as it was being repositioned to block the entrance.

Vito and Father Flanagan had preceded him, as well as Michael, who had brought the other Mercedes from Syracuse.

"Alberto, come in. You have arrived just in time for lunch." Luigi said.

"These are the two young men that you will be instructing. This is Captain Frank Calsase, who will go on the boar hunt tomorrow, and his brother Roger. I understand that you have Walther .380s for them, and some special things for Captain Calsase."

"Yes, I do. After we eat, I will be happy to show them to you. I will admit that I am curious about how well the musket that I have been working on will shoot."

"Captain Calsase, I could not find a suitable original flintlock musket in the short time I had, so I bought a replica Year IX .69-caliber Napoleonic Dragoon musket. Guns like this were used by Napoleon's brother James' troops when he was King of Italy, and by Garibaldi and his Thousand when they invaded Sicily and founded the Italian state.

"Napoleon had restructured the army so that it had units such as infantry, artillery, engineers, and so on. Although he would have fought on the battlefield with pistols and a sword, this musket is what I envision

---

[36] I personally identify most with Alberto, the teacher and instructor who is interested in guns and provides useful instruction to Frank, Roger, Michael, and Vito, just as I would under similar circumstances. As an author I felt the need to do my due diligence and use the tools that I describe.

their equivalent of a Captain would have had made up to use for hunting or perhaps take into combat.

"I took one of Davide Pedersoli's 1777 replica muskets, shortened its barrel, browned the bright-finished metal, and smoothed the action. Like the original, it does not have a rear sight. I did find an original horn powder flask and priming horn for you and made sure that they worked. I also brought balls, powder, and patching material that I understand you Americans use. In combat they used the paper that was around their cartridges for more rapid reloading. I understand that you lube and cut your cloth patches as if you were loading a rifle."

"I do. That gives better accuracy. But let's sit down and have something to eat. Mary is particularly keen to try some of the cheese like that she saw made today, and I certainly want to sample some of the wine."

Lunch at the *Agrituristmo* was less formal than their welcome banquet. Cheese, wine, cut curried meats, sausages, mustard, and breads, along with leafy greens, tomatoes, and peppers, were laid out on a large oval dining table.

The seating arrangements had also been freed up a bit. Nancy, Mary, Angelica, and Cecilia were seated at one end of the table while Luigi, Ronald, Frank, Roger, Albert, William, Alberto, and Father Flanagan were at the other end. Flanagan sat between William and Nancy and had the opportunity to meet the visiting Americans for the first time. Michael and Vito took their plates out to the front porch and ate outside.

"I understand that I am to marry your sons on Friday in Novo. I hope that you are happy about this joyous occasion. This is the first time I have ever done a double wedding." Flanagan said.

"I have mixed feelings about this," Nancy said. "Perhaps we can talk about them later, but for my boys to meet them on Monday and marry on Friday is somewhat abrupt."

"My apologies to you," speaking to Angelica and Cecilia, "but I imagine that you are finding all of this somewhat sudden as well."

Cecilia, who was closer, ventured a reply, "This is a match that Luigi feels is necessary for our safety in these uncertain times. Our grandparents' marriages were arranged, and they worked out. He is a traditionalist and sees no reason why our marriages will not do as well. I admit I think it would have been better if we had a chance to go through a traditional courtship, before we are plunged into something that is going to last for the rest of our lives.

"We have had a chance to meet your sons, and I think that I can speak for us both when I say that we like them. They both seem to be nice men who are physically attracted to us and might even learn to love us."

"The Church has a long history of sanctioning arranged marriages," Flanagan said. "In Ireland, I helped smooth out relations between Catholics and Protestants. Sometimes, the families could be reconciled and sometimes not. At times, the couples had to flee the country to be safe from their own relatives, who felt that their child had betrayed their faith. I don't know if your situation is quite so desperate, and I can see why Luigi would want his daughter and niece safely out of the country. His request is logical, even if this is a rather old-fashioned approach.

"From the talk of guns that I just heard, it seems like Luigi is expecting trouble from rival Mafia gangs. If that restarts the Mafia Wars, that could result in hundreds being killed, including innocents who got in the way. The Mafia has its own code, and if you live within it, things sort of roll along."

"Do you approve of what they are doing?" Nancy interjected.

"Heaven, no. But that is today's reality in Sicily. The Mafia is so strong that it cannot be uprooted, and even if it were, another group would just move in. The Mafia supplies human needs, legal and illegal. As long as those needs remain, the Mafia, or maybe some even worse organization will keep meeting then. This is the case of dealing with the Devil you know.

"My fellow priests tell me that sometimes I speak too freely, but everyone, including those here, is aware of where I stand. I do God's work wherever it takes me – even in the lion's den where I am today."

"The cheese is really good, and I like the fruity wine too," Angelica said to change the subject before either the priest or them inadvertently crossed some line of custom or decorum. "If you eat at the King's table, you do not insult the King," she thought.

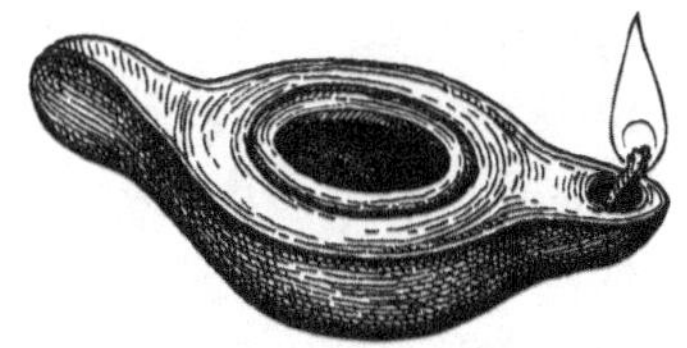

24

On the Range

THE IMPROVISED RANGE WAS set up about a thousand yards from the house where there was a hillside pasture to shoot against. Folding chairs had been set out for Frank, Roger, and to their surprise also for Michael and Vito. Stakes had been driven into the ground to support pieces of cardboard at twenty-five and fifty yards.

"I want each of you to shoot the .380s and the .45s, so that if you get into a firefight in the vehicle you will know how to operate them." Alberto said, sounding much like a Drill Sergeant. "The .45 is much more powerful, and is, in a way, easier to shoot than the .380s. Both benefit from being shot from any sort of braced position, sitting and holding the guns with both hands, for example.

"The way I want you to shoot is like this," Alberto sat in a chair, crossed his legs, and with his right hand holding the gun, held his wrist in his left hand while his elbow acted as a supporting column on his legs. "While the Walther has a double-action trigger that is useful for close-range shots at ten yards or so, I want you to cock the pistol and use it single action. Despite what you see in the movies, you are largely wasting ammunition to shoot at a man-size target much beyond fifty yards. You want to save your shots and make them count.[37]

---

[37] Popular TV shows and movies often show men shooting pistols with their guns inclined in the hand instead of being held straight up and down. That is pure Hollywood, and no way to shoot pistol other than to listen to the gun go bang.

"I want you to carry the guns with a round in the chamber, the safety on, and the hammer carefully lowered on top of the firing pin. These guns have pins with rebounding hammers, and the firing pins have springs that prevent the pin from striking the primer unless the hammer is falling under spring trigger. In addition, the .45 has a grip safety that will prevent the gun from firing unless the gun is gripped in the shooter's hand. Although these guns are pre-World War II designs, they remain among the safest, most accurate, and easiest to shoot pistols of their types. Although the older PPKs in .380 will bite the web of the hand, the newer guns, like you have, will not.

"Captain Frank, this material on the card table is for your musket. The staff at Pedersoli were helpful in assisting me in getting your things together. I have the gun, extra English flints, a tin of Swiss FFg black powder, a powder measure, some hard-cast balls, patch cloth, and a tube of something called Bore Butter, which they say you Americans use for patch lubricant. I also experimented with some beeswax and beef fat to see if I could come up with something more authentic that was not quite so runny, so you can try that as well. For the lock, I have a smaller brass container with a spout for FFFFg priming powder and a ring of tools that includes a small whisk for cleaning out the pan, and a wire for clearing the vent hole. To trim the patch, I included a Beretta pocketknife that has a keen edge. Yet more things are some leather for securing the flint in the cock, a set of screwdrivers, and a range rod for loading and cleaning the gun, as well as a leather 'possibles bag' for carrying your accessories. This gun is much more complex than I thought and considerably more difficult to operate than putting a cartridge into a chamber and pulling the trigger.

"I can't imagine hunting with such a thing, and I am very interested in seeing how well you shoot it.[38] That will determine how close I need to get you to your boar."

If you really want to hit something, grasp the gun the same way every time, and use your sights. Your objective is to hit the target, not see how many rounds you can shoot in a hurry.

[38]   The allure of shooting and hunting with muzzleloading guns is that it does require more skill and effort than conventional cartridge guns. I discuss muzzleloading hunting in *X-Treme Muzzleloading,* and an inexpensive e-book series that now includes, *Muzzleloaders for Hunters, Buying Used Muzzleloading Guns, Shooting and Maintaining Your Muzzleloader, Hunting with Muzzleloading Shotguns and*

"I will need to shoot from the right-hand side of the line to keep from burning someone with the flash from the gun," Frank replied. "It will shoot out a spurt of flame that will be about three-feet long."

"That we can do," and Alberto motioned for Michael and Vito to relocate the table. "In the meantime we will put out the targets – twenty-five yards for the pistols and twenty-five and fifty yards for your musket. No one is to touch the guns while anyone is downrange. Is that clear?"

After receiving an assent from everyone and the pieces of cardboard were positioned, Alberto went from person to person, explaining the pistols' operations. He spent less time with Michael and Vito because he had gone through the same exercise with them and their .45s a few days before but did show them about the Walther PPKs. Although both knew about the pistols from the James Bond movies, they had never shot these high-priced pistols, and had received their training with less expensive Berettas.

Frank used a patch saturated with rubbing alcohol to clean the bore, pan, and frizzen of the flintlock prior to mounting and trimming the flint, which had to evenly strike across the face of the frizzen to give a good shower of sparks. He had shot round ball loads with up to 120 grains of powder from the .75-caliber British Brown Bess musket replicas which were 11-gauge guns, and briefly wondered about the appropriate powder charge for the .69-caliber 14-gauge French musket.

He took the muzzle of the gun and used it to mark a square of cardboard, which he cut out with the point of the pocketknife.

"What's that for?" Roger asked.

"This is to keep the lubricant on the patch from spoiling the powder. When we go on the hunt, the gun may be loaded for several hours, and I don't want to shoot with a weakened load."

"What load are you going to use?" Alberto questioned.

"I think that I am going to start with one-hundred grains of powder, the over-powder card, and then the patched-round-ball. The usual service load for this gun was eighty grains or so, so this load will be somewhat powerful, but the Pedersoli replicas are strong guns."

You are going to need as effective a load as you and the gun can handle because these boars can weigh over six-hundred pounds and fear nothing on

---

Smoothbore Muskets, Hunting Big and Small Game with Muzzleloading Pistols, and Hunting with Muzzleloading Revolvers..

earth. Even a fatally-hit boar can kill a man before it expires, and you will only have a single shot. In the day when these guns were used, some on the hunt would still carry boar spears and swords with crossbars to help fend off a wounded animal. Hunting these big animals is a serious undertaking.

"Gentlemen, I have drawn circles in the middle of these targets with markers. Put in your ear-plugs. Sit down, brace yourself as I showed you, and start shooting. When you have emptied your magazine, Roger, you swap pistols with Michael and Vito and shoot the .45s at the same target. Then take another pistol, and do it again. These guns are like women. Even though they are somewhat the same, they all are a little different.

"Captain Frank, you load and shoot as you need to at both targets until you are satisfied with your load. Take your time. I will let you shoot the pistols later, and you can give us a demonstration with the musket. We are all curious about it."

Even though the shooters were out of sight from the house, the sounds of gunfire could be clearly heard. "You can really tell the difference when that musket shoots," William remarked to Father Flanagan.

"Yes, you can. I have unfortunately heard enough gunfire in Ireland to last me for a lifetime. Hunting and shooting never appealed to me, although I certainly enjoyed a good wild-game meal when it was offered."

"Same here," William said. "My brother Ronald always hunted, and sometimes I went along, but I never really got into the sport as much as he did. I preferred fishing. I understand that there is some excellent trout and salmon fishing in Ireland, and they make a big deal out of it."

"Indeed, they did and do. A person can get into serious trouble poaching on another's stream."

"Do you know that our lives have been threatened if this wedding does not happen on Friday?"

"No, I did not, but the Mafia does have means of applying pressure to get what they want. I don't know if they invented the 'stick and carrot' approach to doing business, but they have certainly perfected it."

"The carrot here is that not only are these beautiful young ladies, but there is also a dowry of 100,000 euros a year. I don't know how you can build a successful marriage like this where we have one strongly independent guy, Frank, who is a Marine Captain, and his less motivated brother, Roger, who are going to have to depend on their wives' income for their futures. Under those circumstances, where is the drive to do anything worthwhile? And you know where this money comes from? I can't say that everything that the family does is illegal, but the majority of the money they will receive is derived from some illegal activity, however Luigi wishes to justify it. As an individual, I sort of like, and respect him; but I don't like where the money comes from. I know the boys are starting to have thoughts about this too, but what can we do about it?"

"While the church is certainly pro-marriage and has for centuries permitted arranged marriages, it is clear that marriage done under threats to those being married or to their families is not sanctioned by the church and would be grounds for annulments. Even so, this does not get your nephews out of this situation.

"The only way that maybe the wedding would be called off would be if the women would refuse, but based on what I have heard, they have already agreed to the match. They want to marry, go to America, and have a chance for a new life out of reach of the Mafia. However, those ties are very difficult to break. Once in the organization, you do not easily extract yourself, particularly if you are blood relatives, as are Frank and Roger."

"So we are finding out," William said.

"This requires some thought. I often found in Ireland that a little Guinness could help the mind think of some interesting solutions to some of these complex problems. I don't have any Guinness, but I do have some Grappa. Would you care to join me for a glass while we go somewhere quiet and talk?"

"I have had it before," William said. "Mario, gave us a bottle to settle our stomachs after our flight."

Flanagan asked Gorgio for some glasses and retired to an old wine barrel and two stone benches which had been set under the branches of a spreading orange tree in the yard.

"Captain Frank, are you ready to show us what that musket can do?" Alberto asked. "I need to see how you shoot at fifty yards to know how to arrange your hunt."

Taking a sheet of cardboard a yard square and his marker, Alberto drew a new sort of target. It showed a section of a huge boar's neck with the back of the head and ears at the upper left corner, two parallel diagonal lines a foot apart extending towards the opposite corner where they were joined by a curved vertical line which represented the body of the animal. Approximately one-quarter the way up from the bottom of the neck, he drew in and cross-hatched a parallelogram.

"Wild hogs carry their spines low on the neck compared to animals like deer. To protect themselves during fights, they have a huge amount of flesh over the tops of their spines and heavy fur. The spinal cord is in the middle of a mass of bone that is six-inches high. A hit with a bullet in that spine will drop the animal, but not often kill it immediately. You need to be ready to have a rapid follow-up shot, or it might go down, get up, and run again. I want to see if you can place three shots in this rectangular area. Use the ramrod in your gun and reload as rapidly as possible, but take your time when you shoot."

So much as possible in the field, Frank cleaned the interior of the barrel out with the jag and alcohol saturated cloth on the range. With the first pass the patch came out coated with heavy grease. He also wiped the gun between shots, but there was a sulfurous smelling sticky black gunk on the patch.

"I never shot a black-powder gun." Michael said, "I did not imagine that the patches would come out looking like that. Used motor oil doesn't look that bad."

"Most of the black stuff is carbon," Frank explained, "but there is also sulfur and other corrosive salts. This is the reasons that these guns have to be cleaned with some solvent that contains water, to dissolve these corrosive materials, and it smells like a bad fart. That is just the way of it."

After running some dry patches down the bore until they came out clean, Frank measured a hundred-grain charge of black powder, and as well as he could dropped it straight down the long barrel. Now he took one of the cardboard wads that he had made and rammed it home. Then he placed a strip of lubricated canvas over the muzzle, cut it off flush with the muzzle, placed a silver-white lead ball over the muzzle, pushed it down with the knife handle, and used the ramrod to seat it on top of the powder charge and wad.

"I'm still not done yet," he announced.

Reaching in his possibles bag, he retrieved the flask of priming powder and closed the frizzen. Keeping the gun level, he walked up to his chair, sat down, opened the frizzen, primed the gun, closed the frizzen, cocked the hammer, and began to pull the trigger. The hammer fell, and the shot fired instantaneously. The blast rocked Frank back in the chair, and the gun's barrel rose with the shot.

"That is a good hit in the neck," Alberto said as he watched through his binoculars.

"I can save reloading time by putting premeasured powder charges into small glass bottles, and putting patched round balls in a loading block around my neck. That way, I can carry everything I need in a pocket and access it in a hurry. When I have everything together, I can reload in less than a minute."

The three shots were fired, and the men went downrange to examine Frank's target.

"Although spread out a little vertically, the balls are within three-inches of each other, Alberto observed. "I had no idea that guns without rifling could shoot that well or that you could hit anything with a gun that doesn't have a rear sight. That is good shooting."

"I think that we can go after one of the big boars that have been giving a landowner real problems. There is a nobleman who has renovated a Norman tower. He keeps and trains dogs specifically for boar hunting. He is getting too old to hunt, but he lets me borrow his houndmaster and dogs, if we have a particularly big boar to go after. For ordinary hunts we often will drive a section of woods and shoot from stands. I have taken Angelica and Cecilia on such hunts."

"The girls shoot?" Roger asked with a note of incredulity in his voice.

"I have been teaching them ever since they were children. They have shot everything from .22s to the 20mm cannon and are quite good shots. Luigi insisted on it. I would say that Angelica is a better shot and more interested than Cecilia, but fellows, those gals can outshoot you any day. The only reason I did not bring them was that I did not I want them to embarrass you."

"That is an aspect of our new brides that I had not thought about," Frank remarked to Roger.

"There are many, many things that you two will find out about Angelica and Cecilia. They are also trained knife fighters. When other girls were being taught ballet and such things, they were taught about fighting knives and how to use them. Everywhere they go, they are very likely armed, and at least carrying a knife. I pity anyone who ever tries to do them harm. They will likely live just long enough to regret it. If these girls must fight, they have been taught to fight to kill."

Michael and Vito took careful note of these comments. If they were going to take these women into custody at some stage, they had best do it with their permissions.

This information was also disquieting to Frank and Roger. Frank wondered if he was going to be marrying a professional killer, while Roger had a movie running in his head featuring Angelica as a black-clad assassin, whose next target was himself. Widows might have a quicker path to U.S. citizenship than divorcees, he thought. An occasional murder in the family might not be out of character. After all, someone was apparently trying to kill them. If not, why all this gun training and seclusion?

Ronald and Nancy had wanted some time to talk by themselves, and now had that opportunity. They said that they were tired and announced that they were going up to their bedroom.

"What are we going to do?" Nancy asked. "Things were sort of all right when we started, but now they are shooting guns, and things are looking worse and worse. If we stay, the entire family might be killed having to do with some Mafia something that we know nothing about, and if we try to leave, Luigi will have us 'meet with an unfortunate accident.' I am worried sick about all of this."

"Me too, but we are in sort of a hopeless situation. We have been unwillingly trapped by our own relatives in something that is spiraling out of control. I am worrying about the boys too. What good are money and an attractive woman if you don't live long enough to enjoy them?"

"Ronald, how can you even think such a thing?"

"We are in a situation with people that, in other circumstances, I could like and respect. But these same people, our relatives, may wind up killing us. Or someone else that we don't even have a clue about might kill us. Maybe there is a way out of all of this, but I don't see it."

Chapter

25

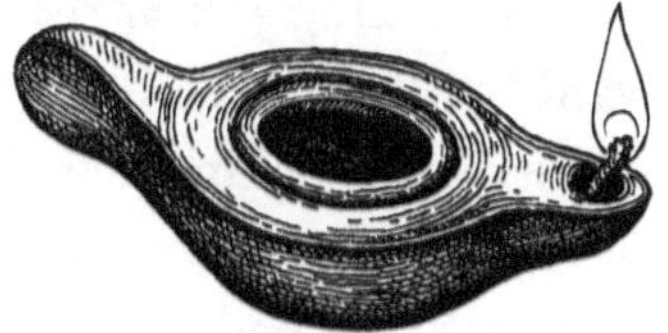

The Roman Villa

LUIGI ANNOUNCED THE DAY'S events. "This morning we are going to visit the Villa del Casale, which is another of Sicily's great wonders from Roman times. This villa was apparently built by a very wealthy individual who had the interesting business of importing exotic animals for the circus in Rome. Also of considerable interest to you, Captain Frank, will be a detailed depiction of a boar hunt with spears.

"In the afternoon we are going to split up. Captain Frank, you will go on your hunt. Roger, I will take you and the family to my villa in Syracuse, where you can rest and start to get ready for the wedding.

"Michael, will the Fiat that you were talking about having painted be ready to use in the wedding?"

"Yes, I believe that it will."

"Have it sent to my villa, and we will use it in the wedding procession. Perhaps Renato can drive it over. He and I have done business for years, and he is invited to the wedding. I will also arrange for him to stay at the villa."

"This was starting to get rather complex," Michael thought. He was supposed to meet the American FBI agents at the parking lot at the villa, but he did not even know what they looked like. He guessed that they would spot him and the limos when they arrived. Even if they made connections, he could not break his cover. This was a deadly game that they were playing. Somehow, he had to let them know the details about

223

the wedding. When he called Renato about the car, he might be able to tell him.

Posing as maintenance workers replacing the flowers in the beds in the sign at the entrance to the parking area at the Villa del Casale, agents Rob Williams and Howard Smith tried to blend in as much as possible with the three Italian agents that accompanied them. Their work truck that the Italians had sent included a command contact center, as well as the listening gear that the Americans had brought.

Stationed five miles away was a group of Italian agents manning a roadblock where they were doing vehicle inspections to check for smuggled goods.

"They are on their way," one of the Italian agents informed Rob and Howard. "They are in the same two limos that they were using before. We just passed them through. We are going to keep this roadblock up until they leave in case someone is following them."

Shortly after, a lime-green van with a painting on the side advertising a Nepalese plumbing firm arrived at the checkpoint.

"A little far from home, aren't you?" While the officer on the road examined the driver's papers, another ran a check on the vehicle and found that it had been implicated in a robbery in Naples, and signaled that the driver should pull over in the inspection lane for a more complete examination.

"Is this really necessary? There is some blocked plumbing up at the villa, and we have been called in to clear it. You know how these tourists feel about going into a bathroom with shit all over the floor."

"Sorry, this will only take a minute. Pull over."

"Maybe you would like a little wine with your lunch," the driver offered.

"Sorry, my supervisor is watching. Pull over in the parking area and open the van."

Inside the van, they found three men, who were all carrying pistols. The driver said, "This is Sicily where the Mafia is everywhere, and even plumbers might be threatened if they worked in a mob-dominated area. We can't be too careful."

Checking, they found that one of the three had an outstanding arrest warrant and the others had either served time or were listed as being suspected Mafia members. This event caused a more complete search of the vehicle, where two sticky bombs made with plastic explosives were found in a tool chest.

Without much ceremony, they were hustled into a paddy wagon and driven away. The van was pulled into a nearby idle quarry site, and almost as soon as it was unloaded, it exploded in a ball of flames.

"What was that?" Nancy asked.

"It sounded like an explosion," Luigi said. "We passed a quarry, and I suppose they were doing some blasting."

Approaching the entrance to the parking area, Luigi observed that a crew was apparently replacing some of the winter plantings around the entrance. The plants included some colorful greens that looked like they could wind up in someone's salad. "Why not," he thought. "If you are going to take all this energy to prepare the ground so that things can grow, you might as well plant something to eat." Had he looked somewhat closer, he might have noticed two paler-looking individuals in the crew who seemed more interested in the vehicles coming into the park than their plants.

Once Michael and Vito had discharged their passengers at the entrance, they had little trouble finding a parking place at the edge of the lot and stepped out of their cars to have a cigarette. When they did, one of the workmen left the work crew and came over.

"Nice limos," agent Williams said in Italian.

"Yes they are. We enjoy driving them," Michael replied.

"Could I join you in a cigarette? I have been out of smokes all morning." the agent asked.

While Michael got one out of a pack that he had in his coat, Williams rapidly confirmed that these were the two Limo drivers that he was expecting by examining a card that Michael slipped him along with his cigarette.

"The roadblock stopped a van full of Mafia thugs that were trailing you. They had bombs made of plastic explosives that they were going to plant on your cars. You have powerful enemies."

"The tour group is going to split up. One of the Americans is going on a boar hunt north of here, the other is going to Syracuse to The Claw's villa, and I suppose all will spend the night there. The wedding is to be at the church at Novo Friday morning at 10:00 AM. That's all I know."

Michael concluded the interchange by stating, "If you ever need limo service on the island, just call us. Here is my card."

This was his first European cigarette, and he had to fight to keep from choking on it. Feeling a little green around the gills, Williams walked back and continued working with the crew.

Although early, the tour buses had arrived and discharged their tourists. Everyone was tightly packed on the wooden walkways that had been constructed to protect the fragile floors. Various groups were being instructed in Japanese, Italian, Chinese, German, and English, with the last being the most popular language.

The first area of the villa that was visited was the baths, which were apparently operated as a commercial enterprise. Before they entered the villa, there was a sign that outlined the position of the more than 40 rooms of the structure and explained the villa's history.

"We Sicilians think of this as our Pompeii," Luigi said. "Both places were preserved by being covered very quickly – Pompeii by ash and this villa by mud. Of the two, this was even more catastrophic in that everything was over in an instant. There was no time to take cover and no warning. A wall of mud and rocks maybe fourteen-feet-high came racing down the slope. The walls of the villa, although rock, were not nearly thick enough to stand the pressure and exploded on impact propelling rocks like catapulted stones ahead of the flow. Inside the flow, it was like being inside a washing machine, except there were blocks of stone weighing hundreds of pounds, mud to clog the mouth and lungs, and utter darkness. Assuming that you might, for an instant be brought to the top of the flow and could gasp a breath of air, you would have been instantly sucked back down into the body of the flow and bashed against any standing obstacle. Death came unexpectedly, instantly, and only the very fortunate few who were somehow out of the direct path of the flow would have managed to survive.

"The fifty or so who might have slept in the villa would have died if the event occurred then, and if it were during a crowded time, say during a festival, the death toll could have been in the hundreds.

"After the mudslide, there were doubtless attempts to salvage any valuable objects that might be found, but this site was abandoned until it was accidentally rediscovered. For archeologists, this was an enormously significant find, and its mosaics were so well preserved and so extensive that it is almost beyond the imagination to believe that they would be replicated today. This is like what you Americans might call a comic book, but done in stone and glass in about the 4th or 5th Centuries A.D., before the fall of the Roman Empire to the barbarians."

As they wound their way through the rooms, Roger kept his camera going overtime. He could see the details in the mosaics as being background materials for some of his paintings, and the challenge of reproducing them in paints excited him. Not only that but the portraits in the medallions on the floors were so good that a person would have no problem recognizing the subjects. After about the third, "Wow. These are so real" comment, he realized the absurdity of his statement, and he kept his eyes on his viewfinder.

Frank was blown away by the quality, varieties, and numbers of animals that were depicted from all over Eurasia and Africa. Although the Romans did not know of the New World, every species of European big game was represented, including boars and bears, many types of African plains game, and even tigers and elephants. There was even a scene of an elephant being loaded on a galley that certainly represented a real event.

"That boar hunt is really realistic," Frank told William, who happened to be behind him in line at the moment.

"It is," William remarked. "You notice that one of the hunters is already down with a wound on his leg, and the others have spears with crossbars so that they have a chance to push the animal away and keep their distance. You take care this afternoon, you may be in exactly the same position. These animals have always been wild, and they are not nearly as compliant as our wild hogs at home."

"I am anxious to give them a try," Frank replied. During much of the tour, Angelica, Cecilia, and Mary were separated from Frank and Roger by Luigi, Ronald, and Nancy.

"What do you think of those outfits that the ladies were wearing in the gymnasium?" Angelica asked Mary.

"They look very practical. They are not as revealing as a Bikini, but they would certainly work. It's a little surprising to me for a culture that wore robes to also have something like this. This was completely unexpected. I also see that the ladies were as particular about their hair styles as we are now. Some things never change."

"Wait until you see the children's section," Cecilia added. "The kids shown are really having fun with an range of real and imagined creatures. In this villa not only did they have pictures of adults and animals to look at, but they also had mosaics of children who looked like them. The family who lived here apparently cared about their children to the extent that they had a nursery and obviously slaves to look after them."

"How many people do you think would be needed to run this house?" Mary asked.

"Considering that everything was done by hand, I suppose that it would have taken a staff of fifty or so to support a family of six to ten." Angelica replied. "You would have had cooks, gardeners, maids, washerwomen, men who worked the grounds, guards, butlers, nurses, handymen to build and repair things, those who worked in the baths, and the list goes on. This one villa was like a self-sufficient city. It makes it all the more remarkable today that people can have these conveniences in their own homes without needing a small army of people to sustain it. These people lived in luxurious circumstances, not doubt about it, but with the loss of personal privacy and the ultimate responsibility of overseeing the lives of their staff. There was danger too. It was in Sicily where the slave Spartacus started his revolt."

"Judging from the numbers of depictions of grapes and of wine making, it is apparent that those who lived here ate and drank well," William remarked to Ronald.

"Yes, they did, but you note that almost everyone shown in the mosaics is really fit. I suppose that this is due to the amount of exercise everyone got just walking most places and getting on with daily life. The only figure that is shown that might in any way be considered fat is the depiction of the Cyclops that Ulysses is offering wine to. He used his legendary wiles to get out of that fix, and we could maybe use a little of his crafty plotting to get out of ours."

"I agree. We could," William assented. "Father Flanagan and I had a talk about that last night, and maybe he has come up with something."

Luigi had by this time moved into the basilica portion of the villa which unlike the previous rooms was paved with marble and porphyry slabs which had shifted during the mudflow.

Angelica explained, "Apparently, this mudslide occurred during a prolonged period of rain that saturated the soils beneath the villa. When the mudflow started, there was enough pressure for the ground to start to move in waves, perhaps as a result of an earthquake. The mosaic floors were flexible enough to survive being rippled like a sheet of paper, but the solid slabs of stone in the basilica could not.

"This large room was obviously an audience hall where meetings could be held by someone in authority. This indicates that this villa, while owned by an individual, also supported the public functions of providing a community bath as well as being the seat of government. Although we now associate the term basilica with a church, this room likely was more commercial and administrative in nature. I could imagine moneychangers, scribes, lawyers, spice sellers, etc., setting up in here to offer their services."

Once out of the press of people on the wooden walkways, Angelica went up to Roger and asked, "What did you think of the tour?"

"I was absolutely awed by what I saw, the artwork, and the glimpses of people's lives and aspirations that we saw. Like your uncle said, this was like looking at a comic book from the 5th Century. I feel sorry for the lives that were so abruptly ended. I know this was over two thousand years ago, but I could not help but cry for them, even though everything that they built was done on the backs of enslaved individuals. I also feel for those slaves who built and saw this splendid villa but could not enjoy it."

"Better to work here than in the galleys, mines, or quarries where a slaves' life might only be a matter of a few years at most. Once sent, there was no escape and no hope for a better future. Are we, really, so much better than they?"

"Signore Luigi, may I speak with you please?" Vito asked.

"Yes," Luigi replied. "What's up."

"That explosion we heard? I spoke to a tour bus driver who was behind us. He said that driver had been told that explosion was from a Mafia van that had been blown up on the side of the road. He said that the driver told him it had been carrying armed men and explosives. I thought you ought to know."

Motioning, Luigi called Michael over and consulted with the two drivers. "Vito, I want you to take Mario and Frank to the farm where he will hunt. The houndmaster, dogs, and some other men will already be there. When the hunt is over, bring them and the boar back to my villa in Syracuse. Roger and I are going in Michael's limo back to the villa. I am going to hire a Taxi for the rest of the Americans. I do not know if that van had anything to do with us, but it might have. I want to do exactly what we have planned, but be very careful about it. Using different vehicles and leaving in different directions will help."

Vito was directed to drive through the picturesque hill town of Piazza Armarina whose central position on a prominent ridge of the Erei Mountains has caused it to be fought over since the time of the Greeks. Although not as adept as Luigi, Mario took on the role of guide.

"There are also some Roman villas here that are among the best preserved in Italy. The town's elevated position in the center of the Island kept it cool during the summer months, and you did not have the problems with what we now know as mosquito-caused diseases that swept the wetter coastal areas."

As the vehicle approached Enna and proceeded further north, Mt. Etna grew more significant on the skyline to the east. "The mountain is 3,300 meters tall, nearly 10,000 feet, and is the largest volcano in Europe. That is snow that you see on its summit now. In the past, caves in the mountain were used to store snow so the Romans and others could have ice during the Summer. It was put in wagons and galleys and shipped all over the island and southern Italy. Once loaded, it was insulated with dry straw and heavy blankets made of animal hair."

When Frank and Mario arrived, they were greeted by Alberto, who had been there almost since daylight. "I wish we could spend more time here, but all I have you for is the afternoon. This is our hosts, Signore Olivito, and our houndmaster, Signore Austolino. The big dog is, appropriately enough, Caesar, and then there is Brutus, Crassus, Cicero, and Pliny. Pliny is the chief scenting dog who will find the boars, while Caesar is the catch dog, and has a heavy metal collar to protect his neck and leather armor. He will only be released after a hog is bayed. Once that happens, we need to get there as fast as possible and kill it before the boar can kill the dogs. Big boars like this often travel alone, and Signore Olivito has shown me where one was seen at daylight. That animal is likely laying up this time of morning after feeding all night."

"I wish I had more time to enjoy this."

"Me too," Alberto agreed, "but I must have you back in Syracuse by this evening. Luigi has something planned for you and your brother.

"You can load your gun here, but don't prime it. We will put it in this case and keep it there until we release the dogs. I am going to be carrying a Sauer and Son drilling, which has two 9X74 R. rifle barrels and a 16-gauge shotgun barrel in case we need to kill that boar in a hurry. As soon the hunt is over and we take some pictures, I need to get you back to Syracuse. I will take care of preparing the trophy and the meat."

"It's a wonderful thing when a hunt plan works out," Olivito said. Listening to the dogs he could tell that Pliny was in full cry, chasing hogs. A few seconds later, he glimpsed him on the heels of a large boar in the valley below, followed by the rest of the pack.

Caesar, knowing he had work to do, was straining against the rope that had him tied to the truck. He was a powerful dog, and no single man could hold him once he wanted to join a chase. "Let him go," Olivito told Mario, who was standing by the truck. When Mario released the dog, Caesar tore down the slope towards the meadow with clumps of earth and grass being torn up behind him.

"Load up quickly. We will drive down. I think that the boar will bay at the foot of a cliff. There are caves in that rock, and if he gets into one of those, we may not be able to get him out. If he fights the dogs one by one, he can kill all of them."

Everyone held on as the old truck roared down the rutted track. Even above the sounds of the engine and things bouncing around in the truck, they could hear the excited barking of the dogs.

"Suddenly, the pitch and tone of the dogs changed. "He's bayed," Olivito said. "He may break and run again, it is early in the chase."

Sure enough. It was clear from the dogs' voices that the chase had resumed.

Another deeper voice was heard from below, "Caesar has joined the chase. It should not be long now before he is bayed again."

Now that they were on a less steep part of the pasture, Olivito jerked the truck off the road and sped overland, dodging large boulders and a few trees along the way.

"It looks like they are in that bunch of trees next to the cliff," Frank said.

"I am going to get as close as I dare with the truck, then we will get out, get the guns ready, and go after them on foot."

A small stream with three-foot banks made that decision for them. Olivito abruptly stopped the truck slamming the gun cases against the walls of the metal boxes in the bed of the vehicle.

"I am glad we had the guns in cases," Frank thought. Nervously fingering his pockets, he located his priming horn so he could ready his gun as quickly as possible.

A dog yelped in pain, "He has tossed one of my dogs. We must hurry; they will not hold him for long."

Frank quickly located his gun case retrieved the gun and his possibles bag, and jumped down into the creek prepared to clamor up the other sides and sprint the two-hundred yards to dogs and boar.

"Stop." Alberto shouted. "We must go together. Going alone would be like charging a tank by yourself."

Although it seemed like a long time, the group, now with guns in hand, were trotting towards the melee which they could now plainly see.

Caesar had grabbed the huge hog by an ear and was not letting go. Cassius was attacking the boar from behind, and Brutus was in front of its face trying to get a bite at its throat. Pliny, blood dripping from one leg, was off to one side barking encouragement. He had done his job, and he was content to let the other, more powerful, dogs do theirs.

"Hurry up," Frank said to his lesser fit companions who were lagging behind. "Let's kill this thing."

The boar had different ideas about who would do the killing and what would be killed. The dogs tarring at his thick fur and hides were little more than minor irritations. Only Caesar, who was hanging onto his ear, was any real concern. He knew from the bullets that he carried in his body that it was the people who were approaching from the front that were his real enemies. If he could break away from the dogs and charge through the line of people, he could likely hook one of them in the legs as he passed, run over another, and get away.

Sinking down on his hindquarters, and then jumping, the sudden movement caused the dogs to shed off him like so many leaves. The boar headed directly for Olivito, whether because he recognized him as the person who had antagonized him before or because he was the only one who was not carrying a gun.

Frank took two steps forward, primed the musket, closed the frizzen, cocked it, and brought it to his shoulder. Quickly aiming at the animal's lower neck, he pulled the trigger.

By the time Alberto shouted, "Shoot" the flint from the white hills of Dover was shaving white-hot pieces of metal from the hardened frizzen and directing them towards the powder in the bottom of the brass pan. His senses detected the heat from the flash, and the smell of burning sulfur before the bullet ever left the barrel.

On it sped towards its target, shedding its cloth patch like a dropped handkerchief. Parting nearly four inches of coarse black fur, the hard-lead-alloy projectile bored through heavy red muscles and tendons, slammed against solid neck bone, drove splinters through the spine, penetrated the flesh on the other side, and, chewed up by its passage, rebounded against the hide on the opposite side where it made a one-inch bulge.[39]

On the hit, the boar's nose dug into the ground and its huge body did a flip, and slid so that when it came to rest, its tail was only a foot away from the houndmaster's shoe.

"Shit," Mario said. "That was close."

---

[39]   Of the 20-odd hogs that I have killed with knives, spears, crossbows, muzzleloaders, and modern firearms, all have been memorable hunts. Many of these hunts are recorded in my books and e-books along with the specifications of the weapons and loads that were used. My most recent hunt featured a modified percussion revolver which took a hog on Georgia's Ossabaw island. This hunt is described in my most recent e-book *Hunting with Muzzleloading Revolvers* and shown on my video, *Alligator Assisted Hog Hunt* on Ossabaw Island. Most of the time, my hunts have been from tree stands, but a number of them have been stalking hunts done with or without dogs. And should you want to know, the dogs are eager for the work. If you question this, try to leave one of the pack behind and see what a protest he puts up.

"Good shooting," Alberto said. "Reload and give it another shot in the brain. It appears dead, but you take no chances with an animal this size. This is your boar, and I want you to take full honors for it."

Frank, his hand shaking from excitement, did as he was bid.

"Now we are going to get you to Syracuse in good time. I am going to prepare your trophy. You may take the gun with you. I will give you the paperwork so that you can fly home with it. Please accept it as a personal gift from Signore Luigi. If he had not already arranged to give it to, I would give it to you myself.

"This boar is going to be part of your wedding feast. So I need to get it cleaned and to the banquet chef as soon as I can. It takes a long time to cook a hog this size."

In the meantime, the dogs had rejoined the group. Caesar claimed the boar and prevented the other dogs from tearing at the carcass, although all of them eagerly licked at the blood that was now emanating from the wound.

"I would like a picture of me, the hog, gun, and Caesar, with Mr. Olivito, if that can be arranged. Take it with my camera so that I can take it home and have the film processed. Roger has a digital camera, but all I have is this old Minolta. They don't even make it anymore, but that's what I've got."

26

𝕵𝖔𝖈𝖐 𝖆𝖓𝖉 𝕵𝖚𝖑𝖎𝖆

CAR MOMENTS HAVE BEEN seized by parents since the first cars were invented as time to have heart-to-heart talks with their offspring. This concept was not lost on Luigi, who now had the opportunity to spend at least a half-hour with the person who was to become his future nephew-in-law.

As soon as he learned that he and Luigi were going to be alone for the trip to Syracuse, Roger was dreading the experience. Compared to what Angelica and Cecilia had done and were planning to do, his own accomplishments were nearly nonexistent. In addition, his lack of success compared poorly to what everyone else in the family had done. "Hell, I can't even cut hair," he thought. This was not an interrogation that he was looking forward to.

"How is your career as a portrait painter going?" Luigi asked.

"It is not going well. I have the skills and knowledge, but I am so meticulous with the details that I am never quite satisfied and so bored with the background material that I can't seem to finish things."

"You know that the great masters often did not paint every stroke of their works. They had apprentices do a lot of the drudgery on the background and then just put in the faces and hands. Traveling painters all over Europe purchased or custom ordered background canvases with all of the tedious work done so they could put out a lot of portraits in a hurry when they visited a town. Not until many years later, when these paintings were sold and exhibited, was it noticed that many portraits by the same artist were nearly identical except for the faces. Maybe what you need to do is to collaborate with someone.

"What I have going on in my studio is a painting that is almost finished. I lack completing the faces on Archimedes and the two Roman troopers, and I would be pleased if you would help me finish them."

"I would be honored. I have been looking forward to seeing what you do and maybe us actually painting together. I also use the old hand-made mineral pigments and would be happy to help you make them up.

"Sorry to change the subject, but what can you tell me of Angelica, the young lady that I am to be married to on Friday?"

"Angelica is a free-spirited young lady that makes up her own mind and usually gets what she wants, as you have probably noticed. Like Cecilia, she was badly shaken by Davide's death. I don't believe that I know the full story about that event, although everyone claims it was an accident. There was a competition between Angelica and Cecilia over Davide, but Angelica conceded. Cecilia and Davide were planning to be married. Davide wanted to wait until he got through with University, but Cecilia would have married him any day. I don't think that either of them have gotten over it."

"Do you think that people are trying to kill us?"

"I don't know. Maybe. I have personal enemies, the family has enemies, and it could be that another family is attempting to move in. It might even be the police or someone who has paid the police. I have my informants, but nothing has surfaced yet."

"I think that we are being followed," Vito said. "There have been two men on motorbikes behind us wearing black outfits and helmets."

"Hand me the pistol. Then pull over and stop and see if they pass us. If they go past and then start to follow us again, then something serious is happening, and we need to do something about it".

"Okay, They are gone."

"They are back," Vito said as he spotted the two figures in his side mirror. "One of them has a gun. It looks like he is going to attempt to pass us on the right."

"Pull over to the right lane, and if he tries to pass, use the car to push him off the shoulder of the road."

Sure enough, the biker approached the rear of the vehicle and drew his pistol as if to shoot out a tire. Vito hit the brakes and turned sharply to the right. The front wheel of the bike hit the side of the car, the bike slipped off the narrow gravel shoulder and careened down the wooded hill towards the stream below.

"That's one. Where is the other?"

"He is stopping. He knows that he has been spotted, and that this is not going to be an easy hit. I think that he has given up."

"Let's hope so," Roger added. "This is not what I envisioned as the actions of the artistic crowd. True, they were sometimes described as cutthroat competitors, but not literally."

"You mean like this?" Luigi asked as he reached inside his coat and slowly revealed a dagger with a wavy twelve-inch blade of patterned Damascus steel which was attached to a grip with a double spiral design on two rounded cylinders like the capital letter "I."

"That is the most wicked-looking dagger that I have ever seen," Roger said.

"The Greeks thought so too. This dagger was used by the early Sicel, who made it out of bronze. The Greeks forbade it's possession. I had this one made out of steel by a blade-smith in Venice who used a waterwheel power hammer that has been used to make blades since the 1400s.

"This knife has taken a few lives and saved many because it is so intimidating that few will oppose its will. Many fights have been stopped and deaths avoided by me just exposing this blade."

"I can certainly see why. It is an imposing and intimidating weapon."

Luigi's descriptions of the painting did not do it justice. The painting was large, even by museum standards. The background of the canvas showed an open door and window with the city of Syracuse on the island below in flames. On the floor was a large sand table on which sections of a cone were drawn. Around the room were models such as the lever Archimedes used to lift entire ships, a polished shield which focused the sun to burn the sails of Roman ships, and his water-lifting screw. There were also large measuring rulers and hinged protractors of two different sizes.

There were three figures in the painting. Two were Roman soldiers. The one in the door held a spear in his hand while the other was standing over the kneeling Archimedes, who was cradling his intestines in his right hand while fingering their folds in his left. His eyes were focused on these, while the trooper standing above him had a bloody sword held high, ready to deliver a fatal blow.

Appearing as if they had been in a hard-fought battle, the robes of the soldiers were torn and in places blackened by soot. Their leather and steel armor was stained with blood and mud. In the manner of the realists, every rivet in the armor and horse hair on the helmet was distinctly drawn.

"I want the young man in the doorway to have an expression of horror on his face because he knows that his older partner is about to disobey a direct order to spare Archimedes' life. He realizes that despite the horrors he has caused and just seen, the least punishment they might expect would be a flogging before the Legion and perhaps something much worse. On the figure with the sword, I want his eyes filled with bloodlust wanting to take revenge on the person who had been responsible for the deaths of hundreds of his comrades during the siege.

"This has been a long campaign and their skins are tanned yellow-brown, contrasted to Archimedes' skin which is clean with more reddish white tones such as a person might have who spent much of his life indoors.

"I like the mummy pigment mixed with cinnabar and white lead for the skin colors. What I need for you to do is to draw in the lines for the facial expressions and help me fill in some of the base layers. The details of Archimedes' beard and stains on the Legionaries faces I will paint later.

"While you do the faces, I will use the same mix of pigments on the hands so that they will be a better match. We have this afternoon and tomorrow to work on it. Let's see how my paints are doing. I will have to freshen them up after they have sat for several days."

With a firm vision of what Luigi wanted him to draw, Roger quickly drew the heads on a large paper pad, so Luigi could give his approval before putting anything on the canvas. He decided that the older Legionaries' face needed some hard lines across a furrowed brow and a broken nose, while his younger companion should have a fresh gash across his cheek.

When Luigi nodded approvingly, he applied some of Luigi's lighter selection of skin tone pigments with a broader brush to the canvas. He could cover the lighter shades with darker ones fairly easily, but not the other way around. Looking at other parts of the canvas as an aid to selecting his brushes, he touched that portion of the canvas with the brush, and when Luigi assented, applied pigment from the palette to the brush and then to the canvas.

"Leave the eyes blank," Luigi said. "We don't have time for those today. I will have to decide on the eye colors and mix those paints another time. For now, let's concentrate on the skin tones while I have these pigments ready."

Appreciating full well the time and efforts that it took to grind these pigments, mix, and maintain them in working condition in this relatively dry air, Roger found that he was developing a real admiration for this man who was a self-confessed killer.

"Dammit," he thought. "I am finding that I really like this guy." With the smell of oils in his nostrils, challenging work that he knew very well how to do, and well-mixed pigments flowing from his brush this was as good a painting experience as he had ever had.

"Could I have a little white wine? I find it goes well with mummy."

"For drinking or painting?" Luigi asked.

"For drinking of course," Roger laughed.

"You certainly may. Go ask one of the servants to bring us a glass. Sorry, I forgot, you don't speak Italian. Help me take my palette off my stub, and I will get us some wine. You will have as much as you want later, but for now, just a glass."

Luigi's palette was secured to his forearm by two leather straps, which Roger carefully unbuckled while Luigi placed the bottom of the palette on a table.

"If I try to do this by myself, I risk tilting the palette and running my pigments."

Luigi returned with a maid who carried a tray on which were two glasses of wine.

"This is from the slopes of Mt. Etna, where we will go tonight. I think that these are some of the best wines in the world, although I will admit that perhaps I am a bit biased in my opinion."

"This is good," Roger said as he felt the warming impact of the alcohol. He involuntarily snorted to clear his nose of the smell of oils, mummy, and acetone. "Just a sip or two for now. I will finish the glass later," he said as he placed it on a table in a corner of the room, well away from the painting.

"May I help you put your palette back on?"

"Please do. It is a bit awkward when I have it loaded up with paint."

By the time they had finished four-hours later, the painting would look to the an observer to have been finished, except for two blank spots on each of the figures where the eyes would be painted and Archimedes' lower jaw. The jaw was outlined in charcoal, but left blank for whatever beard that Luigi might decide to paint in. The faces on the two Legionaries glistened with the oil as if they were freshly washed. Luigi was pleased with the progress that the two had made and remarked, "We will texture and dirty up their faces tomorrow so that they will look like they were engaged in battle."

At the conclusion of their painting session, Roger found Luigi looking at him closely in the eye to the extent that it made him uncomfortable.

"Roger, I need some eyes, and since you helped me finish this painting, I am going to use yours for one of the troopers. I won't need to borrow them for long. Hold still."

Reaching behind him, Luigi took an old Polaroid camera off a table, focused it on his eyes, said "Open wide," and snapped the photo.

Temporally dazzled by the close-range flash, it took a moment while the camera churned out the photo and Luigi tore off the backing to reveal the picture.

"You have a bad case of red-eye here, which when toned down a little might not be so bad for the Legionnaire with the sword. Sorry about the flash. Your eyes will come back to normal in a minute.

"This has been a delightful experience, and I enjoyed working with you," Luigi said. "Perhaps we will be able to do it again sometime. I certainly want you to be with me when I present the painting to the City of Syracuse."

With time on their hands at Luigi's villa before Frank was to return, William and Father Flanagan had renewed their conversation from the night before.

"Did the application of Grappa have the desired result?" William asked.

"Yes, it did. I think that the wedding can be called off if the two women ask Luigi to do it. I have devised a plan where they might be persuaded."

"How so?"

"There are two male strippers, Jock and Julia, who do a comedy act and perform in a club in Syracuse.[40] If we arrange for Frank and Roger to be seen in bed with these men by Angelica and Cecilia, they might refuse the marriage."

"Would the men do it?"

"I think so. This would be a little side gig for a couple of hundred euros for a few minutes' work. They often perform for hire at private parties, so this is not too unusual for them."

"I don't know about the boys though. I'm gay. They have gotten used to that. My brother and I came to terms with that in High School. I don't know if they would go along at all. Time was that an officer could be thrown out of the service for being gay. I think that things have changed a bit now, but Frank would still face something of a stigma if word got out about this incident. He could even be blackmailed about it. I will have to talk to Frank and Roger when they get back."

"How was your hunt?" Roger asked.

"I killed a nice boar as it was charging. It turned out to be a great hunt, but I would have preferred that it had not been so rushed. I can truly say that I have had quite an adventure," Frank replied.

"Me too. Someone tried to kill us on the trip back from the villa where we saw the mosaics. There were two of them on bikes. Vito ran one of them off the road, and the other one quit chasing us. I asked Luigi who he thought was responsible, and he said that he did not know. He said that it could be something personal against him, a rival gang trying to move in, or even a policeman who had been contracted to kill us. With that bomb on the road and now this, someone is seriously trying to stop this wedding. This situation is getting dangerous for everyone, including Dad, Mom, and Sis."

"I wish we could get the hell out of here and take Angelica and Cecilia with us to the states, where we had more time to sort things out," Frank mused. "It is not that I don't like the gals or are unsympathetic to their plight, but I don't want to risk everyone's lives to do it."

---

40 Jock and Julia are fictitious as is their act. They do represent a class of gay performers who work in the world's major cities.

"William said that he might be able to do something with Father Flanagan," Roger related. "I hope that they find a way out without us getting our throats cut. By the way, Luigi always carries a wicked-looking knife with a wavy blade."

"How was your time with him?"

"I found myself liking the guy, and under other circumstances would enjoy working with him, but I cannot reconcile the fact that he goes around killing people, or has in the past. I would suppose that he would say that this was because they threatened him, the family, or some of their illegal operations. In his mind these were justified. I have no doubt that he would kill any of us if he thought he had cause. It seems that our relatives are basically nice people who occasionally kill people, and we are being dragged into it. At the moment, I may be an accessory to murder if the fellow who we forced off the road died. He needed to. He was about to shoot out a tire, but that doesn't make me feel any better about it."

As they were concluding their conversation, William walked up. "I am glad to see you both safely home."

"In as much as Luigi's villa is safe and we are here, I guess that is home for now. Roger had a really close call today, two motorcyclists ambushed the car that he and Luigi were in and tried to kill them. The driver ran one of the cyclists off the road and they made it safely back here. Did you, Mom, and Dad have any trouble?"

"No we did not. It was a little cramped with the four of us in a cab, but we did Okay."

"Father Flanagan has come up with an idea that I would like to talk to you about. Basically, it is that Angelica and Cecilia are to see you in bed with two gay guys that he knows to get them to call off the wedding."

"Say what?" Roger interjected.

"If they go to Luigi and say that they cannot marry you because you are gay, he might give in and call the entire thing off, and we can all go home."

"If this is going to happen it has to happen tomorrow night. We are going somewhere tonight with Luigi" Frank said. "I do not know where or for what, but we are supposed to be there at Midnight."

"This all sounds very mysterious," Roger replied. "If anything can get us out of this mess, I'm willing."

"Me too. Tell Father Flanagan to see what he can arrange."

"Who was that on the phone?" Julia asked Jock after he hung up.

"Do you remember that Irish priest who came from Novo to officiate at our friends' funerals?" Jock asked.

"Yes. He was the only one who would come. No one else would have anything to do with someone who died of AIDS."

"Well, it seems two American guys are in an arranged marriage situation with two girls that have Mafia connections that they want to get out of. One of the women is Angelica who you may know. Before she went to college, she would make the club scene in Syracuse."

"Yes. Yes, I think so. Wasn't she the sharp dresser with the red Ferrari? She is a beautiful gal who has money. Why doesn't he want her? If I were into girls, I would. That is a sharp looking chick with brains, money, and a fast car. What's not to like?"

"I can't imagine. I think that it is the Mafia stuff that that the Americans are afraid of. In fact, they have been told that if the marriage does not take place on Friday, the entire family will be killed – all six of them."

"I can see that might put a wet blanked on the wedding bed," Jock opined.

"Don't we already have something that night? A bachelorette party at the Grand Hotel?" Julia asked.

"Yes, we have, by no less than Donna Carlos. They have apparently booked a wing of the hotel. The bachelor party is going to be in one room, the bachelorettes in another, one with a quieter setting for the older folks, and another for the food."

"We work their clubs, and sometimes they set us up with politicians and later blackmail them. Is this something like that?"

"Since this is being arranged by Father Flanagan, I don't think so, but who knows? He may be being duped in some way. If anything, those Mafia folks are a devious bunch."

"Very true, Honeychild, very true."

"How this is supposed to happen is that we do our wedding night skit for the bachelorettes, then go to one of the other bedrooms, climb in a bed with the two guys, and get seen by their prospective brides, who will then call off the wedding."

"And the men have agreed to go along with this?" "Yes, they have."

"I never liked that bitch Donna Carlos. She is always carrying on like she was royalty, but her mother was a maid who cleaned up kitchens. Are they going to pay us?"

"Yes, two-hundred euros each."

"That will help, because the chances of getting money out of that bitch are poor to nonexistent. They have stiffed us too many times before. Yeah, let's do it."

"I already told them that we would."

"It's on, but we had an unexpected event," Flanagan informed William, Frank, and Roger. "Jock and Julia have already been hired by Donna Carlos for the bachelorette party that is to be at the Grand Hotel tomorrow night. Your bachelor party is going to be in the same wing of the hotel in another room. This is so the security detail can keep an eye on everything. After Jock and Julia have their show, they are going to get into bed with both of you in another bedroom where you will be seen by Angelica and Cecilia."

"At least that is the plan," Frank said. "What's to keep them from gunning us down right there while we are in bed. Those guys are armed to the teeth."

"I will try to keep things calm. I have also enlisted the aid of Mario, who thinks this is just a big joke, so there will be a way out if things go wrong. As bloodthirsty as the Mafia might be, they are not going to have a gun battle in the city's best hotel, particularly as they own a piece of it," Flannigan concluded.

It was pitch-black dark when the two limos were ordered to be brought around to the front of Luigi's villa. For whatever reason, this trip was to include only Frank and Roger from the Calsase family, Alberto, and Estavo. The participants were told to wear some warm clothes because they were going to Mt. Etna.

"Somehow, I don't think that this is going to be a pissing contest," Frank whispered to his brother when they were alone in the car.

"Perhaps Luigi will explain while we go. It seems that he likes to talk when he has a captive audience. I gather he has something serious to say to us." Roger replied.

When Luigi got to the limo, he was carrying a thin rosewood box under his arm that was elaborately mounted with brass fittings. He placed this box on the floor between the front and rear seats and sat facing the two men. Mario got into the front seat with Estavo.

It was apparent to Roger that he was about to be exposed to another in-vehicle lecture from Luigi, but he could take some comfort that this time his brother would share the experience. Had he been given the choice of hearing from Luigi again and facing a charging boar, he thought that confronting a huge hog would have been preferred – teeth notwithstanding.

Once they were underway, Luigi began. "You are going to be awarded a great honor. You are going to have the opportunity to be inducted into a brotherhood that has been established for centuries to protect our island, its people, and its resources. It has its roots in ancient times when the natives of this island resisted the Phoenicians, Greeks, Carthaginians, Romans, Normans, Bourbons, Vandals, Arabs, and some eleven other cultures who invaded our island to steal our treasures, ravish our women, enslave our men and children, and give back as little as possible. Even though the foundation of the modern Italian state began here, Sicily is still considered a colony by the politicians in Rome, and given second-best treatment by a government that takes as much as it can grasp and returns as little as it can get away with.

"This has been our lot. Our family, which some call the Mafia, arose to protect this island and its people. Americans solicited our help during World War II against the Germans, and we gave it. There was even a movement to make Sicily an American state, so we could perhaps better control our own fate. That was declined by your government, and we were left on our own.

"Because of the weak condition of the Italian government after the war, the families became more powerful and started competing among themselves to grab more power. This was a case where absolute power corrupts absolutely, and it did. There were undoubted excesses, and much blood was shed, but things got sorted out and a degree of peace and sometimes cooperation is where we are today.

"Some say that we corrupt politicians and police, but often it is they who come to us for money to finance their campaigns. If we corrupt them, they are willing targets.

"Typically, it may be years or decades before anyone is made in this organization. We are going to a sacred cave on Mt. Etna where we induct new members into the family. I am going to offer you the chance to join us in our efforts to secure for Sicilians worldwide a safe, secure, and just future in an unstable world.

"This sword," he continued as he opened the box, "is a longer version of the blade that you saw earlier today. It was made from iron sands from this island and handled with olive wood nourished by the bones and blood of our ancestors. Although made of steel, it is coated in bronze in honor of our predecessors who fought and died to protect this island."

When Luigi flipped on the interior lights, Frank and Roger could see the sword with its gleaming bronze blade contrasting from a green felt background and richly figured box. The handle like Luigi's dagger was 'I' shaped, but lengthened to be more suited for the longer blade.

"The people who made these weapons worshiped fertility gods, and the designs on the blade are of testes and penises shooting semen which is represented by these parallel lines in the grip."

Interrupting, Frank said. "With all respects, I can't do this. As a U.S. Marine Officer, I cannot join a secret organization. I took an oath to 'Protect and defend the Constitution of the United States against all enemies domestic and foreign,' and that also is presently construed to include the Mafia, regardless of what happened in the past.

"I am sorry, but this is just not something I can do. It is a matter of personal honor, as I am sure you understand."

"I can't either. I don't have the training or the skills to be any good to the family. I am an artist, and I don't want to be associated with anything illegal."

"With that incident earlier today, you already are," Luigi remarked.

"Estavo, pull over for a moment."

"Gentlemen, this offer will only be extended once. You do have the right to decline, and I will respect that; although, I don't know if I like it very much."

"Mario, take the other car and tell the others that we will not be coming. You can tell them that the two Americans declined, and rather than reveal our secrets, I am returning them to the villa."

Turning to Frank and Roger, Luigi said with a degree of iciness in his voice that now matched the temperature outside, "We will never speak of this again, and you are not to tell anyone what transpired tonight. Do not disappoint me again."

After he made them swear, he thought, "Angelica and Cecilia would probably approve of their refusal to join the family, even if I do not. Maybe this is for the best."

Alexie returned to Apachee's hotel room in Palermo to inform him of recent happenings. As he entered the room with his hat in his hand, he was not looking forward to his boss' response.

"What do you mean you didn't get them."

"My man on a motorbike got knocked off the road. He is in the hospital. The plumbing van was intersected and blown up at a roadblock and those men were arrested."

"Dad is staying at Luigi's villa. He can't do anything. He tells me that the wedding is to be in Novo on Friday. You watch those sons of bitches, and you take them out. I want them dead. You hear me, dead! Get out there, and finish your job."

As Alexie left Apachee attempted to shake his fist and howled in a combination of pain and fury.

"If you don't get them, don't bother to come back."

With cries of "Them dead or you dead" ringing in his ears, Alexie was glad to leave the room and escape down the hall to the elevator.

27

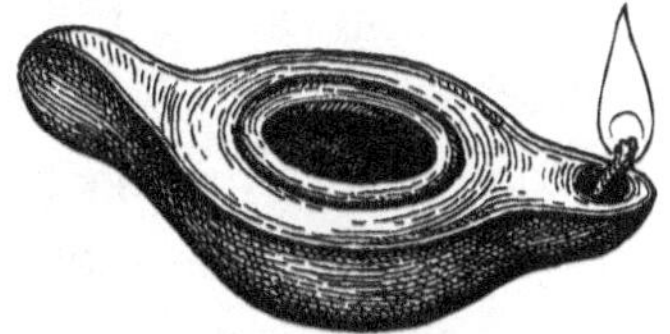

Intrigue

DONNA CARLOS ARRIVED AT Luigi's villa shortly after breakfast, along with a retinue of ladies who would assist Angelica and Cecilia in getting ready for their wedding. She also had the altered wedding outfits that were to be tried on that morning.

She was Queen Bee, and everything around her bused with activity. She was bossing everybody and everything. One minute she was in the kitchen supervising the cutting up and cooking of Frank's boar. The animal was too huge to attempt to cook whole, so it had been cut into sections which, depending on the cut, were to be roasted over oak coals, braised in the oven, or cut up and browned for stews. The fat had also been cut away and was boiling in pots to make lard. Even the head had been boiled, its hair scrapped off, and the glistening pink head placed on a platter to serve as a decoration for the main banquet table.

The wedding cake, which had been ordered the day the Americans arrived, was an enormous piece of culinary construction that consisted of layers having different compositions representing the fruits and nuts from the island. Represented among the fruits were oranges, apricots, peaches, and pears which were coupled with pistachios, walnuts, and hazelnuts with the entire cake covered with an icing that instead of being an ordinary white icing was flavored with lemon to symbolically contrast the sweet and sour sides of matrimony. Topping this cake were two sets of bride-groom figures under a rock-candy crystal arch.[41]

"This is a masterpiece of culinary construction," William said.

"Nothing like it that has ever been done before," Donna Carlos replied. "Luigi and I want this dinner to represent the fullness of what Sicily has to offer to our American guests. Not even the Roman Emperors, the Medici in Venice, or the Popes in Rome ever saw a cake like this. Not only are we going to eat from the boar that your nephew shot, but we are also going to have a variety of seafood dishes and, of course, pastas, rice, wines, cheeses, and breads that are all of local origin in addition to our sea salt, spices, and even our cactus. This will be a memorable meal that will be talked about for generations.

"The reception following the wedding has been limited to two-hundred guests that are going to include ten reporters representing fashion, food, and travel magazines that circulate all over the world. We are going to demonstrate to the world that the family is strong and is not going to yield anything, despite my husband's arrest on trumped-up charges. Instead of trying to hide, I am going to make this an elaborate event so that no one will dare interfere."

"I hope not," William said. "Someone out there is trying to kill us, and Luigi does not know who it is."

"No life worth living is without risks. We'll take care of them whoever they turn out to be. We always have. We always will. The family will go on. We hold our friends close, and our enemies closer, as the old saying goes."

The quiet seclusion of Luigi's villa was now broken by the unrelenting passage of people rushing here and there to fitting rooms, and a near-constant barrage of telephone calls from this contractor or that supplier bringing deliveries and arranging some details of tomorrow's events such as receiving the five-gallon pails of white pear blossom petals that had been flown in from Argentina. A roadblock had been established outside of the compound's gate where heavily-armed guards examined every driver, vehicle, food item, and package.

Luigi had instructed his staff that he and Roger were only to be disturbed in extreme circumstances. Wearing dust masks, the two were

---

[41]   To my knowledge no one has ever seen such a cake. It would be an interesting comment on using local resources to make something memorable for a wedding.

breaking up clumps of the copper minerals azurite and malachite to provide the blue and green that would be used for the eye colors and using the mercury mineral cinnabar to provide the reds that would be employed to paint in the veins and splotches of blood on the weapons and clothes of those engaged in the life and death struggle depicted in the painting.

After the mineral grains were picked to represent as pure a product as possible, they were put into granite mortars and reduced to dust by heavy pestles. Then they were mixed with white lead and oils to achieve the correct tones which were tried on a scrap of canvas on an easel set off to one side to make sure that the desired tint had been obtained before applying their hand-crafted pigments to the painting.

"This is tedious work," Luigi said, "but compared to what is going on outside, I had rather be in here." As if to emphasize his point, a group of shrill-voiced women speaking machinegun Italian passed in the hall on the other side of the heavy oak door. The click of their high heel shoes progressed down the hall and finally faded away.

"The hairdressers were to arrive, and I suppose that those were they. Angelica and Cecilia will sleep sitting up tonight to keep from messing up their hair. I don't know why they get so excited about how their hair looks, but they all do. We older guys feel glad just to have some to keep our heads warm during the winter. Hang onto yours while you can. Your father seems to have kept his fairly well. You apparently have good genes."

Roger unexpectedly discovered he had thoughts of his future uncle-in-law scalping him and making a toupee from his hair.

"Where did the malachite and azurite come from?" Roger asked. "I get my supply from Arizona."

"Most of the time, I do too, although I can occasionally get good materials from Chile and South Africa. I also buy some from the former Soviet republics in the Far East, but that supply is intermittent and irregular. I think that it was Catherine the Great who had an entire room covered with slabs of malachite. So far as I know, that room was destroyed during World War II. I have never even seen a fragment of it".

"Have you ever used smithsonite, that light blue-green zinc-carbonate mineral?" Roger questioned. "There is one mine in Arizona or New Mexico that produces some, but it has been closed for decades. Every few years, rock-hounds bring some of it to the Gem and Mineral Show in Tucson, but it is a sometimes thing. I have a few lumps of it at home. It makes for a good eye color that is not quite so harsh as azurite and malachite."

"I know of it, and see it offered from China occasionally, but more often as rare mineral specimens, rather than as a pigment. One can make it artificially, and I suppose that someone does."

Another bevy of women were heard scurrying down the hall. "They sound like huge rats out there, although that is not a very kind comparison for our Sicilian ladies," Luigi observed.

"All of the ladies are really getting into this wedding business," Roger observed. "I hope Angelica and Cecilia are enjoying all the fuss and attention they are getting."

"First weddings are a once-in-a-lifetime event for women. They get more out of it than we men can hope to understand. It is something like a dog using its nose.

"We can observe the results then he tracks a piece of game to earth, but we cannot really appreciate how it works. So it is with women and this wedding thing."

"For us guys, fifteen minutes in the Magistrate's office and signing the paperwork is more than sufficient."

"I'm sorry. I don't understand."

"In Italy, the wedding is not legal until it is performed in front of a civil official and properly registered with the state. The church proceedings are for the family, the church itself, and as a public event. The magistrate makes some money, the church makes some money, the many venders, suppliers, and entertainers make some money, and hopefully everyone has a good time. Here in Sicily, the time between the civil and the church weddings is not too much of a big thing anymore. The church wedding and formalities may occur years after the couple was married in city hall. It may take that long for a family to accumulate the money and book the places for what they consider a proper wedding. We will take you for the civil ceremony tomorrow, just before your wedding."

"That's nice to know," Roger said. "I did not know what to expect. I suppose just the immediate family will be there."

"Yes. The six of you, me, Angelica, and Cecilia, and that's it. There is not room in the office for many more. We will do that at about 9:00 A.M., and the wedding itself will be at 10:30, as I understand from Donna

Carlos. She is handling all of these details and seems to enjoy doing it. More power to her. I, you, and the others are to be actors in her little play."

"I had no idea that this marriage business would be so complicated," Roger said. "Now let's paint."

Rather than attempting to paint the eyes free hand, Roger observed Luigi select a walking-stick-like rod with a ball turned on the end, place it on a dry part of the painting, brace it with the stub of his arm behind the attached palette, and use the stick as a support for his painting hand. He then delicately drew in each blood vessel with a tiny brush. Even with two hands, he could do no better than this old man with his one hand. The same hand that might one day kill him, if all did not go as planned. "This is like watching an executioner sharpening his ax prior to cutting your head off," Roger thought.

Renato felt a little strange driving Michael and Vito's colorfully-painted Fiat from Palermo to Syracuse. Luigi had gone along with Michael's suggestion that the car be used in the wedding procession from his villa in Syracuse to the church in Novo. He did not know the details of what would happen today or tomorrow after the wedding.

He knew that they would probably go to the city hall in Syracuse and have the civil ceremony. That had to happen either today or tomorrow, but considering Luigi's connections might even take place at his villa.

"I don't really like Fiats, but Michael and Vito did an excellent job of rebuilding it." he thought. "This car is responsive enough to be fun to drive. It has enough power to keep up with the traffic and sufficient agility to navigate the mountain roads and the narrow streets in town."

Although Luigi had offered him a bed in the bunkroom at the villa, Renato had begged off with the excuse that he would find somewhere in town near the Grand Hotel to stay so that he could avoid the noise and fuss of the pre-wedding preparations. "I'll let the young people handle that," he said, "I'll stay in town and free that bed for someone else."

Returning to Syracuse would give him the chance to report back to the AIA with the latest intel from Michael and Vito and see what the AIA strike group could arrange. With only a half-day for planning, they needed as much warning as possible. Ten people were already on their way from Milan. The general approach was that they were to have as little contact with the local law-enforcement agencies as possible to prevent leaks. It would be tempting for any cop who learned about it to tip off his Mafia contacts and earn a thousand euros from a single phone call.

There was also the issue of who was trying to knock off the visiting Americans. It could be anybody or even different groups acting independently. The AIA felt obligated to protect Michael and Vito as much as possible, but the higher-ups apparently felt indifferent if one group of *mafiosi* wanted to slaughter another group so long as they did not endanger the general public. This unseen line was a very hard one to identify and even harder to come up with an appropriate action plan. Once that plan was put into place, and particularly if the military was involved, few, if any, changes would be tolerated. Whatever the results, the plan would go forward or be canceled altogether. There would be few options for fine-tuning as things developed.

Driving up the road to Luigi's villa he was surprised when he encountered a roadblock that was manned by off-duty police and Luigi's own men.

"That is a sharp-looking little car." the policeman observed.

"I am delivering it. It is going to be used in the wedding procession," Renato explained.

"Get out please. We are going to have to search it and search you.

"Bring the dog," the officer shouted.

Renato stepped back as he saw another officer approaching with a large German Shephard that was straining on its leash.

"He just needs to check your car for explosives. He is eager because he gets a treat. Today, he is eating better than we are."

"All that dog is going to smell is drying paint because we just finished the painting yesterday, but let him sniff all he wants. Just let me get my sandwich out. He would likely like that too.

"See, just a sandwich," Renato said, as he unwrapped it to reveal a selection of mixed sliced meats, lettuce, and three slices of tomato.

"Open the doors and step aside. Here comes the dog."

Business-like in his methodology, the German Shepherd sniffed the outside of the Fiat and then jumped into the seat to check the insides. He was momentarily attracted to the spot on the passenger's side where the sandwich had lain but jumped back out and returned to his handler, where he was leashed up again.

"That is a good dog. This is the first time that I have seen one actually work," Renato said.

"They sent him to us from Naples just yesterday when we had a bomb explode in a truck."

"You are free to proceed," the policeman said.

Renato found Michael and Vito in the garage area of the villa polishing their cars so that they would be spotless for the events to take place over the next two days.

"Wow. That guy did a spectacular job on painting the car," Michael said. "I was expecting a checkerboard geometric pattern, but here we have sprays of wedding flowers and scenes of a royal wedding from the 1600s painted on the sides."[42]

"That is just the Sicilian way. The painter took his job very seriously. He said that he would have done more scenes, but he did not have the time. So he ended with a red and yellow checkerboard pattern on the front and rear, the wedding scenes on the doors, and a spray of mixed flowers on the top. He even put a black undercoat under the vehicle and then baked all the paints on yesterday. He said to put a good coat of wax on it. Next time, he said that he would do a better job, if he was still around when it needed it."

Luigi and Roger saw the brightly-colored vehicle come into the compound, but were too engrossed in the details of what they were doing to take a closer look.

"This is sort of like seeing my older brother open a Christmas present that I really wanted to see, but I dared not touch." Roger remarked.

"Concentrate on what you are doing," Luigi sternly rebuked. "We need to finish this today. There is no one else that I would trust to help me with this, and I want to get as much out of you as I can before you leave for America. It may be too dangerous for you to return to Sicily for some time."

Estavo was among those who came to see the new attraction. Addressing Renato, he said "I am sorry Luigi can't come out to welcome you because he is finishing a painting. He told me that you would not be staying with us but would find a place in town."

---

[42] Few of the elaborately crafted and painted donkey carts remain in Sicily. Their place has been taken by painting small Fiats and other cars in the same style.

"That's true. I'll let you younger folks party and carry on."

Estavo took this statement in good humor as he was certainly in no position to be called young, and as head administrator of the villa, he would be much too busy trying to keep everything going than doing anything that remotely might be called "partying."

"I will need to have Michael and Vito drive me back to Syracuse. I want to check out a strange noise that Michael's limo is making, and I need both mechanics' opinions."

"That's fine. I will let the gatekeeper know that you will be leaving. However, I need to have the drivers and the limo back by 5:30 to take people to the bachelor and bachelorette parties at the Grand Hotel."

While on the trip to Syracuse, Michael and Vito fulfilled the real purpose of the drive which was to bring Renato up to date on the events that would be taking place over the next two days.

"To sum up then," Renato started. "There are to be bachelor and bachelorette parties at the Grand Hotel tonight. Tomorrow morning, they are to be married in the civil ceremony at the city hall in Syracuse and then have the church wedding in Novo. Following that, there will be a large reception at the hotel, and then we don't know. Is that about right?"

"Yes it is," Michael affirmed.

"It seems that three attempts have already been launched to kill someone associated with this business, either Luigi, his daughter and niece, or the Americans.

We don't really know who is the target or who is doing it, and Luigi and Donna Carlos don't know either."

"That's it, so far as we know," Vito agreed.

"I suppose that Luigi thinks that no one is going to try anything in Syracuse because it is on an island, and the bridges could be blocked at any time. Although anyone could escape by boat, if they could get out of the middle of town."

"What do the authorities want us to do?" Michael asked.

"Just sit tight and drive them wherever they want to go. We will have to wait for a plan to come down from Milan as to what we will do. What no one wants to happen is to have a mid-morning gun battle in the middle of Syracuse. If we can prevent one of the gangs from attacking the other, we will. Apparently we managed to do that at the Roman Villa yesterday."

"There are hundreds of boats docked around the island. How are we going to stop anyone from smuggling anything they want into the city?"

"We will have to depend on the locals to stop anything suspicious coming into or leaving the town. If the mob hires one of the local fishermen, I think they could get anything onto or off the island that they liked."

"Those with higher pay grades than us are going to have to figure that one out. You two just do what you are asked to do and keep your heads down. I will call all of this in, and maybe someone at headquarters has some other contacts that will let us know what's going on. We can protect the front of the buildings and the streets they will take out of town, but that is about it. They might be ambushed any place along the way, if any group really wants to do it. Once the action starts, we can prevent them from escaping, but they might try something at any time.

"I have a room at the Nautilus Hotel, which is down the alley from the Grand. Drop me off there and get back to the villa. Should anyone ask, the trouble with the Limo was a loose muffler bracket, and we fixed it."

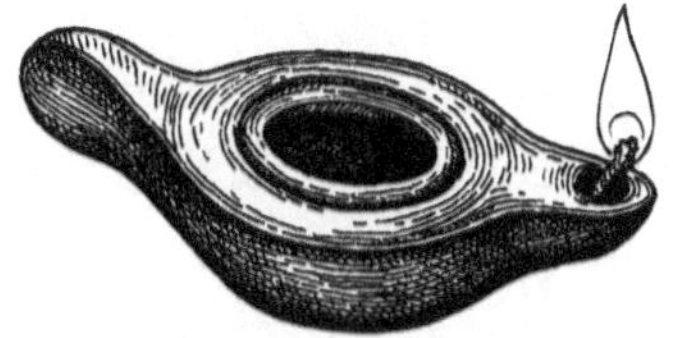

Bachelors and Bachelorettes

ATTEMPTING TO TIE UP all the loose ends in regards to the Wedding, Luigi approached Michael, "I want you to go to Novo in your Fiat, pick up Father Flanagan, and bring him to the Grand Hotel."

William, hearing the order said, "I would like to go with him. It will give me a chance to see more of the island."

"It will be a nice trip, and Father Flanagan is a good conversationalist."

"Give me a few minutes to get my clothes for the party, and I will be right back. There is also something that I feel compelled to do while I am in Syracuse, at the Ear of Dionysius. I think that some of our ancestors were imprisoned there. I have composed a lament for the tens of thousands of Sicilians who left or were driven out of Sicily and were never heard from again. Some were lost at sea, some died in the New World, and others fell to diseases and starvation all over the globe."

"I would like to hear it."

"I have a portable tape recorder, and I will make a recording. The acoustics of the cave should give it an appropriate reverberating sound."

"Michael, take your pistol with you. One never knows these days," Luigi concluded.

"Although this is an older Fiat, it has a new car smell," William remarked as they started their trip on the narrow roads that alternately climbed up switchbacks and then descended through sparsely populated slopes that supported more cactus than anything else on the jagged limestone outcrops.

"It should," Michael replied. "Almost everything about this car is new. Vito and I rebuilt it completely. For a little Fiat, this thing will move. If you like we will get it up to speed when we get off these curvy roads."

Looking down and seeing a nearly hundred-foot drop below them, William responded, "Not right now if you don't mind."

"How do the Mafia families work in the U.S.? Are they like they are here?" Michael asked.

"I really have no idea except what I read in the newspapers. Our family in Louisiana had nothing to do with them that we knew about. It seems that the Sicilian Mafia actually paid for my Grandfather to come to Louisiana. Now, Luigi has called in this debt for what he calls, 'a small favor,' in that he wants Frank and Roger to marry his daughter and niece and get them out of the country. But the boys don't want a life of having to look over their shoulder every minute for fear that someone is trying to kill them. Luigi is offering them not only two of the most attractive women that I have ever seen, but also a dowry of 100,000 euros a year. If they refuse, he has implied that none of us will leave Sicily alive."

A sharp ping on the underside of the vehicle interrupted their conversation.

"There is a motorcyclist behind us trying to shoot out a tire," Michael said. "The same thing happened to Vito yesterday. I am going to see if I can get ahead of him far enough to pull over to the side of the road and nail him when he passes by."

Pressing down hard on the accelerator, the Fiat shot forward, and with the tires squealing in protest, the car rounded the corner while William tightened his seatbelt and held onto the door to keep from banging against Michael as he drove.

With one hand holding the steering wheel, Michael cranked his window down. "When I ask for it hand me the pistol off the seat. Don't cock it or anything, just hand it to me."

After rounding the next corner, Vito saw where a branch road started to climb up the side of the ridge. Quickly pulling into it and slamming on the brakes to stop, he found himself at a slightly higher elevation than the road. As the gravel and dust started to settle, he said, "Give me the pistol."

William did as asked, and Michael quickly thumb-cocked the .45 and prepared to shoot downward at his target while holding the pistol in both hands with his forearms resting on the window sill. As soon as the motorbike came abreast of them, he fired four rapid shots. The ejected brass cases flew clear of the vehicle and landed on the ground.

The first shot went between the spokes of the front wheel, the second hit the fender of the front wheel, the third the engine block, and the fourth exploded the rear tire. The driver attempted to keep the bike pointed towards the centerline of the road, but went off the edge and careened off a bolder. The bike rebounded on impact and came to rest on the cactus and rock-studded slope below, while the driver was propelled into the air to land some yards away.

Returning to the road, Michael sped ahead. "Aren't you going to stop?" William asked.

"I will report the accident anonymously when we get to Novo. Things are too complicated to explain to the local cops. You will understand better in a moment. However, what I tell you must not reveal to anyone else, or it can get Vito and me killed. You see, Vito and I are members of the Italian Anti-Mafia Association, which is a cross between your FBI, CIA, and State Patrol. We wanted to see if a U.S. branch of the Mafia was attempting to link up with the Sicilian Mafia. I am convinced that what you have said is true, that you Americans were brought into this without knowing what was going on. It is possible that we can get you safely back to the U.S., although I do not know exactly how."

"That is going to be very difficult because we are with them all the time and are being watched nearly every minute. I think that the only reason I was allowed to go with you is that they have the rest of the family at the villa." William said.

"Father Flanagan and I have hatched a plot that could result in the two women calling off the wedding at the parties tonight. If they do, maybe we can just have our visit and go home. The boys are willing to go along with it, although they seem to have formed some attachments towards the women. I think that they would be happy to marry them, except for the Mafia baggage that comes with it. I also have reservations about what the Mafia might demand in the future for their support money for Angelica and Cecilia, or what might happen when Luigi dies or is killed. It seems that those who are trying to kill us will settle for whoever they can get."

The police who monitored the entrance to the *Plazza Centrale* in Novo were so impressed with the appearance of the elaborately-painted Fait that they let it into the square when they were informed that the two men were to pick up a priest.

Likewise Father Flanagan, who was enjoying his tea and the best imitation of a scone that he could find, could not help but chuckle to see the outrageously painted beetle-like vehicle navigate between bands of tourists and park in front of the Café. Recognizing William and Michael, he beckoned them to his table.

"You remember Michael, the limo driver," William said. "I came with him so that we could discuss tonight's events on our trip back to Syracuse. As it turns out, Michael has something significant to say, but we can talk about that in the car."

"How are the wedding preparations going?" Flanagan asked.

"You would not believe the money that is being spent on this thing. If I was not directly involved, this would be funny. There is a furious amount of activity including cooking a wild boar that Frank shot, the arrival of a wedding cake large enough to feed the entire town, and guests of all sorts coming in for the wedding and reception. Some of these are Mob Dons from Southern Italy. Donna Carlos, at the direction of her husband, wants to make a big show of this event to prove that this branch of the family is still strong and will not tolerate any interference in their activities."

"Father, would you bless this vehicle? In view of our perils in the past and those that might confront us in the future? We need all the help we can get."

"Yes, I have a little holy water in my travel kit. I never know when I might need it." Making the sign of the cross, Father Flanagan sprinkled some water on the hood and made the sign of the cross and muttered a few words. Because Michael and Vito had not had the time to wax it yet, the water sheeted off the hood, as if to distribute the spiritual essence of the holy water as far as possible.

Alexie, now reequipped with a second plumbing van and with two new men, spotted the Michael's Fiat as it was driving towards Syracuse, as its imitation donkey-cart paint job advertised the presence of a vehicle that was likely going to be used in a fancy wedding.

"Follow that car," Alexie ordered. "That car may carry someone we want."

In preparation for some possible long-distance sniping, this van was equipped with a shooting bench disguised as a plumber's work table with vises on which a sniping rifle could be mounted. Carefully packed away in a suitably beat-up tool box, was a .308 Steyr sniping rifle with scope and silencer. Depending on the target's range, the settings on the Leopold scope could be quickly changed between sub-sonic silent rounds for close-range shooting to high-velocity rounds for longer ranges.

Keeping back, they followed the Fiat into the parking lot overlooking the quarry, and parked so that they could watch a priest and two men get out of the car and quickly walk down to the quarry floor, towards the entrance to the The Ear of Dionysius.

"As soon as a car parked against the rail pulls out, back up against it." Alexie told the driver. "We may have a shot at them."

Almost as soon as he spoke, a car yielded its parking place and the driver deftly navigated the van towards the rail and parked it. Alfaro, the sniper, squeezed into the back of the van and started to unpack the gun and set up his shot. It would be a challenging set-up because of the steep down-angle of the shot.

"This is going to take a little time," he said.

"Hurry," Alexie demanded. "They won't be exposed for very long."

"This rig is not set up for moving targets," Alfaro replied. "I've got to have them standing still."

"Do what you can," Alexi replied.

Wanting to quickly record The Sicilian Lament, Michael, Father Flanagan, and William hustled down the wooden walkway leading to the quarry floor. The Ear of Dionysius is part natural cavern and part underground quarry which had been used for hundreds of years as a prison with its entrance blocked off with iron bars and gates.

The elfin-like ear with its pointed peak soared nearly sixty feet above the dampened earth on the inside of the cave. The opening on one side exposed fifteen-feet of solid limestone which opened up into a larger chamber leading back to the unknown dark recesses of the cave. Scratched on the walls was graffiti, which recorded the names of some of those who had been confined there. While the dampness and coolness of the cave might have been welcomed on hot days, these conditions would have fostered the spread of molds and fungi that could have easily given those who were confined there in close quarters any number of infectious diseases.

"This would have not been a pleasant place to be confined for months or years," Michael observed. Bad as his own imprisonment was in the San Vittore prison, that Victorian-era version of prison life was doubtless much better than being crowded into a cave like so many cattle.

Instead of the whipping posts, racks, and iron gibbons holding the rotting bodies of those who were executed that were placed outside of the barred door of the cave, there were now neatly trimmed boxwood hedges that served to direct visitors to the entrance.

"I think about fifteen feet inside of the ear would be about right," William said. "Father Flanagan, would you hold the little recorder and Michael could you restrain the visitors for just a few minutes? This will not take long."

William sang a scale just to clear his throat and loosen up his vocal cords. It had been a long time since he had performed in public. He was satisfied at the effect and began. He delivered this as a course from a Greek tragedy.

A Sicilian Lament
by Tyson Daniels

Listen, for our constant weeping,
Slaughtered kindred, death unceasing,
The ocean home, their bodies keeping,
Mothers cry against their reaping,
Fathers shout with rage increasing,
Sicilian kinsmen, war releasing,
Violent island, pain recurring,
Bear scars of fire, burning,
Enslaved generations, freedom yearning,
Brutal history, worth mourning,

Countless children, disappearing,
Angry Island crushing, tearing,
Treasure stolen, ever gleaming,
Sicilian blood, forever keening.
Mourn we here, but honor keeping.

"He's singing," Alexie said with a hint of disbelief in his voice. "Shoot him now."

Alfaro had adjusted the two table vises to line up the rifle with the target, mounted the scope on the rifle, positioned it in the vises, bent his lanky frame over to sight in the gun, slipped a round in the chamber, and closed the bolt when a loud pounding was heard on the van's door.

Alexi rolled down the window and there was an old lady dressed in somber clothing holding her cane.

"Are you plumbers? Yes. I need my sink fixed. It has been leaking for weeks, and I can't get anyone to come."

"I am sorry *Nonna*, but we do only industrial work, and we are on contract to someone else at the moment. You need to contact a local plumber. We can't do the work or we would get in trouble with the union."

"Please take pity on an old woman, I can't get anyone else."

Taking his phone, Alexie searched, and found some listings for residential plumbers.

"I have found someone for you. He is Abdulla's Plumbing."

"He is a Turk. He would cut my throat. It would be a sin to have him in my house."

"I don't think so. I will call him for you and set things up."

While Alexie set up the lady's plumbing appointment, Alfaro looked through the scope, sighted in on William and said, "Bang." His shot opportunity had passed.

William's Sicilian lament plaintively reverberated from the cave. He sang in honor of the hundreds of thousands of Sicilians who left the island and were never heard from again by their families and loved ones.

These would have included the mass expulsion of the Jews and Arabs in 1492 by the Spanish and many more who fled to escape persecution, privation, and starvation following wars, internal conflicts, and natural disasters. They left with high hopes for a better future, but many found only death because of shipwreck, piracy, disease, or a hostile reception in their new homelands.

The recording concluded, William received a round of applause from the tourists, and the three proceeded out of the quarry to continue their journey to Luigi's villa.

"That was a heart-wrenching delivery." Father Flanagan said. "I would like to include it in a Mass someday."

"I will send it to you. For an accompanying instrument, there are some Native American flutes that will provide an appropriate haunting, plaintive sound, particularly when played in that cave. The Spanish brought all sorts of things to Sicily from the New World, so the use of such a flute in this context would not have been impossible. Look all around you. With the palms and cactus, this looks like Baja California."

"We had best leave now." Michael said. "I know there is still much to see, but Luigi expects us back before dark, or he will assume that something has gone wrong."

The next morning Ronald and Nancy were still recovering from the events of the preceding days. They were glad to have the opportunity to remain in bed until the chaotic and irregular explosion of noises from the surrounding household made it impossible to sleep.

"They are doing stuff out there, and I guess we had better get up," Nancy said.

"I don't know. There is nothing for us to do but get in the way. The boys are being dressed in their outfits, the girls are having their hair done, and the cooks are working on Frank's hog. I don't know what else is going on, but I don't think that we have any part to play in it until we go to town for the parties tonight."

"Didn't the butler, what was his name? Oh yes, Estavo, it was. Didn't he say that there would be food out all day and that we could go down in our night clothes and eat anytime we wanted — just make ourselves at home."

"Yes, he did. I know that Roger was supposed to paint with Luigi again this morning, but I don't know what any of the others are doing. Perhaps we will find them at breakfast."

Polite nods and *buongiornos* were exchanged as they walked around the quadrangle where trucks and vans were arriving delivering items for the wedding. They were too late to see the colorfully painted Fiat, which had already left, but did run into Mary.

Guessing that their parents wanted to know, Mary said. "Roger is painting with Luigi in the drawing room, William has gone to Novo with Michael in a painted Fiat, and Frank is in the kitchen watching what they are doing with his boar. Among other things, they are cooking the boar's testicles for the bachelor party tonight.

"I never knew they looked like that. They had a thin skin around the outside, like the heart, that they pulled off and then they were chopped up into cubes to be fried – like Rocky Mountain oysters, only chopped in pieces instead of being served whole. They are going to serve them with horseradish sauce. I tried one, and they were a little chewy, but good.[43]"

"Where is the breakfast layout? "Ronald asked.

"It is in that room off the kitchen. They have the main dining room set up for later, but I was told they would be putting out food in the breakfast room all day so people can eat when they can. Angelica and Cecilia ate early, most of the staff has eaten, but the drivers who have been coming in and the guards have been grabbing food all day. I don't know how many people they have been feeding, but it is a bunch. They even made some special coffee for us, so we did not have to drink their strong coffee from those tiny cups."

On a rustic-looking table in the breakfast room, they saw a layout of several varieties of seeded and plain breads, stuffed and plain croissants, crusted fruit breads with a crosshatched crust, looking like a very flat pie, assorted fruits and nuts, a layout of sliced meats, pans of sausage and bacon, and a cook with a hotplate who would cook eggs to order. Luigi was obviously trying to accommodate both his American and European guests.

Ronald was eager to try all of the sliced meats, including some of the liver, blood sausages, and headcheese that he did not often see in the states.

---

[43]   Fried boar testicles are not an original creation of mine, but having access to them I cooked some as shown on my video, *Hog Fries and Testicular Delights a la' Julia Childs*. I do not know if Julia ever cooked them for her New England guests, but I suspect if she did not it was only because she had not thought of it. In truth they are eatable and even tasty with those from young boars being preferred over older individuals.

Nancy was a bit more reserved, and took more of the bread products and rolls and was particularly glad to find more of the goat cheese that they had seen made at the farm.

"Two scrambled eggs, please," Ronald told the cook as he held up two fingers.

"I speak English," the cook replied. "Most of us were taught in school after the war. In modern times, many my age speak Sicilian, Italian, and a foreign language, which is most often English or French."

"I wish our schools in the U.S. did the same. We often have enough trouble teaching English, much less other languages. If we want to learn Italian we have to do it on our own."

"Being on an island and a trading nation, we almost have to know more than one language to get along."

Luigi had thought to feed his guest on plastic plates and forks, but Donna Carlos would not have it. Periodically, stacks of porcelain plates were brought in and the dirty plates taken back to the kitchen to be washed.

After they had eaten, Ronald walked back to the kitchen to check on Frank, and the inappropriateness of his bedclothes and bathrobe was made even more striking compared to the kitchen staff who were all dressed in white aprons and toques.

"Frank, I just wanted to see that you were all right."

"Yes, I am. They are doing some amazing things with this hog. There is even going to be a whole roasted boar's head. I have heard about such things, but I have never seen it. I am teaching them how to do a Brunswick stew. I have to make some substitutions, but it will be a passible product."

"Your mother and I are going back to our room to get out of the way. We have some catching up to do." As he made this statement, he winked, and Frank nodded in understanding.

Mary asked what her parents were going to do for the remainder of the day, and when they replied that they might spend it in bed, she blushed.

"I don't want to hear it," she said.

"You know when we conceived you...," Ronald began.

"Too much information," Mary interjected. "I'll read a book or something. You two go off and do what you need to get done."

"I am going to take another way back," Michael said. "There was an accident on the road with a motorbike, and I suspect that the police have it blocked while they are doing their investigation."

"Was anyone hurt?" Flanagan asked.

"There probably was from what I could see of the bike. The police were already there when we passed." Michael did not like to lie to a priest. But there was no need for him to know that the man on the bike was likely dead, and he had contributed to his death.

Changing the subject, Michael said, "Father Flanagan, William has told me that you and he have a plot to get Angelica and Cecilia to call off the wedding. I may be in a position to help."

"How so?" Flanagan asked.

"Vito and I are undercover cops. We have worked to get Luigi's confidence. So long as we can do something useful without revealing our cover, we can help to get the Americans out of the country, although I do not know when or how. What we want to avoid is having a gun battle in Syracuse or Novo.

"We know that someone, or someones, are trying to stop the wedding by killing those involved. People associated with the wedding have been shot at three times, and there has been one attempt to plant a bomb. Luigi's villa is like a fortress, and everyone and everything is being checked going in and out.

"Nonetheless, more attempts to disrupt the wedding can be expected. The FBI and the U.S. Air Force are involved, although they can take no actions except to defend themselves or you if fired upon. This wedding has come to be an international event."

Turning to William, Flanagan asked, "Are Frank and Roger willing to go along?"

"Yes, they are."

"Jock and Julia are on board too. From what they told me, one wing on one floor of the Grand Hotel has been blocked off. The bachelor party is going to be in one room, and the bachelorettes are going to be in another. The older participants will be in a third room in a tower while a fourth is being decorated to receive the wedding gifts, and a fifth for Jock and Julia to change in. When they return after their appearance at the party, they are going to be naked in bed with Frank and Roger and be seen by Angelica and Cecilia. Hopefully, this deception will cause the women to convince Luigi to call off the wedding. When everything is ready, I will tell Angelica and Cecilia what is going on and escort the two women to the room."

"I like it," Michael said. "If this can be brought off successfully, then there will be no need for us to be involved. I have been designated to escort Mary to the events and will be at the bachelor party, but I do not want to do anything to blow my cover."

"No, you don't," Flanagan said. "The last police informant that I buried was skinned alive and then whipped to death. It must have taken him hours to die. These Mafia folks are not very forgiving if they feel someone has betrayed them, and they have all of the tortures of the Spanish Inquisition and the Aztecs to draw upon. They can be loyal and loving friends but terrible enemies."

This warning, coming from a priest who had seen much violence and delivered as cold, hard facts, caused shivers to run down Michael's spine, as if he could already feel knives cutting away his skin.

A city bus had been rented to take the participants from Luigi's villa to the Grand Hotel. Their departure had already been preceded by vans and cars that had taken the food that the cooks had been working on, the wedding cake, and the presents to the hotel. Thus far, thanks to a heavy hand laid on the events by Donna Carlos and Estavo, everything has proceeded nearly flawlessly. There were things left that had to be sent in later vehicles, but the intermittent parade of cars and vans had proceeded back and forth without incident. Rather than risk having the entire family in a single vehicle, Luigi had them go in the different cars and service vans and reserved the bus for his out-of-town guests.

Michael and Vito had already made shuttle trips to the hotel and were now tasked with escorting the bus into town. That busload of mob figures would be a fine catch, Michael thought, but he had received no word that anyone was going to make an attempt to arrest them at this event – or, at least, not at this stage of it.

After checking on his passengers in the van, Luigi got into the leading Mercedes with Michael and began their trip down the sloping valley to the flood plain below where they would cross the Archimedes Bridge and enter the old city of Syracuse. Luigi touched his hat as a sign of respect when he passed the bronze statue of Archimedes in the middle of the bridge and looked across to see the reconstructed medieval buildings standing on the opposite shore. Boats were tied up everywhere along the walled sides of the island. These ranged from tourist boats to working fishing boats that used the same harbor that had sheltered ships from all over the classical world. Much of the harbor was too shallow for the big tour boats such as plagued Venice, and he had always been happy about that. There was no need for those multistory floating barns to hide the beauty of his city.

"This is our Venice," he announced to Michael. "And as much as I can, I want to keep it that way."

As somewhat befitting the name, the Grand Hotel was in a renovated palace that had served both residential and administrative functions in its day. The hotel's design had retained four large round towers on each corner, which contained mostly decorative slit windows positioned so that fire could be directed towards the plaza below. Now the palace's many halls and rooms had been renovated to provide hotel rooms. Some of the once wide marble-floored halls in the upper stories had been partitioned to provide sleeping quarters. Where the residential portion of the palace on the upper floors provided larger rooms, the renovations were much more in keeping with the structure and provided premium accommodations at appropriately elevated prices. It was in one of these wings that the night's events would be held.

One of the elevators in the richly marbled lobby had been locked so that it could only discharge passengers on that floor. Outside of that elevator door was a matched pair of ornate desks with two large armed men checking the names of those attending against an invitation list. Among those who were invited, were the people who had participated in Frank's hunt and Michael and Vito's boss, Renato, who was booked in the more prosaic Nautilus Hotel.

"Welcome, welcome," Mario said as he motioned Frank and Roger into the room where the noisy bachelor party was already underway. "Ordinarily we would take you around to some of our local clubs tonight, including a gay bar and a strippers' club, but for security's sake everything is here at the hotel. Frank, in honor of your hunt, the boar's skin has been scraped and fried, and the cooks have made you a special dish of fried boar testicles.

"Roger, in your honor, the bartender has prepared a new punch, which is being served from that amphora that has a tap on the bottom which is in the stand in the corner. This is made of juice from our cactus mixed with red Grappa, Champagne, and lemon zest that is cooled with dry ice. He named it The Archimedes in honor of the painting that you and Luigi are doing."

Once inside, Frank found himself being embraced and kissed on the cheek by Olivito, Austolino, and Alberto.

"That was an outstanding shot that you made on that boar," Alberto said. "Congratulations on your taking a true trophy animal. Most hunters who just have a few hours with the dogs, as you did, would not even see an animal that size, much less kill a charging boar with one shot with a flintlock. That gun, by the way, is in a case in the other room with the wedding presents."

"How is Pliny, the dog that was hooked by the boar?" Frank asked.

"Austolino sewed him up and gave him some antibiotics. He said that he would be fine in a few days." Speaking in a mix of Italian and English, Olivito explained how grateful he was that Frank's shot had been so well delivered and had dropped that hog within a few inches of where he was standing. "I was not looking forward to spending a week in the hospital after being ripped and run over by that hog," he said as he grabbed Frank's head with both hands, pulled him closer, and kissed him again.

Roger, whispering in Frank's ear, said, "I thought we might be kissed tonight, but not by a bunch of guys."

Now being led to the corner of the room where the amphora was fuming like Mt. Etna in eruption, wine glasses were filled with the punch and presented to the two grooms-to-be.

"How do you like it? " Mario asked.

"This is dangerous stuff," Roger replied. "It's like those tropical rum punches. They are sweet, go down smoothly, and will slap you down on your butt if you have a couple of them. They also give wrenching hangovers."

"You know no groom was ever hung over on his wedding day. Don't worry. Alberto and I will hold you up if we have to while the priest does the ceremony," Mario said.

"That's fine about me, but what about Frank?"

"I am sure that we can find a pair of willing guys to support him while he undertakes the holy vows and even substitute for you in bed, if need be, on your wedding night. Cecilia and Angelica are beautiful young ladies. In fact, most of us younger guys, and some of the older ones, have lusted after them for years. You two are very fortunate to have them, and we are jealous and happy for you at the same time."

Roger quickly stepped back to prevent another smacker from being planted on his cheek. "We had best get something to eat to put on top of this liquor," he told Frank. "You remember what Mario told us about this Grappa stuff."

"I really want to try some of the dishes that I saw being cooked today," Frank responded. "I think that they may have brought some of the Brunswick stew that I made today. It should be even better now that it has had a chance to sit for several hours."

Arrayed on the table, were steaming covered dishes. One indeed, had the Brunswick stew, and beside it was a dish of white rice that might be used as a bed onto which to spoon the fatty stew.[44] Another covered dish marked "Grooms Only" contained the "testicular delights," as Frank had heard the Chef call them, and other platters had sliced hog tongue, and a spread made of the liver and kidneys which had been cooked, crushed, and mixed with pickles and peppers to make a pate'.

"The way Angelica grabbed me, I don't think that she needs any of these," Roger said as he put some of the delights on his plate. "They had better give us a good bed, or we may break it."

"Cecilia seems to be a gentler soul. I don't really expect that from her," Frank replied as the thoughts of the coming deception crept into his mind. "Dammit, I am finding that I really care for her, and I don't want to hurt her. But I don't want to spend the rest of my life running from the mob either."

"Father Flanagan, Uncle William, come and sample some of this stew. This is a Brunswick stew that I made this morning. It is not quite as I would make it back home, but it is reasonably representative."

---

44   Brunswick Stew is a dish that we Georgians claim to have originated in Brunswick Georgia and consist of smoked meat from the head of a wild hog, other wild game meats, corn, tomatoes, and other vegetables. It is dashed with a bit of hot sauce and vinegar along with assorted peppers, but is kept to a mild heat. I like the taste of butterbeans and okra in the stew, but some decline one or both.

"How would you have done it?" Flanagan asked. "I would have used the meat from a smoked hog's head, mixed it with that of other wild game such as raccoon or deer, and used okra and butterbeans along with corn and tomatoes. In this, we used the neck and shank meat from the hog, the hooves, turkey, and goat with corn and cucumbers along with local tomatoes and peppers. It has a splash of vinegar to give it a slightly sour taste and is a little warm, but not hot by Louisiana or Sicilian standards. And as you are our guest of honor and the one who is going to marry us tomorrow, here is an eyeball."

"This is not the first time I have been so honored," Flanagan responded. "But the eyeballs are for you and your brother, and I must therefore decline."

To demonstrate that he was not reluctant to consume such a thing, Frank put the eyeball on a spoon and popped it into his mouth. When he bit down on it, the eyeball was crushed like a grape releasing a flood of salty slightly acid-tasting fluids over his taste buds – not unlike the taste of boiled peanuts.

"Brother, your turn," Frank said as he offered the other eyeball to his sibling.

"Frank you were always cooking up some strange stuff. Remember the palm grubs?" As he always had on his brother's culinary dares, Roger put the eyeball into his mouth and chewed contemplatively. Even if it had tasted like a mix of coal tar and black-strap molasses, he would have got it down, if for no other reason than not to have his brother embarrass him in front of his Sicilian cousins.

"It's good," he replied, and this comment received a round of applause and laughter from the room. "Why do I always let Frank get me in situations like this?" he asked himself.

Across the hall, Angelica and Cecilia's attentions were focused on Donna Carlos who was with Nancy, their future mother-in-law. They were having a deep conversation about the wedding. At this stage, they didn't really want or need to know more details. They had endured being fussed over all day by the tailors, hairdressers, nail artists, and their friends who were often making useless suggestions, such as things they ought to do on their wedding night. They found themselves wishing that this wedding thing would get done with. It had not even happened, and they found themselves getting tired of it. They would be glad to be in a position where they could run more of their own lives even though marriage would offer additional, and likely unexpected, restraints on their activities.

"I wonder if Roger will make me sell my car," Angelica mused. "What does a painter need with a red Ferrari?"

Luigi had reserved the left rear tower room on that floor as an intimate space to entertain his Mafia associates. Because of the room's thick stone walls and heavy door, and a guard outside, he could be assured that whatever was said within would not be heard by anyone else. Unknown to him, the single sheets of glass which had replaced the original leaded glass windows turned out to be ideal sound-transmission surfaces because the wedge-shaped walls of the shooting slits focused the sound.

In order to adapt the room to modern use, the wooden scaffolding that would have allowed the defenders to stand at the window level nine feet above the floor had been removed, and a round conference table installed. This table was made from the island's trees with multicolored wedges of wood being inlaid in the top of the table in the pattern of rows of wooden diamonds, which increased in size towards the edge of the table that was covered in padded black leather. The visual effect was like a harlequin's umbrella with a black rim laid flat on the floor. The table was so large that it had to be brought through the narrow passage to the tower disassembled, and then reassembled in the tower. The whitewashed interior walls were partly covered with tapestries depicting scenes from ancient Syracuse, including some showing Archimedes' inventive means of defending the city such as levers used to lift galleys out of the water and the shields employed to burn the sails of the Roman ships. One blank section of the whitewashed wall was left undecorated so that a centrally mounted projection box could use that as a screen to project images for business meetings. These references to Archimedes made this room one of Luigi's favorite places in the entire city. Sometimes he wanted quiet, so he would come in, lock the door, and think.

Agent Rob Williams attempted to use filter dials to cut out the background noises, while Howard Smith adjusted the window-length black antenna to focus on a slit window on the tower of the Grand Hotel across the street. From their position in Renato's room in the Nautilus Hotel, the antenna focused on a slit window that was only twenty-feet away.

"Rob, are you hearing anything?" Smith asked.

"Only chatter in Italian and Sicilian. I can make out a word or two here and there, but my Italian is not good enough to make out much more. Wait, I hear the sounds of chairs being moved. Maybe someone is going to speak. Yes, apparently Luigi is going to say something."

"Members of the five families, I would like to welcome you to the weddings of my daughter Cecilia and my niece Angelica to two Sicilian men whose families left the island generations ago and have now returned." Luigi began. "While they are of our blood, they are not members of the family and do not wish to be. Since their arrival, four attempts have been made against their lives. I do not know who is responsible. One group who attempted to plant a bomb in our cars has been arrested. Two others have been injured or perhaps killed when they attacked our cars. Thus far, because of the skills of our drivers, no one on our side has been hurt.

"Although Don Carlos and Leo, are temporally in prison, our family is strong. Should anyone attempt to attack us again, be assured that there will be a terrible retribution should any harm come to members of the family or our American visitors." With this statement, Luigi reached in his coat and drew his flame-shaped dagger, slapped his prosthetic hand sharply, and laid the dagger on the table.

"You all know this blade and what it has done. All it has stung are now dead. On the heads of my mother, child, and all the saints should any continue to seek to harm me and mine, it will once again do its terrible work, even though I might die while exacting my revenge. It is a dreadful curse to be hunted down by a person who has no fear of death. I have lived my life, loved my women, fought, strived, and won. Now, I only want to see my daughter and niece married and perhaps hold my grandchildren. Anyone who attempts to deprive me of that will suffer the consequences.

"I would now like to share with you my great work, that was just finished today with the assistance of my new nephew-in-law. Please dim the lights."

When the lights were dimmed the suspended projector turned on and hummed. Then, The Death of Archimedes appeared, projected on the curved wall. "As an artist I am all those who appear in the painting. I am Archimedes, examining his own guts with seeming indifference to the burning city below or the fact that he is about to die. I am the rage-filled Legionnaire about to exact a terrible revenge on a person responsible for the deaths of hundreds of his fellow troopers, and I am the spearman standing in the doorway recoiling in horror at what his Sergeant is about to do and the consequences that can result for disobeying the orders of his General to spare Archimedes' life.

"This marriage with the Americans will result in absolutely no change in the family's operations, how things are run, or the projects that we may have in progress. I have no desire to return to the Mafia Wars of the nineties. Those were to no one's benefit, and a lot of good men were killed, including my own brother. I am representing the family's interests. I know how to fight, and I will. Let this wedding proceed without any further interference, and things can proceed as they have. Should you elect to further endanger me or mine, I will not quit going after you so long as I draw breath."

At the conclusion of the speech, many muffled and confused voices were heard, but significantly no gunshots.

"I can't tell what is happening now, but that was quite a speech that Luigi gave. He told the members of the other Mafia families to quit bothering him, or else. I will have someone transcribe the speech into English in case there was something I did not get, but he really told them to lay off or risk starting the Mafia Wars up again."

As the meeting dispersed, Don Augustino went up to congratulate Luigi. "I am pleased to see that you are getting your daughter and niece married. It is more difficult getting a match for women."

"Thank you. Where is Apachee? I was expecting him."

"You know how young men are. He got into a fight over a woman and got cut. Nothing serious, but bad enough to keep him in bed for a few days after the wounds heal."

"I'm sorry to hear that. He would have enjoyed this. Give him my best regards."

"I surely will tell him all about it," Don Augustino replied with a toothy smile.

"Take it off. Take it all off." Were the shouts that were coming from the room where the bachelorette party was in full swing. Jock was dressed in black tails, a cummerbund, and bow tie while Julia was wearing a sleek floor-length electric blue dress with sequins, spike heels, and a black skull cap with a single peacock feather.

They had concluded a comedy skit depicting a newly married couple exchanging sexily flavored banter before beginning a tawdry tango. Their clothes were held together with Velcro strips and with each turn, a glove, sleeve, or portion of the pants or dress would fall away. As each piece was discarded and thrown to the crowd, it would be searched to recover the party favors that were pinned to the fragmented garments.

The wear and tear on the garments was severe, as the women's competitive nature would sometimes overcome decorum, and they would act like women at a sales table for discounted diamond jewelry. The longer strips of dress and leg pieces were particularly troublesome as two or perhaps three people would grab portions of them pull in different directions ripping the garments. Once, Donna Carlos had to intervene to keep the event from turning into a brawl.

A portion of the dance floor had to be roped off to keep the frenzied ladies from ripping pieces of clothing off the performers long before the sexual tease part of their act became obvious. Over the years Jock and Julia had perfected this set to the extent that they knew which rip of dress or trouser would come off at each turn in the tango and how many steps would be required, and consequently how large a room they would need. Being in an apartment, rather than a ballroom, their movements were confined, and instead of a full-fledged tango their act had devolved into more of a bump-and-grind type of performance, which was not so artistically satisfying to either of them.

One-by-one, as the pieces of clothing were dismembered, two-inch strips were peeled away to reveal progressively more bare flesh, like disassembling a Venetian blind slat by slat. When the strip over Jock's right breast was pulled away, it revealed a male nipple that was flat against a muscled chest, as was expected. However, a quite different result was obtained when a corresponding strip of Julia's costume was removed. Instead of the pert tight breast indicated by the costume, there was another muscled chest was revealed, with a pasty with a propeller stuck on the nipple. For the first time, some members of the audience discovered that this ostensibly attractive young dancer, with her short haircut, was a slim young guy in drag.

Excitement built as more and more strips of the clothing were removed from the dancing figures. The final reveal was the bow tie on Jock and the necklace pendant on Julia, which slowly pulled down to show the breastbone, belly button, a fringe of pubic hair, and was then torn away showing a flesh-colored speedo filled with a straining phallus.

This is when the round of "Take it off. Take it all off." erupted from the room. Looking at Donna Carlos for guidance Jock saw a definite head shake and said, "Sorry ladies not tonight. But for twenty euros you can have a peek."

As they circulated around the room to get a drink, the straps of their speedos accumulated a row of twenty-and-fifty-euro notes. It was not the exposure of their sexual organs that they minded so much, it was being scratched by the fashionable, but functionally useless, long fingernails that bothered them. It felt like they were being assaulted by a hungry school of piranha as they felt hands all over their bodies. After finishing their drinks, they wrapped themselves in a towel and went out into the hall for their second gig of the night.

"I think that this one will be more enjoyable," Jock said.

"You know that it is those sex-crazed young women that pay the bills," Julia replied. "How else is a gal like me supposed to make an honest living?"

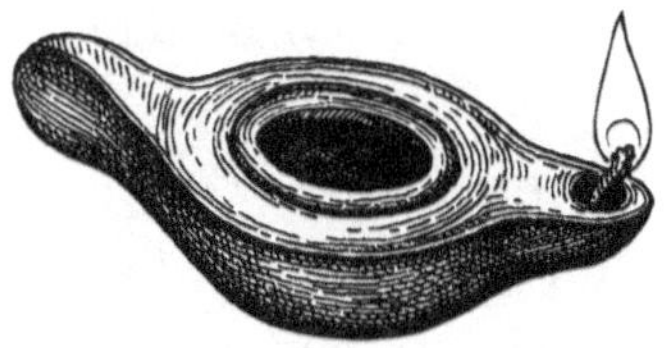

29

𝕭etrayed

LYING NAKED TOGETHER IN bed was a new experience for Frank and Roger. "I don't recall that we ever did this before," Frank remarked to Roger. Mom and Dad always had clothes on us. Sometimes when we were both small, I remember us being put into the same tub and bathed together, but so far as I can remember, we always had something on in bed, even when you were in diapers. In the daytime they might put us in the same bed for naps, but never naked."

"How are we going to handle this?" Roger asked. "It gives me the creeps to think about it."

"Well, I guess we are going to have to play like we are in a porn movie – just thrash around and show some skin and butt – maybe like we were wrestling with them. I think that the best way to think about it. Greco-Roman wrestling – like they did in the time of the Greeks. You know the saying, When in Rome…"

There was a rap on the door, and in came Father Flanagan, Jock, and Julia. "Frank, Roger, this is Jock and Julia who I told you about. I will go get Angelica and Cecilia. When I come in, I will turn on the lights and find you all thrashing around in bed. Jock and Julia don't speak much English, so first, I will help you work things out. You want to make it appear that you were being intimate without actually having intercourse."

"What I have talked over with my brother is that we all get in bed together and do a sort of wrestling thing, and turn over in the bed with maybe a few grunts, groans, and slapping noises to make it sound real," Frank said.

"Do you want to do a practice?" Flanagan questioned.

"No," Roger said. "Doing this once is going to be hard enough."

"Come on, Roger," Frank said. "We need to have at least a run through to make it look good."

"Not this time. If we got to do this thing, let's do it." and he waved his arms to invite Jock and Julia to get into bed with them.

Flanagan explained to the two performers what had been agreed and that they would do a sort of wrestling with the sheets off the bed. When he returned, he would rattle the door and fiddle with a key to give them time to get into a supposed mode of realistic passion before he opened the door and flipped on the light.

On seeing their temporary bed partners, Jock remarked in Italian to Julia, "It is a pity that they are straight. They are great looking guys. I would take either of them in a moment."

As she took off her towel and speedo and climbed into the right side of the bed with Roger, Julia nodded in assent.

Roger felt his throat tighten and his mouth go dry, with what he could only describe as a bad case of stage fright.

"Don't worry, it will be all right," Julia said in reassuring tones.

Although spoken in Italian, Roger guessed the intent, and it did comfort him a bit. He was ready for this brief little show to be over.

The bed was large enough to hold the four of them comfortably, and Frank found himself wondering how many threesomes and foursomes had occurred between those sheets. He felt Jock beside him and tried to imagine in the dark that it was Jane, his ex-wife. Maybe for a moment, in his mind, it was.

There was a rattling of the key in the door, and the figures in the bed started moving like logs tumbling over each other. With limbs entangled when the lights came on, there was a shriek from Cecelia and a disgusted "humff" from Angelica as the door slammed shut. This was followed by the sound of heels rapidly striking the marble floor as the prospective brides ran down the hall, trying to put what they saw as a scene of unspeakable horror behind them.

Their little micro-play completed, the four guys arose from the bed with Jock, fully stimulated from the night's activities, expressing a throbbing erection. Frank motioned Jock and Julia back into bed, and picking the covers off the floor, threw them back over the amorous pair.

"Let's get dressed and get out of here before these two get started," Frank said.

The two brothers quickly redressed and combed their hair before stepping back out into the hallway. Not wanting to immediately return to the bachelor party, they stepped into the room where the wedding presents were displayed. There, they saw the aprons and vases with the Moor Sultan and his Christian lover's heads on them, household items, and salt and bread for their new home.

"I feel rotten that we had to deceive the two girls like this. In many ways, I like them both," Roger remarked. "But I don't want to run and hide from the mob for the rest of my life, and I don't want their blood money either, regardless of how much I could use it."

"I know the feeling. The family over here has treated us well. Here is the musket that I shot the boar with that they were going to give me. Now I suppose that they are as likely to shoot me with it as gift it to me. I know that Angelica would. Cecilia is more reserved. She would more likely poison us than shoot us."-

"That's a comforting thought," Roger replied.

Angelica and Cecilia had run across the hall and locked themselves in another room's bath while they tried to sort things out.

Cecilia, wiping her eyes with a towel, said, "I don't know why I am crying. We really don't know these guys. They could be gay or bisexual or devils for all we know. I feel hurt, betrayed, and wounded. I really ache in my heart."

"I am just mad. I know gay men, and I like some of them. It is not so much that I care that they might have slept with men before, but not on the eve of our wedding. It's like catching your future husband making love to one of your bridesmaids, only worse. At this moment, I feel like I could kill them."

"What are we going to do?" Cecilia asked. "We can go to Luigi and call off the wedding, but all this money has been spent, the guests invited, the wedding reception arranged, and the family would lose face. You know how these Sicilian men are. They can play around all they want, have mistresses, etc., but if their wives do, they get stoned or locked up in a nunnery."

"I have always wanted to be a teaching nun," Cecilia said.

"That may be fine for you, but it is not for me. We have to go and talk to Luigi and Donna Carlos and get this business called off tonight. Tomorrow will be too late," Angelica confirmed.

Returning to the bachelor party, Frank and Roger found that the entire room was darkened with periodic eruptions of uninhibited laughter as footage of their recent activities was being continuously replayed against a wall. There were shots of Jock and Julia climbing into bed with them, the lights going out, and then coming back on, showing them in their simulated lovemaking and then switching to the looks of disgust and horror on the brides' faces as they observed for a few seconds and bolted out the door.

Slapping them both on the back, Mario said. "That was a fine joke. That was even better than taking you to the gay club like I had planned. Look at the expressions on their faces. This will get five million hits on the internet tomorrow. You will be famous."

"How did you film us?" Roger asked.

"There are recording cameras in all of these bedrooms. You never know when we might find some useful bedroom activities to capture. We use old-fashioned film so the poor bastards we catch doing something wrong can buy the film from us. That is how this little game works,[45]" Mario replied.

"I want that film. That could ruin my military career," Frank said.

"Yes, it could, and you shall have it. That will be my wedding present to you. That is the best joke that we have ever played on a prospective bride."

"It is not us I am worried about. What did that do to Angelica and Cecilia?" Roger interjected. "They could be really hurt by all of this."

"Don't worry," Mario said reassuringly. "Luigi and Donna Carlos were in on it too. They will straighten it all out."

Now that the meeting with the Dons was over and the parties were winding down, Luigi and Donna Carlos were sharing a drink at a table in the hall as they wished their departing guests good night.

---

[45]   With today's technology filming through two-way mirrors has been replaced by the use of tiny hidden cameras used by those who wish to capture clandestine footage.

Spotting them, but not wanting to appear distressed, Angelica approached her Uncle. "Something has happened, and we need to talk."

"Whatever in the world might that be?" Luigi remarked to Donna Carlos.

"I assure you I don't know," she replied. "This should be the happiest night of their lives, and they appear disturbed."

"Excuse us for a moment," Luigi replied. "My daughter and niece have something to tell us. We will be in this room over here."

"Father, Uncle, Donna Carlos," the two started off simultaneously.

"One at a time please," Luigi said with an uncharacteristic smile creeping across his face.

"We can't marry these Americans. They are gay. We just caught them naked in bed with Jock and Julia."

"Maybe they were tired," Luigi replied.

"No. No. They were, well making love or whatever they do," Cecilia said. "We saw them. Father Flanagan was there too."

"I can't torture you any longer." Donna Carlos said. "What you have observed was a clever bachelor party joke that apparently everyone but you knew about. They were just play-acting. They were not having sex. This was something cooked up by their Uncle William and Mario. Poor Father Flanagan got duped into going along. It was all a joke."

"With all due respect, Donna Carlos, a joke?" Cecilia asked. "A joke! Angelica was mad to the point of killing them on the spot, and I can't say that I would have done much to stop her."

"Uncle, how could you have let this happen if you knew about it?" Angelica asked.

"With all we have been going through, I felt that a little levity would be in order. This was an event that everyone will remember for as long as they live. This will be talked about for generations.

"Now, let's go meet your husbands-to-be and patch things up."

Trying hard to calm her enraged passions, Angelica replied. "Patch things up from what?" she questioned. "We have hardly even exchanged a dozen words."

"That, you will do tomorrow," Luigi said. "What the brothers did makes no difference. The wedding is tomorrow."

"I heard what you two did," Mary shouted when she saw her brothers in the hall.

"That was the worst thing that I ever heard of to do on the night before your wedding. You were supposed to go out and get drunk or something, but not bed down with two gay guys. I don't know if Angelica or Cecilia are going to do this, but I sure will."

Approaching her brothers, she pulled back as if she was standing on a pitcher's mound and gave Frank and then Roger stinging slaps across the face. Neither of them tried to fend off the blows.

"We deserved that, but we were trying to get us out of this mess," Frank said. "Sis, you still swing quite a punch."

"You should know. You taught me."

"Where are Angelica and Cecilia?" Frank asked. "We certainly want to talk to them before tomorrow. I know we hurt them. I don't know what to tell them, but I need to say something before we stand before the priest."

"You had better think of something good," Mary admonished. "Something very good indeed."

"Maybe the truth," Roger volunteered. "That is all we have."

"Here comes everybody," Frank observed as he saw his mother, dad, sister, uncle, Angelica, Cecilia, and Father Flanagan coming down the hall.

On seeing Frank and Roger, Angelica pointed a finger at the two brothers and started a bombastic attack in Sicilian during which she called them snakes in the grass, slime molds, piles of shit, spineless, shiftless, worthless, limp dicks not fit to be stable hands, along with some less easily translated Sicilian curse words.

Although Cecilia was the only one who could understand what Angelica said, there was no doubt that Angelica was one very mad lady who had been mortally embarrassed and was going to tell someone about it.

"And that goes for me too," Cecilia said as she looked Frank straight in the eye.

"Where can we talk this out in private?" Father Flanagan asked.

"The only room in the hotel that I know is not bugged is the conference room in the tower," Cecilia volunteered. "That is where my father holds his secret meetings."

Walking towards the tower, William motioned to Michael to join them. "We may need to use those limos for something," William explained as he summoned the limo driver who was known only to himself to also be an AIA agent. Whatever happened, it would have to be Michael to disclose that fact, not him.

When the group walked through the narrow passageway and made the right angle turn to enter the tower conference room, Frank was reminded that those who had lived in this palace were not well-liked by the people they ruled, and their home-fortress might have to be defended at any moment.

The hotel staff had not had the chance to clean the room from the earlier meeting, and a cart containing liquor and another with some crackers, spreads, bread, and sliced meats along with chilled fruits and vegetables remained.

"I don't know about the rest of you, but I could use a drink," Ronald said. "Could I fix something for anyone?"

"I will have a Bourbon and Coke," Angelica said, "Not too strong though, that punch is still working on me."

A general series of assents came from the group except for Cecilia, who said that she would stick with the white wine.

The fact that, for the first time during the entire week, the American family and the two prospective brides had a chance to be together out from under the watchful eyes of Luigi or Donna Carlos was not lost on the group.

Ronald's pouring a round of drinks and Nancy's passing around a plate of sandwiches gave Ronald the feeling that this group of diverse individuals might have the possibility of becoming a family. It was almost as if they were having Holy Communion.

"Angelica and Cecilia, if this is to be, I would like to welcome you to our family. This wedding has come as quite a shock to Frank, Roger, and us all. Nancy and I think you are beautiful young ladies who would likely make wonderful wives for our sons if it were not for these Mob connections that we knew nothing about until we arrived a few days ago.

"There have been several attempts on our lives. Your dad-uncle Luigi has made us an offer, that in the terms of the old Godfather movie, 'that we cannot refuse.' This is not the best way to start a marriage, as I think Father Flanagan would agree. Still, before tonight, I got the feeling that things were happening between both of you and my sons. I would have preferred that everyone had more time to work this out, but this is the situation that we are in."

Uncharacteristically, Roger, rather than Frank, spoke next. He walked up to Angelica gently took both of her hands, looked her in the eyes, and said, "I was a participant in a terrible joke played on you, which I regret doing. For the record it was all an act. Nothing happened between us and Jock and Julia except that they were paid performers doing a sex scene like in a movie. I didn't know that we were being filmed or that it would be shown to everyone else. Mary gave us both a slap across the face for even considering such a thing. You can do the same. I deserve it."

Closing his eyes, Roger waited for the blow, but instead received a gentle kiss on the lips.

"Thank you," he said. "What we hoped was that you would talk your uncle into calling off the wedding, and we could all get out of here alive. This would sound funny if it were not so deadly. Someone out there is trying to kill us. There have been four attempts on our lives. Two men have been injured and are maybe dead. This is not the kind of life that Frank and I want to live, and neither of us can support you with fast cars, villas, and those kinds of things.

"It is not a matter of whether Frank and I love you or not. How the hell are we supposed to know, after only seeing you for four days and hardly speaking to you? I respect you, I feel for you, and, sorry mom, I would certainly make love to you in a heartbeat; but is this enough to last the rest of our lives? Are we going to be hiding from some mobster or other for things that we never did? Is this what our marriage is going to be like?

"I enjoyed painting with Luigi and helping him finish his Death of Archimedes. Without question, I respect his art, his skill, his management abilities, and what he has done. In any other circumstances, I would love to have the opportunity to work and exhibit with him. Hanging over everything is the thought that he might use that knife he carries to kill us all if this wedding doesn't go as planned. It doesn't look like there is any way we are going to get out of it, so I am willing to go through with it whatever happens. We will make the best of it for five years and after that, if we find we make each other miserable, then we will divorce and go our separate ways."

"Well said, Brother. That goes for me too," Frank said as he took Cecilia's hands. "I feel that I know you and what you have gone through. I have an overwhelming desire to protect you and keep you safe and help you get over Davide's death. I can never replace him in your heart and don't want to. I would be very pleased to be your husband and take you as my wife for so long as we have together in this world."

With these words Cecilia collapsed into Frank's arms and allowed him to give her the hug which he had wanted to do since their first meeting.

Seeing the outcome, Father Flanagan found himself pleased with the immediate results, but brought things back to reality when he asked, "I will be happy to do the ceremony in the church after morning mass. But the real problem is, how to keep you safe? I know that Luigi is going to hire guards and check everyone going into the wedding. No one will be allowed in unless they have an invitation.

"The danger to you is going to be on the road from Syracuse to Novo and from the Grand Hotel where the reception is to the villa. Ultimately, you will be together while we take you back for your flight back to the states. That is a longer trip, and you could be ambushed anywhere along the way."

"I may have some suggestions about that," Michael said. "I can't give you the details, but I feel confident that I can get you safely back to the States."

This unexpected statement brought a quizzical look from Ronald, who thought, "There is more to this driver than I thought. Otherwise how would he dare to promise such a thing?"

"Did you catch all of that?" Rob Williams asked agent Howard Smith.

"Yes I did. The Air Force base where I am staying is only a short distance from Syracuse. We can put them on a C-130 and fly them to Germany and, from there, they can drive or be flown elsewhere. Do you think that we can get Frank and Roger and their wives in a witness protection program for a few years?"

"Maybe, but they are not really witnesses, are they? Who would they testify against – their own father? And even if so, they have committed no crimes in the U.S."

"Still, didn't we give asylum to Stalin's daughter? I suspect that she was under protection for a few years."

"True, but if we are going to take them into protective custody we need to get things started. Renato will be back in a few minutes, and we can fill him in."

Luigi felt an unfamiliar bulge in his coat pocket. Reaching in to discover what it was, he extracted an envelope that someone had slipped into it. Scrawled on the front were the words, "Luigi open tonight."

Death has been dealt in many ways in Sicily, and he held the envelope up to the light to make sure there was no deadly powder concealed inside. Seeing only the outline of a single sheet of paper written in black ink, he went to a table and concealed from the others extracted his dagger and slit the envelope. To perhaps anyone else but Luigi, the contents would have been chilling, but to the cagy ex-enforcer, this was just an everyday piece of business.

Luigi,

Three contracts have been given. One is to conceal a bomb in a carton of Lucky Strike cigarettes that will be put on the Air France plane that is to fly the Americans back from Rome when it stops in Damascus. There will also be an attack on your cars when the Americans make their trip from Syracuse to Palermo.

That is what I know of. Someone else may try something in Syracuse or Novo.

We have been in many battles together and come out of them.
Good luck to you and yours,

Take care.

"Estavo has some contacts with Air France in Italy, and he can tip them off about the bomb," Luigi thought. "The road attacks will be much more difficult to defend against, and I am going to have to call in the Carabinieri to protect the public highway. I know the usual ambush points very well, and maybe they can keep them from setting up in them. It is that they might shoot at us from a farmhouse beside the road that worries me."

Chapter

30

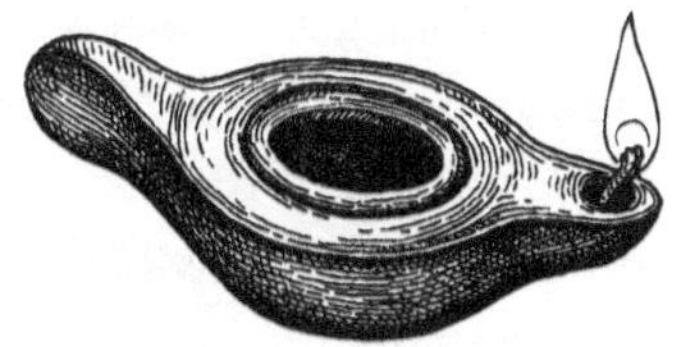

𝖂edding 𝕯ay

RONALD AND NANCY CALSASE again awoke to the sounds of a frenzied household getting ready for the unprecedented occasion where two women who had been raised as sisters were to be simultaneously married. Because of the involvement of so many relatives, friends, vendors, part of the protection force, and others who had been impacted by the Mafia during their lives, this event had almost risen to the same heights of celebration as Saint Lucia's day.

The cars and buses that were to take the wedding party to the City Hall and the church in Novo[46] were lined up inside the compound. Instead of the vehicles being all black, as might be the case for a funeral, the outrageously painted Fiat and Angelica's red Ferrari added splashes of color.

Angelica had insisted on driving the car herself, saying, "Everything else about this event has been planned by somebody else. If I am to participate, I am going to damn well drive myself to it. If anyone objects, they had better get out of the way."

This time even Luigi agreed because it was far easier to give in to his strong-willed niece on this point, than have to fight with her over every other detail of the complex events that were about to unfold.

---

[46]   My fictional town of Novo is a composite taken from several Italian towns in eastern Sicily including the very real Noto and Savoca which is the location of the church used for the wedding in The Godfather movie which is called the Church San Nicolo/San Lucia.

While most of the attention was paid to Angelica and Cecilia, Frank and Roger were being fussed over by Mario, who had accepted the role of making sure that his two cousins were properly prepared to the point of having their handkerchiefs properly peaked in their jackets and the two .380 Walther pistols stored in their inside pockets.

Mary gave her two brothers a final inspection before breakfast and remarked, "For two yard birds from Louisiana, you look passable." In fact, they had a look of restrained resplendence which, while lacking the frills, laces, and ornate collars of the nobility from the Spanish Baroque, they cut handsome figures fit for a ballroom.

Luigi was also being prepared for the events. As befitting the acting head of the family, his outfit included a dark suit with shoes that had a mirror polish, a cummerbund made of ballistic cloth, a sash across his white shirt with the red and gold colors of Sicily, held on the shirt by an enameled pin of the flag, and his jacket had also been lined with the same bullet-resistant Kevlar fabric.

After telling her brothers that they were to stay clean, Mary recalled that her mother had an expression she used when she was getting the children ready for church, as she dressed one and then the other. "If you don't stay clean, I am going to hang you on hooks on the wall until I get you all dressed." She never did, but the thought of her actually doing it was sufficient to bring compliance, as the boys were forced to nervously sit together on a sofa until everyone was ready to go.

Covering their finery with bathrobes, Frank and Roger went to the breakfast room to eat, before what was to be the start of a very long day. "Eat up Brother," Frank remarked. "This is like going into combat. You never know when you might have a chance to eat again. However this turns out, this is going to be a very busy day."

Even though the room where the women were being dressed was across the quadrangle, the shrill sound of women's voices could be heard reverberating across the courtyard. "I wonder how Cecilia is taking this? She does not strike me as the type who likes being fussed over."

"I know. I got that sort of impression too. I suspect that Angelica, on the other hand, is eating it up. They are two quite different women. Do you suppose that we got the right ones? You know that pickled onion made the choice for us."

"I think so. I guess so. I hope so. I feel close to Cecilia, and you are going to have a handful with Angelica. Who knows, maybe we should do a foursome some time?" Frank joked.

"That's fine with me," Roger retorted, "but I think our Sicilian gals and their families are a bit straitlaced for that. Although they trade in all kinds of sin and vice, they are a conservative bunch among themselves. Cecilia, for one, would never agree."

Across the courtyard, Nancy was having a discussion with Donna Carlos about American wedding customs. "We need to have the brides have something old, something new, something borrowed, and something blue for luck."

"If anything will bring these pairs luck, then by all means. I think that Luigi may still have something that belonged to Cecilia's mother. We can loan them the pearls we are wearing and for blue what about matching garters? I will call and have them delivered to the church."

"That can work," Nancy agreed.

When the pair approached Angelica and Cecilia about the last-minute additions to their wedding outfits, they were putting on slips of Kelvar ballistic cloth while Mary was helping them adjust the straps of the heavy garments.

"These are heavy and they are hot," Angelica said.

"Who knows what might happen today," Mary responded, in an uncharacteristically solemn tone. "You may be in real danger, and these will help keep you safe."

Coming from anyone else, Angelica would have rejected this suggestion out of hand, but the earnest words and concerned look from her future sister-in-law were persuasive.

"I agree. Thank you." Angelica said as she gave Mary a gentle kiss on the cheek.

On receiving the warning letter the night before, Luigi had called a contact that he had with the local Carabinieri warning of the impending attacks on his family. This information was relayed to the AIA in Milan and to Chief Detective Roscotti, who was already in Syracuse.

In a cryptic telephone call Roscotti told Luigi, "I would like to wish you and your Americans the best of luck with the wedding tomorrow. Take an umbrella, I hear that it might rain. It looks like the weather will be fine for your relatives to fly out tomorrow. My friends in America were concerned. Their tickets will be at the airport. I look forward to meeting everyone at the reception."

Roscotti had communicated with Agents William and Smith, who were in Renato's room at the Nautilus. Renato was, in turn, to let Michael and Vito know of the extraction of the Americans on a C-130 from the American Air Force base the following day. Michael and Vito were also told to prepare to leave to start their rotating assignment with the FBI in the States.

"This was going to be just like in the war when the Americans and Mafia were working together to drive the Germans out of Sicily," Luigi thought. "Circumstances make for strange bedfellows. Whoever would have thought that I would have the AIA and the American Air Force protecting me?"

Traffic going into the city was already starting to build up when the marriage party left for City Hall. Since only the immediate family members were going to attend the civil ceremony, the bus with the guests would not leave for the church in Novo for another half-hour.

Vito's Mercedes, with a load of bodyguards, went first. They were to park and guard the cars. The area in front of the municipal building and the halls inside were protected by the city police, while the Carabinieri looked out for suspicious activities on the roof tops and waterfront. Of all the assignments, the large expanse of waterfront docking for pleasure and fishing boats was more difficult to patrol. Still, to the practiced eye, the groups of boats that were nearly always parked in the same areas were well known, and a strange craft seeking a berth was reasonably easy to spot. This was particularly true when their docking appeared to take one of the valued mooring places which was like stealing a parking spot at an apartment building. Italians do not argue quietly, and any sort of disturbance was a cause for investigation as was any unloading of sealed boxes by those who were inappropriately dressed for life on the waterfront.

Side streets leading to the City Hall were temporarily blocked as the four-car motorcade proceeded into town. Following the leading Mercedes that Vito was driving was Angelica's Ferrari with her and Mary, the Fiat now driven by Roger also carried Frank, and then another Mercedes with Ronald, Nancy, William, and Cecilia.

"Michael said that he and Vito had brought this car up to the standards of a rally racer, and I believe him," Roger said. "It is very tight, responsive, and feels like it wants to run. I would like to take it out on the road and see what it can do."

"If we have to get out of here in a hurry, you may have to," Frank responded as he heard the sound of a helicopter flying overhead. Looking up, he saw that it had police markings. "It looks like police are shadowing us, I hope that is a good sign. Few are likely to attack us if they think that they are going to be instantly spotted."

The group of vehicles picked up speed as they approached the bridge that was to take them to the town square near the center of the island.

"So far, so good," Luigi said to Ronald as they approached the Archimedes bridge. But unsaid was his thought that a bomb might have been planted days before somewhere along the road, to be detonated at any time by remote control. This was not a comforting thought, but he kept it to himself. He knew that if he was going to attempt to make a hit under similar circumstances, an innocent-appearing act like flipping a light switch in a nearby house would be sufficient to initiate an explosion that could take out a car or even a tank. This was an act that, decades ago, he had done himself near this very spot, in front of a checkpoint that the Nazis had set up at the bridge. "What an ironic way that would be to have one's life end?" he mused.

Four more blocks they were at the *Plazza Centrale*. The entrance barriers had been removed, and the four cars were pulled up in front of the City Hall.

Ushered up the steps and into the building, the two couples found themselves facing a desk behind which sat a man in his fifties wearing a crumpled and soiled grey suit with two stacks of papers that appeared to have been already filled out.

Shoving a stack before each of the two couples, the man behind the desk handed them pens and motioned for them to sign.

Once they did, he said in Italian, "You are married." He then waved both hands in a brushing-away motion as if he were shooing flies that was accompanied by a rapid burst of Italian which indicated that they should leave immediately.

Frank said to Luigi, "Isn't he supposed to say some words or something?"

"He said that he and the rest of the town were in danger by us just being here and to 'get the hell out as fast as the Devil can carry us.' I am sorry that this was not a more pleasant experience, but you are nonetheless married."

"That was something of a bummer," Roger remarked to his brother, as they drove across the square to leave for Novo. "We did not even get to kiss our brides."

"I guess that that comes later, at least I hope so." Frank replied. "Those Mafia bastards would like nothing better than to kill us now, before our wedding night. They delight in that sort of irony. Stay sharp. You may have to get us out of here in a hurry."

Leaving the island of Ortygia, they did not return the way they came but went north to highway A-12 which would take them part of the way to Novo along a high-speed four-lane highway. No one thought that anyone would plan an attack on the heavily trafficked highway, but the danger would come on the narrow two-lane road that would take them to Novo which constituted half of the trip.

"The car runs well, I am not having any trouble keeping up with that big hog of a Mercedes, but could never catch Angelica in that Ferrari," Roger said. "Wow Frank. This marriage thing is going to take some getting accustomed to. I should have said 'my wife in her Ferrari.' How long did it take you to get used to the concept that you were really married?"

"It is awkward at first, but these things sort of come in time, maybe a month or two, before you really feel that the marriage has sort of took, and you both start feeling really married."

The closer they got to their destination, the more rustic the countryside became. The road seemed to be a little wider than it was in Roman times with stone walls being used to border the fields lining both sides of it. Scattered throughout the countryside were abandoned and sometimes ruined stone farmhouses where families had given up their rural lives to seek better-paying jobs in Syracuse, Catania, and other parts of Italy. The few farms that appeared to still be operational were worked by the old and young, with maybe some younger relatives coming to help out on weekends and during harvest season. Many had been so frequently subdivided the small plots became increasingly unprofitable to operate and were sold to corporate interests who cleared the walls for orchards, vineyards, and, where possible, fields.

"I am not worried about those isolated buildings hundreds of yards away. What worries me are those that are close to the road," Frank said. "That is where the locals really loved to ambush us in Iraq. This was especially true if they could gain some elevation advantage and shoot down on us."

Almost as if he were prophetic, a rifle bullet tore through the roof of the Fiat, missed Roger's head by an inch and exited through the glass window.

"Put your head down and drive." Frank ordered.

Roger did as he was bid, and he hit the accelerator to give the sniper as fleeting a target as possible. The second shot blasted through the side of the car and would have hit any back-seat passengers.

A rip of machine-gun fire erupted from above as their escorting helicopter laid down a barrage of fire into the farmhouse. The entire convoy sped on. Fortunately none of the vital components of the Fiat had been hit, although the painted flowers on the top now looked as if they had a bee sitting on them and one of the figures on the painted door had a head ventilation problem.

"Welcome to combat, Brother. Do you feel all right?"

"My heart is racing, I'm trying to catch my breath, and I guess the impact of what has happened is just seeping into my system."

"You are doing fine. Concentrate on your driving. When we get to a place where the convoy can safely stop, we can switch over, and I'll drive. Right now just drive. The more you think about it, the harder this experience will hit you. There is a clear area ahead. We can pull off there."

"We can't stay here, but for a moment, is anyone hurt?" Luigi asked.

"Roger is okay, just a little shook up," Frank replied. "The car took two hits, but nothing vital. I'll drive us in," Frank said as he got out of the car as Roger moved over to let his bother in.

Angelica and Cecilia, in their wedding dresses, approached the little Fiat with a sense of dread, that one or both of their new husbands might be dead or injured.

"The bullet just missed me," Roger said. "I have heard of shotgun weddings, but this is getting a little extreme. I didn't expect to be married to the tune of sniper fire and gunships – maybe there is a country song in there somewhere. We are sitting ducks standing here. We need to get gone."

Now that everyone was seen to be all right, there was no argument. Luigi explained the events to Ronald, Nancy, and the rest of the family as the cars resumed their journey to Novo.

The sky had cleared. They drove through green fields set in rolling hills with red-tile-roofed stone houses dotting the countryside. There were a few pencil-shaped Cedars of Lebanon punctuating the landscape, along with the Mediterranean cypress interspersed among the groves of olive, citrus, and pistachio trees. Except for the immediate circumstances of being shot at, this would have been an idyllic day in a beautiful setting that to Roger cried out to be painted.

The scene and events brought something of a revelation to Nancy, who thought to herself, but did not dare express to Luigi. "This is a bloody island. Everywhere we go, there has been murder, killing, slaughter, and death on an unprecedented scale for thousands of years. We are all cannibals. We walk on their bones. Every bite of food we eat contains the very elements that made up their bodies and now fertilize the soil. We breathe in their bodies with the dust we inhale. Now, like it or not, we are part of them, and they are part of us. Looking at Luigi across the way, she sent a mental message. "I understand. Now, finally, I understand how you feel. You could be none other than who you are. This land, this island of blood and death, has made you so."

Luigi, feeling Nancy's eyes on him returned the look and smiled, as if to say, "Message received. Thank you."

Bypassing Catania and approaching the ancient town of Novo, the topography changed to a craggy landscape dotted with steep hills formed by old volcanic necks associated with the enormous and very ancient volcanic center of Mt. Etna.

The Romans knew the world of volcanoes, and they gave this type of mountain its name from the Island of Volcano, named for Vulcan, the Roman God of Fire. Mt Etna was treated with great respect. It belonged to a time even before the Gods, and if they had a sense of forever, this enormous mountain and its many sister vents, which were now represented by vertical pillars of stone weathering out of the softer ash, carried the concept of times that were unimaginably long ago. It was on top of one of these pillars that Novo was located.

The town could only be accessed by a narrow road with many turns, which could be defended by relatively few men. Its weakness lay in the fact that it could also be surrounded by large forces that could starve the population out. Although it could capture water in cisterns, little food could be grown on the craggy outcrop, which had sprouted homes, shops, and churches.

Novo's height and difficult approaches provided security, while its access to the sea and the naturally enriched volcanic soils of the lower slopes of Mt. Etna provided the most consistently fertile area of the island. Believed to contain the Forge of Hephaestus by the Greeks, the mountain's slow-flowing basaltic lava had overwhelmed anything that it encountered. The intercession of saints and other holy figures had been often solicited to stop flows approaching towns but had only modest successes. Flows even reached Catania and filled the moat of the Norman fortress in 1669, and that flow was only blocked by the thick stone walls of the structure.

The church where they were to be married was located up a narrow street. The bus carrying the wedding guests had already discharged its passengers in front of the church door and parked in a pull-off area of the roadway five-hundred feet below the town. As the caravan from Syracuse approached, everyone got out of their cars, and the drivers took their cars to the same area. In Angelica's case, one of Luigi's guards took her car to the parking area.

Luigi came down the stone steps to meet her. He helped her balance in her high heels and wedding dress as she climbed the stairs to the portico for the church. Cecilia and the rest of the family had already been hustled inside.

31

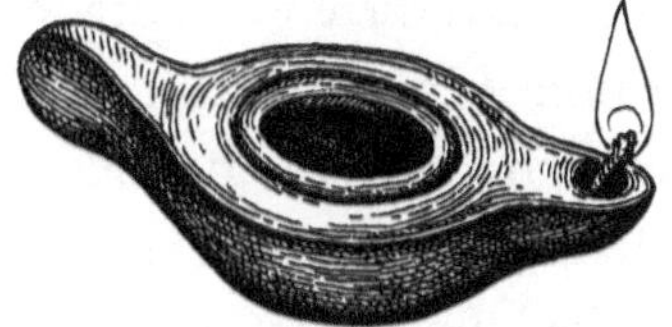

Holy Matrimony

THE SAVOCA CHURCH WAS a scaled-down version of the fancy basilicas that the Americans had seen on their tour. This church was dedicated to Saint Lucia, and contained a stone sarcophagus made of a white and red marble breccia containing the Saint's remains. Among other holy figures represented on the walls of the church were statues of Saint Michael, Saint Vincent Ferrier, and Saint Anthony the Abbot with a staff leading a pig.

This church served the needs of those whose lives revolved around generations-old patterns of traditional living. They felt honored to make or donate embellishments for their church, just as they would to have their children freshly scrubbed and in clean clothes for mass.

Recent renovations included installing modern steel and wooden pews and alterations to the central altar, which was now flanked by carved, twisted marble columns. Instead of a cross behind the altar, there was a framed painting of Christ in glory receiving the eyes of Saint Lucia on a silver platter in his right hand, and a white branch in his left representing the spirit of the departed Saint. Each year a festival honoring the Saint is held where she drives out a figure representing the Devil, and her martyrdom is reenacted including the gouging out of her eyes by Roman soldiers and having her body torn apart by oxen.

Square columns of white marble supported the roof of the structure, which matched the color of the brides' wedding dresses. As befitting clothing that had to be worn all day and Cecilia's inclination for a more modest style of dress, they did not feature the open backs and prominent display of the breast chosen by some of their contemporaries. They had slightly flared skirts that were not quite down to the floor, a detachable train which flowed behind, and on their tall hairdos there was a drape of white silk, secured in front by a rhinestone-festooned comb which framed their faces.

The nave beside the high altar did not contain holy relics, but rather photos from The Godfather movie, which used the same church to represent one that might be found in an isolated rural town. This church was one of the few that were available to Donna Carlos when she was arranging the wedding and had the additional advantages that it would be a place that the Americans might have some affinity after having seen it in the movie.

A last-minute delivery was made to the door. When Donna Carlos opened the box, she found the two blue garters that she had ordered. Angelica and Cecilia were seated on the left-hand side of the church and put them on. On the other side of the holy water containing basin, the grooms were likewise being readied with fresh white carnations prior to their trip to the altar.

"What do we say?" Roger asked worriedly. "We have not had any rehearsals."

"Don't worry," William replied as he finished pinning the flower on Roger's lapel. "There are two priests. One will do the wedding in Italian, and Father Flanagan will repeat it in English. He will just ask you some questions, and you reply."

"Do you have the rings?" Frank asked.

William replied, "The altar boy, who is one of your young cousins, has them. He will give them to you on a velvet pillow when the time comes. They go on the second finger of the left hand. If it does not fit, just exchange it with your brother. Don't force it on. Don't drop it on the floor and have it roll all over the church."

"I have butterflies in my stomach, I don't know which is worse — getting married or getting shot at. Right now, I am thinking that this marriage business is worst."

Suddenly, a female figure dressed in black broke out of the group of women, and purposefully ran towards the men on the opposite side of the church.

Brushing hard against the edge of the stone basin that contained the holy water, she staggered slightly and ran towards Luigi, who turned to meet the attack.

"You Mafia bums, you killed my Davide," she shouted as she pulled a knife from her sleeve, and instead of attempting to stab with an over-hand thrust, drove its point towards Luigi's stomach with all of her body weight behind the thrust. Luigi staggered under the onslaught.

Flora Francaviglia was thrown backwards half a step and was about to deliver another thrust when her wrist was grabbed by Rodrigo, and the knife clattered noisily to the stone floor.

Luigi examined himself to make sure he was not injured by the unexpected attack, and after he was helped on his feet responded to his attacker.

"Mrs. Francaviglia, I assure you that I had nothing to do with Davide's death," Luigi said. "I loved him too. I would have been proud if he had married Cecilia, as they had planned. Now it is time to let these two fine young people get on with their lives.

"Rodrigo, you and Paolo take her home and assure her that nothing is going to happen to her over this. I truly understand and appreciate what she is going through and can assign no blame to her."

Saying, "I bleed for Davide too," he picked the knife from the floor and cut himself across the right cheekbone. He then leaned forward to catch the blood on a handkerchief, which he pressed to his face to staunch the flow.

The details of this disruption of the ceremony were not fully observed by Father Flanagan and Father James from the front of the crowded church. After he saw that three people were leaving the church, he assumed that whatever had transpired was under control, and signaled for the organist to start the processional. The music indicated that the families and the couples should start their walk with the ushers between the closely packed attendees, towards the open pews at the front of the church.

This closeness bothered Frank because he knew that almost every man in the room was probably carrying a weapon, and it would be very easy for someone to shoot them at very close range as they walked by. Those several layers of ballistic cloth had protected Luigi, and he hoped that it would not be necessary for him to find out if his jacket would stop a bullet.

Now it was his turn to be walked to the altar, and Mario was the usher that would guide him, but Luigi was still cleaning up, and a Band-Aid smeared with a cream from Donna Carlos's handbag, was being attached to his face. He would have to wait a bit.

Cecilia came next, then Roger, Angelica, and Frank. The painting of Saint Lucia loomed larger in front of them, and the symbolism of being married before the depiction of a martyred virgin Saint was not lost on her. "I wonder if that is a suggestion as to how we are going to wind up dead with our eyes plucked out. Not a particularly pleasant thought for my wedding day," she thought.

She concentrated on placing her feet and heels carefully so as not to catch her shoes on the helms of this unfamiliar long garment. She knew that she would have to kneel at the altar and was happy that her skirt was large enough to allow her to do that, although getting up would be a little more problematic.

Witnessing the assault on her father from Davide's mother, Cecilia felt tears running down her cheeks as she began her travels towards a marriage to a man she hardly new. This should have been her and Davide's day – a person, that she had fantasized with about being together for the rest of their lives.

Michael who was acting as her usher, whispered, as if he were Davide himself, "Be strong. It will be all right," and he gave her arm a reassuring squeeze.

"I don't know if I can say the words," Cecilia replied.

"You will. You are Sicilian, you will get through this," Michael replied.

Without hardly seeing or realizing it, Cecilia found herself kneeling before the two priests, with Frank beside her.

While some marriages that the prospective brides had seen on American movies allowed the couples to compose their own vows, such deviations were not allowed in the Catholic Church. Marriage was to be done by the book, whether it was being conducted in Sicily or Seattle.

To make sure that no detail was omitted, Flanagan held a red-bound *Roman Ritual* in his hands from which he would read the ceremony, which contained distinct segments depending on whether it was part of a Mass or held at some other time, as was the case here. Several times during the ceremony, the brides and grooms would be asked questions, to which they must deliver appropriate replies. No one in that church had ever seen a bride or groom refuse when they were before the priest, but this was an unusual wedding under unusual circumstances. Both sets of brides and grooms had to agree to be married, or there would be serious repercussions.

The organ was a treadle-pumped version from the late 19th century, and had a wheezy, breathy sound as if the young organist who was doing hard physical labor while playing, as he was. He pumped out the music for Psalm 127, which was being sung in Italian by an octet of singers. Their rendition of the song evoked memories for Nancy, who knew sufficient Italian to pick out the stanza, "Your wife shall be a fruitful vine enriching your abode." She also caught enough of it to realize also catch the references to children flourishing like olive trees bearing fruit.

Ronald, who had less of a musical ear than his wife, could read Italian reasonably well, but had considerably more trouble picking out the words, particularly as they were being sung rather than spoken. The first part of the ceremony struck him as especially appropriate, as each bride and groom were asked in both Italian and English if this marriage was done freely and that they were not being coerced into the union. Cecilia, who had seen and participated in more weddings than anyone else, knew this question was coming, but it caught the prospective grooms flatfooted.

"In fact, the wedding was being forced on them in the most aggressive manner," Frank thought. "But what in blazes can I do about it now?" Frank stumbled through his answer, and the word that finally emerged was a group of sounds that said "No," but more nearly resembled the noise a person would make as if he was punched in the stomach.

Cecilia also had trouble with the question, and softly replied "No. Before God," she thought. "I have said what I know not to be true, but it is the best for all of us. God have mercy on us all."

Being somewhat forewarned, Roger and Angelica had time to mentally process the fact act that they were already married at City Hall an hour ago, and replied in a more deliberate manner that this union was of their own free will.

Having the ceremony done in two languages delayed the proceedings, and now that his bleeding had stopped, Luigi walked down to the altar and stood behind the kneeling couples. Even if the knife had been sticking out of his back, he was not going to miss this wedding.

In light of recent events, it was difficult for the two couples to keep their minds on what the priests were saying. Their portentous words faded into a background drone while they mentally prepared for the next phase of the ceremony where they must again give a response.

"I've got this man, and it is too late now to do anything but make the best of it," Angelica thought, as she cast a glance in his direction. He responded with a nervous glance. "Hell. He is as nervous about it as I am. I guess being nearly killed on your wedding day will do that a fellow."

On and on the ceremony seemed to go, as the couples' knees were starting to pain from being in that position so long despite the padding on the kneeling rail.

The critical question from Father Flanagan finally came. "Do you Frank take Cecilia, here present, for your lawful wife according to the rite of our Holy Mother, the Church?"

"I do," Frank replied.

"Do you Cecilia take Frank, here present, for your lawful husband according to the rite of our Holy Mother, the Church?"

Under the watchful eye of the two priests and the invited guests in the small church and with Christ in Glory and the disembodied eyes of Saint Lucia looking down on her, she replied, "I do."

The identical questions were asked to Roger and Angelica and they likewise replied that they would accept each other as husband and wife.

To confirm what they had just said, Flanagan asked that the couples join their right hands and now repeated the familiar phrases that they had expected from the outset. The grasping hands gave the couples a sense of joint purpose, and they looked each other in the eyes. For the first time since they arrived at the church, they smiled at each other as they exchanged honest looks of happiness. The feeling that "this might honestly work," swept over them. It did not feel so strange when Frank said to Cecilia and Roger said to Angelica:

I take you for my lawful wife, to have and to hold, from this day forward, for better, for worse, for richer, for poorer, in sickness and in health until death do us part.

Cecilia responded that she would accept Frank as her husband, and after Roger and Angelica had exchanged vows it was time to move to the next segment of the ceremony, which involved the blessing and exchange of rings.

This was the part of the ceremony that bothered Roger the most. With two couples, there were four sets of rings, all of which were different sizes.

Then the grooms and brides had to repeat:

In the name of the Father, and of the Son, and of the Holy Spirit. Take and wear this ring as a sign of our marriage vows.

When the time came the ring bearer presented the rings on the cushion to Frank, who selected the smaller one on the right-hand side and slipped it onto Cecilia's finger.

"Wow. It fit," Frank thought.

Cecilia, in turn, put the ring on Frank's finger as she repeated the blessing.

Relieved that this exchange would work out, Roger selected the smallest remaining ring and placed it on Angelica's finger. As she reciprocated, Angelica gave it a twist as she slipped it over Roger's knuckle as if to say, "Now stay there."

Four rings had been exchanged and four blessings rendered by the two couples, and the end of the marriage ceremony was in sight.

Following a reading and response evoking the Lord's blessings on the new couples, Flanagan read a passage wishing the couples a long life, salvation, and at the end of life entry into Heaven. Then, he administered the Eucharistic Liturgy, and the new couples shared their first Holy Communion to solidify their oneness in love.

The marriage concluded with the Prayer of the Faithful, after which the brides and grooms were helped to their feet and stood on unsteady legs for a few moments to regain their balance while pictures were being taken and congratulations given.

To their surprise at the front of the church, they were showered with pear blossoms, rice, and small coins, which, as Cecilia later told Roger and Frank, represented fruitfulness, happiness, and wealth. They were preceded by a brass band. Police were stationed alongside the road and watched the crowd very carefully, looking for anyone or anything suspicious.

At the parking area, a spread of tables had been put out, containing food and wine for the wedding guests and townspeople. But the brides and grooms quickly got into their cars and proceeded back to Luigi's villa, where they would change before the reception at the Grand Hotel that night. For the return trip, Luigi wanted to split up the convoy, in hopes of making them a more dispersed target.

This time the couples paired off with Angelica and Roger riding in her Ferrari and Frank and Cecilia, riding in the Fiat. "I've raced on these roads, and I know them," Angelica said. "We four will go back in the Ferrari and Fiat and get back to the villa long before you arrive." Michael, with his .45, was in the Fiat's back seat to provide a degree of protection.

Playing something of a shell game, the couples milled about among the vehicles before Angelica and Roger started off in the Ferrari, selecting some narrow streets that were too constricted for the larger Mercedes to follow.

"Can Frank drive?" Angelica asked.

"Yes, but the little Fiat doesn't have the horsepower to keep up with you."

"The way we are going favors small agile cars over fast ones, I am going to take you back through olive groves in the hills," Angelica responded.

The departure of the two colorfully painted cars was noted by four men in a black Mercedes sedan. This car was not as large as the limousine versions that Michael and Vito had been driving. It was as wide, although not as long. This was a car that could cruise at one-hundred miles-per-hour on the Autobahn.

Alexie took his flip phone and punched in the number of Apachee's hotel room while they got the car underway.

"They're leaving the church in a Ferrari and a Fiat."

"Go get them sons of bitches. I want them dead before they sleep. Kill them all."

Roger had the premonition that this drive back to Syracuse might turn out to be more like the movie scenes where a stagecoach was being chased by a bunch of bandits on horseback that he remembered from his childhood. Even the country looked the same. The only thing about it was all he was armed with was a Walther .380 popgun.

"If we get into trouble, all I've got is this little pistol."

"Luigi gave us more than that, Angelica said, look in that case in the back."

When he opened the violin case, he found what he and Frank grew up calling Tommy Guns, except this version of the Thompson submachine gun was loaded with military box magazines instead of the drum magazines so often depicted in the movies.[47]

"Do you know how to shoot this?" Roger asked his new bride.

"Sure, doesn't everybody?," Angelica answered.

"No. I can't say that everybody does. This is not a conversation that most married couples have on their wedding day."

"We will get around to those kinds of things later. Put a magazine in, and lay it back in its case. I don't want you shooting up the car."

Roger was immediately impressed by the weight of the gun. It would be very difficult to shoot from any position except with him hanging halfway out of the window or straight out the side in which case the hot empties would be bouncing around all over the cab. The only other option would be to shoot straight out of the front or rear windows. His only really practical way to effectively use the gun would be to get out of the vehicle and shoot from the ground.

"I can't shoot this thing from the car. It's just too big."

"I know" Angelica said. "If we are followed, I am going to put you out and then you can shoot at the other car as it drives by. Trust me."

Michael, looking out of the rear window of the Fiat, saw the black Mercedes on the road behind them. The thought "Friend or foe?" came through his mind. This was definitively settled when a shot from the vehicle hit the Fiat's roof, adding another bee to the bouquet of flowers.

"Don't you dare shoot up my car," Michael said as he leaned out of the window to attempt to get a clear shot at the vehicle. Remembering what Alberto told him, he knew that he had to select his shots very carefully. With the car bumping up and down on the road, and swerving around the curves it was very difficult to line up the sights on the Colt 1911 to hit the

---

[47]　The Thompson submachine gun was used more commonly by allied troops with a long box magazine rather than the much slower to load and bulkier drum magazines.

middle of the radiator where he was aiming. Loss of coolant would generate steam to obscure the driver's vision and ultimately stop the vehicle.

Finally he felt that he had a reasonable shot, and fired. The bullet plugged both the radiator for the air conditioning and the main unit, throwing water on top of the hot engine block, releasing a billowing cloud of steam. The Mercedes momentarily slowed as the driver poked his head out of the window and continued his pursuit.

Expertly working the gears, Angelica rounded three switchbacks going up the side of a ridge which was planted with olive trees on both sides. To aid in harvesting the crops, the orchard was cut by a steep path which went down the slope of the ridge to enable carts to be positioned in convenient places to gather piles of olives at the ends of the rows.

"Hold on," Angelica said as she stopped the car then turned off the road through the olive trees. Branches whipped against the side of the car as it bumped over rocks on its way down. On a lower row of trees a workman, seeing the approaching car, pulled the donkey and its cart off the path just in time to let the bouncing vehicle complete its descent.

"We are getting to your ambush point. Get the gun and jump out when I stop."

Angelica slammed on the brakes. Roger felt his back rebound against the console. Catching his breath for a second, he opened the door and dismounted. Angelica then eased the now dusty and scratched Ferrari back onto the roadway.

Seeing Angelica's rapid departure off the road, Frank did not know if he dared do the same. The Fiat did not have the weight or footprint of the larger car and less ground clearance. If the drop became too precipitous, there was a chance that the car could go end-over-end and roll down the hill like a bowling ball.

"Hang on, everybody. Here goes," Frank shouted as he turned the Fiat onto the cart track. Coming up, Frank could see a pointed rock sticking up in the middle of the cart track. Gunning the car he purposely hit two smaller rocks with his front wheels, which gave the car a little lift with the effect that it bounced on its springs, became airborne for a second, and then crashed down with the skid plate catching the impact. As sparks flew the car slid forward off of the rock with the front driving wheels clawing at the rocky soil.

Frank spotted Roger too late and missed his turn back onto the road. The Fiat took a bounce off the road and started down another section of the cart track. Now slowing, Frank stopped before he reached the next level of the switchbacks only to discover that he was hung up.

"I will give you a push," Michael said as he got out of the rear seat. He grabbed a nearby piece of fencepost, put it under the rear bumper and, using the post, eased the car sufficiently far forward that the front wheels could gain traction. With dust and rocks flying, the car wormed its way back onto the road. Once again pointed downhill and on more solid ground, Michael gave the tires a quick look and told Frank, "Everything looks fine. Let's get out of here."

Angelica had briefly stopped to let the Fiat catch up and was relieved to see it pull up beside her. I was afraid that I was going to have to come back and get you," she called out.

"What's Roger going to do?" Frank asked.

"He is going to try to ambush that car with a machine gun."

"My little brother is going to do what?"

As if to answer, they heard a rip of submachine gun fire and the sound of a car going off the road and exploding. They could see the flames billowing up between the trees.

Taking the Fiat, Frank went back up the road to pick up his brother. He found him with the Thompson hanging limply in his hands watching the burning car below. Screams were coming from the car. Frank took the gun from Roger, slapped in another magazine, pointed it towards the car, and gave it a burst of bullets. The screams stopped.

"That is a terrible way to go," Frank said. "But they were trying to kill us. What else were we supposed to do?"

Roger, shaken, allowed Frank to put him in the car and drive him down to his bride who was waiting below. The only words Frank heard above the sound of the engine and the noise of the tires on the gravel road was, "Let's just go home."

"Whoever it was who was after them. They certainly get full marks for persistence." Frank told Cecilia as they resumed their trip. "Poor Roger is catching hell. He has never been in combat, and now, he is in the midst of it. This is one hell of a way to have a wedding."

"It will be better, I promise you," Cecilia replied consolingly.

Despite their interruptions on their trip back to the villa, they arrived before the remainder of the wedding party had returned.

Luigi, seeing the condition of the Fiat, ordered that new glass be installed that afternoon. Michael and Vito patched the holes in the roof, and Roger helped them match the paint. Getting out of his stained clothes and doing something with his hands allowed him a much-needed opportunity to unwind. Their adventures on the trip back to the villa were the last thing that he wanted to discuss with his parents. The less anyone knew about that, the better. After all, the big reception was tonight, and he would have to play the part of the happy bridegroom for Angelica's sake, if for no others.

Chapter

32

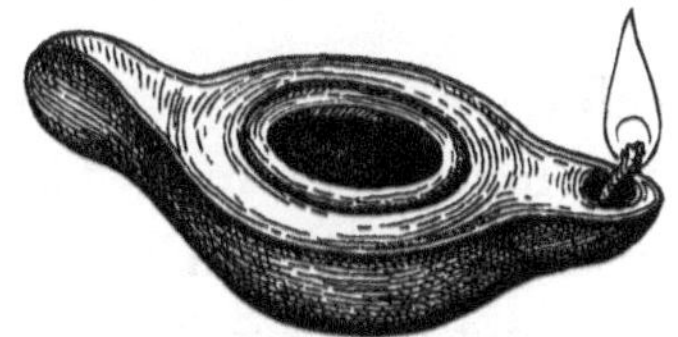

The Reception

AS ESTAVO PRESENTED A card to Luigi, he said, "I have a Signore Roscotti from Milan to see you."

"Show him into the drawing room. I will be there in a minute."

Roscotti, the former soccer player who had the erect statue of a field commander, had never imagined that he would be in the home of one of Sicily's major Mafia figures as anything other than an arresting officer. He had been put in an untenable situation of using state resources to protect members of a criminal organization, and he must find a way to deliver something in return.

He knew Luigi's reputation as a feared enforcer who had undoubtedly killed people in his long career, but felt that he knew nothing of the man himself or how to deal with him. Instead, he found himself in the midst of a household going through the turmoil of a Sicilian wedding. Except for the guards on the gate and two men who were patching up bullet holes in a colorfully painted Fiat, this could be a scene from any well-to-do family going through their wedding day trials and traumas – albeit a bit more serious than most.

Approaching the large painting that dominated the room, he walked to the front of it and saw that it represented a scene that he quickly identified as The Death of Archimedes, even though no nameplate had been attached. He saw the kneeling figure on the sand table holding his guts, and thought, "How appropriate for a painting by a Mafia enforcer."

It is full of terror, death, fire, and destruction. It struck him as a painting that could have only been done by someone who had experienced such events in real life.

"I was admiring your painting," Roscotti said as Luigi entered the room.

"I just finished it with the help of my new American nephew-in-law who is also an artist. I plan to present it to the City of Syracuse."

"It is an impressive piece of work, but I am here to tell you about our plans to get the Americans out of Sicily. There are C-130 cargo planes flying from the American Base at Sigonella every day. Those who have been trying to kill them may make an attempt somewhere on the road to Palermo, and having them fly from and to military bases will allow them to land secretly in Europe and the U.S. The FBI has arranged that the couples are to go in the U.S.'s Witness Protection Program to start new lives in America."

"Have you discovered who is trying to kill them?" Luigi asked.

"Not exactly, but everyone who we have picked up and the vehicles are from the Naples area. It appears that someone with Mafia connections there is responsible."

"You know that Sicily was once ruled from Naples, and the family there is apparently trying to do something of the same thing now that you have arrested Don Carlos and his Segundo. Some of them are even staying in this villa.

"It is obvious that you are expecting me to deliver something in return. What do you want?"

"The family in Naples is getting more violent, as you have seen. I want evidence and witnesses so that we can bring them to justice. I also want to shut down the drug traffic in Sicily and southern Italy."

"I can give you information about the Neapolitans and the drug trafficking, but be careful about what you wish for. The Mafia families in Sicily have kept rivals from Russia, South American, and Asia from moving in. People want this stuff, and if we do not supply it, there are others who will."

"Nonetheless, I have to produce something significant for all this expenditure of people, time, and money."

"You realize that this is likely to get me killed."

"Yes, but isn't that what you expect to happen anyway? I hear someone tried to stab you at the wedding – a local woman. This was not the first time. Someone, someday, is likely to kill you. I'm sorry Luigi, but that is the life that you have chosen."

"I don't know if it was so much chosen as it was the life that circumstances and some accidental events forced me to live. I agree to your terms. I want you to help me get my daughter and niece out of Sicily. "

"Very well. Tomorrow morning we will have a C-130 on the runway at Sigonella. An escort will be waiting to bring them on the base. The cars with the brides and grooms will be driven on board the plane, flown to Germany, and then to England and the U.S. The couples will be given new identities, and the vehicles will be given new serial numbers and plates.

"Bodies are going to be put in one of the limos, and it will be blown up on the road. Then, a report will be made that the couples were killed, funerals held, and the remainder of the family can safely go home to resume their lives and mourn their dead. This is the plan."

"Where are you going to get bodies?"

"We will have six unclaimed bodies from Rome flown in. All of the information that will be released will be about the new couples' tragic deaths on the day after they were married. Newspapers all over the world will pick up this story. It is too juicy for them not to print. They will even run some of the wedding photos. This will have to be a convincing subterfuge to work."

"One other thing. The Ferrari and that Fiat are too obvious. They need to be repainted tonight – maybe dark blue or something like that."

"I can have that done in my garage while everyone is at the reception, although Angelica, my niece, and the Fiat's owners are not going to like it."

"Unless they want to be blown up in their cars everyone needs to go along with it. They can do whatever they like with them when they get out of the country, but for now, those vehicles need to disappear. I have diplomatic plates for the vehicles with me."

"Give them to me. Estavo will see you out. There are some things that are going to happen here tonight that you do not need to see."

Roscotti now knew more about Luigi The Claw. He had first heard about him when he joined the AIA a decade ago. He had no doubt that he was dealing with a dangerous individual who could be anticipated to protect his interests by any means possible. He did not know what would happen to Luigi's Neapolitan house guests, but he suspected that they would not enjoy the experience.

"Luigi, remember that I need them alive. You can threaten them all you want, but they cannot be physically harmed."

"How would you like to live in America?" Luigi asked Michael and Vito.

"We were planning on maybe moving there some day and setting up a Limo rental business in Chicago, something like our cousin has here," Michael replied. "What's going on?"

"I want to get Angelica, Cecilia, and their husbands out of the country. I have arranged that instead of them going to Palermo as everyone suspects, they will be go to the American air base at Sigonella, and the U.S. Air Force will fly them to the States and put them, and you, in a witness protection program. Not only will you have new businesses, but you will also have new lives and new identities."

"We have worked hard to get our mechanic's certifications at Mercedes and Fiat. Can these be swapped over to our new names?"

"Yes they can. If the FBI can't arrange this, I will. These are large programs with hundreds of students going through them every year. Should you ever go back, you will have to look different – beards or something."

Exchanging looks, they nodded their heads in agreement.

"One other thing, though. You are going to have to repaint the Ferrari and Fiat tonight. Something like glossy royal blue and black."

"We just had the Fiat repainted and waxed it," Vito said. "The only thing we can do is to spray paint over the wax. That paint won't stick unless we can cut the wax off with rubbing alcohol or gasoline. I don't know about the Ferrari, but I suspect that it will need the same treatment – to say nothing of the time it will take to mask off the windshield and chrome."

"I have gallons of alcohol and acetone in my studio to get you started while the spray paint can get here from town. Estavo is the only one that I can trust to help you."

Luigi gathered the participants in the coming drama into his study and stationed guards outside of the door and windows.

Present were all six members of the Calsase family, Michael, Vito, Alberto, and Estavo. Luigi began. "Several attempts have been made against our lives, and I now know who was responsible. That is a matter that I will deal with.

"Arrangements have been made for the new couples to be secretly flown back to the States on board a U.S. Air Force plane from the base in Sigonella and put under the protection of the FBI witness protection plan in the U.S. along with Michael and Vito.

"The hard part of this is that Ronald, Nancy, William, Mary, and I can have no contact with them for at least five years. They will have new names, identities, and new lives.

"There will be a car bombing on the road to Palermo, and the newspapers will report that the brides and grooms along with their driver and an escort were killed, while the rest of the family escaped. There will be publicity in the newspapers and funerals held here in Sicily.

"I am sorry that these events are unfolding this way on what I was hoping to be the happiest days of your lives," Luigi remarked collectively to the Calsase family.

"Everyone involved is going to be called upon to make some personal sacrifices. Tonight is the last night that you may ever have together as a family. Try to make the most of it."

"Damn and double damn," Ronald interjected. "You mean we won't be able to see our own children for five or ten years."

"I am sorry, but that is how it has to be for your own protection. You, your wife, daughter, and brother will be able to continue your lives, but there can't be any direct contact. There likely will be an arrangement between third parties at the FBI so that mail can be interchanged between you, but there can be no direct links that someone might intercept.

"Roger and Angelica, you two can go to a university in England where you are not known and continue your studies and maybe set up your own businesses in art supplies and restoration architecture.

"Frank, you can start some sort of business in the U.S., and Cecilia can become a qualified teacher, something she has always wanted to do. All of you young people will have a chance for a new start. Please take advantage of it."

"I don't like it, but I suppose that I will have to go along with it," Nancy responded. "No parent should have to bury their own children, even if it is make-believe."

Roger said, "I feel that I ought to say something, but I can't put anything together. Frank, do you have anything to say for us?"

"No. Not really," Frank replied. "It seems like everything is out of our hands except to say that we love our wives and want to do the best for them." With that statement, he reached over and grasped both Cecilia and Angelica's hands and squeezed them.

Letting go of Frank, Angelica stepped aside and threw her arms around Roger, and pulling themselves together, kissed him firmly in the mouth. Taking her cue from her cousin, Cecilia grabbed Frank and kissed him.

As the door opened and the meeting dispersed, the two couples were left in passionate embraces. It seemed to everyone that nothing more needed to be said.

After scrubbing off the grime from their morning's activities, the new couples were once more resplendent in their newly cleaned clothing and outfits before returning to the Grand Hotel for the reception. Before their departure, Luigi had the photographer take a series of shots of the two couples and their families at the villa.

While the grooms wore the refurbished outfits they had on at the church, minus the accumulated dust and smoke from the road and gunfire, the brides were attired in new white gowns. Angelica's was a backless dress that revealed the tops of her breasts, was tightly fitting around her hips, but expanded at the bottom so that she would have freedom of movement when she danced. Cecilia's outfit was more conservative, although a bit more revealing than her wedding dress. Just as significantly for the girls, their hairdos were refreshed for one last public exposition of the hairdresser's art.

Luigi once again called for a meeting in the tower room before the banquet-hall doors were opened. Luigi started the meeting. This gathering was different in that five of his men were standing around the walls.

"Gentlemen, contrary to our agreement, the pact for cooperation between our families has been broken, and another attempt has been made against my family. According to our code, there is only one way this can be resolved, and that is by a vote of us all. I now know who is responsible, and they are in this room.

"I call for a vote of this group to exact retribution from us on all of this family in repayment of their treachery. It is my intention to turn them over to the Federal authorities, although I have every right to take their lives, according to our code.

"Their offenses include a machine-gun attack on a family reception and three attempts with snipers and cars on the road. One person gave me a warning of more to come, and only he will be spared. Will he please stand and step back from the table?"

Don Augustino's uncle, an 80-year-old white-haired man stood and supported himself by leaning on the back of the chair and a cane. "I wrote the note. I did not agree with what they were doing." As he spoke, Luigi's guards stood behind the remaining three representatives from Naples.

"Is what I have accused your other family members true?" Luigi asked.

The man raised his left hand in assent and replied, "Yes, it is true. I tried to stop it, but each of these three was involved. They also gave information that caused Don Carlos and Leo to be arrested. They have betrayed our code. They also carry poison for tonight," he said as he placed a glass vial of cloudy liquid on his plate."

"You are going to die for this. I am going to live to see you dead," Don Augustino quipped.

"I'm old. I will die soon anyway, but at least I will die with honor."

"As I can only act with your consent, I call for a vote. Do you agree?" A quiet round of discussion circulated around the table followed by raised hands which indicated consent.

"Gentlemen, you may leave. Enjoy the evening. I will join you later."

Luigi nodded this head, and the men quickly pulled the men from Naples to their feet and searched them. The three were quickly disarmed, and had their pants and underwear pushed down to their ankles. Glass vials were recovered from two of the men, but not from Don Augustino, who attempted to draw a pistol, but was stopped.

"Who did you give your vial to?" Luigi demanded, pulling his knife from his sleeve and drawing its blade gently across the Don Augustino's nose, but turned so that the edge did not cut, but was fully visible to his eyes."

"Let us go and I will tell you."

"I think you will tell us anyway."

Luigi produced a length of wire padded with rubber and cloth with two grips on the ends. When this was placed around Don Augustino's neck, he replied.

"One of the servers."

"Which one?"

"An older one who is balding, with green eyes, and a fringe of reddish hair. He wears glasses."

Pointing to one of the guards, Luigi said, "Find him, and bring him here. He will join our little dining party."

Shortly after a struggling man was brought into the room, searched, and forcefully sat in a chair.

"You were given poison to put into a dish. Which one did you put it in?" Luigi asked.

"I did not have a chance to put it into anything. I still have it," he said as he pulled a thin vial out of a shirt-sleeve pocket. I was going to put it into the American's stew because the strong spices would disguise the flavor."

"Bring the stew in. Enough so that everyone can have some."

Addressing the waiter, Luigi asked, "Was anyone else trying to poison anything?"

"Not that I know of," the waiter replied.

"Just in case, you are going to join these gentlemen for the banquet. I will let the kitchen know that you have suddenly fallen ill, and they will be short one member of the staff."

"I could not let you all leave without your fully enjoying the meal. You will eat everything that is set before you. Before we get started, is there anything else that was poisoned? If you tell me now, you will save us a lot of trouble, and you, considerable discomfort. We will start with a little wine and stew. Should you refuse to enjoy our hospitality it is a shame that even today people choke to death on meatballs." Enjoy.

"Report to me immediately should our guests have any reservations about their food," he ordered as he left the room.

A long table was set at the head of the room for the immediate family while round tables in the center of the ballroom were for the guests. The tables circled an expanse of the dance floor. The guests were served sliced wild boar from Frank's hog with lamb as an alternative dish for those who did not feel so venturesome or did not eat pork. A side table held some of the more exotic dishes, such as Franks' Italian rendition of Brunswick stew, fresh sausages from the hog, fried pork skins, and a crackling corn bread with peppers to represent the American's Louisiana traditions. Dominating the ends of the table were the wedding cake on one side and the whole roasted boar's head on the other. The boar had a red apple in its mouth and pimento-stuffed olives for eyes.

Large volume items that might conceal a bomb had been searched. The cake had thin metal rods run through it from various angles to detect anything solid, and the boar's head skin had been lifted to examine the skull. Only after every item had passed the inspection of Luigi's men was it brought into the ballroom.

The tasting of the food and inspections of the ballroom had delayed the serving of the plates. To provide entertainment, the members of the family were brought into the ballroom to be introduced by a DJ who supplied appropriate music. As it was not played at the church, a rendition of Here Comes the Bride was played for Frank and Cecilia and Roger and Angelica to the standing applause of everyone in the room.

William had chosen to appear in a caftan that he had purchased that was decorated with lemons and wore a cap made of matching fabric. The flowing caftan concealed the .45 that he had borrowed from Michael, who was occupied repainting the vehicles back at the villa. Of all the people in the room he would appear to be the least likely to be armed, but the 1911s had always been among his favorite firearms. The other one was carried in a black man-bag by Frank while the bags carried by Angelica and Cecilia contained the .380 autos. Alberto had fitted a back holster with a 9mm Beretta for Roger which allowed concealment even under a tight-fitting jacket.

Some of the guests seated at the tables were dressed in traditional Sicilian costumes, with the men wearing knee socks and red string ties, which contrasted with their bloomy black trousers and white shirts. The women were wearing colorful blouses and long flowing skirts that had sufficient volume to swing away from the body as they danced. They also each wore a small drum attached to a sash over their right hips.

Father Flanagan, now in his regular black suit and clerical collar, rose to give the blessing. As he mouthed the words and crossed himself, he thought, "I don't know if I have done the right thing or not. But they do seem happy, and maybe things will work out all right in the end. It is all in God's hands now. These Americans are innocents in the wilderness. He has protected them thus far."

These thoughts caused him to include in his blessing, "And may the mercy of the almighty God keep and protect these young people who are starting out on their life's journey together, wherever it might take them."

After the blessing and everyone was settled in their places, a series of chuckles went around the head table when it was noticed that before each of the grooms and brides was a small silver bowl containing a single red pickled onion. As it turned out, Donna Carlos had a sense of humor.

Frank remarked, "Our U.S. states have state flowers and even state vegetables, I guess that we as a family are going to have pickled red onions on our family crests."

"I have dealt with these things before," Roger said as he first placed his knife behind it and then stabbed it with a sharply tined fork. "It is sweet and sour at the same time." He concluded.

"The pork tastes a bit differently," Ronald remarked.

"I saw them cook it, Dad," Frank replied. "It was rubbed with oregano along with salt, pepper, and a little local honey mixed with vinegar, so it is not like our tomato or mustard-based bar-b-que sauces."

"I like the sliced and grilled vegetables with the ravioli and marinara sauce," Nancy said. "The mix provides a welcome change over the butter and salt that we usually use. That is when we don't fry them."

"Here comes the seafood mix, which is my favorite," Angelica said. "Husband, Roger, I am not sure what I am going to call you yet, have some of the squid and octopus and let those tentacles and suckers remind you of how tightly I am going to hold onto you. I am not going to let you go."

"We have plenty of seafood in the states, too," Frank said to Cecilia. "I will be happy to introduce it to you. What are these? They look like crayfish."

"They are salt-water crayfish from bays around the island. Sometimes, we eat them chilled and raw with seafood sauce, but these have been lightly cooked. They are somewhat like shrimp, but they are slightly sweet even without anything on them."

"I will have to try those," Ronald remarked. "You too boys. You have been brought up with crayfish all your lives and should know something about them by now."

Taking and dipping them in the sauce and munching on them simultaneously, a series of yums was mouthed around the table.

"If they are that good, I will certainly try some," William said. "For a meal like this served to hundreds of people, this is coming across as very good indeed. Please pass me the bread basket, I am really enjoying the local breads. I suppose that they pick up a fresh batch from the bakery each day for their meals."

"That is the custom," Luigi remarked. "With the bakery's products being so accessible and so inexpensive, it really does not make sense to take the time to bake at home, although some still do."

"Do you bake?" William asked Angelica.

"No." She replied. "We always had cooks, and anything special came from the bakeries."

"You might want to get some recipes. Although there are a few bakeries in the states in the larger cities who do breads like this, most do not if there are any bakeries at all. Frank and Roger were taught how to cook, but they don't know much about baking – me neither, for that matter. If you are going to have your favorite pastries, you are going to have to learn how to make them or settle for breads that could be a week old by the time you get them. They are more like museum exhibition pieces and are not to be compared with the real thing warm from the oven."

Luigi rose and tapped on a microphone to signal silence. "Honored guests, I would like to introduce you to Frank and Roger Calsase, who have, during the past few days, proven themselves to be worthy Sicilians by killing this wild boar that we are dining on with a flintlock gun, and protecting their wives from mortal danger.

"Gentlemen, will you remove your coats." They were assisted so that their backs never faced the audience. "I would like to present you with these sashes which carry the colors of our homeland that you may wear with pride as representing us wherever you go."

With these remarks, Angelica and Cecilia came forward and helped their husbands put on the unaccustomed garments.

"At least they are not turbans," Roger remarked. "We would never get those on right."

"Gifts may now be presented to the brides." With this statement a line of men who were sometimes accompanied by their wives came forward to give their best wishes to the couple and put envelopes of cash into the white silk bags carried by Angelica and Cecilia. These bags had differently colored drawstrings as they would be taken away and examined before the envelopes were opened. This was a precaution in case some biological agent had been put in the envelopes. Even the bank notes were picked up with tweezers and scanned with ultraviolent lights to detect any potentially harmful substances.

Among those presenting gifts was Davide's brother Paolo. What he presented to Cecilia was a single two-euro coin. "This coin is the one that you gave Davide. I am sorry about what my mother tried to do. I know you loved my brother, and he loved you. He would be happy for you now," Paolo concluded with his eyes tearing up from the maelstrom of emotions that he was feeling. Before he could embarrass himself further, he turned and left.

Cecilia slumped as if she might faint. Frank grabbed her and returned her to her seat at the table. He then stood by Angelica and continued to collect the envelopes in her bag and receive the congratulations from those still standing in line.

"What happened?" Frank asked as he returned to his seat.

"It was a shock seeing Paolo. This coin was the last thing I gave Davide on his birthday. The day he was killed. He said that he would keep it next to his heart. It broke me up to be reminded of all of that, but I think that I am getting over it."

"Have a little wine, maybe that will help. This is supposed to be a happy day, and we need to put on a brave face. I never knew Davide, but I do know that he would want you to be happy and enjoy your wedding. It is almost over. Soon, we will be able to wind down and just be ourselves. For now we still have our little play to perform. I need you to help me get through this too. I really love you, and we are in this together. Sometime tonight, I suppose that we are going to dance."

As the efficient servers brought and took away the plates, the time came that the elaborate wedding cake was to be cut by the brides and grooms. The couples went to the side table and stood on each side of the cake so that each could ceremonially cut the cake simultaneously. The photographer had quite a task framing up the shot, but once that was done, servers cut slices from the enormous cake and distributed them to the diners.

William appreciated the artful construction of the cake in that its different layers contained the fruits and nuts of the island. He wanted to sample each layer, but he settled for one slice that contained pistachio nuts and apricots, which he found to be an unusual, but tantalizing, combination of flavors and textures.

"In a way, it is a shame to eat this cake," William said. "This is really an eatable masterpiece. It deserves a place of honor in a museum."

"I certainly agree," Roger said. "It is simultaneously culturally appropriate and significant. I am sure the reporters who are covering this event will make note of it."

"All of this stuff is a bit over-the-top," Angelica remarked to Roger. "I wish that it was all over and we were alone in bed where we are supposed to be."

"I know. I want that too, but we have to go through the motions. With all we have gone through, I feel almost as close to your uncle as I do to my own father. If I were him in these circumstances, I would have probably done the same thing for my daughter."

As in ball rooms, which might host trade shows and conventions, the room was dotted with drop-down TV sets that could project images from a stage back of the main table. The TV sets flickered, came on, and on the screen was a large rectangular object covered with a cloth. Standing before the painting was Luigi and the director of the Museums of Syracuse.

"Before the dancing, I would like to present to the City of Syracuse my newest work, The Death of Archimedes, as a gift to the museum to remain forever as a tribute to our city's most famous son who aided in the defense of his city against the Romans," and the drape was pulled away revealing the painting to the public for the first time.

This unexpected event caused the sounds of a collective shock to go through the audience who were simultaneously repulsed and attracted to the painting.

"Thank you for the offer of your magnificent painting. However, before I can accept it, I must have the approval of our artistic committee and directors. It must be evaluated on its artistic merit and historical significance before I can add it to our permanent collection."

With those remarks, the TV sets were turned off, while murmured voices speaking in Italian emanated from the now darkened stage.

Roger, feeling that Luigi's painting might be refused on artistic ground, rose to stand by Luigi's side while a muted but raging conversation was taking place between his uncle-in-law and the director.

Seeing Roger, Luigi told him, "The Director does now want to take the painting because I did it. He says that the members of his board will likely reject it on artistic grounds. He thinks they would call it a large, but insignificant, work of an amateur that is unfit to hang in a gallery dedicated to the masters who produced paintings from past centuries. He also brings up a real problem that people might try to damage my painting and others in the museum because of things that I have done in the past. People who cannot attack me might attack my painting or the museum itself. He said that maybe ten years after my death he could hang it, but for now he dare not accept it.[48]"

"This is a painting of great artistic merit and significance and deserves to be displayed in a museum here in Syracuse." Roger opined. "I suppose it could go to a museum somewhere else, but that is not what you want. If you will permit me, I will keep this painting for you and arrange for it to return to Syracuse ten or twenty years after your death. Angelica and I would be pleased to do this for you – not only because we are now related, but because this is a magnificent work of art, that by all measures, should be exhibited here."

"Thank you Roger. I will consider it." Luigi said.

The presentations of the couples and announcements having been concluded, members of the audience started to gather on the dance floor as a caller announced that the tarantella would begin. Instead of the DJ

---

[48] Museums worldwide are very picky about the art they accept for exhibit. The art must suite the general purpose of the museum, have proper providence, and generally serve some useful purpose in the museum. With much stolen and looted art remaining from World War II, some, offered to museums, is now being returned to their original collections or owners' descendants.

putting on a record, a man in traditional dress with an accordion stepped to the center of the floor.

Angelica and Cecilia attempted to pull Frank and Roger to the dance floor, but both refused. Saying that they did not know the dance and speaking little or no Italian could not understand the calls.

Jock understood the problem, found Paolo, and approached the main table. "I will be happy to lead the dance with Angelica while young Paolo will dance with Cecilia, if you will permit us."

Frank and Roger shared a look of relief that they would not be seen as a pair of stumbling fools trying to master a complex dance without ever having a chance to practice it. They had not grown up with this traditional wedding dance, as had the island's natives. "It looks like we owe Jock another one," Frank said. "I am glad he is here."

At first, the pairs of dancers lined up in parallel rows of men and women who faced each other and bowed. Led by the two couples, they proceeded to form a ring around the room, and then making an arch, the front couples stood, allowing the remaining dancers to pass between them. As they did, the women raised and waved white handkerchiefs above their heads. Then, as in a square dance in the U.S., the caller announced progressively complex moves whose final result was the dancers switching partners and taking a whirl on the floor until everyone had danced with everyone else. Then the parallel lines of men and women were reformed, they bowed again to each other, and the dance was concluded.

Returning to their seats as the DJ put on some slow dance music, Angelica and Cecilia reclaimed their husbands. Angelica told them, "Now, it is our turn. We must lead the dancing."

With feigned reluctance, and too much protesting, Frank and Roger allowed themselves to be pulled to the floor by their wives. Once they were position, the DJ put on a slow waltz and the pair of dancers glided effortlessly across the floor and were joined first by Ronald and Nancy, then by Mary and Roberto, who was standing in for Michael, who was back at the villa repainting the cars. After a time, Luigi came onto the floor and danced with his daughter and niece and, in parting, gave each of them a kiss on the cheek.

Luigi then left the dance floor as he had other guests to attend to. He stepped into a phone booth and phoned Roscotti that he could pick up his delivery in the tower conference room on the seventh floor of the hotel, and it would be wise to bring a trash can or two, because these men might have a need to pee and vomit.

When Roscotti arrived, he found the men bound in chairs with their pants around their ankles. They offered no resistance as they were escorted out of the building and into the waiting squad cars parked outside of the Grand Hotel.

Passing through the lobby, they heard the sounds of music and voices coming from the ballroom off the first floor but had no inclination to join the party or say their goodbyes to Luigi. They felt lucky to be alive, as they knew the next time they saw him could be the last moments of their lives. They had been condemned by their own, and there were no arguments or appeals to be made.

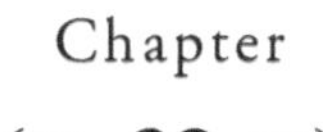

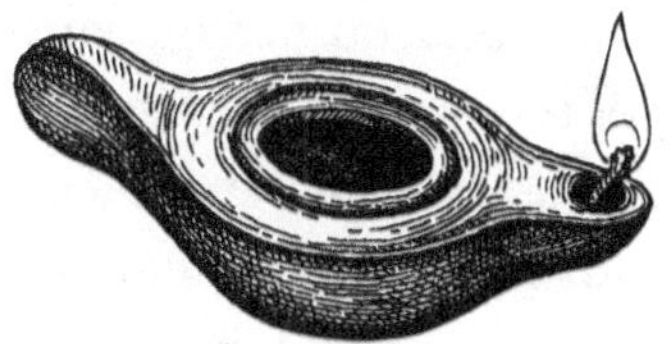

33

Together

THIS ETERNALLY LONG DAY was nearing its end. Frank and Cecilia and Roger and Angelica finally found themselves behind locked doors in rooms by themselves.

Cecilia sat at a dressing table, and looking at the long central mirror, started pulling the combs out of her hair while Frank assisted.

"You look beautiful," Frank said. "Let me help." He removed the comb and drape and carefully started undoing the pins, which allow her flowing hair the freedom to expand in volume and began to fall.

Feeling that Frank's tugs while doing this unaccustomed task might get too violent, Cecilia said, "This hairdo took hours to put together. You are not going to take it apart in seconds. I appreciate your help, but let me do it."

Frank remembering how Mary was always fiddling with her hair when they were younger, replied, "I know. Mary could do it. Where is a sister when you need one?"

"She is only two doors down. I'll go get her if you want."

"I don't think so." Cecilia replied with uncharacteristic firmness. "We are finally in a bedroom alone, and I want to keep it that way."

Next door, separated by a stone wall, things were progressing a little faster. A pile of mixed men's and women's clothing lay on the floor, and two naked bodies were savoring each other on the bed.

"I've been wanting to do this ever since I first laid eyes on you," Angelica said to Roger as her hungry lips first nibbled on his neck and her hands rubbed down his ribcage, hesitated for a moment over his hips, and then fingered the pubic hair around the base of his hard throbbing penis.

Rolling over on top, Roger let Angelica's hands guide his shaft inside her waiting vagina and when he felt the entrance, pushed, which solicited a sigh of shocked satisfaction as he pushed in, partly withdrew, and pushed in again in the manner of the rutting bull that he felt he had become.

Not wanting to ejaculate too soon, he slackened his pace, but Angelica would have none of it and arched her body to meet his assault.

As they moved on the antique bed, it began to emit a series of rhythmic creaks accompanied by exhales of breath from Roger and groans of pleasure from Angelica. With so much pent up anticipation, the climax came suddenly and explosively to them both, and they collapsed in each-others' arms.

Roger, still not recovering from his release, lay back panting while his heart beat in his chest. "It had been good with Matilda, but this is the best that I have ever had," he said silently to himself.

After getting up, Angelica went to the bathroom and returned with a towel, whose corner she had dipped in warm water, and proceeded to gently fondle and wash her husband's genitals.

"Your balls almost disappeared when you were large," she said. "Now, they are back. What? You've got three of them."

"Not really," Roger said. "The third is what they call a hydro cyst. I have had it since I was a teen. It is benign and doesn't really mean anything. My dad and Frank don't have them. Just me – special I guess."

"I think that it's cute. I'll think of it as my own little special testicle." Angelica said, as she gently fondled him.

"How did Dick do?" Roger asked as he lifted his now-limp member. "He does not look like very much now."

"Not as deep as a well or as wide as a church door, but will serve," Angelica quoted, delivering the Shakespearian remark with a bit of fun in her voice.

"Men are always wanting to know that, as if it was the most important thing in the world." But you know it is not, at least that is what Father Flanagan would tell you."

"What is a celibate priest supposed to know about sex?"

"They are men too, you know, and everybody tells and discusses everything with them, whether they are supposed to know anything about it or not."

"I guess. Can you sleep? We are going to have a very long day tomorrow and a flight to the states. We may not see a bed again for a couple of days."

"I suppose, maybe sex again in the morning? Just for the record, new husband, that was wonderful. I think that we can make this marriage work. Hold me until we fall asleep."

"It sounds like Roger and Angelica have already started," Frank said to Cecilia after she had let down her hair and turned on the bench to face her husband.

"She was always the impetuous one. I hope that Roger can handle her. Your brother is going to have a time with her, although I think that she has come to think that she really loves him. I hope so."

"What about us? Do you think that you have come to think that you love me?"

"I think so," Cecilia said as she started to loosen his tie and unbutton his shirt.

"I think that we have entirely too many clothes on."

"I agree. Let me help you."

Cecilia stood and Frank gently undid her straps and slipped them over her shoulders, letting the dress fall to the floor.

Cecilia pulled the shirt off Frank and pulled his undershirt off over his head. Frank then dropped Cecilia's slip and, undoing the back of her brazier, removed it, leaving them both standing and bare-chested. Reaching up with both hands, he brushed his thumbs across her nipples, causing her to shiver in excitement.

Stepping away from the pile of clothing, Cecilia undid Frank's belt, and his pants fell to his shoes. She then knelt and untied his shoes, and one by one removed his shoes and socks. Stepping away from the accumulating pile of now unnecessary clothing, Frank now stood before his wife, clad only in his jockey shorts while she wore only her underpants.

As Cecilia's hands reached inside his waistband and slowly peeled the shorts down from his hips, a line and then a forest of pubic hair emerged, until the now-erect penis pointed upward as it sprang from confinement.

This slow tease was all that Frank could stand, and he lifted Cecilia by grabbing her across the waist and while kissing her on the mouth, carried her to the bed. There he sat her down, pulled off her panties, and kissed her on the navel.

The pair then climbed into the bed and, clasping each other in a lover's embrace, proceeded to make love with first, Frank on top and then Cecilia riding his shaft as if she were a rodeo rider on a bucking horse.

Their antics were dimly heard by Angelica and Roger next door, who drifted away to sleep with the knowledge that now, in all respects, all of them were truly wed.

"Do you think that they did it?" Nancy asked Ronald, as they lay together in bed.

"It sure sounds like it. After all that we have gone through and will go through over the next few days, I sure hope so. It is not like the boys were sixteen-year-olds. They have been through the mill before, been hurt and now should know how to make this marriage thing work. Even though they have known each other for only a few days, there seems to be something developing between them. I don't think that the sex part of marriage will present any problems. It is all of this Mafia and gang business that is going to impact their marriages in ways no one can foresee. We will just have to hope and pray for the best.

"Want to?"

"Yes, I do," Nancy replied. "We might as well make this night a family event."

The act, while perhaps not as intense as the lovemaking done by their sons, was nonetheless performed in the manner of well-practiced partners who had learned over the decades how to please each other. When they were finished, the household was quiet, and even the villa itself seemed to sigh as all its inhabitants settled down to a night of well-earned rest.

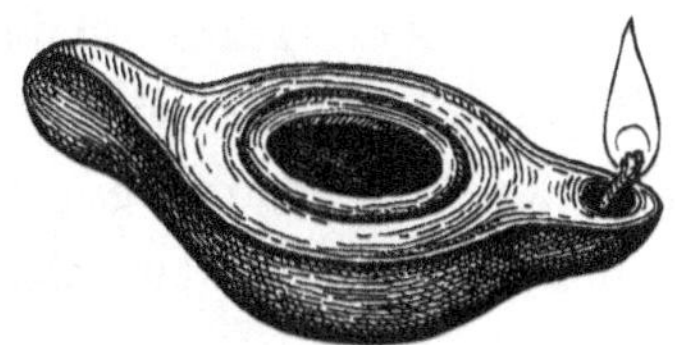

34

The Departure

A SHARP SERIES OF raps were given on the doors of the Calsase families' rooms before dawn.

"I guess this starts it," Frank said as he got naked out of bed and turned on the lights.

Cecilia, rubbing the sleep from her eyes, pulled the sheets up around herself and really looked at her husband for the first time. Tan, tall, well-muscled, and handsome, she thought, "He is gentle, kind, good looking, brave, and he says that he loves me," she thought. "I certainly want him physically, and I am finding it hard to think of a future without him. Oh Mary, Mother of God, and my dear Davide, please look over us and keep us safe," she silently prayed.

Frank went to the bathroom, and when he was finished, he heard another sharp series of raps on his brothers' room next door. He wrapped a towel around himself and opened his door.

When Frank stepped into the hall, he found Luigi saying to Roger, "We need your clothes to put on the bodies and your suitcases to put in the limousine. Everything must be there – just like nothing had happened, and you were flying home with your wedding clothes and presents. That includes your rings, passports, everything. Everything must be there to give the authorities no doubt that those bodies are yours, and there is no need for an autopsy. Here are duffle bags to put a few things in to keep you for four days. Everything else will be provided to you when you get to the States."

"Our wedding rings too?" Angelica questioned from inside of the room.

"Yes those too. I can't think of any reason that any bride would not be wearing them the morning after her wedding.

"Even the money you were given must be in the bags, as you would have had no time to exchange it between last night and this morning. I will replace it."

"It's going to be like we were never married," Angelica protested.

"Child," Luigi said. "It is not this stuff that makes you man and wife, it is the love that you pledged to each other and the love that you had last night that has made you married. There is no time for speeches, but believe me, you are married, and this fine man here, who I have really come to like, is your husband."

Luigi concluded by grabbing first Roger and then Frank by the shoulders, and pulling them to him, kissed them on the cheeks.

Walking back into the room, Frank asked Cecilia, "Did you hear all of that?"

Michael and Vito had the gruesome job of dressing the corpses and putting them in the car before it was loaded on the 18-wheeler that would take them to the site where the explosives were already planted in the road. Little did the few early morning drivers realize that the blocked off section of the highway had workman working all night to plant a powerful shaped charge that was sufficient to destroy a heavy tank, much less a Mercedes limo.

"I didn't know that I signed up for this," Vito said, as he pulled Frank's jacket onto the stiff arm of a corpse. "Are we going to put clothes on the women too?"

"There is no one else but us. The fewer that know or see anything about this the better. I am sorry about what's going to happen to it. It is a nice car."

"Well, at least it is not our car."

Unexpectedly, William and Mary walked in, and William was the first to speak.

"Luigi told us what you were doing, and we are here to help. We assist the funeral directors at home all the time, getting people ready for burial."

"I didn't know that hairdressers did that sort of thing," Michael said.

"It is a specialized skill, and we do it," Mary replied. "It is the least we can do for these two women, whoever they were, would be to treat them with respect. They are gone, but their bodies are going to be used to provide a safe future for my brothers and their new wives. I want to help."

"Vito and I have already dressed the guys, but if you want to help take care of the women, that would be fine," Michael said. "There was something about us working on them that seemed to be, well, just not right."

"I am sorry that you had to repaint your car," William said. "You had it looking really nice. Whoever did it had done a beautiful job. I took some photos of it. Whenever it is safe, I will get them to you somehow, but for now, that Fiat needs to look like thousands of others.

"Does Angelica know what happened to her Ferrari?"

"I don't know," Vito replied. "It is over there. We tried to do as good a job as we could with spray paint. We had a hard time getting through the wax job, but we got enough paint on it to make it look reasonable. It is not up to a factory job, but it will pass."

"We need to hurry. This car needs to leave before dawn with the suitcases and everything in it," Michael said.

"One truck left last night," William said. "I don't know where it was going or what it was carrying, but we need to get moving here, as distasteful as our task is. As soon as the bodies are ready, this truck needs to roll."

While hardly the languorous romantic interlude that couples would expect the morning after their weddings, Frank and Roger, with the aid of their brides, had packed and carried their bags to the courtyard to be loaded in the vehicles.

When they went into the breakfast room, they found that Ronald and Nancy had already eaten and were ready to leave.

"We have to go now so that we can be on the road behind the limo when it is blown up," Ronald said. "Boys, I do not know if we will ever see each other again. Angelica and Cecilia, we have come to love you too, like you were our own. Ten years from now, maybe we can laugh about all of this. Once we all get back to the States, they are going to send us a message that you have arrived safely. We have got to go. Give us some hugs, please, and let us get on our way. I hate it, but this is what we have to do to keep you alive."

William and Mary, after having completing their macabre task, had showered and redressed. Coming out of their rooms nearly simultaneously, they ran up to the remainder of the family to say goodbye to the two brothers and their wives.

After another round of fraternal hugs, Alberto announced, "I need all of your weapons. You must now all play the part of innocent Americans, and you cannot have weapons on you when you go to the airport or the Air Force Base. The truck with the car has already left to get that vehicle into position just before you arrive. Stay at least a hundred yards behind it when it is blown up. Then, drive closer and get out of your vehicles, act confused and distressed. Finally, back the vehicles away from the fire and wait for the police to arrive. You will cancel your flight reservations home and return to the villa to prepare for the funeral.

"I will have cars of armed men ahead and behind you, should they be needed. They will leave as the police are arriving."

The number of wedding guests at the villa had been much reduced. Three of the Neapolitans were now in custody, and the fourth had returned to Naples before the banquet started. The other guests were instructed to remain in their rooms because the Americans had to make an early flight from Palermo and would be leaving before dawn. With the vehicles moving around in the villa's courtyard with limited visibility, it was too dangerous to also have guests trying to leave. A breakfast would be held in the dining room at 7:00 A.M., after which a bus would take them to Syracuse, Catania, or Palermo. Each departing guest was sent home with a bottle of Luigi's estate-bottled wine.

Frank had already experienced several going-away-to-war departures and felt the usual tinge in the bottom of his stomach as he saw the taillights of his parent's limousine go through the gate and disappear into the darkness. Roger was less prepared. Sure he had left home to go to San Francisco, but this was a deeper, more wrenching feeling almost as if he was going to throw up as the realization hit him that he might never see his parents again. He knew he wasn't supposed to, but tears started running down his cheeks, and he wiped them away with his fists like he did when he was a child.

Coming beside his brother, Frank pulled him close and said, "Everything is going to work out all right." He then extended his other arm out to Cecilia and pulled her to his side. Witnessing these events, Angelica came, took Roger's hand and placed it on her hip, and allowed him to pull her closer. The four stood, side by side, with the first glints of dawn from the rising sun behind them casting light on the low-hanging grey clouds in front of them. With the car's lights disappearing from view, Frank announced quietly, "Let's load up."

"Go straight and go fast," Luigi told Angelica. "My men will escort you out of the city. They will be replaced by police who will take you to outside the Air Force Base. Then the Military Police will take over and escort you onto the aircraft. As soon as both cars are on board, it will take off. Once you leave the city, this entire thing should be over in about half an hour."

Looking around for her car, Angelica did not see it until Michael drove it out of the garage, "What have you done with my car?" Angelica shouted.

"It's not my fault!" Michael said. "Luigi said that the FBI ordered it done, and I had to repaint the Fiat too," he replied as Vito drove the now black Fiat out through the doors. "We worked most of the night to get them done while you were at the reception. I'm sorry if we smell. We did other stuff too, and that stink is still on us."

"Well, at least I will have my car," Angelica said. "Get in the back, I'm driving." There was little room to spare in the back seats of either of the two vehicles. Michael was wedged in somewhat sideways between the rear seat and the rear glass while Frank and Vito sat in the front seat of the Fiat, with Cecilia in the rear.

With a Land Rover in front, then the Ferrari, Fiat, and an older utility van in the rear, the group left the villa attempting to look as much as possible as part of the normal traffic flow of a metropolitan area. Their passage through the awakening city was reasonably rapid, with only a few delivery trucks having an early morning start and some more activities around the docks. Again crossing the Archimedes Bridge, they headed not towards the high-speed access to Palermo but over smaller roads more generally towards Novo and then northeasterly to Sigonella.

They were picked up by a police escort and sped up. Abruptly, the lead police vehicle slowed and turned off onto a side road.

"He's leading us into a trap," Angelica shouted. "That road doesn't go anywhere. I know them." Not waiting for consent or discussion, she floored the gas pedal, and the car shot ahead. Seeing Angelica's move and concurring with her opinion, Vito also accelerated the Fiat to the point where he quickly put some distance between him and the trailing police vehicle.

"We are still ten miles from the base," Angelica said. "We can outrun them if the Fiat can keep up."

"Vito will stay with you on these roads but can't catch you on the straight-a-ways," Michael shouted from the back.

"I wish I had that Tommy gun again," Roger said. With that comment, a shot rang out from behind, which could be heard over the engine and wailing sirens.

"Well, that declares their intentions. They want to kill us," Michael said. That shot came from the Police car. I hope that everyone in the Fiat is all right. We put some extra metal in it that would stop a pistol bullet. It seems to still be driving fine."

"I think that it is time to call for assistance," Michael said as he pulled out a U.S. military radio and turned it on. "If they have relays on these hills, we can get through."

"Escort Group, this is Red Onion, Over." "Escort Group, this is Red Onion. Over." "Come in Red Onion, this Escort Group."

"We are being attacked by police vehicles. We are approaching Vizzini. Over."

"You are fading out. Understood. Needing assistance. Repeat location. Over."

"Approximately one mile northwest of Vizzini. Over."

"Say again. Over."

"Get that Huey in the air," the duty officer ordered. "Have them fly towards Syracuse so they can intercept the target somewhere along the way."

"I can't reach them. We need to get on a high point," Michael told Angelica.

"There is a ridge crest coming up," Angelica said. "It overlooks the valley where the base is. We have to go down a series of curvy roads. What do you say? Switchbacks. They can shoot down on us from the top of the road."

"That's good to know. As soon as we get on top of the ridge, I will try again."

Intermittently, more shots were heard. Some were directed towards the Ferrari and others at the Fiat, depending on which vehicle the shooter thought he might be able to hit.

"What are they shooting at us?" Roger asked.

"I hope just maybe their service pistols," Michael said. "If this was just an escort mission, they would have to talk their superiors into supplying them with anything else."

As soon as they reached the ridge crest, Michael tried again. "Escort Group, this is Red Onion. Over."

"Red Onion this is Escort Group. Repeat location. Over."

"We are descending the switchbacks on the ridge about a mile northeast of Vizzini. They may try to shoot down on us from the top of the ridge."

"Understood. Puff Dragon did you copy? Over."

"Loud and clear. Estimated ETA five minutes."

"We can stop out of sight and hope that they stay on the ridge crest and let the helicopter have an easy shot at them or push on and hope that they miss us as they shoot," Michael offered.

"We should stop." Roger said.

"If we do, they will catch up and maybe cut us off somehow. If I push it, maybe we can clear the dangerous parts of the road before they can get ready. Can the Fiat keep up?" Angelica questioned.

"On these roads it can," Michael said.

"Try it," Roger agreed. "If we can make it two levels down before they can set up, we will be so far away that their chances of hitting us with their pistols will be fairly slim."

With one vehicle following closely behind the other, the two cars successfully made it past the first of three switchbacks while their opponents were putting fresh magazines in their Beretta 9mm handguns.

"Do like what we were taught. Pick a spot on the road, and when the vehicles are coming by, shoot at that spot and keep shooting until our magazines are empty. Let the cars run into the bullets," the older gunman advised.

Unseen by the drivers of the two cars but visible to the two gunmen, a semi pulling a heavily loaded trailer was starting to climb the series of switchbacks from below. Ahead of it were two cars, carrying commuters heading to their jobs in one of the coastal cities.

"Maybe we don't have to do anything," the elder gunman observed. "At the speed they are going, they may run themselves off the road or crash into one of the vehicles."

"Get ready. This is going to be our best chance to get them," the head gunman said as he braced his pistol against a signpost, aligned the sights on the middle of the road, and prepared to squeeze the trigger. As soon as Angelica's Ferrari, came into view, he started shooting. The first shot hit the roadway in front of the car. The second bounced off a front fender, and the third caught a bit of the rear bumper. His companion shooting faster from a less steady position was bouncing bullets all over the roadway but did register one hit on the roof of the Fiat.

Under fire, but still in control of the vehicle, Angelica slowed to take the next turn and hit the brakes when she spotted the approaching car. Avoiding a collision by hanging close to the rock wall from which the road had been blasted, she again pressed the accelerator and sped down the road towards the next turn.

In the Fiat, a bullet penetrated the roof and for the second time busted the driver's side window, throwing glass fragments into Vito's arm. This caused an involuntary jerk, and he nearly pulled the Fiat into the oncoming car, but he managed to recover.

"Damn. Lost another window," he said in a joking manner.

The car, which Angelica had so narrowly avoided, was now visible to the two gunmen, who stuffed their pistols under their coats and took a stance as if they were peeing off the precipice. The flashing lights on the police cars caused the approaching vehicle to slow and stop and ask what was going on.

Waving them to pass, the elder policeman said, "Just admiring the scenery," as he finished zipping up his trousers.

"You should do something about those two cars.

They nearly killed us driving like that," the driver said. "There is no way we can catch them," the policeman replied. "We are just waiting to pick up the pieces when they crash."

After dodging the first car and then the second one on what was turning out to be a harrowing drive, Michael looked below and could see a large, obviously heavily-loaded truck working its way up the road. Although signs on the narrow roads indicated that only local truck traffic was permitted, this warning was commonly ignored by truckers, particularly those who might be carrying an overload or something that they did not want to go through the inspection points on the main highway.

"We have to pull over somewhere," Michael said. "There is a big truck coming up."

Angelica assented and found a cut-out on the cliff side of the road for the cars to pull into, where they stayed until the truck, with gears grinding, labored up the road. Then they proceeded on.

Once the vehicle left, the gunmen looked down to see that the two vehicles were now on the road heading across the flatlands below and were impossibly out of range. They were startled by the abrupt, whomp, whomp, whomp, of a helicopter behind them, and a booming voice from a bullhorn, ordering them to put their hands on top of their cars. Facing an M-60 machine gun sticking out of the Huey's door, they were not inclined to offer resistance.

"Red Onion. This is Puff Dragon. Over." crackled over the radio.

"Roger Puff Dragon, this is Red Onion." Michael responded.

"We have solved your little problem. Should you need us again, call. Have a nice day. Over."

"Roger, Roger," Michael replied.

"For a guy that was never in the military, you did very well on the radio," Roger observed.

"I did have some practice, and I have watched a lot of American films," Michael said. "Many people would be surprised at the skills that they really do have that they have learned from the movies and TV."

"True," Roger said. "Very true. Now let's see if our ride home is on the tarmac."

"Tarmac?" Michael asked.

"Runway," Roger replied. "Whatever you call it. It had better be there, and we had better be on it and off this island today. You don't know who you can trust, and those Neapolitan gangsters are still after us, no matter if they are in jail or not. How is that possible?"

"I don't want to scare you, but they have put out a contract on you and your brother. They will pay anyone who kills you. This is not something that they have to arrange themselves. In fact, they like it that way. This is a game. A Super Bowl for murder, if you like. That is why all of these machinations are necessary."

Simultaneously, on A19 approaching Enna another part of the drama was taking place. Temporarily, all eight lanes of the highway had been blocked, which allowed the 18-wheeler to discharge the doomed limo over the bomb and continue its trip to Palermo.

When the other cars were safely out of the way around a curve, the bomb was exploded. Even though they could not see the explosion, the concussion was sufficient to ring their ears, and they could feel it on their bodies. This was followed by a rain of debris, which sounded like a hailstorm. Metal, burning materials, bits of paper, clothing, and body parts were scattered over the roadway. Clear spots were shoveled to represent the places where the cars would have been and debris thrown over the tops of the cars which were then driven to those spots and then backed away.

"Nancy, Mary, close your eyes and don't look," Ronald said. "There is no reason for you to have to see this."

Look or not, the stench of burning flesh seeped through the air-conditioning units into the car.

Traffic on the other side of the median was now allowed to continue, and cones and yellow tape was being put over the right half of the right lane to allow the traffic and gawkers to see as much as they wished as they passed by. Soon, the sound of approaching sirens was heard as the accident investigation arrived. These officers were almost immediately followed by reporters and photographers who quickly settled into their usual Mafia bombing modes of reporting, which had unfortunately been honed by long practice.

The TV crews arrived. They wanted to capture the essence of the story from as many people as possible, including the Calsase family whose wedding and reception some of them had covered the day before. This was news. This was big news, and they wanted to be sure that they had their share of it.

To say that the entire family was in a state of shock would be an understatement. Nancy and Mary cried and sobbed for the cameramen, while Ronald and William tried to console feelings that were inconsolable. This was horror and carnage that they had never seen before.

Ronald remarked to the person who he judged to be the officer in charge of the investigation. "Just get us out of here. Back to the villa or somewhere. I don't care. We all will be happy to answer your questions later, but not here. I need to contact the American counsel."

Since the vehicles were material evidence, they could not be moved until the police photographers had a chance to document the accident and the investigative team had collected the evidence from an area the size of half a football field. Using fire extinguishers, the flames from the burning car were subdued, and finally went out when all of the combustible parts of the car had burned down to the last fragments of melted plastic, which emitted strings of black oily smoke and acrid fumes. This helped to mask the smell of burning flesh emanating from the bodies in the vehicle.

By the time the investigating officers arrived, the bodies had been almost completely reduced to skeletal material, outside of parts of the upper torsos and limbs that had been blown from the vehicle by the explosion. Even these were fragmentary, and it was difficult to determine whether they belonged to men or women. So much as possible these were identified as belonging to Man one, Woman one and Man two, Woman two, and so on.

"So far as I am concerned, you can just throw these in a garbage bag or leave them for the crows," an officer remarked. "These Mafia hoods deserve nothing more. If they want to kill each other, so much the better. Then, we don't have to fool with them."

"Now, Now." Chief Investigating officer Broccoli responded. "These are people too, and they deserve a degree of dignity. Let's wrap this up as quickly as possible so we can get the road open."

Approaching the gaggle of media who had been confined to one section of the road away from the investigation site, Broccoli decided that he had sufficient information to give a preliminary report to the media.

"This was an apparent Mafia bombing of a group going to the Palermo Airport from a wedding that was held yesterday in Syracuse. There were six killed in the car. Two sets of brides and grooms, a driver, and a bodyguard.

Both the grooms were Americans, and their brides were Sicilian. All were killed instantly by the force of the explosion. There will be a more detailed report tomorrow when I have more information. That is all for now. Stay away from the accident site. After my team has gathered the evidence, you will be allowed in to take your photos, but stay behind the yellow lines. The bodyguard was carrying a gun, and there may be unexploded rounds in the vehicle." Walking away, the officer declined to answer the barrage of questions coming from the reporters.

After two hours work and realizing that he had more than sufficient evidence to document yet another Mafia killing, Broccoli ordered the vehicles towed back to Syracuse where they could be reclaimed at the city impoundment yard. What cleaning up on the vehicles that could be done would be done by the wind and crows. Somehow, that gave him a sense of satisfaction, that a degree of universal justice had been obtained. It was time to grab a beer, sit down with his family, and watch some soccer. An Italian team was playing Manchester United, and that always promised to be a good game.

A crow, attracted by a shiny object on the roadside, picked up a one-carat white diamond and swallowed it. As a grinding stone in his gizzard, it would serve him for the rest of his life and was put to immediate use grinding the bits of flesh he was finding nearby.

35

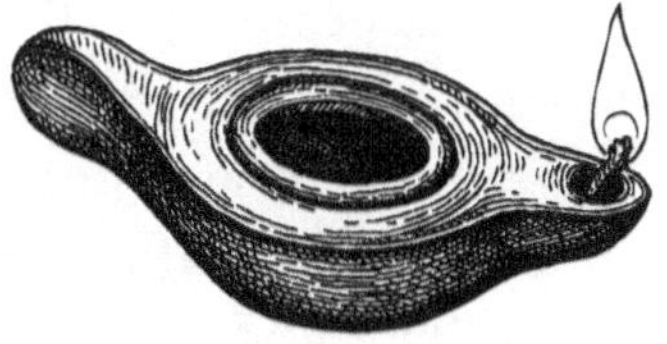

Sigonella

AS FRANK KNEW FROM passing through the base before, the Joint Air Force-Navy base at Sigonella was a modest affair compared to some others. However, it had likely hosted nearly every U.S. military aircraft made from World War II to the present.

Those stationed on the base could bring their dependents, and the U.S.O. arranged for inter-base competition between the school football teams. Unlike some of the larger installations, such as Naples, the small number of students made it impossible to have offensive and defensive squads. The same boys had to perform both duties.

This circumstance resulted in a girl being made quarterback of the team because she could throw better than any of the boys, and she did land some touchdown passes. The crux came when the Sigonella team was pitted against the team from Naples, who not only could field full teams, but also had much larger players playing defense.

Not wanting to take the chance of being outplayed by a girl, the team collectively decided to injure the girl quarterback to put her out of competition for the season. Although some team members later expressed regret for their unsportsman-like conduct, a late hit put her on the injured list for the remainder of the year.

Frank chuckled, as this incident reminded him of a basketball team from North Carolina called the Top Sailors, who likewise were shorthanded and recruited girls to their team. As the story went, and he was never able to confirm it, the local school board was so tight-fisted that they refused to furnish new uniforms for his players, saying that too few participated to matter, and that the entire basketball program should be dropped.

In protest of this action, the coach convinced the parents to let their players play topless, and the team became the Topless Top Sailors. Their games became instant sell-outs. The co-ed team started winning because the guys on the opposing teams were so distracted, they stood around and watched the topless girls make basket after basket without putting up anything but token resistance. This was considered an unfair advantage, and the other coaches protested, forcing the Topless Top Sailors to play more fully dressed.

The coach won, in that funds for new uniforms were somehow discovered, and if his funding was ever threatened again, he said that he would hold exhibition games to raise the money he needed, or so the story went.[49]

Now on the open road and in full daylight, Angelica could see escort vehicles ahead, and when directed slowed down and pulled over. Envelopes containing their new passports, driver's licenses and airplane tickets were handed to the couples and to Michael and Vito.

"You can look these over on your flight," the Captain said. "Let's get you out of here. Your C-130 is on the runway. Drive straight in on the ramp, and the Loadmaster will strap you down. Then take your seats on the sides of the aircraft."

Very quickly, they passed the guardhouse at the gate, passed the administrative and residential areas, which still included some World War II structures, entered the wire around the airfield, and headed for the enormous plane on the runway. As they approached, they heard the engines wind up, sputter, fire, and then one by one, the huge propellers started to rotate blowing dust back towards the vehicles.

The Fiat was loaded first. When Vito stopped and put on the emergency brake, the Loadmaster had already started putting shackles around the axles and, using a come-along, alternatively tightened the front and rear wheels.

"You hurt?" the Loadmaster asked as he noticed Vito's bleeding arm.

---

[49] Delicious as it might sound the story of the Topless Topsailers is fiction. It was first broadcast on my podcast radio show Hovey's Outdoor Adventures on WebTalkRadio.net. That show is still available on the web.

"Just some glass fragments," Vito replied. "Get me a first aid kit when we are flying, and I will take care of it. A little alcohol and bandaging is all I need."

While walking back to secure the Ferrari, he said, "Get strapped in. The pilot will take off as soon as the load is secure." With that statement, he activated the controls to raise the rear gate, and as he did the inside of the cabin darkened, until he switched on the interior lights.

After securing straps to the Ferrari, he gave it a perfunctory kick in the right front tire and satisfied, strapped himself into his seat. "Ready for takeoff," he told the pilot through his headset. He noticed the bullet holes and broken window and thought, "It looks like they damn-well better get out of here. Somebody doesn't like them very much."

"Prepare for takeoff," the pilot radioed back on the intercom. The engines revved up, and the aircraft started moving down the runway. The sets of dual wheels started to roll as the wings and fuselage started to rhythmically creak, strangely reminding Roger of the lovemaking that he and Angelica had done the night before. This was the first non-stressed sexual thought that he had that entire day.

Roger shivered and put his arms around Angelica, who picked up on the electricity passing between them, and for the first time read his thoughts. "Humm. There is no doubt what he has in mind as she thought about the Mile-High Club. "Who knows, it might be fun."

She remarked to Roger, "Yes, it is something devilish to think about, and I would like to as well, but maybe we had better wait. This is going to be a very long flight – a very long flight indeed husband mine."

Frank looking at Cecilia, said. "We will be lifting off in a few minutes, and we are going to be starting a new life together, it looks like in San Diego, according to the paperwork. You are the new Mrs. Richards. Roger have you looked at your paperwork yet?"

Tearing it open he pulled out the papers and said. It looks like Angelica and I will be leaving you in Germany. We have been accepted to study at Oxford in England-I in the fine art department and Angelica in the architectural department. I will have a junior instructor position in mineral pigments, and can take courses, while Angelica can work on her architecture degrees. We are on full scholarship, and will get a stipend from a Swiss bank. We are Richards too, so I suppose we are still brothers.

We have been taken care of, but I can't really say more about it," Michael said. "Vito and I have come to regard you as family, and we will miss you all. I am going to stop talking before I start crying. I need to stop anyway to keep from losing my voice trying to talk over these engines."

Now airborne and settled in, the Loadmaster came by with a basket full of earplugs and a first aid kit for Vito, but before they had a chance to put them in, he said, "Some things were sent ahead for you that are already loaded on. There is this large crate, probably a painting or something, to be off loaded with the couple going to England. There is also a long slim box to go with the couple that is going to the states. For each couple, there is a crate containing some porcelain vases. I was also to give you gentlemen these two boxes."

Opening his box, Frank saw a note written by Luigi. "These are the rings that you exchanged at the wedding and the engagement rings. I managed to get substitutes for the others."

Paying no attention to what the grooms were doing, the Loadmaster continued. "There are also some lunches put up for you, with some ham sandwiches and soft drinks. Sorry, no alcohol on the aircraft."

Roger put in his earplugs and opened the box. Taking out the three rings, he put his wedding ring on his finger and slipped the two rings on Angelica's finger while mouthing the words, "With these rings, I the wed."

For the second time during their Sicilian trip, Frank said, "Brother, you did good," and replaced the rings on Cecilia's finger while repeating the vow. This re-affirmation was accompanied by the roar of engines that sounded sweeter than an ensemble of harp-playing angels.

Returning with blankets and pillows, the Loadmaster informed them, "We are about five hours from Frankfurt. Now that we are in the air, you can sit in your cars, just don't start the engines until we drop the loading ramp on the runway. Then, we will unload the Ferrari, painting, and couple going to England. After we fuel, we will take the other pair to Dover, Delaware. From there, I don't know. Get some sleep if you can. I am going to dim the lights and leave you alone."

Michael and Vito, seeing what was obviously about to take place, passed conspiratorial looks, and Michael announced, "I think that Vito and I will be more comfortable up front somewhere. Can you find us some seats?"

"Sure can," he replied. "Just follow me." With that Michael and Vito said goodbye and followed the Loadmaster to the front of the cavernous aircraft.

"Frank, it is a little tight in the Fiat. Why don't you and Cecilia try in the Ferrari first, and then we can swap off, say about Belgrade?"

"We may not take that long," Cecilia said, surprising herself for making such a remark.

"Speak for yourself," Frank replied. "We are still trying to figure out to get this thing done."

Mostly undressing outside of the vehicle, Frank and Cecilia climbed inside the Ferrari.

Sitting inside the Fiat, Roger and Angelica tried not to look back in the mirrors, but when they glanced up an occasional arm, foot, and glimpse of an arched naked back could be seen. Roger took his blanket and draped it over the windshield. "Let's let Brother and Cecilia do their thing while we do ours."

By the time Frank and Cecilia had emerged from the Ferrari, condensation had obscured all of the windows. Taking a towel from their duffle bag, they dried off quickly in the cold aircraft before redressing.

"I'm sorry, Roger, we left a bit of a mess in there."

"That's all right. Roll the windows down, and the car will dry out. Angelica and I took care of things too. I'm hungry, let's get into those box lunches."

Once again buckled into the side seats, the couples had an in-flight picnic.

Not long after, the pilot announced, "Prepare for landing," and the sounds of the heavy landing gear being let down reverberated through the aircraft. There was a resounding "thunk, thunk," as the wheels locked into place. After the Ferrari had been rolled out, the new couples exchanged their parting words.

"I don't know when we will see each other again," Frank remarked to Roger.

"Me neither. We can't go home. Maybe we can do Christmas in Iceland or New York or somewhere, depending on where we are."

"Whatever, we'll work things out."

Frank put his hands around Cecilia's shoulder as they prepared to re-board the C-130. Once more, they watched a pair of taillights disappear as darkness descended on the English countryside. They were about to start a new life in a new place, something that was altogether unexpected only six days ago.

In Apachee's hotel room in Palermo the telephone rang. Apachee turned on the speaker phone, and listened intently.

"Dad arrested and those bitches got away. I'll get those sons of bitches, I swear I will."

With these words he took the telephone receiver and bashed it against the telephone while howling in anger and pain.

Chapter

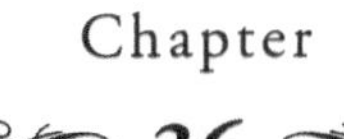

36

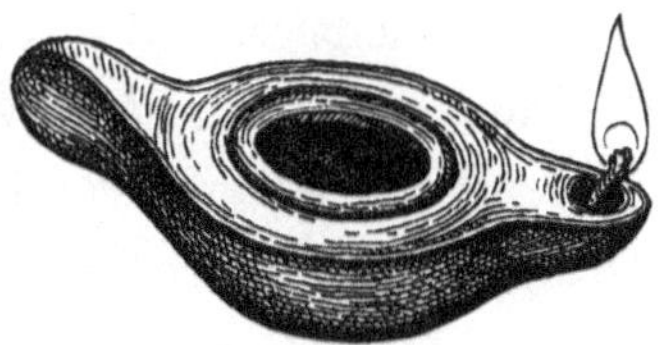

𝔈pilogue

TEN YEARS LATER, A young Sicilian was seen pushing an elderly man up the ramp to the Syracuse Museum of Fine Arts in New York State.[50] Pushing the button to open the automatic doors, the young man headed towards the reception counter where tickets to the exhibit were sold.

The young man told the cashier, "I am Paolo and this is Signore Luigi. We are here from Sicily to see Assistant Director Richards. Here is his card."

The card on stiff white stock carried a single name, Luigi and the drawing of a strange-looking knife with a wavy blade and an "I" shaped grip. Beneath was the title "Fine Arts and Antiques, Syracuse, Sicily," along with telephone and FAX numbers, but no address.

"Just a moment. I will inquire if the director can see you." She pushed a button on her phone and said, "There is a visitor from Italy named Luigi who wants to see the director. He is in a wheelchair. Should I send him up?"

A few minutes later, her phone rang with the instructions, "Have a security guard escort them."

---

[50]   The setting for this museum is modeled from the Everson Museum of Fine Arts which is located in downtown Syracuse, New York. It was designed by world famous architect L.M. Pei who also designed the Glass Pyramid at the Louvre. The museum was completed in 1968, and the collection relocated after having been housed in two previous buildings.

351

The receptionist looked a little surprised at the response and called one of the security guards. "Take them over to the elevator and show them to Director Richards' office."

As requested, the guard took them to a service elevator, which was large enough to hold several wheelchairs, and whisked them up to the top floor which contained the museum's administrative offices.

In the halls were some newly-arrived crates and boxes that were soon to be installed for a new rotating exhibit, and the guard helped Paolo navigate the chair around the obstacles. Unlike the wide double doors in the exhibit area, the doors to the upstairs offices were standard doors and a bit tight for the chair. The two men had to lift and turn it a bit to get it around the boxes and through the door.

An assistant had her offices in the front room of the director's offices. This room was decorated with framed posters from past exhibits.

As they entered, Roger rose from behind the desk and walked to the door to greet Luigi. Roger motioned for the guard to leave and close the door behind him.

"Signore Luigi, it is good to see you after so long. Who is this young man that you have brought with you?"

"This is my assistant Paolo, who danced with Cecilia at your wedding."

"Yes. I remember very well. I thought I recognized you, but you have grown over the years. I last saw you as a boy, and now you are a man."

Unaccustomed to being spoken to directly, Paolo stammered out a "Thank you" in response.

Turning now to Luigi, Roger asked, "How are you, and how have things been in Sicily?"

"Don and Donna Carlos are dead. Mario and Rodrigo are running the family business, and we have had good times and bad as usual. I have cancer, and they sent me to the Mayo Clinic, and while I was in the States, I decided to pay you a visit."

"I am so very glad that you have come because I have something to show you as well as tell you about us. Angelica and I finished our studies at Oxford, and we were both offered positions here. She consults and teaches architectural restoration, and I teach classical painting. As a family, we are well, healthy, and thriving. Angelica and I have a son and daughter, and Frank and Cecilia have two sons. Mother has unfortunately died of pancreatic cancer, and dad moved to San Diego to be closer to Frank rather than come here to snow country. For the past few years, we have met somewhere for Christmas."

"What does Frank do?" Luigi asked. "I know he could not go back to being a Marine."

"After the funeral, his ex-wife received a settlement from the Marines. Frank started a business selling and recycling remote control units for TV sets and expanded that into a full-time job. Cecilia got her teaching certificates, and she is a leader in the effort to unionize California teachers to get proper support for immigrant children."

"How about your uncle, William, and sister Mary?"

"They still have their shop in Baton Rouge, although William is not actively doing much at the moment. He developed some leg problems, and his mobility is restricted. Mary married, and they have one girl. Mary, and her husband, who is a fertilizer salesman, live in Mom and Dad's old house in town. William and Tim have a house, and he published a book on Sicilian-style Louisiana cooking, including some of the foods that you introduced us to over there."

With that statement, he put an album of pictures in Luigi's lap and said. "Look over these. I need to mix up some paint in my studio. I will be just a few minutes. We have some unfinished business to take care of."

On his way out, he told his secretary to close the modern paintings section of the permanent exhibit.

Gathering a palette, brushes, paint, and solvent he returned to his office.

He announced to Luigi, "We have a painting to finish," as he helped Paolo push Luigi out of the door through the crowded hallway and back to the elevator. Passing exhibits of modern ceramic and paintings, and a traveling exhibit from the Metropolitan Museum of Art, they entered a gallery. There, displayed on a wall was a heroic sized painting, The Death of Archimedes. In contrasts to the modern theme of the majority of the paintings, this one was done in the distinct style of the Italian Baroque.

"I have a recorder, and I am going to ask you some questions to which we both know the answers. But I need a voice record of your response that will be transcribed, and we both will sign so as to provide undoubted providence for the painting done by you and the late Roger Calsase, who with his new bride, was killed in that Mafia bombing ten years ago.

"I understand," Luigi replied. "Now that you mention it, I never did sign it."

"We are going to take care of that right now."

Going into the gallery, Paolo pushed Luigi close to the corner of the canvas. Luigi bracing his right hand on his prosthesis wrote two lines on the bottom of the painting.

"It is done," he said. "Now, pull me back so that I can see it." That done, he looked at it anew, as if he were examining a painting that he might purchase.

"It looks a little different hanging on a gallery than as it did in my studio," he said. "I remember it. I remember the smell, the wine we drank, and your finishing the faces. Thank you, Roger. Thank you."

"I go by Bob now," Roger said, "one of those accommodations for modern times."

"I don't have long. A matter of a few months, the doctors' say. I want my collection split between the museum in Syracuse and the one here. I want you to have a copy of that painting to remain here while the original goes back to Italy, as was always intended. Paolo can help take care of that. After I am gone, I want you to teach Paolo about the art world and how to make a living at it. He is interested, and he is talented. I do not know what part in it he might play, and maybe he doesn't know himself. But if anyone can help a young artist find his way, I think that it is you."

"Paolo, tell me true. You have gone through some terrible events these past ten years. Is this what you really want? I can help you if you are willing, but I cannot magically inspire you to take what you don't want to receive. Do you want this?"

"More than anything," he replied. "Then I will do it," Roger replied.

"I don't want any of you to come to my funeral. Memories are long in Sicily, and someone may yet try to kill you. This will be our last goodbye. Is Angelica here?"

"She has a class right now, but I will get her."

While Luigi and Paolo waited, Roger's secretary typed up the document in two copies. When Roger returned with his wife, they were ready for their signatures. The documents were quickly signed and exchanged.

Angelica expressed delight at seeing Luigi, and despite the awkwardness of hugging someone in a wheelchair, she bent over the arms of the chair and gave him a hug.

"Roger and I have been catching up. He has told me about everyone and that you and Cecilia are doing well. He showed me the photo album of you all. I am so very proud of you."

"Come home with us and see the children," Angelica said.

"I can't. It would put you all in danger. I took pictures of all of you from the album. That will have to do. I need to get back to New York to catch my plane back to Italy. Let's say our goodbyes here. I don't want you to go down to the parking lot with me."

With that, Roger and Angelica each took Luigi's hand and Angelica bent over and gave him a kiss on the cheek. Paolo again navigated the automatic doors and pushed the chair through them and down the ramp to the curb where he waited for his cab.

"I don't suppose that I will ever see him again," Angelica said with tears starting to well up in her eyes and stream down her face. She took the handkerchief from Roger's pocket and dabbed her face with it.

Two shots rang out from the museum's parking lot, and the sounds of car tires were heard as a yellow cab sped down the street.

Roger rushed down the winding staircase to the main floor, past the receptionist's desk, and out the door. He found Luigi limp in the wheelchair with Paolo lying on the ground, trying to staunch the blood that was pouring out of his leg. Roger whipped the belt from his paints, and fastening it around Paolo's leg, cinched it up to stop the bleeding. Between the efforts of both of them, the blood flow was slowed. Then Roger said, "Someone call the police."

"I already have," a young man wearing a hoodie replied. "I got a picture of the cab with my phone. I saw it all."

"Stay here, the police will want to talk to you."

Now giving his attention to Luigi, Roger stood and looked at the front of the chair. There were two bullet holes squarely centered on either side of the breastbone and Luigi was panting, exhaling blood with each breath. He was making no attempt to stop the bleeding. "Let me go, he said. "It's time. Look after Paolo. Get us both back home."

With those words, Luigi, called The Claw, died.

The next day Roger returned to the gallery after giving statements to the police and making sure that Paolo was recovering at the hospital, Roger returned to the gallery. He walked by the Modern Gallery and unhooked the chain from the posts that had blocked entry to that portion of the exhibit.

Seeing that apparently something new had been done in the gallery, two early visitors walked by, but all of the same paintings were there. Only the most discerning eye would have noticed that signatures had been added to a large painting called The Death of Archimedes. The new signatures read:

Luigi of Syracuse
Roger of Louisiana, 2004.

Paolo, on crutches, stood amidst a growing number of grave markers on his mother's farm outside of Novo. After having a funeral in the old German bunker, he was ready to bury the antique Greek amphora, which now contained Luigi's ashes.

Luigi's funeral had been attended by friends and foes who sent flowers in tribute or celebration of the old man's death.

Though threatened to be defrocked by the church for his close association with Mafia figures, Father Flanagan presided over the funeral. At the event he saw the aging but now well-known faces of Mario and Rodrigo, who he had stood by at this very spot ten years before when he had officiated at Davide's funeral.

Should one-thousand years hence some archaeologist be excavating the site, they would be surprised to find the burial of an ancient Greek amphora invaded by the roots of a huge, wild grape vine. What was unusual was this urn contained a rusted wavy bladed dagger made of fine Damascus steel. It had been buried under a single stone inscribed "Luigi" which had a similar dagger carved on its surface.

"This man," the archaeologist might explain to his students, "has returned to the soil that reared him." Picking a grape from the wild vine, he might bite it and savor the green taste of the unripe fruit, which left a sharp, somewhat metallic, aftertaste in his mouth.

THE END

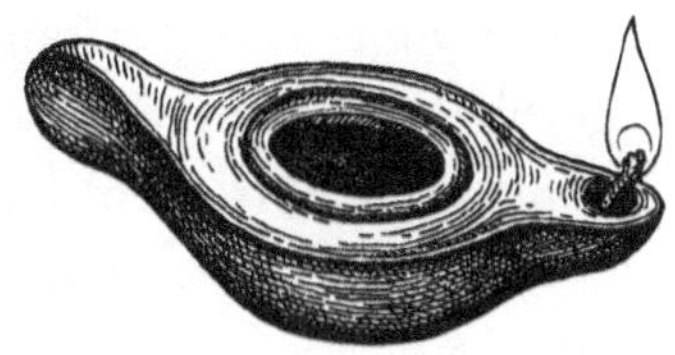

Creating the Novel

TWO SICILIAN FAMILIES WITH blood ties, but vastly different experiences, are thrown together by a series of events that do not go as planned when two dissimilar sons from the American side of the family discover when they arrive on Monday that they are to marry two of "the fairest flowers of the island" on Friday.

As a writer, I'm often asked how I come up with such a plot, the characters, and the places that I describe. Any writer bases what he writes about from his own, and others,' experiences which is what I have done. I briefly stayed with an American family of Sicilian descent who lived in Louisiana, and they described a trip to the island to visit some of their relatives.

Another family living in Mississippi had handsome sons who were having marital difficulties. Borrowing some elements from the movies "Father of the Bride" and "The Godfather," I conceived of the general storyline of a dark comedy which could investigate why an organization like the Mafia could have such a profound hold on a culture and how to use my fictional characters to relate the events and examine some significant issues that would resonate among readers and viewers.

The book also allowed me to investigate other issues by incorporating a gay hairdresser uncle who goes on the trip and two dissimilar brothers who are thrust into marriages with two beautiful gals. One of the women is the niece of the acting head of the Mafia and the "wild child" of the family, while the other has serious thoughts about becoming a teaching nun. Following the vendetta killing of a young man that they had known since childhood, they were willing to do anything to get away from the endless cycle of death and bloodshed, even to the point of marrying two Americans that they had never met.

One of the prospective grooms is a portrait painter, who has an uncertain future in this age where a photograph can be printed on canvas and framed to give an exact rendition of the subject. He has tried to dabble in any number of artistic projects, but never managed to finish anything, even the portrait of his own mother. In contrast, his brother is a Marine officer who served in the Second Iraq War as an airstrike coordinator after an injury prevented him from flying ground-support missions.

Unexpected aid is offered by Father Flanagan, a transplanted Irish priest sent to Sicily to bring some peace to the eternally fighting Mafia families. Because he is the most conveniently available English-speaking priest on the island, he has been selected to do the ceremony.

I have always had a strong interest in archaeology, and the passage of seventeen different cultures through the island has left a historical legacy that I could not ignore. Our family tours the island to become acquainted with their cultural heritage and visits many of the famous sights including historic Greek and Roman ruins and dramatic natural features such as Mt. Etna, the largest active volcano in Europe.

In May, 2019, I made an eleven-day trip to Sicily that was not only useful in discovering settings on the island, but also in sampling the food and wine. The most valuable thing of all was interacting with the people and picking up interesting, and unexpected, details of local culture to use in the book.

One thing that I was looking for was what the Greeks described as a dagger with a 'flame-shaped blade' used by one of the ancient Sicilian cultures three-thousand years ago. As each culture pillaged their predecessors' tombs, few of these bronze knives have survived, and I could not find one in any of the Island's museums. This dagger was considered the 'terror weapon' of the day and thought by the Greeks to be unsuitable for 'civilized warfare.' Since I own Hovey's Knives of China, I had an understandable desire to make such a knife. It is used as a weapon of intimidation by Luigi, The Claw, who has been brought out of retirement to be caretaker of the Mafia operations after the two principals have been jailed by Italian authorities.

As a boy, Luigi fought with the resistance against the German occupation of the island and lost his left hand. After the war ended, he worked with American archaeologists doing salvage excavations in Syracuse. It was discovered that he had a talent for drawing, and Luigi was taught to paint in order to make truer renditions of the objects that were being discovered than photography would allow. He has taken on the task of completing "his great work" a heroic-sized painting, The Death of Archimedes, using ancient pigments, but is having problems finishing it because he was never taught to draw human faces. This slant in the novel comes from me being a professional geologist with interests in mineral-based pigments.

Similarly, I have published a number of books on hunting with muzzleloading guns, and I could not resist having one of the brothers go on a boar hunt with a flintlock muzzleloader from the Napoleonic Wars. I have taken an Italian boar with a muzzleloading gun and cooked the head, as well as the testes – items eminently appropriate for a wedding feast. A 1777 Dragoon musket was purchased from Davide Pedersoli that I built from a kit, which I will hunt, and ultimately use in the movie.

Plans for this project will hopefully include a movie, now that the screenplay has been finished. One advantage of thinking about all three at once is that scenes can be written into the novel that would have been much more difficult to portray without visiting the locations.

This is a work of fiction and any resemblance to anyone, living or dead, is purely coincidental.

I received significant financial support from Ron Lanzo and Ron Lanzo Jr. who were among the early backers of the project and contributed to the completion of the manuscript. I would also like to thank Frank Fazio for his comments and corrections, particularly about aspects of Sicilian culture. Tyson Daniels made many corrections and editorial suggestions during his month-long review of the book which were of considerable value in rooting out many of the First-Edition's errors in addition to contributing the lyrics to The Sicilian Lament, and to Viad Onee who proofread the manuscript.

Whitehall
Wm. Hovey Smith

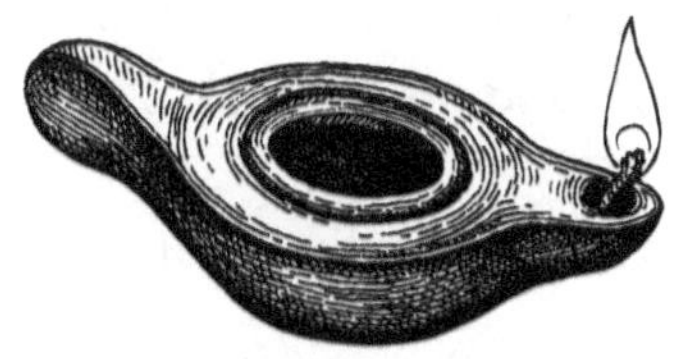

Other Works by the Author

Archer's Bible Presents Practical Bowfishing, Stackpole, 2004

Crossbow Hunting, Stoeger, 2006

Backyard Deer Hunting: Converting Deer to Dinner for Pennies per Pound, Author House, 2009

X-Treme Muzzleloading: Fur, Fowl and Dangerous Game with Muzzleloading Rifles, Smoothbores and Pistols, Author House, 2012

Create Your Own Job Security: Plan to Start Your Own Business at Midlife, Profit, An Imprint of Whitehall Press-Budget Publications, 2018

Make Your Own Job: Anytime, Anywhere, At Any Age, Stratton Press, 2020

The above titles are available as softcover and e-books from distributors of on-line content worldwide.

The Short-Shot series of books below are inexpensive editions of specialized books about muzzleloading hunting that are also available from distributors of on-line content.

No. 1. Muzzleloaders for Hunters: How to select a muzzleloader that fits your hunting style and pocketbook, 2013

No. 2. Buying Used Muzzleloading Guns, 2020.

No. 3. Shooting and Maintaining Your Muzzleloader: How to make your muzzleloader most effective and keep it working under almost any conditions, 2013

No. 4. Hunting with Muzzleloading Shotguns and Smoothbore Muskets: Smoothbore guns let you hunt small game, big game and fowl with the same gun, 2013

No. 5. Hunting Big and Small Game with Muzzleloading Pistols: Using single-shots, double barreled pistols, and revolvers for taking game, 2013

No. 6. Hunting with Muzzleloading Revolvers: Modern powders and bullets have made these pistols effective game killers, 2019

No. 7. Muzzleloading Guns for Self Defense. How to Defend Yourself with Muzzleloading Rifles, Pistols, and Shotguns When You Can Own Nothing Else, 2020

No. 8. Building and Restoring Muzzleloading Guns: Building and Using Historic Guns and Their Replicas, 2021